Reviews for The Night Nurse:

"A propulsive and twisting thriller."
     - **Daniel Kalla,** author of *The Last High* and *We All Fall Down*

"Oh. My. God. It's fabulous. Absolutely smashing novel ... captivating, cerebral and tangible ... the magic took over and I was utterly immersed in the world of Jackson Teague, Nurse Wendy and the others."
     - **Bacchus Books review**

"Refreshingly different! What a great story. Unique premise and interesting characters. I especially liked that, other than the villains, the 'good' characters were smart and figured things out."
     - **Amazon review**

"This is so tightly written that you will be horrified one minute and laughing the next."
     - **Goodreads review**

Also by Tony Berryman

MASSAGE THERAPY THRILLER SERIES:
The Night Nurse

Co-written as Trigger Jones

ADVENTURE SCI-FI SERIES:
Gravity Doesn't Lie
Atmosphere Meltdown

ON BORROWED TIME

TONY BERRYMAN

Twintree
Books

ON BORROWED TIME

the second massage therapy thriller

Paperback original published by Twintree Books / May 2025

ISBN: 978-1-77713-356-6
Also available in ebook

Cover design: Evgeniia Gurcheva
Cover photo: Shutterstock.com

Printed in the USA and Canada

For Eric
my memento mori

Chapter 1

Jackson saw the attack but thought nothing of it. Not right away. Few people were exiting the North Vancouver Seabus terminal this late on a wet October evening, so when the slim man speedwalked out of the gate and veered into the older gentleman in front of him it was hard to miss. Slim guy corrected course and headed for the street without so much as a backward glance. The older man grunted, then recovered and carried on through the turnstiles. Jackson shook his head and hustled to catch the evening's last harbour crossing.

The ramp to the Seabus gave a dull clank as he crossed. His autumn jacket drooped from the rain that had slicked the dark streets. He'd taken the day off from his massage therapy practice and spent the afternoon and evening doing what he did every October 5th. He'd visited the North Vancouver container docks his father had monitored, the Port Authority building where his father had worked. Then loitered with his memories at the street corner where his father had met a street punk's blade. Five years ago tonight.

Knife attacks don't take very long. Don't need to be big, flashy affairs. But they always leave a scar.

He and the older man were almost alone in the back half of the ferry. Jackson sat at the back and could see the man's round, neatly-coiffed head over top of a seat near the doors. Partway across the harbour he heard the man give a small exhale of surprise. The man shifted aside his waxed canvas raincoat and look down towards his side. That was all.

When the Seabus slid into its Vancouver dock and Jackson got up to leave, the man rose slowly out of his seat. Not entirely out of character for a senior pushing 70, but something about his movement caught Jackson's professional attention. He favoured his right side. His right arm stayed close, an instinctive guarding posture. Maybe he had a cramp.

The man kept the slow pace on the long skyway over the rail tracks to the station's street entrance. Despite the cramp he walked with a natural spring in his step, easy in hips and knees, remarkably lightfooted for someone his age. His right arm stayed curled in by his side. Jackson matched speed a few steps behind the guy, concerned. The rest of the passengers kept going, oblivious.

The signs became more and more obvious. The man's right leg swung less than his left, giving him a limp that got worse with every step. The spring faded into a plod. He hunched over his right side as whatever was wrong began to seriously hurt. Jackson heard his breathing get shallow and hurried.

Jackson picked up his pace. When the man canted towards the right at the end of the skyway, he caught the guy's arm and guided him to the floor. "Whoa, you're hurt. All right if I look?"

The man's eyes were blue, startlingly clear. He had a round, smooth face below salt-and-sand hair. He looked more like 40 than 70, much different than Jackson's guess. Those blue eyes stared off into the middle distance, seeing a realization Jackson wasn't privy to. His voice was light and soft, tinged with a European accent, maybe German or Dutch. "That man, just before I ... thought I'd lost them. The boat ride was nice. He must have ... didn't even feel it." He huffed a dry laugh, then pulled his focus onto Jackson. "A ginger! Freckles and all. Double recessive gene, not your fault. Thank you, yes."

Ignoring the implied prejudice, Jackson lifted the man's arm away from his right side. There it was. A slit went right through his coat, with a sticky redness at the edges. Whoo boy, he thought, as he peeled back the jacket and lifted the perforated shirt.

The knife—stiletto, maybe, the puncture was only an inch wide—had made a clean in and out, a surgical attack. Just below the last rib, just off the midline. A kidney shot. It was amazing the guy had made it this far. And amazing that he wasn't bleeding like a slashed hose. Even on the skin, there wasn't much blood. The wound was seeping, not gushing.

As he watched, the slit stopped bleeding altogether.

"This is serious," he told the man. "I'm going to call you an ambulance." He reached for his phone.

The man placed a hand on his arm. "No need. Just get me to the front door, please. I suspect—" a look of hollow regret saddened his face—"a ride will be waiting for me. Help me up?"

Jackson took the man's left arm and helped him back to his feet. He looked steadier than he had a moment before. "You sure about this?"

"Yes, let's go. Wait." The man looked around, then collapsed back to the floor again, taking Jackson with him. He rolled to one side, glanced around again, then shoved a manila envelope deep inside Jackson's rain jacket. Face angled towards the floor, he murmured, "Deliver this, please. Your hands to his. It's more important than you know. Only to him. Tell no one. Tell me you will." He gripped Jackson's arm hard. "Tell me."

"Okay, whatever," Jackson nodded. "Let's get you on your feet." The man seemed to accept that. He rose, appearing to let Jackson help him back up. His stamina was incredible.

Whoo boy, thought Jackson again. He tucked the envelope under the back of his belt, out of sight.

Without another word, they passed through the doors and into Waterfront Station. The long, cavernous building was almost deserted this late at night. The street exit waited across the short axis of the building. Downtown Vancouver glistened outside as rain pelted the windows.

The man's voice was soft in his ear, only a whisper through stilled lips. "By the time I knew, it was too late. I was out of time. Heh. ironic."

He held onto the man's arm with one hand and kept his other wrapped around the man's waist, holding him up. The man's strength had evaporated after that moment in the hall, and Jackson worked hard to keep him up. With every step, his hands registered a weird sensation he'd never felt before. The guy was somehow hard to hang onto. Like he was poorly assembled and sagging out from under Jackson's grip.

"I could call the cops," Jackson began.

"No. No good," the man mumbled, now saving his breath for the journey.

This was nuts. Jackson made up his mind to call 911 the moment they were outside. But as they neared the front doors, a familiar ambulance siren wail came pealing through the glass. Lights flashing, a white and red cube truck sailed around the corner and rocked to a halt directly in front of them.

The abrupt movement brought Jackson's condition out from its closet inside his head. The patterns of the night jumped into his vision. He could see the ambulance's path down the street as a brilliant, phosphorescent green streak against the rainy night. Faint lines from corner to corner gave a lovely highlight to the truck's boxy symmetry, wonderfully bisected by the thick, red ambulance stripe marking a diagonal from back to front. The fancy eagle seal on the door was a touch off-center, shimmering a faint orange to Jackson's inner eye, a small jarring note in the otherwise clean design.

Not helping, he told his pattern sense. He shoved it back into its closet.

Just before the doors the man whispered once more, a breeze of words Jackson strained to hear. "Tell them I'm sorry."

The man stumbled again, and would have collapsed if Jackson hadn't been holding on tight. Again, he had the impression that something was wrong under his hands. It was like the fellow wasn't put together very well. But there was no time for detailed assessment.

Two paramedics jumped out of the ambulance. One headed for the truck's back door as the other ran towards Jackson. In the moment before they reached their patient, Jackson squeezed around the guy's midriff with one hand and ran his other up and down the man's left arm. Then the paramedics took him and laid him down on a wheeled gurney.

It was the quickest of assessments, but Jackson's brief rub had revealed two things. The soft tissues of the man's arm were loose under the coat sleeve, as if he'd recently lost significant weight. And he had a small lump on his side, under the last rib. Interesting. But, in this situation, not useful.

One attendant began strapping the man down as the other examined the wound site. "Stab wound, as reported," he said to his coworker. "We'd better make this a rush."

Paramedic Two was busy with straps. A lot of straps. Relieved of his burden, Jackson stood back and watched. Paramedic One needed scissors to cut away the man's shirt for access. Jackson could see the scissors on the back of the attendant's utility belt, shining silver in the night. It took two seconds of patting around for the attendant to find them. The attendant pulled a bandage from his bag, one of those four-side adhesive pads, and literally slapped it on over the bloody cut.

No bedside manner at all, not even the usual questions. Tonight's ambulance calls must be seriously backed up.

"I know first aid," he said, taking a step in. "Want some help there?"

"No, we've got it," said Paramedic Two. They positioned for the lift into the back of the open truck. The man on the gurney, now obviously both exhausted and resigned, looked over at Jackson and frowned. Then shook his head, once. "Thanks for your assistance," said the attendant. Then, "How did you say you found this man?"

The dark night took on a tinge of electric blue as Jackson's condition slipped out of its closet again. A gust of wind slanted the rain past the streetlight and the movement made a thousand tiny meteor trails dance at the edge of his vision. The two attendants, now both standing over the gurney and facing him, shimmered with steel-grey intent. Shoulders wider than hips, feet planted in ready positions. To a casual bystander they'd look like two healthcare professionals focused on their job. Jackson saw two coiled springs focused on him and made a decision.

"I found him in the lobby there, heard you coming and helped him out. Looks like he's really hurt. Good thing you got here so fast."

Paramedic Two took a moment to absorb that, scanning Jackson's face. Jackson turned to the older man, immobilized on the tiny bed. "You going to be okay?" he asked.

The gentleman gave a weak smile and nod, both in answer to the question and, Jackson was sure, relief at his performance. Paramedic One asked, "Did he talk to you, drop anything?"

"No, nothing. Good luck, guy." Jackson turned his back on the scene, a surprisingly hard thing to do, and headed away. After a long moment he heard the attendants bustle the stretcher into the ambulance. The siren blurted up again and headed into the night.

Not in the direction of any hospital Jackson knew of, and he knew them all.

Chapter 2

GLIMMERING TORNADOS OF ENERGY

Five minutes after Jackson got home, Marilyn buzzed the intercom. A rush of excitement lit him up from the inside as he opened the apartment door and she stepped across the threshold. They were four months into their thing and his heart still went on a wild ride whenever she came over. They wrapped each other up and squeezed hard. "Welcome home, cop," he said into her ear. "You're officially off duty."

"Hey, Freckles." She pushed him back into the apartment and kicked the door closed. Her mouth landed on his hard enough to tap his head into the wall. He kissed back, letting both of them satisfy their hunger for as long as he could stand. Then he pushed her far enough away so she could see his face.

"Hey, Legs. Ow," he said, glancing down. A Leatherman and a black, tactical baton hung off her belt and jammed into his midriff.

"Oh, right." She peeled herself off him and turned down the hallway towards the living room, and the bedroom door beyond. She looked over her shoulder once to make sure he was watching, then popped the clasp on her belt. The hardware slipped off her hips and dangled by her right hand as she rounded the corner.

Of course he was watching. He allowed the inner door to his pattern sense to crack open and Marilyn's walk bloomed into a dazzling symphony of movement. Her short brown ponytail bobbed in time to her steps. Her triathlete's legs ate up the hallway with leopard symmetry, no sign yet of the veteran policeman's lopsided gun swagger. Tiny, glimmering tornados of energy spun away from her feet like they wanted to leave the floor with each bouncing step.

He could help with that.

A half-hour later, Jackson looked out from the wreckage of his bed at the line of clothing that stretched towards the living room. "Good day at work?"

She reached down and grabbed a sock. "Pretty standard. Putting out fires, mostly. Ahmed and I caught a few domestics, rode a patrol through District 2 from the warehouses to the docks, did a whack of paperwork. The usual."

"So, all that energy was just for me."

She poked him in the shoulder. "Of course. The last part of the workday can't go by fast enough." Lifting onto an elbow, she looked down at him. The question was in her eyes. "My overnight bag is in the car."

He grinned. "Sure, bring it in. Spend the night."

He put the bedroom back together and marvelled at his luck as she went outside. The last six months had shaken his world. In the springtime his obsession with patterns had flared out of control after three years of careful management. When he started seeing patterns in the deaths of his elderly patients, Marilyn had shown up at his door in her full Vancouver Police uniform. She and her partner, Ahmed, had come very close to locking him up for his own good.

Then she'd followed a slender thread of trust and been there for him when the shit hit the fan.

A great doctor with the right meds had reined in his condition again, but he'd come close to a terrible edge. It had left him feeling broken in a way; far too broken to risk sharing his life with anyone.

Then Marilyn had called. Kept calling, and slowly fostered a deeper healing.

Now here they were. His condition was back under control. A woman was in his life, a miracle he'd almost given up on. His travelling massage therapy practice had recovered to the point that he was paying the bills again. And Marilyn had brought her overnight bag.

"What's this?" he heard her call from the living room. She was looking at the wrinkled manila envelope on the low coffee table.

"Oh. Weird thing this evening." He put some water on for tea and recounted the story of the injured Seabus commuter, the spontaneous ambulance, the attendants with the bad vibe. "The guy gave this to me and asked me to deliver it. Said it was important."

Marilyn kept her eyes on the envelope. "So he gave it to you?" she asked.

"Practically jammed it under my coat, actually."

"Hmm." She sat on the couch. "That coat over there? The beige one?"

"Yeah. The one that looks rained on."

"And what colour was his coat?"

"Dark brown, one of those waxed canvas jobs. Expensive. Why?"

She was looking at the table, not him, hands in her lap. "How did it happen? Step through it for me."

Frowning, he did. "I helped him up, like this." He mimed the action on the living room floor. "Then he collapsed again. No, actually, he looked around first. I went down with him. He looked around again, like he was lost or searching for something, then jammed that under my jacket." He demonstrated.

"Hmm. Left hand or right?"

"Left, of course. His right arm was still clamped to his side." He showed her the posture, practically feeling the man's wound as he did.

"And what did you hear?"

"'Deliver this for me, it's important. Your hand to his. Tell no one.'" It was like he'd said the words himself. "Yeah, pretty much exactly. Nice interrogation work."

Marilyn brushed off the compliment. The carefully neutral voice was gone, replaced with something a bit harder. "He told you to tell no one. Anything else?"

"Well, yeah. Not then, but while we were walking. Something about he thought he'd lost them, and being out of time."

"He was hurt, maybe stabbed, you said. An ambulance appeared out of nowhere. Did you call it in?"

A niggle of discomfort started up in his gut. "And say what? That I helped a hurt guy get to an ambulance and saw him be driven away, but it looked wrong? That didn't work out for me so well before."

She had to nod at that one. "Okay. Still. Didn't any of that seem suspicious to you?"

Jackson said, "Of course. All of it. But by the end the injured man was in the back of an ambulance and there was nothing left to report."

"Except for this." She pointed towards the envelope lying on the table. "Whatever it is, that man wanted to keep it out of the hands of officials. Or people with official connections."

"Really?"

"Yes," she said. "He fell and rolled so the security cameras wouldn't see him give it to you. He was worried about whoever had access to those cameras. Have you looked at it yet?"

"I just got through the door when you buzzed. What's to look at? It's an envelope."

She reached to pick it up.

He stuck out a hand to stop her. "Aren't you worried about fingerprints, DNA, that kind of thing?"

She glanced over at him. "You stuffed it down your pants."

"Oh. Yeah."

The envelope crinkled as she picked it up and examined it, flipping it back and forth. It was thin, not the best quality. She spent a moment pondering the message on the front, neatly lettered in black Sharpie: Deliver to – J Harrowman – 1301 Kootenay Street. After inspecting the back of the envelope again, she grinned. "It's from a dollar store. Their glue's not the best."

She retrieved her Leatherman, flipped out the knife and gently slid it into a loose gap under the flap.

"Hey," Jackson said, "that's not for us."

Marilyn sat back and lifted an eyebrow. "Really? You want to hand deliver a suspicious package that was given to you by a complete stranger in dubious circumstances without checking it out?"

"Uh," he replied, "when you put it that way."

Working slowly and carefully, she slid the blade back and forth under the flap, lifting a bit more each time. She was right. The glue came away with a minimum of fuss. Once it was open she handed it back to him to do the honours.

He tilted the contents out onto the table. Out slid a ziplock baggie and a few sheets of paper. "Don't touch," said Marilyn as he reached for the bag. "Just look." She took out a pen and teased the baggie out onto the table. Inside was a small, silver cylinder with rounded ends, about an inch long. It had a dull sheen, like it was made of some exotic metal. Other than that, it looked like nothing more than a capsule of allergy medicine.

The papers were upside down; she grabbed a second pen and used them like chopsticks to flip the pages over. The first three sheets of paper were crammed with technical notes and what looked like chemical formulas, with a lot of what Jackson recognized as benzene rings.

The last sheet was gorgeous. Someone had done a pencil sketch of the back of a hand, three fingers outstretched with the index finger and thumb tucked out of sight. It was a classic anatomical drawing, with the skin removed to show the intricate webbing of fascia, muscle and bone that lay underneath. Small artistic flourishes adorned the edges of the sketch, whorls and curlicues on each side and scattered circles and diamonds below the wrist.

"Ew," Marilyn commented.

"No, it's beautiful," he corrected, leaning in. "The human body's an incredibly complex piece of work. Fascia drawings like this really highlight the engineering."

"Grab your phone. Take photos of all these." He did as instructed, and she did the same with hers.

"So," said Marilyn as he slid everything back into the manila envelope, "when are you planning to deliver it?"

"What? No, I figured I'd drop it in the mail or something. Now that I have an address."

She spun to face him. "Did you agree to deliver it? And tell no one?"

A red flush warmed his freckles. Damn it. "I may have. Just to get the guy moving."

"Well then."

He waved at the papers. "We have an address. They're in an envelope, for heaven's sake. It's practically begging for a postage stamp."

Now she was peering at him, just like the injured man had. "Jackson. You made a promise."

A flutter of irritation prickled under his skin. The last thing he wanted to do was get involved, but he knew better than to let it show. She was right. "All right, okay. Tomorrow morning's open. My schedule's only about half full these days anyway."

Marilyn studied the flap on the package for a moment, then went hunting for a glue stick. "Well then. Looks like we have an appointment in the morning."

Chapter 3

UNTIL I'M FINISHED WITH THEM

The package's delivery address led them to a secluded commercial district tucked between a neat, sunny neighbourhood and a row of trees concealing the highway. 1301 Kootenay was a bland, two storey building footing the dead-end street on grounds that had to be at least an acre, with a parking lot to one side and a scattering of trees and benches on the grass out front.

The architect had dressed it in Vancouver industrial chic standard: tan stucco with a metal-framed glass front door near the parking lot and two rows of tinted, inset windows stretching across to the other end. Discreet white lettering spelled out Blast Dynamics on the top left corner.

Jackson pulled his Subaru into the lot as Marilyn craned around in the passenger seat to get a good look at the outfit.

"Pretty decent security," she said. "Sensors in the pavement. You can barely see the cameras. And nothing short of a breaching charge is getting through that door."

"Blast Dynamics." He pointed to the lettering. "Maybe that's what they make here."

The front door's glass was green-tinged and uncommonly thick, set into a strong frame. A numbered keypad sat inside a small weather shield at chest height beside the door, with a small glass plate beneath. Thumbprint reader, Jackson guessed. Above the keypad was a doorbell.

The moment he pushed the bell the door clicked open, letting them into a broad, airy lobby that extended up both floors. The decor was a pleasing mix of concrete and pale wood above and forest-green carpet below. An expansive reception desk and a scattering of comfy, upscale-modern chairs gave the space an open and welcoming feel, and a stairway against one wall provided access to a second floor balcony fronting a row of offices. A young woman in a grey blazer smiled at them from the desk.

"Welcome to Blast Dynamics," she said as they approached. "May I help you?"

Jackson said, "Uh, yes. I have a delivery for Mr. Harrowman."

"The CEO? Certainly. I can take it here." She held out a hand.

Head of the company? He felt foolish, but a promise was a promise. He gave her his best rueful, apologetic smile. "I'm sorry. I have instructions. Hand to hand."

He braced for a gatekeeper's argument, but after only a brief pause she said, "Okay. One moment please."

She murmured into a handset, then put it down. "Right this way."

She took them up the stairs to the second floor and then to an empty conference room, said that it might be a bit of a wait, and left.

They loitered there for around twenty minutes. A bank of large windows showed them the back of Blast Dynamics, three long wings that extended to the trees. The highrises of downtown Vancouver glittered in the distance. The opposite wall sported three framed pencil drawings that immediately drew Jackson's attention. They were lovely anatomical sketches—a foot, a shoulder, and a gracefully-curved neck, all minus the skin and emphasizing the structures beneath.

Jackson admired the artwork, then flipped through a small stack of magazines on a side table. "Hmm," he said, holding one up and waving it at the drawings. "Not explosives after all." The magazine was the Journal of Histopharmacobiology, and he'd have needed a medical dictionary to read the article headlines on the cover.

"Explosives? Not even close!" an exuberant voice announced from the doorway. A tall, lean, forty-something man in dress slacks and rolled up shirtsleeves strode into the room, leading with his hand. He had racquet-sports shoulders, an amazing head of black hair shot through with veins of white, and a squash-player's grip. Jackson returned the handshake with his massage therapist's best.

"Jonathan Harrowman, co-founder and CEO of Blast Dynamics. The company name was my idea. You see it driving by, you think we make things that go boom, am I right? A nice little layer of obfuscation there. Quite proud of it."

Marilyn gave his hand a shake and asked, "So what is it you do here, if you're not blowing things up?"

Harrowman gave her another thousand-watt smile, genuine and infectious. Jackson saw Marilyn's face brighten, an instinctive response. "Not here. Come in to my office." He led the way to a door at the end of the hall.

"Fibroblasts!" Harrowman announced as he took one of the four plush seats on this side of a large oak desk. Pale wood bookshelves and wainscotting accented the terra cotta carpet and walls. A small secretary desk to one side was piled high with correspondence. Another anatomical drawing hung behind the desk, this one a study of the deep fascia that surrounded and held the heart. He waved them to the other chairs. "Early stage biomedical research, but promising, very promising. Fascia is perhaps the least-understood tissue in the human body. Disorders of fascia affect every system we have. Conversely, improvements to fascia can potentially have widespread benefits."

Marilyn's face had fallen into the pained-yet-patient expression she put on whenever Jackson waxed eloquent about obscure medical details. "Sorry, you lost me," she said. "Fascia? Isn't that part of a house?"

Harrowman spread his hands. "My mistake, I'm always starting at step ten instead of step one. Your friend—Jackson, is it?—seems to know what I'm talking about."

"Registered massage therapist," Jackson said, and flipped out a business card. "I have a travelling practice throughout the city. I work with fascia every day."

Harrowman took the card and examined it, impressed. "Indeed you do. Perhaps you'd like to cover the basics?"

Jackson turned to Marilyn. "Fascia is what holds us together. It's our connective tissue, although it's so much more than that. Fascia wraps around muscle and nerve fibers, around our bones and organs, around everything. It forms tendons and ligaments. Sheets of it wrap around entire sections of our body, distributing forces when we move and do things. It's slippery, and allows all our various parts to glide against each other. Loose fascia fills the gaps between blood vessels and every other tissue, allowing the space for nutrients and metabolic wastes to get shuttled back and forth. Fascia provides the battleground for our immune system to fight invaders. It supports and nourishes every specialized tissue we have, from our eyeballs to our toes. In fact, if you took out every specialized tissue and just left the fascia, you'd still have the complete form of a person." He stopped for breath and looked over at Harrowman.

Harrowman plucked a rubber model off his desk. It was a spiky thing, about six inches across, like a grapefruit sprouting wobbly, tapered points. "Excellent summary. Tell me, what is fascia made of?"

"It's simple as hell, but also amazingly diverse and complex," replied Jackson, warming to the topic. "At its simplest, fascia is fibers, cells, and gels. Collagen fibers provide the structure and strength. Ground substance is the gel that bathes and lubricates them, mainly hyaluronic acid. Different types of fascia—tendons versus loose fascia, for example—get their properties by the density of fibers, what direction they run in, and the amount of hyaluronan."

"Good! Now, where does fascia come from? What makes it?" Harrowman asked. He tossed the model up and down like a baseball.

"Fibroblasts," Jackson gave the obvious answer, pointing at the model. "They make the fibers. Fibroblasts, fasciacytes, and a few other cells make the hyaluronan. If there's plenty of lubrication and not many fibers, you get loose, disorganized fascia, like the stuff in between organs. More organized fascia is thicker and all lined up, like organ sheaths, tendons, and ligaments."

"Right on the money!" Harrowman beamed. He tossed the model to Marilyn. "And therein lies a host of potential problems. Too many fibers, or too few, or not lined up properly, and you get limitation and disease. Too much or too little hyaluronan, same thing. When your fascia doesn't function optimally, every part of you suffers."

"Sounds like fertile ground for research," Marilyn said. "So, what's your take on it?"

Harrowman gave them that thousand-watt grin, leaned back in his chair and made a show of crossing his arms. "See this?" he said, lifting his arms up a bit. "My lawyers taught me this. Apparently I talk too much about my work. Whenever the conversation moves on to details about what we do here, I'm to cross my arms and remember the phrase, 'intellectual property.'"

Jackson and Marilyn both laughed. Marilyn said, "I noticed the building security on the way in. I suppose that's part of it all, too."

The executive pursed his lips and wrinkled his brow in a grand, theatrical frown. "You noticed! How disappointing. We paid good money to be invisible here. But to answer your question, yes. The lawyers and the investors insisted on it. Blast Dynamics is working on some truly miraculous therapeutics, but we're still years away from clinical testing. It's a very sensitive time. Any leak of our methodologies or formula could be devastating. Could be the end, if another company picks it up and runs with it."

"I thought there were patents and things to keep that from happening," Jackson said.

"There are," Harrowman admitted, "but in order for a patent to be useful, you have to enforce it. Unfortunately patent disputes often come down to who has deeper pockets for the better lawyers. And in that regard, I'm afraid, Blast Dynamics would lose out. So although I can't tell you anything about my ideas or our research, let me say that fibroblasts, like all other cells, are not immune to damage and decay. Just like everything else, they get old. They malfunction. They break." He uncrossed his arms and leaned forward, the twinkle shining clear and bright in his blue eyes, and dropped into a stage whisper. "That is, until I'm finished with them."

Jackson felt a chill run up his spine. He still had no idea what these people were doing, but Harrowman's enthusiasm was catching.

"All right, enough of the sales pitch. Excuse me, but it's become a reflex." Harrowman sat up. "I believe you have a delivery for me?"

"Oh, yes." Jackson remembered the brown envelope, still in his hand. "It comes with a bit of a story."

He related the Seabus incident—the stabbing, the secret handoff, the old man's apology. He left out the part about the ambulance being fake, saying only that the ambulance was waiting for them when they reached the street. That got a sideways look from Marilyn but she didn't contradict him.

When he was done, Harrowman let out a low whistle. "You had an intense night. I can't say I know anyone who matches that unfortunate man's description. Certainly no one I know has been hospitalized or attacked. Well," he moved to the leather chair behind his desk, "let's see what was so important."

Jackson handed it over. Harrowman slit the envelope open and let the contents fall onto the blotter on his desk. First, he picked up the small metal cylinder in its ziplock bag and turned it over. Raising a single eyebrow, he set it aside. Then he looked at the papers covered in dense scientific notations. He looked at them harder, turning them over and examining the tightly-written formulas and chemical equations with a sharp intensity. "Where did you get these?" he said, not taking his eyes off the papers. His voice had lost its humour.

Jackson went through the story again. "Then the ambulance drove away," he finished. "That was last night. It only seemed right that we deliver these personally."

Harrowman said nothing, just kept flipping the papers over and studying the symbols. He dropped them, picked up the drawing of the hand and studied it. Marilyn spoke up. "Those notes are way beyond us. Obviously they mean something to you. What are they?"

Jackson saw Harrowman put his face back together. The intense look had been edging towards a dark anger. Now he did a quick rearrangement, and by the time he lifted his eyes from the papers back to them he was his professional, affable self. Not quite as pleased to see them as before, but still it was an impressive show.

"Oh, these? I'm not sure, but they look like rough notes on a new way to synthesize glycoproteins. I'll have to study them to be sure, but it looks as if your mystery man was some kind of amateur scientist. He probably wanted my help to patent a new process. Unfortunately, the existing lab synthesis is cheap and easy. It doesn't really need improvement."

"So they're pretty much worthless, then," said Marilyn. She stuck out her hand to get them back.

"Probably, but I'm sure the man will show up eventually to press his case. I'll hold onto these until then." He scooped up the cylinder, sketch and formulas and dumped all of them into a drawer of his desk. Jackson heard a click as the drawer closed shut.

Jackson pointed to the illustration on the wall. "Those fascia studies are amazing. I've never seen them done in that style before. Are you the artist?"

A touch of warmth reappeared on Harrowman's face. "Yes, in fact. I picked up the habit in grad school. When biochemistry made my eyes cross I'd head over to the dissection lab and sketch."

"And that one?" Jackson pointed to the now-disappeared drawing in the locked drawer.

"Not mine, I assure you. I've done the hand, of course, but that's a completely different style than my sketches. Much nicer, in my opinion. I'm just an amateur." Harrowman folded one long leg over the other and tried to look relaxed. "I'd guess that the artist was our mystery man. A shame he didn't give you anything else. Any clue to who he might be, or anything."

"Sorry, that was all. I wish we could be of more help. Well. I guess our job here is done. It was nice meeting you, Mr. Harrowman."

"Jonathan, please." Now the smile was back in all its dazzling glory. "You know, here at Blast Dynamics we're setting up a corporate culture that values employee wellness. A weekly chair massage would fit right in. Lab work can be stressful, and not very ergonomic, I'm sad to say."

Bingo. "I do office visits," Jackson said. They spent a minute working out a price, then set a weekly time slot. This was perfect.

Jackson's appointment calendar still had some holes. A day a week at Blast Dynamics would fill out the schedule nicely.

"Let's get you introduced around, then," Harrowman said. "How about a tour of the place?"

Chapter 4

TWO DOLLAR TOUR

Harrowman escorted them back to the first floor lobby and handed them off to Dr. Harold Dunn, a hulking mailbox of a man in a lab coat who looked none too pleased for the assignment. Harrowman apologized about other commitments, told Jackson how much he was looking forward to his first chair massage, and hurried off.

Dunn shouldered the menial task of conducting a lab tour with a resigned grace. He pivoted on his heel to face them (no spinal mobility at all, Jackson recorded for future notes) and swallowed each of their hands in his. "I'm the chief scientist for Blast Dynamics," he said in a whisky-barrel monotone, "and co-founder. Jon probably forgot to mention it. Call me Harold. Come on, let's give you the two dollar tour."

For all his reluctance, Dunn was an amiable and informed host. They began on the ground floor by the welcome desk. A door off the atrium led to a row of glassed-in offices dedicated to human resources, accounting, and two rooms labelled Investors and Regulatory. Dunn introduced Jackson to everyone from maintenance men to administrators as the company's new massage therapist, to exclamations of delight from most of the office staff.

The second floor held Dunn and Harrowman's offices and a series of meeting rooms off the balcony. Jackson chose the boardroom they'd waited in as his massage room and leaned over the balcony railing to book it with the receptionist for every Tuesday.

"Now for the fun part," Dunn announced as he led them back downstairs. He looked older than Harrowman by a few years, with ample evidence of grey rising up his temples into thinning, close-cropped brown hair. He had a broad, solid face and large hands, wizard's eyebrows, and deep folds under his eyes. From the measured pace of the tour Jackson figured Dunn seldom hurried about anything but would be the type who rarely slowed down and never stopped.

They'd passed three doors set deeply into niches in the back wall of the office block. Jackson remembered the three extensions they'd seen from the boardroom. Now Dunn led them to the first one. It was an imposing, windowless steel slab with another keypad and thumbprint reader. He turned his back to them as he went through the security procedure.

"The working part of the operation—and for God's sake don't tell the front-office staff I said that—is divided into three separate wings. Jon and I did the initial drug discovery in our own lab. Then Jon drummed up some investors and we built this place. Wing One is for compound optimization and archive."

The door whooshed open and Dunn led them into a small but well-appointed anteroom lined with lockers and shelves. He handed them hooded Tyvek lab overalls, safety glasses and booties. The overalls had Visitor stencilled in bright orange letters across front and back. He got them to lock their phones into small cube lockers. "No recording devices allowed, for obvious reasons," he said by way of apology.

The next door opened into a long, straight room that could have doubled as the set for a space station. White walls, black counters, and brushed-aluminum cabinets stretched the room's length under full-spectrum LED lights. Clear acrylic dividers separated workstations. Lab equipment of every kind filled the space, from glassware to computer monitors to tube-covered white boxes. Jackson reached back to his high school chemistry class and recognized fume hoods, a sterilizing autoclave, a bank of high-end microscopes and what he thought might be a centrifuge. The rest of the equipment was beyond him. All of it looked expensive.

The room was beautiful. Everything was in its right place. The lab had been designed by an expert to be both practical and elegant. Despite the volume of equipment it looked neither crowded or cluttered. Jackson felt a warm glow of pleasure just being here.

"Wild," he breathed. "So this is what a working lab looks like. I can't even imagine the price tag."

Dunn pointed at something that looked like three futuristic, stacked breadmakers capped by several glass bulbs. "That one's about a year's salary. Jon's found us some investors who really want this venture to succeed." The trace of a smile was back on his lips. He waved a hand at the half-dozen scientists at work in the room. "Here is where our biochemist team brainstorms new iterations of the original formula, runs initial stability tests, catalogs and archives them."

"I thought Blast Dynamics already had the idea. That's what got you going in the first place." Marilyn looked as awed as Jackson, her eyes everywhere.

"We're actively exploring the original theory Jon and I came up with," Dunn replied. The smile dropped off his face and he tried for nonchalant, which looked more like brick wall to Jackson. "By the way, how much did Jon tell you about our work here?"

"He remembered what to do," Jackson reassured him. "He crossed his arms, said intellectual property a lot, and told us the basics. Mostly, he and I discussed the properties of fascia."

Dunn's faint smile returned. "Good. Jon's enthusiasm gets the better of him sometimes, but the security message seems to be getting through. We've had no data leaks, and it needs to stay that way." He levelled a look at Jackson. "You'll be required to sign a non-disclosure agreement. And expected to take it seriously."

"Not a problem. From what little I know already, your work sounds really exciting. It deserves every chance to succeed."

Marilyn asked, "Is IP theft really that big a problem?"

Dunn walked them down the main aisle, murmuring greetings to the scientists and slapping a few shoulders. "Yes, it is," he answered. "Companies like ours can rise on the strength of a new idea, and vanish in a day if that idea gets 'independently discovered' by another, larger company. The pharmaceutical industry is worth hundreds of billions of dollars a year. All major outfits have their own research arms, and they often buy up smaller labs to get their intellectual property legitimately. But no one, large or small, is above taking a shortcut now and then." He sighed, an eloquent comment on the state of the industry. "Corporate espionage is alive and well in Big Pharma, I'm sorry to say."

They reached another door at the back of the long room, this one mostly glass. The space beyond was filled with close-packed metal shelving. "Reminds me of a library," Marilyn said.

"That's because it is," replied Dunn. "Promising compounds are archived here, in a strictly controlled environment."

They exited through the anteroom and retrieved their phones from the lockers. "Dump the booties, but keep the suits on." Dunn led them back into the main building and over to Door Number Two, another imposing barrier.

The second door opened onto a similar anteroom. "This is our lead optimization and DMPK lab," Dunn said as the inner door opened with a quiet hush. "That's drug metabolism and pharmacokinetics. Here we take the promising compounds and try to break them. We test them on single-celled organisms and tissue cultures, and see what might actually work. We're just beginning this phase now."

Lab two was all steel and white enamel, stuffed with another fortune in high-end equipment. Aside from a more complicated fume hood and a cluster of computer stations in the far corners, Jackson was at a loss to identify anything. About a dozen scientists worked at various stations throughout the room.

"So I get what fascia is, I think," Marilyn said as Dunn took them down the room. "It's all the strings and sheets that hold us together, and the goo that makes everything slide around. Stuff can go wrong with fascia, I suppose, like with anything else. But is it worth all this?"

Jackson looked over at Dunn. "Kind of a good question, actually. Fascia is important, it's the support system for everything our bodies do, but you guys must have put millions into this place."

"Tens of millions," Dunn replied. "Seeing a new therapeutic from discovery through to production can take ten years and a billion dollars, and that's being conservative. Is what we're developing worth it? Jon and I think so, and so do our early stage backers."

He pulled out a stool and sat down, inviting them to do likewise. "Now I come to the part where I'm careful what I say. As are we all, aren't we?" His voice raised to boom off the walls of the lab.

"Yes, Mr. Dunn," droned the lab techs in the room, not even looking up from their tasks.

"A silly grade-school exercise," he continued in his normal tone, "but useful as a reminder. What I can say is that your summary of fascia's importance is fundamentally correct. If a system in your body is working well, that's partly because the fascia beneath and around it is healthy. And vice versa. A disorder of your fascia, by definition, will affect the system it supports.

"Back in our original lab, Jon and I started messing with fibroblasts. We developed some theories that might change our understanding and treatment of disease, and worked those into a unique chemical formula. There's a long road ahead of us that can't be rushed before we're ready for clinical trials, and we have to guard our intellectual property closely, but it looks promising."

Dunn's face remained taciturn, but deep within his brown eyes Jackson saw the same glint of excitement he'd seen with Harrowman.

Jackson felt it, too. The atmosphere in the lab seemed electric with the potential behind their work. "That sounds thrilling, all right," he said. "Which disease are you targeting, if I can ask?"

Dunn leaned forward until the lab stool creaked. This time the excitement in his eyes reached his face. "All of them."

He resumed the tour, walking them deeper into the testing lab. past more machines. "But first, baby steps. Take the original idea and discover stable variations. We have over a thousand iterations now. Run each qualifying lead through a hundred tests, both in vitro—" he gestured at a rack of test tubes "—and in silico." He pointed at the computer workstations. "The surviving candidates get put through a hundred more, and more after that."

"Then it's on to human testing?" asked Marilyn.

Dunn allowed another emotion to touch his face. Jackson interpreted it as a mix of surprise and frustration. "Clinical trials? No, like I said, those are years away. There are a dozen more steps to go through first, and waves of governmental oversight and approvals."

Dunn's lab coat buzzed. He pulled out a small phone and glanced at the message, then stabbed out a reply. As he did so, Jackson felt his ears pop. The door at the end of the long room opened and closed with a smooth hush. A youngish man in a hooded Tyvek suit, surgical gloves and face mask stepped through, his full attention on a small, white box he carried in both hands. He placed it down by a woman stacking glass dishes inside one of the futuristic white boxes.

"No luck, Dorey. The mass spectrometer shows these as still contaminated. Run the next batch through an extra filtration, okay?"

"Reggie, I need you." Dunn beckoned the young man over. "I have to take care of something. These two are on a basic lab tour, and this one—" he gestured at Jackson "—is going to be our in-house massage therapist. You know what to show them. Finish up for me, thanks." He nodded at them both and was gone.

Reggie said "Of course, Mr. Dunn," and snapped off a pair of surgical gloves. His handshake was fast and strong. "Reggie Mancini, molecular biologist, senior lab manager and tour guide, at your service. So, what have you seen so far?"

"Most of it, I think," Jackson said. "Harold told us a bit of what you're shooting for here. It sounds fantastic."

Reggie nodded, setting a headful of black curls bouncing under his hoodie. "Old Well-Dunn is a little sparse with his words. Still, I have to watch what I tell you. Corporate piracy and all, you know." He winked as he said it. "You haven't seen the clean room yet. Come on over."

He led them to a window set in the end wall. The glass was thick and lined with metal mesh. More security. Beyond lay another white room, dotted with the most exotic equipment yet. A couple of fully-suited lab techs were focused on tasks inside.

"Here's where we do our materials handling and testing," Reggie said. "These first two rooms are mostly prep work, making the initial ingredients. In there is the kitchen where we cook the stuff, then test what we've got. That's the exciting room."

"Can't do shit in there without the slave labour out here," called Dorey.

Jackson smiled, but listened closely. The exchange sounded like good-natured banter. That was a plus. He'd done some massage work in toxic office environments before, and doing stress-management chair massage in a place where everyone hated their job was like throwing a cup of water on a burning building. So far, Blast Dynamics seemed like a pleasant place to work.

"We probably can't go in," commented Marilyn, staring through the glass.

"Hah!" Reggie snorted. "Old Well-Dunn would blow a gasket over the security breach. Nobody wearing a Visitor suit gets anywhere near the action. But aside from that," he got serious, "we protect our samples. When a promising drug candidate comes along, we don't want to miss it because we were sloppy."

As Reggie talked, Jackson saw his eyes flick up and over their shoulders to a clock Jackson had spotted on the wall. Reggie was polite and professional, but he obviously wanted to get back to work.

Jackson stuck out his hand. "Well, thanks for the tour, Reggie. You've been generous with your time."

Reggie brightened up and turned back towards the anteroom. "My pleasure. I'll show you out."

In the long corridor behind the offices Jackson's curiosity got the better of him. He pointed down the hall. "We haven't seen door number three yet."

"Oh, that? Come on." Reggie took them over and worked the number pad. The anteroom for this lab felt cooler than the first two, unused. Reggie stuck out his hand for the inner door.

"Don't we need jumpsuits?" Marilyn asked.

Reggie laughed. "Definitely not. This lab isn't commissioned yet. And once it is, trust me, we won't be worried about a few stray hairs."

The first thing Jackson saw as the door opened was a long row of cages near the far wall, large enough to hold a dog. A rack of rat-sized cages sat on the counter halfway down the room. A central island held more of the upscale lab equipment, but the room's main purpose was crystal clear.

"Once we're done with molecular testing and process purification, we'll seek approval for in vivo tests," Reggie told him. "Then Lab Three will get opened up. That won't be for a few years yet, though. One step at a time in this business."

They spent a moment looking in, but there seemed no reason to tour the room. After a few more pleasantries Reggie took them back to the receptionist and they said their goodbyes.

Once outside, Jackson tugged Marilyn onto the stretch of grass between the building and the street. "Let's go over here, I want to check this out."

A dozen big trees threw islands of shade over the expanse of smooth lawn. Autumn was already well underway and the leaves showed off a blaze of reds and yellows above their heads. A few cedar-slat benches, and an artistic one in faded pink, sprouted from the grass among the trunks.

"Hah! Thought so," Jackson said as they stopped by it. The bench was a single web of formed plastic, its strands flowing in graceful arcs from backrest to seat. He sat down on a thickened, solid pad, ran a hand over the gleaming flesh-coloured plastic, found it firm but with a bit of give, and laughed. "Tough but springy. Perfect! See how the strands go every which way, the open spaces between them all different sizes? But still it looks right somehow. Feels right."

"Uh, sure," said Marilyn, sitting next to him on a second pad. "They put some solid chunks in for the seats, that was a good idea."

"Not solid chunks. Look closer. This one's rounder, and the one you're sitting on is longer. It's fascia. Loose fascia, with a fibroblast and a fasciacyte. I love it!"

Marilyn gave him a 'you're such a nerd' eye roll and got up to leave.

On their way back to the Subaru Jackson pointed a thumb back at the building and said, "So, what do you think?"

Marilyn shrugged. "I think I'll set up an investment alert for when this operation goes public. As for the rest of it—nothing. We delivered the package, we had a look around. I'd say mission accomplished and case closed."

Relief washed through him as a knot untied itself in his gut. The last thing he needed was any complication in his life.

He'd had one weird night, that was all. Case closed. By the time they reached the car he was whistling.

Chapter 5

NO MORE MISTAKES

The pale gold of the afternoon light was descending into an early dusk, but he could still see the vines. He'd harvested the grapes himself a week ago when Autumn's crisp touch first brushed the fragrant air of his garden, and now the leaves were showing their first edge of yellow. He studied the vine in front of him, traced its path with his hand. The vine was headed down for its long sleep. The trunk that had birthed it was brown and knurled, rich and scarred with long years, one of his oldest plants.

He found himself refusing to see how much the trunk resembled the hand that caressed it. Weakness, always there to be discovered and crushed. He ran his eyes from trunk to hand, let in and acknowledged the inevitable lesson.

Markovic stepped up behind him, the only man on Earth he'd allow to do so, and held out a phone. "For you, Uncle."

"Tell me," he said into the thing.

"It's done. The ambulance arrived in time. The patient was attended to."

The vine in front of him had done its summer's work. Was it time for the pruning? Grapevines were touchy. They needed to be cut back to allow for the new growth. But prune too soon and the plant's life would weep out, weakening the next summer's crop. Don't prune at all and you had a useless mess. He paused with the secaturs, considering.

"You told me you had Sachs under lock and key. Always accompanied outside the lab, no contact with anyone. What happened?"

"He asked to go for a walk in the woods to clear his head. They took him to Lynn Valley and he out-hiked them. We searched and watched, but he stayed out of sight. When our man saw him headed for the last Seabus he took action. The ambulance attendants picked him up on the other side."

An honest mistake, a decent recovery. "So everything is in order, then."

"There was—a small problem. A bystander, a young man. He helped Sachs off the Seabus, walked with him a fair ways. The old guy gave him a package."

His grip on the phone tightened. He ordered himself to relax. "Tell me you picked up the bystander."

The line hissed with a moment's silence. "I wasn't there. The attendants let him go. They knew nothing about any package. But they took his picture."

"A picture. Of one stranger. In a city of two million." He lifted the secaturs, positioned their jaws around the dying branch.

"We know who he is, Uncle. We did a reverse image search. It was easy, he has no security at all. And he's got red hair and freckles. The search took no time. He's a massage therapist. We have his name and address. One other thing."

"Tell me."

The man on the phone said, "He came to the lab this morning and handed over the package. Then we hired him. We're his new clients. But I'm sure he knows nothing."

"How sure? What was in the package?"

The line hissed again. "Enough to get some attention, but nothing that points to us. Still, I can't be a hundred percent sure. What do you want to do, Uncle?"

He felt a glimmer of the old rush, the high of watching a

campaign's hundred moving pieces as the deadline approached. But this wasn't his game. A reverse image search. He wouldn't have thought of that. "This is your operation. What's your decision?"

He could practically hear the man's chest swell. "We should watch him, Uncle."

"So watch him."

"I'll need help."

That was fair, and good judgment to ask. "You will have it. Franko, Donnie and Johnny are finished watching Sachs. I will retask them to this. Markovic will see to it."

"The Three Stooges? They've already lost one man. Their failure with Sachs caused all this."

"Respect!" He snapped the correction through the line. "They are family. They are loyal. Use them for the skills they have. You must learn this."

"Yes, Uncle. It should only be for a few days. Until we're sure the massage man knows nothing."

"No more mistakes. The time is getting close. We must be perfect now."

"Yes, Uncle. No more mistakes." The line went quiet.

He handed Markovic back the phone and placed his attention on the vine, but found it difficult. The family's future rode on the back of this venture. They had lost so much to the barbarian invaders, those unprincipled hotheads who had invaded the city, brandished their guns and announced, 'all this is ours.' The family had been beaten, stripped bare and shoved to the sidewalk. Forgotten. The acid of that defeat burned in the back of his mouth.

This one project would bring the family back to life. Or finish them.

He pulled back the secaturs. The vines would not be pruned today. Not yet.

Chapter 6

DANGEROUS HAPPINESS

Marilyn's voice came through his phone with a rush of background noise. "I'm coming over, all right?" She was in her car, probably already halfway here.

"You bet," Jackson answered. "Bring your toothbrush."

"Got it. See you in fifteen."

He made a quick scan of his apartment. It was spacious by Vancouver standards, eight hundred square feet on the first floor of a red brick apartment building near the foot of Balsam Street, close to Kitsilano Beach. The kitchen and bathroom were clean. No renegade underwear in the bedroom. Everything seemed neat enough.

Good. Now for the real check. He shifted his vision a little, allowed the vigilance in his mind to relax.

As always, it caught his breath. Lines, angles and arcs flowed into being across the entire apartment like a clear geometric overlay of shimmering light. The major pieces of couch, coffee table and dining table anchored the living area with a deep ochre glow. All three were offset to each other in a complex set of angles that shimmered a pleasing ocean blue. Chairs, lamps, bookshelves and side tables occupied their perfect places, ideally placed in relationship to walls and windows and intermeshed with their neighbours.

The apartment danced with an intricate fractal symmetry he could both see and feel.

He glanced back down the hall to the door. A tiny shelf on the wall held a notebook and pencil, the notebook aligned to the shelf and pencil aligned to them both.

He stepped over and, with a flick of a finger, knocked the pencil askew. The touch of chaos glimmered an angry green. The sight of it pricked at his mind, but he let it be. He was able to let it be.

Both he and the apartment were ready for Marilyn's visit. So unlike the first time she'd been here.

In June, thanks to ineffective pharmaceuticals and a stress level bordering on terror, he'd been at the mercy of his condition. His mind had been laid bare. He'd seen the patterns behind everything, all the time, fascinated and drowning in equal measure.

His pattern sense had drawn evil into his life. He'd called the cops, of course, tried to explain it to Marilyn, standing shoulder-square in his living room with her partner Ahmed.

He remembered the crushing realization, in the middle of his statement, that it was not going to end well.

They hadn't thrown his ass back in the psych ward. But they'd come close.

Enough of that, he chided himself. Marilyn believed you. That time's over. She's coming. She's bringing her toothbrush.

His pattern sense still blazed, almost unchecked. He was enjoying it, he realized. But it was still a dangerous happiness. He may have his condition under control now, thanks to a persistent doctor and some good meds, but it could easily become far too much of a good thing.

He checked for her car from the living room window, ten feet above the sloping sidewalk of Balsam Street and a couple of buildings up from Cornwall Avenue. The sliver of city outside his building glittered with movement. The last of the commuter rush was finding its way home. Cars tooled up and down the street looking for parking. Pedestrians dodged puddles from the recent rain on their way to Cornwall's string of restaurants or crossed the avenue to Kits Beach. Every moving thing left shimmers of phosphorescence where it had just been and shone slim echoes of light to where they might be going. The sight was beautiful.

No silver Jeep yet; Marilyn must still be on her way. His pattern sense flashed a brief red, highlighting a champagne Toyota compact parked next to the fire hydrant up the street. A man's head stuck up over the seat in the semi-dark evening. Probably waiting for someone in another building. The guy was either brave or foolhardy. One driveby from Vancouver's camera-laden parking enforcement team and he'd be facing a hefty fine.

Still no Jeep. He closed the door on his condition and turned for the kitchen. He had time to pull dinner out of the fridge.

He almost lost the beef stroganoff over the side of the stove when his apartment door rattled to a loud knock. "Shit," he muttered as he hustled down the hall. He opened the door to a stern-looking Marilyn, toothbrush in one hand and a strip of duct tape in the other.

"You really should do something about your building security," she said, waggling the tape. Then she was inside his arms and giving his ribs a healthy squeeze. "Smells great in here. I went for a run after work. I'm famished."

The stroganoff passed muster, Marilyn shovelling it in while she talked around the mouthfuls about her day. "Started off pretty normal," she said, "you know, paperwork and the neighbourhood cruise and a couple of domestic calls. Caught a shoplifter walking down the sidewalk, his backpack just crammed with stuff. Still had price tags sticking out the top. Then," her hazel eyes sparked, "we got a call to assist."

He knew his cues by now. "Really? Assist with what?"

"Arrest of a known gang enforcer. He's a wiry little guy, but he's been mean since the day before he was born and knows how to win a fight. VPD suspects him in at least eight strongarm events and two murders, but we never had sufficient cause to pick him up. Until last night. It seems he went a round with his girlfriend and she decided to give us a call. Their place was loaded with evidence, including both murder weapons. So we geared up and headed for the docks."

He cleaned up some sauce with a chunk of sourdough. "Why does it always seem to happen on the docks?"

She laughed. "I know, right? This bust had nothing to do with the shipyards, he was down there selling a Harley to a stevedore. Of course, with somebody like that, you don't walk up to him swinging a pair of cuffs. So we did a triple S on him."

"Sun, sand and serenade?" he ventured.

She laughed again. He could get used to that sound. "No, but I'm going to tell Ahmed you said that. Stage, surround, swarm. He never saw it coming. We had twelve gunsights pointed at him before he could so much as twitch. Of course, he got in a couple of licks during the takedown. But he's gone now, for good."

Jackson jerked his head up, looked her over. "You okay?"

She pointed to her side. "Bruised rib or two. You can kiss it better in awhile." She finished her last noodle with a slurp and winked. "Like, maybe, now."

They took the time to clear the dishes. He could see it, the tiny way she favoured her right side. "You enjoy your work, don't you?"

"Yeah, I do," she replied, rinsing a plate. "Not the getting kicked in the ribs part. But taking bad guys off the streets, definitely. Especially the important ones." She was silent a moment. "So this afternoon I made a few enquiries around the building. About helping out with Organized Crime."

He paused, dish in hand, as a chill rose up from his toes. What to say? Vancouver gangs had taken a turn for the ultra-violent in recent years, shooting at each other in the middle of town with no care for collateral damage. Still, this was her job.

More than that, it was her calling, he was sure of it. But the thought gave his stomach a lurch.

"Why there?" he settled with.

She flashed him a frown. "As opposed to what? Traffic enforcement or school liaison? I want to make a difference, Freckles. A big one." Kitchen in order, she took his hand and pulled him to the couch. They sat. "Jackson, do you even know the scale of what we're facing? No, I suppose most people don't. Today's gangs don't just peddle drugs and girls on the street corners and call it a day. That's what everybody sees, but it goes way deeper than that. They're international, global. Borders mean nothing to them. Cars, drugs, people, clothes, information, money, weapons, you name it, they'll get it and move it. Organized crime siphons up billions, and I'm talking just in this country alone."

"Uh, wow," he said, about the size of the problem and, even more, the passion that had lit up her face. "But you guys take them down all the time, don't you?"

"Sure," she replied, "after hundreds of hours of police work and an eye-crossing pile of paperwork so they'll actually stay behind bars. But more always take their place. And we seldom get near the real money." She stared into him. "You know where that money comes from, right? All those billions?"

He thought about it. "Dealers? Pimps? Users?"

She laid a warm hand on his knee, keeping up the stare. "From us. All of us. That much money is a serious hit to the economy regardless of where it leaves the system and gets into their pockets. These organizations are leeches and they're bleeding society dry. And what do they do with those billions? Think really bad things, then think worse."

She lifted her hand from his knee and sat up straight. "I know it's tough, but I got into this job to do what's right, not what's easy. I can do little bits of good on patrol, one person at a time. Or maybe I can help out in bucketloads. I'm going to push for Organized Crime."

A jolt of fear went through him at her pronouncement, but by now he knew Marilyn well enough to keep any arguments to himself. "Let me know how it goes."

She laughed, giving him a smack on the arm. "You'll be the first to hear, silly. Now, I believe we had some plans." She jumped up and jerked him off the sofa.

At the door to the bedroom she stopped him with a hand on his chest. "Turn it on."

Well, okay. He let his vision shift, allowed the inner door to open.

Marilyn lit up as her body's energy and geometry came alive. The spark in her eyes flared. Her hand on his chest threw off waves of a beautiful green, not pushing him away but somehow drawing him close. Bright lines of silver arced towards him from the balls of her feet, revealing her whole body poised for a leonine pounce. Her right side pulsed with a touch of red guarding, but she'd spoken truly, her ribs were only bruised. He'd kiss them better, and more.

This was going to be good.

"Oh yeah," she murmured. She closed her fist around his shirt and launched him through the door.

Later, as Marilyn dreamed her way past midnight, he stumbled to the kitchen for a drink. Outside the window Vancouver was drenched and glistening again, but mostly empty and quiet. His pattern sense, still keen, flashed a burst of electric blue at a sudden movement up the street. The Toyota by the fire hydrant was just pulling away.

He went back to bed with that car on his mind and a twinge of unease in his heart.

Chapter 7

STOP THE CLOCK

Georgia stepped up to the mirror on her side of the double bathroom to begin her morning routine. Jackson was coming over soon to deliver her biweekly massage, so the makeup would wait. No use getting it all over the face cradle of his massage table. But there was plenty else to do.

Looks like this didn't come cheap. Or easy.

She started with water. Always water, the elixir of life. Her glass had stood on the shelf all night with its cargo of ionized glacier water, releasing any toxins picked up from its plastic transport bottle. She plinked in three fat teardrops of liquid trace minerals, wonderful for the nervous system. Her hand reached over to the bottle collection beside the sink and came back with the multi-vitamin, the extra B's, the gleaming omega 3 oil capsule for brain health and dose of nicotinamide riboside for DNA and telomere repair. She tossed them to the back of her throat, lifted the glass and drank it down. A top-up from the decanter in the corner and the glass went back on the shelf.

Only eleven more glasses today and she'd be at optimal hydration.

Next up was her mouth. She gave her teeth a thorough clean with the non-fluoride toothpaste and extra soft brush, ran a stiffer brush over her tongue to chase away the night film, then gave it all an antibacterial rinse. Her hand reached over to the bottle collection again, and this time came back with metformin and resveratrol.

The door creaked open behind her. Charles came in, sliding past to stare bleary-eyed into his mirror. "Morning, Heart," he mumbled. He'd come up with that endearment when they were still in high school. The simple term, and even more the man who said it, still warmed her soul.

"It's morning, all right. Sleep well? How was the shift? I didn't hear you come in." Which meant that his evening stint as an emergency room doctor at St. Paul's Hospital had gone late, but she knew he liked to tell her about it.

"It was nuts. The gangs are at it again. Three gunshots and a stabbing, all from the same bar. At least no bystanders were caught this time. I had to spend an extra hour with one of them. A single entrance wound, but his abdomen was a mess. Can you believe they've found fragmenting rounds? Nicked his aorta, lacerated his small intestine, basically exploded his liver. Kept me up past my bedtime." He yawned into the mirror and started in with a comb.

"Did he make it?"

"Nah. We boxed him." Charles was matter-of-fact about it, a mental switch she'd never been able to understand. "His body's in the morgue. His soul is no doubt sweating bullets somewhere trying to explain his life choices."

She picked up a brush and began on her own hair, which took a little longer than his. She needed one more capsule to complete the morning supplement regimen. Her left hand slipped over to the bottle collection as her right kept going with the brush.

Charles noticed. Of course. She could hear the professional mask slip over his voice, so non-judgemental it hurt. "Any new ones lately?" he asked.

She made her hand complete its journey, return with the supplement, which she dry-swallowed. "No, nothing new. You've seen all these before. You've cleared them for my use." Unlike her husband, her filter wasn't nearly so professional. Even she heard the tinge of resentment in the words.

He sighed. "I love you, Georgia. I just want to make sure you're safe. You run across some crazy ideas sometimes. A magazine article, a new podcast or pseudo-study, and suddenly a pill shows up on your shelf or you're off to try some new therapy. All I ask is that I check them out first. So you don't get hurt. That's all."

She felt the old sadness tug at her eyes, frustrated that they still had this argument, even years after they'd made the agreement. "I know, Charles. I just want to make sure I'm happy and healthy for a good, long time."

He'd started on his teeth, mashing at them with a brush full of fluoridated poison, no care at all. She was sure he wasn't going to keep them past seventy. He didn't try to speak around the rising foam, but the force of his actions spoke volumes. Waves of irritation poured off him.

Which transmuted her sadness to a flash of anger. "Really, Charles. I'm not doing anything new. You've already researched and approved everything here, which you'd know if you bothered to look at the shelf instead of interrogating me. I'm living up to our deal. And in case you forgot, you promised not to get so grumpy about it."

He spit, wiped the remnants off his face, then turned to face her. "Grumpy? That doesn't begin to describe what I feel about this, Georgia. Look, I get it. You want to be healthy as long as possible. Me too. So we eat well and get some exercise and look both ways before crossing the street."

His professional filter was gone. Now, standing by the sink in his pyjamas, with a fleck of toothpaste on his cheek the only flaw on that Clark Kent face she'd fallen in love with as a teenager, she saw the man behind the doctor. The man who had done the schooling, spent the days in the libraries, worked the insane hours. The one who was convinced he knew what was best for everybody else. His voice hardened into that patronizing tone she hated.

"But that's not enough, is it?" he said. "To live well and healthy for as long as we can. Grow old gracefully and try to stay out of assisted living. That's not good enough. You want to stop the clock, Georgia. Stay young forever. And I'm telling you, Heart, it can't be done. Precious few of us make it to a hundred, and nobody gets past 120. That's just the truth of it."

She reached for the eye cream, so rich in hyaluronic acid it gleamed. "The science is advancing." They were deep into the old argument they'd had dozens of times, and the words tumbled out of her. "More money and real attention is aimed at life extension now than ever before. Breakthroughs are made every day. People are reaping the benefits of it, right now. And I'm going to be one of them."

"My point exactly." He turned to face her. "They're breakthroughs. Maybe. Or maybe not. They haven't been tested, Heart, haven't been approved. There's a system for all of this and it's there to keep people safe. You just have to give it time to work."

"Time? I'm 34, Charles. How much time do I have to wait? Ten years? Twenty? Fifty? So I can use the approved treatment when I'm seventy, instead of listening to all the testing and discovery that's happening right now, and taking advantage of it while I still have some youth to save?" She finished up with her eyes, placed the small bowl of cream back in its place, and sighed. "Don't worry, I've checked everything out with you. I know you want what's best for me. But give me a little credit for knowing what's best for me, too. By the way, Jackson's coming over soon. We'll be set up in the living room."

"Jackson! I forgot. Great, haven't seen him in over a week." Charles turned back to his mirror.

In the bedroom she pulled on a sweatshirt and shorts, easy to drop come massage time. She reviewed the conversation, checking it over. She'd made no promises, said no lies. Charles had vetted every supplement currently on her shelf and every therapy she'd already been to. She hadn't broken their agreement.

Not yet.

Chapter 8

Make me young again

Jackson didn't bother to knock, just flipped open Georgia's front door and levered his portable massage table through the entrance. "Hey guys, I'm here!" he called into the house, and headed for the living room.

The dark-stained wood floors and matching thick trim around the doorways set off Georgia's choice of warm-whites and roses for the walls, making the place welcoming and cozy. Charles made good coin as an emergency room doctor, but the house was Georgia's. She came from old Vancouver money. Her job, if it could be called that, was to socialize with the city's elite and convince them to donate to various charities and cultural events. This living room had seen eye-wateringly huge sums talked out of some of the biggest pockets in the country.

He slid his massage table out of its bag and snapped it open with a few practiced, reflexive moves. Two flicks and a tuck, and Georgia's table was covered with thick flannel sheets.

"I'm here, too," she said from the base of the stairs, coming down from the bedrooms. "Nice to see you. How's Marilyn?"

They chatted for a few minutes, catching each other up on the week's events. He spent a few minutes recounting the Seabus incident and the lab trip. "So at least I picked up a new office client out of it all," he finished. "Should fill out the schedule a bit more."

"That's wonderful! Almost back to normal."

"Pretty much." He added, "Marilyn's interested in moving up the ladder at the VPD."

"Good for her," called Charles from the door as he came down the stairs.

"Of course she is. She's not going to stay in one place for long." Georgia busied herself taking off a sock. She kept her back turned to Charles, who disappeared into the kitchen. "So, how many drawers is she using?"

"Drawers? Sometimes she brings her toothbrush, if that's what you mean."

She glanced over her shoulder, some kind of look in her eye. "Her toothbrush. Well, it's a start."

Nothing more was forthcoming, so he let it slide. "Here, let me look at you."

Georgia stood in her bare feet and loose workout clothes and squared herself to him. "Just relax, that's it. Now turn to the side, please. And once more." He stepped back, let himself relax slightly, and switched from conversational sight into assessment mode.

The body before him sprang into bright relief, a miraculous assemblage of 206 bones, hundreds of muscles, dozens of movement vectors, all woven together by its fascial webs. He saw the minute tilt of Georgia's head towards her right shoulder; to be expected, she spent most days with her right ear glued to a phone. The muscles of her shoulder arced gracefully up to their attachments at the back of her neck and skull. Their strength was balanced by the prominent sternomastoid muscles that sloped down to the delicate dip at the top of her sternum.

The fascia that wrapped those muscles and enveloped her neck also swept down in a lovely and elegant spiral. So the sideways tilt of her head also turned it a little to the left.

Her right foot turned out a little. A faint glimmer of yellow restriction flowed down to her ankle and up to her hip, brighter at the knee where it all began. Jackson had worked on Georgia for a couple of years and knew the story. She'd slipped on a kelp-covered rock when she was eleven trying to keep up with the boys at an upper-crust summer camp on the Sunshine Coast. She'd given her medial collateral ligament and surrounding muscles a good pull. The fascia had responded by becoming thick and tough. It didn't slow her down much then, but had grown more prominent with the passing years.

"How's the knee?" he asked.

She grimaced. "Oh, you know. Same old, same old."

Not even close, he thought. His steady work over the past two years had made a world of difference. Today he'd nudge it along a bit more.

"Okay. I'll step outside and let you get situated." Once she called him back in he turned the corner of the sheet, starting with her leg. "Let's see if we can do some good."

Georgia snuggled into the facerest. "Do your thing, Jackson. Make me young again."

He slipped into the rhythm of his work. Left hip, thigh, knee, calf, foot. Working through the skin and into the muscles, feeling for tight spots, watching the movement of the limb on the table as he massaged. Just the usual minor tensions of daily life, easily swept away. He re-draped the leg and moved over to the right.

He rocked the leg a little. The pattern revealed itself, the limitation wrapping like a bandage around her knee and reaching around to the front of her thigh, keeping her leg from free movement. His hands felt the thickened restriction as an area of tight skin, resistant to his work. As above, so below. Fascia connected everything, fed everything. When deeper structures tightened up you felt it on the surface.

His fingers pressed in. Fascia demanded patience, so he didn't hurry. He turned and pulled until he could feel where the tissues were most restricted—along the knee's inside edge, in a thin but strong ribbon that wrapped up towards Georgia's hip. His other hand found the southern end of the restriction, partway down her calf. He pulled and twisted, testing the area's give, and found a short glide with a hard stop, like he'd hit a brick wall. Back at the top of the restriction he anchored it with one hand and applied firm pressure with his fingers. Then he pressed deeper, and pulled slowly down towards Georgia's calf.

And again. And again, varying direction as the fascia released.

The hard restriction lessened and softened. By the fourth pull he felt that the fascia had gone its course for today. When he tested it again the brick wall had turned into a more natural elastic spring.

More work, from light stroking to deeper massage, set the fascia into its new configuration and worked out the muscles. He moved on to the rest of Georgia's session, encountering little more than everyday tensions.

When she was up and dressed again she tested out the knee. "Better," she said. "Not gone, but it moves more than it did."

He smiled. "These things take time. But really, you're doing great. Keep up the good work and you'll last forever."

Charles, done whatever he'd been doing in the kitchen, passed by the opening to the living room and heard Jackson's comment. He hustled up the stairs, but not before Jackson saw a look of dark anger suffuse his friend's face.

Chapter 9

ENNUI

Ruling Vancouver's crime world had its occasional perks. Shaheen took a break from the interrogation to catch his breath and enjoy the moment. The bare rock walls of the sub-basement filled the cavern with a dark, midnight scent. Sharp-angled hexagonal pillars emerged from the native stone, spaced around the circular room to join up with the ribs of the vaulted ceiling. None of it structural, of course, but he'd brought over an architect and stonemasons from Isfahan to give the room an authentic flair. He'd let on that the fancy decorations would impress the special guests allowed into the club's sub-basement for the most elite parties.

It impressed the guests, that much was true. But he'd fashioned the traditional decor entirely for himself. So he could watch the looks on their faces when they were dragged into this most soundproof and forbidding of rooms.

The chamber was cool, with barely enough heat to push back the underground damp, but he felt a bead of sweat trickle down the scar on his back. It had been months since he'd had this much fun. The early days on this wet coast had been exciting, to be sure. Breaking ground in the new territory, announcing his arrival in Vancouver to the existing operations. Giving them the opportunity to step aside. Then showing them what modern warfare really looked like, the latest tactics coupled to an ancient ferocity, when they inevitably didn't.

Ah, what glorious times. But then peace had descended on his life like a wet blanket. Work had become an everyday routine: move products, manage shipping, guide his people, collect the funds, and report to his superiors. He'd begun to fall victim to that most corrosive of emotions: ennui.

Back to business. He turned to the center of the room, to the young man standing in the middle of the gaping lion's mouth of the floor's mosaic. Just a grown-up boy, really, playing at being an adult. His youth was evident in the artfully torn jeans, the fancy, glitter-coated basketball runners, and the frilly attempt at a beard. His grey designer hoodie with the New Canadians patch lay crumpled in the corner. Three thick gold ropes draped around his neck and down his thin chest, an advertisement to the world that the New Canadians were an outfit worth belonging to.

Nothing wrong with that, Shaheen thought. Maybe a little obvious.

The bright gold chains were a nice complement to the thin streams of red dripping down from the lashes across his chest. Shaheen would have to remember that colour combination for his next remodel. The somewhat more substantial chains that ran from the boy's wrists to the rings in the floor trembled slightly, letting off a faint, pleasant jingle.

"Now, Ruffalo, you really must do better. What you've told me I simply cannot believe. You picked up the precursor chemicals from the ship, yes? All twenty barrels?" The daintily-whiskered chin dipped in a yes. "Then you were halfway to Surrey, on your way to our facility, in the middle of the night, when three men—it was three, right?" A mumble, which Shaheen took to be another yes. "They made you stop, shot your partner in the head, and drove off with the entire shipment. Tell me again, please, how you survived this terrible thing."

The man-child started in on his 'I don't know, happened so fast' lie when Shaheen held up a hand, struck by a thought.

"Ruffalo? Where did you come up with that name? Surely your mother didn't call you that."

The boy flinched into silence at the sudden movement. His eyes ignored Shaheen's raised hand. They flew instead between the small, leather whip in Shaheen's other hand and the bull mastiff watching with a Cerberus stare from the edge of the circular room. The dog's breath steamed gently in the coolness of the sub-basement. "Uh, no, name's, um, Leonard. Ruffalo, you know, from the actor? I thought it sounded, uh, better."

Shaheen shook his head. "Leonard. Never be ashamed of your heritage, my friend. That's a fine, strong name. Now tell, me, Leonard. About the thieves. About how I'm to believe you're not one of them. And be strong."

At the encouragement, the boy found a shred of courage. He stiffened his spine and glared sparks from red-rimmed eyes. "Fuck you say, Shaheen. The delivery's gone. They plugged my man Fallon, pasted his brains all over the truck, and pushed me into the ditch. Why? Fuck if I know, they probably didn't want to waste the bullet. Did my man Fallon tip someone to the meth chemicals run? How the fuck should I know, but I hope he fuckin' did, you psycho freak. None of it ever got down to me, I can tell you that. You think Fallon tells me shit like that? I'm bottom rung, I lift and carry. And now he's fuckin' dead and I'm in a, what is this, some kind of medieval dungeon? Come on, man, it was a robbery, these things happen. I. Know. Nothing, got it? You're lookin' for a truckload of ingredients, you ask management, not me. I got no idea, none. But I hope Fallon ripped it off under your fuckin' nose, and—"

The noises went on, but Shaheen's attention went to the door, which had opened. His lieutenant came into the chamber and walked over. Leonard, emboldened by Shaheen's inaction, began to shout. He leaned close to hear what his lieutenant had to say.

"We found it where you said, under a bush marked by a small

gold chain on a branch. Ten thousand in hundreds. They bought him cheap."

He clapped his lieutenant on the shoulder and shook his head. "No imagination at all. Thank you, my friend."

"One more thing. News from the maintenance man," he rumbled into Shaheen's ear. "Your instinct was right, putting him into the research facility. The Croats aren't finished. The Uncle definitely has ties there, one of his main people helps run it. And something has happened. A massage therapist came to visit the lab yesterday. Now the principals are—agitated. So is the Uncle. We checked up on the therapist and saw one of the Uncle's men watching him."

"Ah," said Shaheen, and his fingers flexed on the handle of the whip. A warm delight spread through his chest as he felt ennui recede into the shadows. "The Uncle. I'd thought we'd beaten him and the rest of the Croats out of the game entirely. Apparently not. How many men does he still have?"

The lieutenant answered, but Shaheen couldn't hear. The noise from the center of the room had reached a screeching volume. Young Leonard had found the strength in his real name, and was using it. The mastiff, excited, had risen to its feet. This was good. Young men should feel their power. From strength came truth, and Leonard was still professing his ignorance to the vaulted ceiling.

Professing the truth of his deceitful nature, blissfully unaware that the payment for his betrayal was in the vault upstairs.

"Enough." Shaheen reached around to the small of his back, drew the Sig Sauer pistol from its holster. The lieutenant stepped back to the wall. The Sig jumped in his hand and a thunderclap echoed around the room, announcing the end of a life. Chains rattled down to the tiles as the boy's blood drained into the lion's mouth on the floor.

"What would you like me to do?" The lieutenant nodded to the body.

Shaheen was riding the wave now, the wave of complexity, of twisting courses. "Let's have some fun. Chop off his foot. Leave it laced into that ridiculous shoe and throw it into the middle of Georgia Strait. That always creates such a wonderful stir. No, wait," another idea arrived, "have the dog chew it off. That will entertain their forensics team."

"And the rest?"

"Make sure his own mother could never find it. Then find that truck. Purchase satellite footage through our engineering firm if you need to. Those barrels are worth millions." Shaheen motioned to the dog, who he had never named, and tapped on the boy's right calf. With a single bark and a series of loud crunches, the mastiff went to work with those remarkable jaws.

"What about the other thing?" The lieutenant raised his voice over the ripping sounds.

"Give the maintenance man his bonus. If the Uncle believes this massage therapist is worth his attention, then we shall watch the watchers. Put some men on it. And find out more about this therapist."

Chapter 10

SIDE STREET SHUFFLE

After Georgia's session, Jackson spent the day setting up his massage table in two downtown condos and three more Westside homes. The traffic was its usual tangled mess, but he'd learned a trick or two and made it through his rounds without difficulty. Overall it was a full and satisfying workday.

Except for the followers.

A silver Honda Civic had slid out of a parking spot a block away from Georgia's and stayed a discreet three cars behind him all the way through downtown. It had followed him between patients, back over the Burrard Street Bridge and partway through his Westside run, always three cars back, barely in sight.

Glaringly obvious for its perfectly methodical obscurity. But it never came close enough to actually be threatening, and he was left gritting his teeth, unable to report it.

He scanned the parked cars as he left his last massage a block off Arbutus and 41st, but didn't see the Honda. Three blocks down Arbutus a phosphorescent swoosh of bright green momentum in his rearview mirror caught his attention as a shiny black Mercedes bulled its way out of 38th and into the line of cars.

Three cars back from his.

Irritation bloomed into anger. At 33rd he took advantage of a break in the flow and goosed his Subaru onto the cross street. The sedan made the turn from the wrong lane to keep up, to a chorus of bleating horns.

That did it. Borrowing a Gene Hackman line from an old spy movie he muttered, "Let's see what you've got." He patted the Subaru on the dash for luck, pulled a hard right and jammed the pedal down.

He was a traveling professional. He booked sessions all over town, every day, and could navigate most of Vancouver's streets from muscle memory. Whoever the hell these guys were, they were playing on his turf, and he was willing to bet they'd never played the side street shuffle.

The Subaru scooted halfway down the block in seconds. Another twist of the wheel and he swerved left into the long alley that paralleled 32nd Avenue.

It was close quarters, a single lane between backyard fences dotted with trash cans and garage doors. He saw a yellow flash highlight an obstacle ahead, his pattern sense spotting an encroaching recycle bin before he did, and swerved to avoid it. The Mercedes hadn't seen him dodge into the alley but they were paying attention. He heard tires squeal as it overshot, spotted him, and backed up to make the turn.

He rocked onto the next street, slotting himself between some loosely spaced cars, commuters heading home at the end of their day. They weren't pushing the speed limit and he had to stomp on the brakes hard. Behind him, two cars back, the Mercedes did the same.

They cruised downhill through a couple of lazy corners, everybody behaving themselves. Jackson knew a straight section was around the next bend—not a long one, but it didn't need to be. The car in front of him crested the corner. An instant before the straightaway came into view he pushed the pedal down and willed his condition to show him what he needed to see.

The barest green flicker illuminated the path ahead and he went for it. He caught the expression of stunned outrage on the old woman ahead of him as he blasted past her and nearly clipped her bumper on the re-entry.

The Mercedes tried the same move, but they were already too late. The straight stretch ended and a panel van rounded the corner. Horns blared as whoever was following him pushed the old lady to the curb in their effort to not get accordioned.

He was clear. More gas, two more fast corners, and he knew he'd lost them. "Hah!" he yelled at no one, clapping the Subaru on the dash again. He found Blenheim Street and turned back towards home.

Which was when he realized that, although he'd won, he had already lost. The champagne Toyota compact had been parked on his street the night before. They knew where he lived.

Once the anger faded he felt well and truly spooked. "Teague, what the hell are you doing?" he muttered on his way into the apartment. On his way through the door he straightened out the pencil on its little shelf. He'd only just got his life back after a summer of chaos. The last thing he needed was to antagonize ... whoever they were. He didn't want any trouble right now, of any kind.

They started it, said a hard corner of his mind.

Well, whatever. He had a date to keep. Marilyn was making dinner tonight. He rushed through a quick shower and change, eager to get to her arms and anxious to save the meal. On the way out the door he pocketed his toothbrush.

By the time he reached Marilyn's Yaletown condo building, unmolested by followers, the weirdness had vaporized in the heat of a growing anticipation.

"Freckles! Just in time!" Marilyn met him with an oven mitt and a wooden spoon as the elevator doors opened on the seventeenth floor. "How the hell long do you have to stir risotto?" He laughed and rushed in to save the kitchen.

The marinated pork loin was more than passable and the risotto turned out creamy and delicious. She'd over-steamed the carrots and peas, but butter covers all sins. During the meal their conversation spanned the range, as it often did. They covered climate change, the latest misdeeds at Vancouver City Hall, his visit with Georgia, her morning helping a young woman and child go from a life on Hastings and Gore to a single-room-occupancy shelter in a quiet corner of East Van, casual racism in the streets, and the weather. Jackson felt himself relax as the food and the company warmed his insides.

"I saw some cars today," he filled a lull in the conversation as the memory of the sedan came back to him.

"You're a traveling therapist in Vancouver, I'd imagine so," Marilyn replied deadpan. "Any in particular?"

"A black sedan. Before then a silver Accord. And last night a champagne Toyota, outside my apartment." He told her about the patterns, the strange movements and timings, the brief chase. "I have no idea why, but someone's watching me," he finished.

"But not right now?" she asked, taking another forkful of risotto.

Good question. He got up and went to the window, scanned the pavement seventeen floors below. "Don't think so. Hard to tell from up here."

"Wild," she said, then got quiet.

"Really. I'm not imagining this, Marilyn. If this is even a thing. All I'm saying is that there have been these cars doing weird things around me, and I get a creepy feeling about it. That's all."

"I know what you said. But in a city that's crammed with cars, don't you think a few of them are going to do unusual stuff? I mean, have you seen the drivers out there?" She nodded towards the window. As if on cue, they heard a distant screech and metallic thunk from the streets below.

That got a smile from both of them. Still. "Yeah, there's chaos everywhere, and yeah, I see it. But it's like background static, you know? Normal, oblivious people doing normal, oblivious things, I don't even see that anymore. It's like watching dust motes dancing in the sunshine, right? After a minute it's like they're not there anymore and you're looking for something more interesting. But this isn't that."

He got up and went over to the window, motioning her to follow. She did, with a touch of reluctance. Seventeen floors below, Yaletown buzzed with the evening rhythm. Richards Street glittered with the headlights of stopped cars, backed up behind the accident that was now surrounded by red flashing lights. Over to the left, Nelson Street sliced between two other residential towers, and they could just see a small piece of Helmcken off to the other side. It was typical city grid layout, all one-way streets, and everyone was trying to get somewhere—to home, to a restaurant, to somewhere else entirely.

Jackson let himself see it, really see it. Then he pointed.

"Do you see that?" he said, gesturing to the accident. An SUV had tried to push a turn and crinkled the door of an obstinate compact, maybe a Hyundai. Police had traffic control going and the other cars trickled past in systolic pulses. They heard frequent honks and bleats from the inconvenienced drivers. "See the rhythm to it, the on-and-off flow?"

"Sure," Marilyn replied at his shoulder. She didn't sound sure, or happy.

"See the really impatient one? The car that's going to cause a second accident?"

That caught her attention. She leaned closer to the thick curtain of glass that ran from floor to ceiling of her condo and stared down. "No, I don't."

"That red thing, looks like a Tesla. About ten cars back from the wreck. He's all lit up, yellow sparks coming off him in all directions. See how he's riding the brake, nosing around, looking for a way to pass?"

She was trying, and he was grateful for that. In truth, the

shifts the red car was making were slight ones, but he hoped she saw. "Nope," she said at last. "It's just like all the others, Jackson." Now a touch of concern was in her voice.

This better work, he told himself. "All the other traffic? It's doing normal stuff. I hardly even see it, just a blue blur, everyone doing what they're supposed to. But that guy stands out because he's doing something different. See? He's coming up to the accident now. He's going to squeeze past it like all the others, but he's not going to be happy about it. The second he's past, he's going to cut into the other lane and clip the fire truck that's just coming around the corner now." They saw and heard the big engine, red lights dancing, swing wide off Homer Street and barrel into position behind a police car.

She leaned forward some more. Do it, Jackson wished down at the red car. A cop waved the driver past. They both saw the red car surge away from the accident in a burst of speed. It almost tagged the car in front of it, then dodged left into the newly empty lane. By some miracle, the driver weaved past the rear bumper of the fire truck without a scratch and was gone, getting a few more honks for his efforts.

"Well, almost," he muttered.

"Yeah. Almost." Marilyn was back behind his shoulder now. "There are patterns everywhere," she said, leading them back to the meal. "You know that, maybe more than anybody. But, Jackson, just because you notice a strange pattern, that doesn't mean it's out to get you."

He sighed. "That black Mercedes today? I led it on a cruise. You know what I can do. High speed, corners, alleys, the whole bit. Marilyn, it stuck to me like glue."

She frowned. "You're not supposed to tell me stuff like that. But yeah. That's weird."

They tossed some small talk back and forth over pecan pie from True Confections. The air between them warmed as they did the dishes in the tight quarters of her cockpit kitchen. She flicked soap suds at him and asked, "Did you bring your toothbrush?"

"No, not tonight. I have some early work tomorrow. First day at the new gig, that biomedical place." It was a lie. His toothbrush was in the pocket of his jacket in the hall. "I should go."

"Oh. Have fun tomorrow. Tell me how it went over dinner?"

"Sure." They kissed goodnight and he left. A block away from the building a silver Honda Civic flashed into view behind him. He refused to see it.

Chapter 11

A MOVIE STAR'S BUTT CHEEKS

Jackson proved to be as popular at Blast Dynamics as he expected. Office massage was an occasional treat for him and a welcome respite from the office routine for his clients. In comparison to his regular work it was quick, easy, and fun.

Blast's front door procedure had changed since his first visit. The receptionist met him at the door to buzz him in, checked his ID with an apologetic air, and clipped a Visitor tag to his shirt. As he shouldered his massage chair through the glass doors and into the lobby she pushed the button on her headset mic. "He's here," she announced. A moment later Harrowman himself crossed the balcony and came down the stairs with his hand out.

"There were some discussions over the scheduling," he informed Jackson as they headed towards the boardroom. "I know of at least one arm-wrestle. All in good fun, we've fit in everyone we could. But I'm first, of course."

They both laughed at that one. The person footing the bill always went first.

Harrowman, or maybe Dunn although Jackson doubted it, had made some effort at festivity. The boardroom lights were dimmed in favour of more natural light from the windows. Catered treats and mini sandwiches adorned one end of the long table. Most of the chairs had been pushed into a corner to make room for Jackson's work.

While Harrowman helped himself to a profiterole Jackson

liberated his massage chair and clicked it into place. A complicated piece of wood frame, tension wires and padding, it was built for easy opening and simple use. A forward-facing seat, knee supports, chest pad and curved face cradle allowed the client to rest easy while giving Jackson clear access to their back and neck. He glanced over at Harrowman, adjusted the chair for a tall person, and said, "Ready."

Office massages were fifteen minutes long, clothes-on and straightforward. Jackson had given the CEO a quick once-over while he'd set up and seen nothing unusual—a tall, aristocratic, moderately athletic man, torqued microscopically to his dominant right side, but showing no obvious challenges.

The first sweep from Harrowman's neck to his mid-back told a much different story. The man was stiff as a board with tension, totally jazzed. Harrowman hadn't said a word about it, so neither did Jackson. He simply got to work, trying to do some good in the limited time they had.

"That's marvellous," Harrowman mumbled into the facerest. "How long have you been doing this?"

Jackson rattled off his curriculum vitae as he worked. "So now I split my time between office massage and home-visit therapy," he finished. Harrowman could use some more involved help; maybe he'd take the hint. The iron plate of the CEO's trapezius finally softened, and Jackson went a level deeper, worked his knuckles up either side of the spine.

"I suppose you're busy," Harrowman said, his voice sounding slower and more relaxed. "When you're not rescuing strangers on ferries."

A thrum passed under Jackson's fingers. Harrowman's trapezius tensed up again, just for a moment, practically bouncing Jackson's hands off the man's back. That was interesting. He took a moment to smooth them out again, then moved up to the neck.

"Yeah, I guess," he chuckled, keeping it light. "Though my schedule always has room for more."

Harrowman laughed. "Spoken like a true salesman! I just might take you up on it. Oh, did you ever hear anything more about that fellow on the Seabus? I must admit, the story you told has stuck in my mind."

That wave of tension again, a polar opposite to the casual nonchalance in Harrowman's voice. He was much more than curious.

"No, nothing," he replied. "I guess he never came by to get your help with his patents?"

"Not yet. Perhaps when he works up his nerve. Or gets out of the hospital, if he's still there." Another wave of tension, and Harrowman's trapezius was rock hard again. "Still, your little adventure made for quite the tale. I bet it's gotten you a drink or two at the pub."

Another laugh, through musculature so tight Jackson was worried Harrowman would strain something.

"Oh, not really," he answered. "I don't get out much. Besides, another man's misfortune isn't really my story to tell."

Harrowman lifted his head out of the cradle and turned to glance over his shoulder, pausing Jackson's work on his neck. "That's remarkably sensitive of you," he said, and settled back in. "Not everyone has that kind of respect."

"Comes with the job, I suppose," Jackson said. "Client confidentiality is drilled into us in college."

The stress in Harrowman's back let go a notch. The session continued in silence, and a few minutes later Jackson finished up with three long sweeps. "That's good for now."

"Marvellous," Harrowman said again, bouncing off the chair. "Top marks. We couldn't fit all the staff in today. Let's get you back again this week. Arrange it with Kelly on your way out."

Twice in a week, excellent. The CEO could sure use the help,

Jackson thought as he readied for the next client. So could his bank account. But a tiny, paranoid corner of his mind whispered that the invitation felt like another version of being followed. Because this session had definitely felt like an interrogation.

Next up, unsurprisingly, was Harold Dunn. "Good, you got a Visitor pass," he rumbled, spotting the tag Jackson had relocated to his belt. Jackson readjusted the chair for Dunn's sizeable chest and forward-leaning head and invited the big man to take a seat. "Don't usually go in for this," Dunn said. "It's for morale. Just a quick rub, that's fine."

Jackson smiled and said, "Sure."

He loved these types. As he'd noted before, Dunn had the flexibility of a refrigerator. Anybody with eyes could see the loads of tension through Dunn's back and neck, his body fairly groaning under the strain. Jackson planted a foot on the massage chair's bottom rung as an anchor and leaned into his work.

It took all of the fifteen minutes. The big scientist tried to strike up a conversation several times, but after the first minute lapsed into a deep silence. When Jackson did the final sweep and pronounced him done, he got up from the chair with considerably more ease than he'd sat down.

"You certainly know a thing or two," Dunn managed as he reached for his lab coat. "What sort of training do you people get?"

"Registration exams, and before that a college diploma," Jackson rattled off. "Anatomy, physiology, pathology, clinical theory and ethics, hands-on classes, clinic hours. Nothing like a PhD, but it'll do."

That got him a laugh. "So, no biochemistry or lab work," Dunn said.

"Hah! Not even close. That's hard science. Too many numbers, if you ask me, not really relevant to what we do. Our training takes a more hands-on approach."

The rest of the day was a parade of office staff and scientists, all of them happy to see him. The sandwiches and snacks dwindled. Around noon a maintenance guy meandered in to check the light bulbs, but declined Jackson's offer of a massage in a singsong Filipino accent. Both the lab workers and the office employees had typical desk-work complaints—tight, forward-leaning necks, rounded thoracic spines, knots of pain by their shoulder blades. Bread and butter work for a traveling massage therapist.

And they talked. In bits and pieces, from a dozen different perspectives, he got an insider's overview of Blast Dynamics. Everybody, from data analysts to admin assistants, was excited about the company's prospects. Every single one of them was nervous about the venture failing.

From the lab workers he got a picture of the difficulty behind the science. They were doing bleeding-edge work, each advance a victory against long odds. All of them had mad respect for both of the company's founders, who drove most of the lab's innovations and discoveries.

From the accountants he learned about the dizzying ups and downs of venture financing. Blast's fortunes swung from nerve-wracking scarcity to warm abundance and back as skittish investors were alternately spooked and reassured. Early stage pharmaceutical research was a razor's-edge journey, it seemed.

They told him all of this without once stepping off the line of corporate confidentiality. All the staff, he noted, now sported clip-on security badges.

The day's last massage was Reggie, the young lab manager who had finished his and Marilyn's tour. He slapped his badge onto the conference table and took his position on the chair with the confident strut that Jackson figured was his default setting.

"Whoo boy! What the hell did you do?" he said the moment his face hit the cradle. "The moment you left the other day old

Well-Dunn went ballistic. He's got this place locked down tighter than a movie star's butt cheeks."

Jackson laughed through his initial assessment. He'd worked on movie star butts.

"Really," Reggie continued. "By the next morning we all had these things." He waved a hand at the badge on the table. "Photo, signature, and they're RFID-tagged, most of the staff don't know that little cherry. Dunn's tracking every step we take all the way through the building. Security watches us go in and out. Wouldn't be surprised if there's a pinhole camera and a mic in here somewhere."

Jackson's hands discovered a fine specimen under Reggie's polo shirt. He was about Jackson's height but heavier. Jackson's bike riding and massage work had given him a lean form. Reggie, he suspected, preferred the weight room. The young scientist's muscles were well-developed without being rock hard, a pleasure to work on.

"All I did was deliver a package. Harrowman didn't seem all that interested in it." Not exactly true, but that was the impression the CEO had tried to convey.

"Must have been some package. What was it?"

Jackson gave him the short version of the incident on the Seabus, followed by his visit to Blast Dynamics the next day. "The envelope held weird stuff," he said. "Some kind of chemical notes, a little metal capsule thing in a baggie, and an anatomical drawing. I handed it all over to Mr. Harrowman. He said the notes were worthless."

Reggie whistled. "So the guy slipped it to you? Then disappeared in the back of an ambulance? Sounds like a Liam Neeson moment."

Jackson nodded as he switched from thumbs to an elbow. "It was pretty surreal. But over before it began, you know? Only exciting in retrospect. I'd recommend you get a real massage someday, by the way. You're in great shape, but a few spots could use some work."

"I like to stay fit," Reggie said. "This feels great, maybe I'll do that."

"Mancini," Jackson said, making a connection. "Your family wouldn't happen to own—"

"Manny's Laundry. Sure, all three locations. My grandad was the Laundry King of Little Italy back in the day. Keeping Commercial Drive Clean, that's the family motto." Reggie nodded into the facerest. "Wasn't for me. I found my way out. Now I run the lab here."

Jackson thought back over the day's conversations. "Everybody here seems really excited. You think Blast Dynamics is going to live up to the hype?"

Reggie's black curls bobbed in the face rest. "The stuff we're working on? If those two in their fancy offices stop courting investors long enough to get back in the lab and help us crack a few nuts, it's going to change the fucking world. Providing we don't get poached."

Jackson snagged the last profiterole on his way out the boardroom door. Kelly the receptionist plucked his Visitor tag off at the front desk and, true to Jonathan Harrowman's wishes, rebooked him for another session.

Jackson drove out of the parking lot on a high. His appointment book and bank account were getting healthy. He'd enjoyed the day's work. Blast Dynamics had a general air of optimism around the place, and Reggie's words pinged around the inside of his head. Maybe he'd speak to Harrowman about taking some of his payment in shares.

His good mood lasted for ten blocks. Then he caught a glimpse of a champagne Toyota in his rear view mirror.

Chapter 12

Kicked your sacred cow

Tuesday was hill day, and that meant the North Shore. Jackson strapped his and Charles' road bikes to the rack on his Subaru and they drove over the Lions Gate Bridge in the back-and-forth rush of morning traffic.

The trip across the huge bridge, a kilometre and a half long, no longer frightened him. Four years before, when the obsession with patterns erupted from nowhere in his mind and lit up the entire world with a mesmerizing display of shimmering force, he'd ended up standing at the center of the bridge, captivated by the intricate, impossibly connected dance of the city and harbour beneath him.

Today, he drove up onto the span with nothing more than a flicker of appreciation at the edges of his vision.

They'd been talking about everything and nothing during the drive, friend chatter. Jackson loved these conversations as much as he loved the workouts. He and Charles went way back, long before Georgia had caught Charles' eye at a society fundraiser, and he had no other friendship that went as deep.

As they neared the bridge Charles got quieter, then the conversation stopped as they passed the center of the arch. Charles kept his eyes forward but Jackson could feel the attention on him.

"Still watching, I see," he said, as they started on the downhill slope to the looping turn into West Van.

"Was I?" Charles glanced over. "Professional hazard, I guess. Sorry about that."

"S'all right. Really. It's nice to know you've got my back." Which was the truth, as far as it went. If you had a demon in your head you could do worse than have a doctor look out for you.

He navigated the Subaru through West Vancouver to the base of 21st Street, parked and unslung the bikes. From here it would be a straight, pedalpumping ride up through the shiny, well-tended West Van neighbourhoods and the shiny downtown shops that serviced them, until they got to the curving streets and high hedges of mansionland farther up the slopes. From there they'd hop onto Cypress Mountain Road. The leg-burning lungfest would continue all the way to the ski hill at the top of the mountain.

It was a magnificent way to spend the morning.

Blast Dynamics was still on Jackson's mind. As they loaded up extra water bottles he asked, "What do you know about fascia?"

Charles paused, then shrugged. "It's what you cut through to get to the good stuff."

That stopped Jackson cold. He gaped. "What the hell?"

Charles howled. "Kidding! Massage therapists are so touchy; you look like I just kicked your sacred cow. An old surgeon I trained under in med school used to say that. Nowadays we pay a little more attention to connective tissues. Fascia contributes to some diseases, either by restricting movement or blood flow. It can be its own source of misery, too. Did you know that fascia actually has nerve fibers and pain sensors? Sometimes people think they have sore muscles when, in fact, it's their fascia that—" he grinned. "Yeah, you probably know that."

"Yeah, maybe. Asshat. Anyway, I had this really weird thing happen the other day." He retold the Seabus story, his trip to Blast Dynamics with Marilyn to deliver the package, and his massage day at the lab. He left out the part about the scary ambulance attendants, and didn't mention the cars at all.

"That's incredible," Charles commented. He'd stopped laughing.

"I know, right?"

"No, I mean it's not credible. I was working in the ER that night and we had no one by that description come through the door. St. Paul's is the logical hospital to take a patient from the downtown. Your man never got to us."

"Huh." He still didn't mention his reservations about the ambulance and its attendants. As close a friend as Charles was, Jackson omitted much mention of his pattern sense in their conversations.

They rode. He and Charles had decent bikes—slippy carbon fibre frames, razor-thin wheels and gear cassettes capable of handling the hills—but the Cypress climb was a workout all the same. He felt his quads and calves go through the usual routine. First they woke up, surprised to be called to action but ready for the challenge. Then the switch as the initial energy stores were depleted, the muscles called for more, and his heart and lungs kicked in. He began to breathe, taking in deep and even pulls of the crisp autumn air. That powered some more beautiful performance, all the way through mansionland and the first turn onto Cypress Mountain Road.

As the uphill wore on the third change happened. His muscles, called upon to exert more energy than they had access to, started to complain. Unable to flush out the metabolic wastes as fast as they were made, his quads, calves and gluts began to burn. He could feel the pulse in his legs and chest as his heart did its best to speed up the inflow of oxygen and outflow of trash. His lungs, fully engaged now, did their best to keep up to the rest of it.

He was fully operational, all systems pushed to maximum capacity and stretched to exceed and grow. The very air around him was alive and his tires sang against the road.

With a jolt that wobbled his front tire he realized where the pinch point was. These workouts always had a plateau—you pushed to get better and stronger, then found the point beyond which you simply couldn't improve. The lungs couldn't grow larger, the heart couldn't pump more. Oxygen and energy couldn't get from blood vessels to muscles fast enough, and the metabolic wastes couldn't get back out and away.

The systems wanted to grow and meet the challenge. The problem was, they didn't have the space.

Fascia was holding everything back. Before lungs could grow, their fascial envelope had to expand first. Before heart and arteries could move more blood, the fascia that supported them had to get more supple and elastic. All nutrients, all waste, moved through fascia on their way from capillaries to cells. Only as fast as the fascial web allowed.

Could that be what Blast Dynamics was up to? Could they make fascia work better, adapt faster? Jackson knew from his own massage work that fascia was sensitive and workable, but it took time and patience, so much patience, to make any real change. And when fascia grew thick, stubborn, hardened, its effects were felt far and wide. If Harrowman had found a way to improve all of that ... he thought again about asking for shares in the company.

The final push to the ski hill parking lot was almost level. His cardio leveled out and swept some of the burn from his legs. Ahead of him he could hear Charles puffing as they both clicked into higher gear and cruised into the mostly empty lot. This early in October there was still no snow on the mountain.

"Hey," he asked, once they were off their saddles for the fifteen minute break before the downhill run, "how are you with chemical formulas?"

Charles shot him a look, both amused and curious. "Lousy. I have people for that. Why?"

Jackson pulled some folded sheets of paper from his cycling bag. He'd printed the photos of the formula pages from his phone.

"There's something I'd like your opinion on. Quietly, nothing official or anything. In fact, if you could keep it pretty close to your chest I'd appreciate it. I grabbed some shots of the package Marilyn and I took to Blast Dynamics. These are the formula pages. Can you look into it?" He grinned. "I have a good feeling about this one. Call it due diligence."

Charles folded up the wrapper of his power bar, stood up into a long, lean stretch that turned the heads of two women strolling by, and took the pages. "Yeah, sure. I'll see what I can make of it. Ready to burn some brake pads?"

They mounted up and pointed the handlebars downhill. As the wind began to hum past his ears Jackson felt a surge of optimism about the future. Business was looking up. Marilyn was in his life. Maybe an awesome investment opportunity had just come his way.

Chapter 13

It'll be a mercy

"The dude's, like, normal." Johnnie stood on the far side of the lab counter, meeting his eyes and delivering the bad news in his stupid Americanisms from the safety of distance. "Goes to work all over the place, goes to his girl's, goes home. Right now he's riding a bike up Cypress Mountain, if you can fuckin' believe it, so we figured we'd come and report."

Johnnie nodded his oversized peach of a head as if agreeing with himself, showing off an excellent view of the premature bald spot in his blond buzz cut. Donnie, almost invisible behind Johnnie's right shoulder, bobbed along. Franco, the only actual Croatian in the trio, stood a little apart and had the decency to look glum.

The Three Stooges. Stopping their surveillance to report nothing. He'd expected no more.

"You tailed him to Blast?"

"Yah," said Franco. "Saw him carry in his massage thing. Stayed the whole day. Went home."

"Very good. Where was he the day before?"

Franco didn't need to read from a notebook to answer. That was something. Or maybe he couldn't. "Working, doing his massage thing. That boy covers the ground. A house in Kits, two downtown, more around Arbutus. Then back home. Changed into decent clothes and went to his girl's for supper."

Donnie spoke up, his high-pitched Irish brogue a

counterpoint to Franco's gruffness. "His girl's a garda, thought ye'd wanna know."

That was interesting. He'd wondered about her, when the two of them had shown up at Blast the other day, but hadn't thought to follow up. "What did they talk about?"

The three of them glanced at each other, confusion on their faces. Johnnie spoke up. "You mean, when he went over to her place?"

"Yes."

This time it was Franko. "She's seventeen floors up a Yaletown highrise. We wasn't gettin' in the door, much less putting an ear to her keyhole."

All right, they had a point. Still. He didn't like the thought of police. "So he's normal. Boring. And now he's out for a bike ride."

"Right," offered Donnie, "him and that boyo, they look pretty tight. Both of 'em on savage road rigs, look to cost a penny, I can tell you." The other two bobbed some more in agreement.

He stared into Johnnie. "You said nothing about a friend."

Johnnie flinched his eyes down at the long, black counter. "So he's got a pal. Some doctor type, works in the emergency room downtown. They're out for a ride, not doing nothing."

"Anything. Not doing anything. But they're talking, too, aren't they? And you're all here."

"Hey now," complained Donnie, taking another step back behind Johnnie's shoulder. The kid could disappear if he turned sideways, but still felt the need to hide. That was nice. "We watched, like you said. Wasn't nothing about any eavesdropping. Besides, what are we supposed to do, ride along real slow and follow them? Ask them to speak up a little?"

A low moan from the other room stopped Donnie's whining. He turned away from the Three Stooges, took a step over to the small window and looked into the animal testing lab. This one was a scaled-down version of the one at Blast, a third the size and without most of the fancy equipment. Just a row of cages and some measuring devices, a few microscopes for tissue analysis. But the macroscopic results were all that really mattered. A second moan, quieter than the first, drifted in from the female subject partway down the right-hand wall.

His latest attempt to fix the problem had failed. The subject was declining, same as the others.

Back to the challenge at hand. "I did say watch, didn't I? Very well, I can't fault you for obeying orders. Still. A cop, and now a doctor. It could all be fine, and it might not. We don't know which."

He thought about it, drawing looping doodles onto the countertop with his finger. This was his project, the Uncle had said so. He knew the family's straits. Everything rode on his success. If he needed to take action, then so be it.

"New orders, then. The boy is still on his ride, yes? Then go to his place. You're going to search it." He gave them specific instructions on what to do and what to look for, watching as their eyes widened, then narrowed with purpose. "All right. What are you waiting for? Get on about it."

As they scurried for the exit a third moan reached through the Phase Three lab door. "Franko," he called. The stocky Croatian stopped but didn't turn around. He could see the man's shoulders tense. "Make the call for me. It's time for the ambulance."

Once he was alone he went for one final look through the window. He checked the calendar. There had been some variability among the patients in the study, but the results were broadly the same. Good results quickly, within a day or two. Spectacular results shortly after that, and lasting for weeks. The Ponce de Leon implant performed beyond all expectations.

Then, around six weeks, the first signs of failure. Too much of a good thing. Which proceeded down a ladder of equally spectacular decline, culminating in this. Ten weeks into the clinical trial it was all over.

The subject lay on the floor of the barred enclosure, unable anymore to stand. Ragged blotches discoloured her loose, hanging skin. A few last patches of hair dripped from the scalp like laundry on a windless day. She stared up at the window, somehow still able to see him looking back. He could tell that her eyes used to be blue.

"Bastard," she managed in a hoarse croak. The effort brought on a coughing fit and a tooth hit the floor.

He turned away. Eight weeks. The therapy's parabolic curve took roughly eight weeks before the first signs of the downslope became unmistakeable. He had eight weeks from launch day to make the Ponce de Leon count. To make the family rich.

Lots to do. He grabbed the stupid security badge, in the RFID-proof faraday pouch he'd shoved it into, and left the lab to get back to the bigger lab at Blast before he was missed.

"I dunna think this is a good 'un," murmured Donnie as they hustled away from that godforsaken place. "Whadd'yall think?"

Franko glanced left and saw the darkness all over Johnnie's face speak for itself. "Like it or not, the Uncle's put him in charge," he said. "We do what he says, down to the letter, and that's what we're going to do." He plucked a small phone from his pocket. "Don't mean the Uncle can't hear about it."

Johnny pointed at the phone. "Uh. Don't you have another call to make first?"

Franko felt the acid in his gut go sour as he punched in the number. He'd had to call it often in the past couple of weeks. "Yuh. That I do. It'll be a mercy, you ask me."

Markovic was a fine lieutenant, handling the details when he was otherwise occupied. Like now, when he was in the den playing with his granddaughter, little Daniella. Minding and watching more than actual playing, as she was plunked down on the Persian carpet with a jumbled combination of Lego, plastic logs and a doll's tea set, and his knees refused to let him join her. Daniella was four now, still rounded with baby fat but growing out of it fast. In the odd moments when she glanced up to make sure he was still there her eyes shone with love and happiness.

A happiness he was determined to preserve. So, when Markovic edged into the room and nodded, he got up to take the news outside. "What is it?" he murmured by the shelves in the library.

Markovic, impassive behind his thick, black beard at the best of times, kept his voice low as well. "A call from Franko, Uncle. They have new orders and he thought you'd want to know. The surveillance has revealed nothing. Now they have to break in to the massage therapist's place and search it."

His first impulse was to snatch the phone out of Markovic's hand and start yelling. He was still alive after all these years because he'd learned early to conceal his first impulses. But a home invasion? An escalation, at this stage of the project? Stealth and secrecy had been their friends all along. This was a huge risk. What if the therapist came home early? What if his woman, the cop, dropped by for a visit? Donnie and Johnnie were known to the police. All three of them were known to Shaheen and his men as soldiers of the Croats family.

Police interest at this delicate point of the venture would be a disaster. As much as it chafed to admit it, even to himself, renewed interest by the New Canadians would be worse. He'd worked hard to project the image that the Croats were finished, only a few shreds of import-export income left to sustain them, not enough to catch Shaheen's interest.

In truth, it wasn't much trouble getting the image across. Last year's lightning war had been terrible on his organization. When packs of young, brash smeckeri from all over the world had muscled their way onto his streets calling themselves the New Canadians, he had failed to see the danger.

They'd opened fire on the sidewalks, in full daylight. Twenty men lost, connections cut, almost all the Croats' territory gone in one awful month. He had been beaten. Ready to pack up the family and return to Croatia. Until the new idea had come along.

Daniella called for him. He leaned out around the corner of the door and smiled at her, providing the reassurance that he was still there. Because that was his place—the family anchor, the guardian. Which was why, when the new plan had come along, strange and audacious and full of the promise of redemption, he had said yes.

Now this. Was it worth the risk? They didn't know what the massage therapist knew. Had Sachs told him something in those moments at the Seabus terminal? The existence of the package was potentially harmful enough, but had the massage therapist and his girlfriend been stupid? Had they kept a copy? Given their questions at Blast Dynamics, and now Jackson Teague's ongoing presence at the lab as part of his business, the question wasn't ridiculous. Teague had shown a curiosity that their plan could ill afford.

But an invasion. Would the Uncle ever have done such a move in the old days? Had he ever been that foolhardy, that bold? Of course he had. But now he felt that most unfamiliar of emotions. He was uncertain.

He glanced back into the living room at his granddaughter, who'd brought some of her dolls into the play. Children, always exploring something new. He vaguely remembered the feeling. But, every day, life reminded him that he had gotten old.

And so he'd placed this project in another's hands. Never

mind that he didn't understand the science. He knew that, of all the troubles they faced, he was perhaps the greatest risk of them all.

Oh, he still had the family's respect, he knew that. He could continue to lead the Croats, bully and growl his way past any argument and hold on till the end, but his discipline forbade it. He could not stare the truth in the face and say, fuck you. He needed a succession plan. He needed to bring someone else up to the top. And this project had given him the opportunity.

"Franko's waiting," Markovic murmured, holding out the phone.

Trust was the first step. He took the phone. "Do as you were told. Thank you for informing me, but he is your commander on this project. Do it."

He nodded to Markovic and headed back to his dear Daniella. He had paid out some rope. Only time would tell if there was a noose for them all at the end of it.

Chapter 14

Nine figures huge

"Get the lead out, we're obvious as hell out here." Johnnie never broke a sweat when they were picking up a shipment at the railyard, or keeping dealers in line with an occasional popped elbow or busted leg. Only when their business took him into the world of the straights. Like it was doing right now. A cold droplet trickled down the middle of his backbone. He glanced up the hallway of the solid, old apartment building. No sign of the landlady yet.

"Hold the horse," Franko murdered another saying with his thick Croatian accent. He hunched over the apartment's deadbolt and fiddled with those stupid little lockpicks he loved so much. "I did fine with the front door, no? One more second."

Scritch, scritch. A bunch more seconds passed with no change. "Aw, feck this shit," said Donnie, way too loud for Johnnie's comfort. "Outta the way." Without waiting for Franko to move he stepped forward, leading with his heel. One crunch, the tinkle of some hardware hitting the floor on the other side, and the massage therapist's door swung wide. "Piece a cake." Donnie swaggered past Franko and flicked the little lockpicks, now dangling in midair from the big man's hand, with a finger as he passed.

These two are gonna get me put away again, Johnnie thought as he followed Donnie. I'm still on parole. Franko brought up the rear and closed the unlockable door behind them.

The kid was neat, he'd say that much. They were in a scrap of a hall with a bathroom and closet off to the left, a decent-sized kitchen and living room over to the right. The bedroom led off the living room and the big picture window gave a good view of the sloping Balsam Street sidewalk. The kitchen was spotless, not a dish in sight. The living room looked like a magazine cover, if the magazine was Early Millenial Standard. Even the books were tidy on the shelf.

"Whoa, hold up," he said, placing a hand on Donnie and Franko's arms. The other two paused without a word. He soaked it all in, then made up his mind. "This kid's sick in the head."

Franko wrinkled up his face. "He's going to die? You can tell that from this?" He waved a hairy arm around the place.

"Nah, not like that. He's OCD. Has to keep everything clean, everything in its place, or he can't stand it. See? Everything's neat and he wasn't expecting company."

"Righto on that. Or he'd have left us tea and biscuits." Donnie cracked a smile at his own joke and Franko grumbled something that might have been a laugh. Then Donnie's smile got nasty. "He's really gonna hate that we stopped by."

They all laughed at that one, but Johnnie didn't let it go on too long. "Go on, you know what to do," he gave the instructions. "We're looking for a few sheets of paper, maybe with fancy symbols on them, like advanced math or something. Maybe some photos. Maybe in a big brown envelope. Get to work. But keep it quiet, the landlady's around here somewhere."

They all knew the drill. Donnie started with the sofa, Franko down the hall by the door, while Johnnie took the kitchen. Not much noise, but they checked everywhere the massage guy could hide a sheet of paper. They'd tossed a fair number of places before, only one of the many jobs they'd done for the Croats over the years. The Three Stooges, Johnnie knew that was their nickname in the family. But they were family, as much blood as the Uncle's wife and kids, and had been there for the good times. They were still here now, when the good times had all but deserted them.

"Sure hope we find somethin' nice," Donnie said as he felt the sofa for loose seams. "The Uncle could use some luck."

"It will take more than luck. More than whatever we can give him," Franko growled. It seemed like he was always in a bad mood these days. "Them New Canadians got us good last year. Shaheen, he's a smart one. He didn't touch the Uncle or his family. Just killed enough of us to take the business away."

"That'll be his mistake," Johnnie said, opening the fridge and checking behind the eggs. "The Uncle's still pissed, and don't you go discounting the Croats just yet. I wouldn't be surprised if we get the order someday. Open up the gun cabinet and take them all down. That Shaheen first, crazy bastard."

Donnie shook his head, flipping cushions. "In that nightclub of his? You'd need a demn bunker buster to root him outta that hole. Besides, the New Canadians aren't just a local group. They're transnational, right? This one in Vancouver's only a branch office. You take out Shaheen, they put some monster on a plane who's even worse to replace him. You take out the whole operation, they send over a planeload. No, the Uncle's got it right. Lay low, do what you can with whatever they leave you."

They moved on to the bedroom. "Keep looking, you two." Johnnie found the kid's laptop, flipped it open and messed with it while Donnie and Franko unmade the bed. "You're both wet blankets, makes me tired just listening to you. I got no business telling you this, but I heard a little bird in the grapevines the other day. I—"

"Tut!" said Donnie, holding up a hand. They all shushed. Donnie was the youngest of them, still a pup, and had the best ears. In a moment Johnnie heard it, too. Light, uneven footsteps, the rattle and ding of too much jewelry, and an off-key humming of what Johnnie supposed must be Italian opera.

The landlady, making her rounds.

He snapped his fingers and pointed. Franko slid out of the bedroom and down the hall to the door, still hanging slightly ajar without any operating hardware. He eased it shut and held it.

The humming and jangling made its way around the corridors, fading and growing. It grew stronger and closer. The three of them held their breaths as she stopped on the other side of the massage therapist's apartment door.

When the humming cut off mid-aria, Donnie leaned down and pulled a black leather sap from his sock. Johnnie didn't like it, but knew that it might be necessary. Donnie knew what to do with it, at least. When his sap whispered against your ear, he could put you to sleep for a minute or an hour.

"Who dented my door?" they heard a scratchy, sangria-blurred voice come through the wall. Franko, who'd been holding the doorknob shut, placed his shoulder against the door and leaned into it. A second later the knob rattled. Franko held it rock-steady.

Then the door thumped. She'd pushed it. Franko's shoulder didn't budge, but his eyes widened in surprise.

"Locked up," they heard her mutter, "not like last time, bad time that was, splinters everywhere. Even in the boy's mind." She hiccupped a laugh, then shushed herself. "Oh, you be quiet, Constanza, you bad girl. He's a nice boy. All better now." A flurry of footsteps receded back down the hall, and the terrible humming resumed and faded into the distance.

Franko breathed out a sigh and let go of the door. Donnie slipped his sap back where it belonged. "Let's get this done," Johnnie waved them back to the bedroom, "though I'm sure there's nothing to find."

"You heard a little bird," Donnie murmured as he tore apart the kid's closet. "You said so. In the grapevines, and we all know where they are. So spill."

Johnnie'd hoped they'd forgotten his slip. But what the hell, they were his friends. They were family, and needed a pick-me-up. "I don't know specifics or nothing. But that stuff in the lab? It's big. Like, nine figures huge, and real soon. It'll put the family right back on the map. Fuck, we'll be kings of the city. Then, I imagine, we'll buy us a bunker buster." He grinned at the thought.

Franko frowned. "Whatever they make in that lab, it don't work. Even the old scientist tried to run away. You sure about all this? I hear nothing."

"Like I said, I wasn't supposed to hear it either. But I did. The Uncle was talking to Markovic. Big plans, with a big payoff at the end."

"All fine and good, boyo, but when might this end be ending?" Donnie had a glint in his eye. He'd lost a brother to the New Canadians and had been looking for payback ever since.

"Soon. That's all I know. They both sounded excited about it. Now get back to work, before that drunk bitch does another round."

Chapter 15

A KALEIDOSCOPE OF BRILLIANT GLASS SHARDS

Jackson plucked his bike off the Subaru, wheeled it through the back entrance of the apartment building to the lockup, then headed upstairs to his place. The cycling shirt and shorts had dried and stiffened on the drive home. He couldn't wait to peel them off and hop into a good shower.

The door opened at the first touch of his key to the lock. "What the—oh no," he breathed.

Unbidden, his pattern sense sprang to life. The apartment had been trashed. Books and papers littered the floor. Furniture had been moved. His kitchen cupboards lay open and violated, their contents dumped on the counters. He took a step in, then backed out. The chaos slashed his eyes, a kaleidoscope of brilliant glass shards in his mind.

He fumbled for his phone and called. She answered on the third ring. He heard a keyboard clicking in the background. "Hey, Freckles. Good thing I'm at my desk. This better be a booty call."

He could hear the shock in his voice and hated himself for it. "I've been broken into."

The keyboard sound stopped. "How bad is it?"

"Bad. They moved everything. It's like a bomb went off."

"Oh, Jackson." Then the cop came back. "Any sign of them? Where are you now? Are you safe?"

He gave her the details, no immediate danger. "Good. I've got Ahmed sending a unit over to your place, they'll be there as soon as they can. So—how are you? Everything all right?"

Her question chafed, but he was glad she cared enough to ask. At least the irritation put some strength back into his voice. "Yeah. Fine. It hurts to look at, but I can handle it. But really, what the hell? Spooks in cars and now this? Two weird things in a couple of days. You'd think the universe doesn't like me or something..."

Tumblers lined up in his head and a door opened onto blackness, sending a cold chill down his spine. "Fuck. At least they didn't find what they were looking for."

"What? You did an inventory? I thought you just got there, haven't been inside yet."

"No, I haven't been inside. But I took the printouts of that Seabus package with me to show Charles. They didn't get them."

"Jackson." He heard the computer keys click again. "There's been a rash of break-ins around your neighbourhood in the past month. They're taking whatever they get their hands on. Stuff that's easily pawned. I'm sure they'd have no interest in a few sheets of paper."

"Marilyn." He mirrored her scorn. "This was done by whoever's been following me. I just got back from a bike ride and I didn't see them all morning."

"They're not—"

"Oh come on," he interrupted. "First the Seabus, then the cars, now this?" He leaned back in through the apartment door, looking at the carnage even though it hurt. "Mostly I see papers thrown all over the place. My TV is still here. I—" he leaned in further. "I see my laptop. It's been moved but it's still on the table. These weren't addicts or thieves. My place wasn't robbed, it was searched."

Silence on the other end of the line. Then she said, "Okay, those are some good observations. Listen, the unit will be there in about fifteen minutes. Don't go in and start tidying. They know what to look for, probably already know who did it. While you're waiting, why don't you pop another one? Up your meds, just for today. Your place must look terrible. I'm sorry this happened to you, Jackson. Once you can get in there and make a list of what was taken, we'll start looking for it. I'll be over as soon as I'm done work, okay?"

"Yeah. Sure, okay." For the first time in their relationship he hung up without saying goodbye.

"Again!?" A whiff of sangria and patchouli swept over him from behind as the landlady, Mrs. Castelli, rounded the corner and stormed towards him. She'd been eavesdropping. "Broken into? Again? Not good, Jackson, not good! I saw this earlier." She pointed at a small indent on his door, just above the deadbolt and shaped like a heel, the bangles on her wrist jingling. "I pushed your door, it was solid." Her eyes got round, the pencilled eyebrows rising towards her steel-wool hairline. "They must have been there! Holding the door! So close!" Her hand fluttered over her chest, then a finger flew out to wave at him. "You call police! No police, no insurance to fix all this. You call them, right now!"

"They're on their way, Mrs. Castelli," he said. "And I'm sure you were in no danger."

"This city. Getting more dangerous every day." The bangles danced again as she waved her hands at him. "This is twice, Jackson, twice. You get broken into, nobody else. I like you, but this—" she nodded at the door and all the menace it implied. "Three times, you find another place to live."

She left him alone with an open door and a cloud of bad perfume, the cell phone dead in his hand. He was supposed to wait. Take more meds and wait. And never let this happen again.

Like there was a fat lot he could do about any of it. A wave of what he could only describe as helplessness watered his eyes as he leaned his back against the corridor wall. Underneath it, a small, hard knot of indignation burned like the start of a bonfire fire in his gut. It was all that held him upright.

Chapter 16

The game has changed

Marilyn hung up the phone after Jackson's abrupt departure and tried to scrub the worry from her mind. Jackson had sounded tense on the phone, almost manic. So much like her brother. She still remembered the day, when Andrew had been seventeen and she barely twelve, that he'd told her about the men watching them. Unseen to all but him, waiting in the darkness of the alley. She'd been so young then. Hadn't known the fear-sweat on his forehead for the raging paranoia that it was.

The day they took her brother away had been the second most painful day of her life. Topped only when she'd heard of his death at the hands of another patient on the institute's lunchroom floor, eight years ago this week.

Ahmed, pounding on his own keys at the next desk, said, "He'll be all right. He's made of tough stuff, your man. Quit fretting, you have an appointment to get to."

"You're pure gold, you know that?" She swept her fingers through the shoulder-bobbed mess she called a hairdo and gave her face a quick rub to clear the cobwebs.

"So Gordon keeps telling me. Now get your ass moving. The future is waiting for you."

The meeting was in Staff Sergeant Dilly's office down the hall. She swung through the door and thrust out her hand. "Sergeant. Thanks for putting this together."

Delores Dilly (Delly Dilly to anyone who was tired of living) was sitting in one of her visitor chairs next to a stranger. She was in tightly-pressed uniform shirtsleeves, as always, and carried the air of a supportive but faintly disapproving older sister, as always.

Dilly and the stranger both rose. "You're the one who pestered me for it. This is Sergeant Rockford."

A slender, unsmiling man in plain clothes, tall enough to hurt her neck looking at him, stepped forward and enveloped her handshake in both of his. "I'm pleased to meet you," he said in a deep, slow voice. "I understand you're interested in the Organized Crime Section. I'm here to talk you out of it."

Well. "But, I thought, I mean," she looked from Rockford to Dilly and back. Neither of them were laughing at the joke. Okay then. She took back her hand and claimed Dilly's chair. "I guess we'd better get started, then."

Rockford sat back down next to her. A folder lay on Dilly's desk beside him—her personnel file. "Looks like you've had a busy few years, Constable," he began, flipping through the pages. "All the usual courses, excellent street work, a few commendations for investigations. An all-round, solid performer."

"Exactly. Just the sort of—" He held up one of those huge hands to stop her.

"That's fine, but you know as well as I do that the interesting stuff is in the fine print on the back pages. Like this note from Staff Sergeant Dilly here," he turned to an assessment report, "that says you're often spotted wandering the halls. Nothing wrong with that, of course, and you're never late for shift or anything. But the general opinion is that you're shopping around. Looking for opportunities and other sections that might take you out of the beat cop life and into something else."

"Like the Organized Crime Section." Despite herself, she was starting to get steamed.

That got her a trace of a smile. "Yes, for sure. It does show a certain initiative. An interest in other aspects of policing. Maybe a slight disdain for normal procedure when it comes to transferring between Divisions. Last Spring you got noticed by the Emergency Response Team. Which you got seconded to, I see. For precisely seven days." He glanced up under his brows. "Didn't end so well, did it?"

"Not my fault," she said through her teeth. "I was a trainee in the right place at the wrong time."

"True enough," he admitted. "But you see what I'm getting at. First ERT, then OCS. Then what? Is something else going to catch your eye?"

He closed the file, settled back in his chair and folded his hands over a knee. "Organized Crime isn't especially fun or exciting, Constable Mathers. It's not a short term commitment. It's a long game, with plenty of investigation for comparatively few arrests. We can't have you signing on, then roaming the halls in a few months looking for something else."

"This is what I want," she started, but Rockford held up a hand again.

"Not finished yet. Your record shows some combat skill, a few tussles on the job, even an injury or two. You've come under fire and discharged your weapon. Although the bomb maker got away." He tsked, a sound Marilyn found distinctly annoying. "Do you know what I see when I scan these incidents?" He opened her file again and waited for an answer.

"That responding to domestics is a high-risk venture?" She tried to keep the growl out of her voice.

Rockford chuckled. "Ain't that the truth. But no, Constable Mathers, that's not what I see. Some of your bumps and bruises came from getting between couples, sure. But this one a few days ago, down on the docks. And these from last year. And that bomb-maker shooting, too." He flipped through the reports. "The highest-risk incidents, the ones that gave you more than just bruises? Those were your brushes with organized crime."

His gaze was rock-steady on her face. "It's not like it used to be, you know. The game has changed. New players are moving in from all over the world, and they don't play by the old rules. At one time, believe it or not, these violent psychopaths kept a certain kind of civility. They kept the violence off the streets and out of public view. There was a certain back and forth with the police, because too much exposure in the press or the courts was bad for business. The old bosses kept things low-key.

"Now, the new gangs are the real bad boys. They're flashy, ultraviolent, and don't care one bit about collateral damage or the publicity it brings. They've got a war going on with the established OC groups, and I can tell you they're winning."

Rockford paused. Knowing a test when she found herself in the middle of one, Marilyn kept her trap shut and waited. After a moment he continued. "So that's my second point, Constable. Organized Crime is slow, methodical, careful, because it's also more dangerous. We don't rush in. We don't tolerate hotheads and fast guns, because that kind of cop gets us killed. Us," he leaned in, "and our families. Do you understand? When you join OCS, you're not the only one doing the investigating. The bad guys keep files on us, too."

He sat back in his chair. "So you see, Constable Mathers. We don't want a dilettante who's looking for the next big thrill. We don't want anybody who might put us all more in harm's way than we already are. And we don't want anyone who isn't prepared—fully prepared—to accept an increased level of risk, to themselves and their loved ones." With one long finger he levered the file closed. "Your turn."

Marilyn pursed her lips, nodded. "Yes, I see what you mean, Sergeant. These are the bad ones. As you know, I've met the type. Some of them hurt people for a living. Some of them do it because they like to. And they're not above hurting cops. I've heard those stories." She took her turn to lean forward, placing an elbow on

Dilly's desk. "But you know who else they hurt?"

Rockford waited, impassive. She answered. "They hurt everybody. These guys make millions—hell, billions—by poisoning the streets and ripping off every level of business. They're into everything from pickpocketing to insurance fraud and stock market scams. They use that money to make themselves stronger, swing votes their way, edge themselves further into society, invent new ways to make even more. They do all this from cities and ports all around the world while we try and catch up with the international shell game, working our way through jurisdictions and laws while they dodge and weave and laugh. They're leeches, Sergeant Rockford, and they are sucking society dry.

"You want to know why I've been wandering the halls, as you put it?" She was in full swing now and worked hard to keep her voice down, but he'd offended her. "I do good work on the street. But I only help one person at a time, one situation at a time. Beat cops are firefighters, sir, running from one call to the next and putting out the blaze. Have you seen the statistics? There are more blazes now than ever before. Society is in trouble, Sergeant, and more and more people are feeling the pinch. I'm tired of putting out fires. I want to catch the arsonists. I want to work on the source."

She'd run out of breath and out of words. Somehow she'd worked her way to the edge of the seat. She slid back and waited.

"Told you so," said Sergeant Dilly without elaborating.

Rockford frowned. "I see," he said at last. "Thank you for listening to me, Constable, and for speaking your mind. I'll be in touch." They all stood. He shook hands with them both and was gone.

Marilyn eased the door shut after he'd left. "Delores, what the fuck was that?" she asked quietly.

Dilly shook her head. "Can't say another word, Marilyn. All I did was arrange the meeting. The rest of it is beyond me. You spoke your mind, like I knew you would, and that's that. We'll just have to see." Her face gave nothing away. "I believe you have fires to put out. Dismissed, Constable."

For the rest of the day Marilyn tried to get the interview—rebuke, refusal, whatever it was—out of her head. She failed.

Chapter 17

CURED EVEN BEFORE IT BEGINS

The cops that Marilyn sent to cover the break-in were polite, professional, and swift. Once they'd checked things over they invited Jackson in to see what had been taken.

Which, as far as he could tell, was precisely nothing. Even his laptop was still on the table.

"Guess you got lucky," one of the cops commented, a shaven-headed Dwayne Johnson wannabe with extra-large sleeves covering his biceps. "Maybe your landlady scared them off. We'll get the report to her in a day or two. If you find anything was actually taken, or if they come back," he handed Jackson a card and that was that.

All through the interview and inspection he kept his condition under lock and key. He didn't want to see the disorder in his place with anything more than his normal sight. He also kept a firm hold on his tongue, determined not to make the same mistake he'd made with Ahmed and Marilyn five months earlier.

No way was he going to tell these cops that he knew exactly what the thieves had been searching for. Anything connected to the incident on the Seabus. He'd only printed the pages for Charles, and kept the rest of the photos with him on his phone. His laptop, which had definitely been abused, was a thick Dell dinosaur that he used for streaming movies and, behind passwords, his clinical notes. It had nothing on it for the bad guys to find.

Once he was alone he spent an uncertain minute divided between the mess in his living room and the one in the kitchen.

"Just start somewhere," he muttered, and picked a Robyn Harding thriller up off the floor.

A couple of hours later Marilyn showed up to help, chocolate in one hand and overnight bag in the other.

In the morning they spent a wonderful hour chatting over coffee in a spotless apartment, then both went their separate ways to work.

He had two new clients today, referrals from Georgia's extensive friends and acquaintances list. The first patient, Griff Townsend, lived in a Kitsilano townhouse not too far away.

Apparently too short a drive for anyone to tail him.

When a trim, 30-something Ryan Reynolds lookalike opened the door to his knock, Jackson knew this was going to be a fun session. He used specimens like this as an anatomy refresher—underneath his thin turtleneck sweater Griff was ripped, with a minimum of body fat, every muscle defined and available for examination.

"So you're Georgia's friend. She gives you the highest recommendation. I don't know why I didn't think of this before, come on in." Griff led him into a spacious and elegant living room, shuffled a small table out of Jackson's way and handed over a piece of paper. "Here is the history form your website gave me."

"Thanks. So, Griff, is there anything specific I can—oh. Wow." The form was a standard case history, an automatic download for new patients to his scheduling service. The first thing that caught Jackson's eye was the birthdate. Griff was 47. Second, under Medical History, was a problem in his early twenties. Griff had been diagnosed with Type 2 diabetes. Third, under medications, was the list.

It was impressive, to say the least.

Griff was smiling. "What caught your eye?"

"Let's start with this. Diabetes?"

He nodded. "Yes. That was the beginning of it all. I was, let's just say, a less than healthy child. My school nickname was Butterball. By the time I was nineteen I had trouble getting up a flight of stairs. When I was twenty-three my doctor informed me I had diabetes. He put me on a raft of pills and said I might not live as long as I wanted to." He pointed to a corner. "That day I went out and bought those." Perched on a tiny, slanted shelf, all by themselves, was a worn-out pair of Nike runners.

"I'd say you turned things around a bit. I don't see many of the usual meds on this list. Just metformin." Jackson pointed to the form, naming a common last-generation diabetes drug.

"Three years after the diagnosis I'd dropped some weight, changed some habits and didn't need them anymore. That was a relief, I can tell you."

"But you kept the metformin. And added all these?"

Griff stood and began adding hand gestures to his conversation, moving into lecture mode. Jackson stole a quick glance at the line for Occupation. Sure enough, it said 'Teacher.'

"Yes, that's right. It was the life expectancy thing, my doctor telling me I might not have much. I went home and researched everything I could about diabetes and how to shake it. Metformin is a simple, generic drug that moderates how much glucose the body produces and how it is used. But doctors started noticing that patients taking metformin lived longer than others. They had less of certain cancers, too. Studies confirmed it. Now metformin is being looked at the world over as a life extension drug."

"Wild. And the rest of this?" Griff had listed over fifteen different substances, from herbal remedies to supplements only listed by their chemical name.

He gestured to a forest of bottles visible on a counter through the kitchen door. "That's my regime. I started digging into longevity research. Most of what ages us doesn't need to happen, or not nearly so fast. Bone loss, joint destruction? We can help that right now, and not by replacements. Cognitive decline? Keep using your brain and take a few things to protect it. Bad skin? Keep your fascia healthy."

He was pacing now. Vitality rippled off him in waves. "Good diet, exercise and lifestyle are the foundation of a long and healthy life. Nothing else works without those. But once they're in place? There's so much more you can do."

Jackson was impressed. "So you're forty-seven? Looks like it's working. How long do you think you'll live?"

Griff laughed and waved towards the window. "That depends on how terrible the traffic gets. I ride a bike everywhere, and in this city that's a high-risk lifestyle. But really, that's not how I think of it. I aim for healthspan, not lifespan."

"I get that. Aren't they kind of the same, though?"

"Close." Griff got serious. "One thing your case history didn't ask for was family statistics. Both my dad and mum died in their fifties. None of my relatives, on either side, have ever made it past seventy-four. So yes, I do think about the years. But I always remember an old joke about health nuts by the comedian Redd Foxx. When my time comes, I want to look really silly, lying in a hospital bed dying of nothing."

The massage was straightforward maintenance work. Griff had a couple of old muscle tears from lifting weights and a loose ankle from a running sprain. Other than that he had the springy, flexible body of a thirty-year-old and was a pleasure to work on. They set up a schedule of weekly massage for the first month, then monthly sessions after that.

Jackson's second patient lived in the middle of his traveling range, in an industrial-chic space on the third floor of a blocky building near Quebec and Third. Nothing in the rear view mirror caught his eye during the ten minute drive; either the followers had given up or they'd switched vehicles again.

Abe Tremblay's voice buzzed him through the door with a "Hey, yeah, elevator's straight ahead." Bypassing the sound studio on the first floor and the game developers on the second, the elevator door opened into Abe's concrete-and-ductwork open penthouse.

Abe himself, it turned out, was founder and majority owner of the gaming company. "I like a short commute, right?" he joked, part of a nonstop patter he'd begun the moment the elevator door closed. Abe had mixed-heritage skin, a brilliant smile, and the beginnings of some fine dreads in his brown hair. He never stopped moving, including his tongue. So far, Jackson had learned that Abe was alpha-testing some new code for a first-person shooter app, preferred afternoons to mornings, loved his panoramic view of the North Shore mountains and was on his third company, having birthed and sold the first two at a handsome profit. Not bad, Jackson thought, for someone who looked to be Jackson's twenty-six.

"This'll be for you. Your scheduling app's not too shabby, maybe I'll crunch you a new one if I get a minute." He handed over the case history and Jackson gave it a scan.

He wasn't quite as surprised this time, but still. "You're older than you look," he commented, doing the math from Abe's birth year. He was in his early thirties. Not a huge difference from Jackson's estimate, but Jackson considered himself to be a skilled observer.

"Yeah, thanks! I get that sometimes. Expect I'll be hearing it a lot." Abe beamed at the compliment.

"Tell me about these." Jackson pointed to the list under the Medications section, long enough that it continued to a second page. It made Griff's history look paltry by comparison. Metformin was on there, plus a couple more he recognized from Griff's list.

"My stack! Yeah, that's what keeps me young. Health supplements, mostly. They keep the machine in top form."

He was struck by a subtle difference in what Abe was saying. "Right, so you're working to extend your healthspan," he ventured.

"That's one way of looking at it," Abe said. He stopped moving and got focused. Jackson could see some of what made Abe a CEO. The walls of the room seemed to fade backward as he found himself listening intently. "There's healthspan, and that's all good, staying a hundred percent for as long as you can. That means no disease, right? But get this—what if old age itself was a disease? I mean, all of it. The wrinkles, the fuzzy head, loss of strength and flexibility, the freakin' hair, man. Arthritis, heart disease, the big C. What if all of it, the whole works, was not necessary? Not inevitable? Cured even before it begins?"

Jackson gave his professional-detachment nod. "Well, yeah, that's a pretty big if. But that's life extension. See how long you can go before things fall apart. So long as you don't get hit by a bus." He chuckled at his own joke, but Abe's smile had vanished.

"Gotta look both ways, right, that's for sure. But no, man, I'm not talking life extension. You know the target longevists have in sight?" Jackson shook his head. "120. That's the longest anyone on record has ever lived, give or take. That's the hard stop to human existence. And the only way anybody's got there is by accident, by not falling apart quite as fast as the rest of us. But look at them, man. Look at all the oldies. They're broken. Used up and waiting for the batteries to run out. They're old, Jackson my man. And that. Doesn't. Have. To. Happen."

He waved a hand at the list. "These? They'll help me live long enough for the real thing to come along. Plenty of people are working on it. Silicon Valley brains, dot-com funding. Best of the best, right? Won't be long before someone cracks the longevity code. Then old age will be a thing of the past." He winked. "Not long at all, is my bet."

"Wild." Jackson's work in people's homes had given him glimpses into a hundred different lifestyles. He'd learned not to judge any of them. "So, what can I do for you today?" he asked, moving the session onto safer ground.

Abe Tremblay wanted maintenance massage as well. He wasn't nearly as well-muscled as Griff, but he kept himself in shape. Jackson found the typical coder tensions in neck, mid-back and forearms, but no real inflammation or challenges.

What he did find was phenomenal skin. No doubt the guy ate well and drank enough water, but Jackson's hands felt more than that. Abe's skin was fine textured and silky smooth. It was like working on the soft and pliable skin of a child.

What he didn't find were significant problems. Everywhere Jackson found a knot, it was in the muscle and responded almost instantly to his touch. None of Abe's tensions had reached the point of thickening and toughening his fascia. The tendons where his hand and forearm muscles attached to the elbow, always a hazardous and stubborn spot for coders, had no roughness or inflammation. The fascial sheaths that surrounded and held the muscles of his back and neck were completely fine, unaffected by the muscle tension within them.

It was the easiest massage Jackson had given in years.

"Almost done," he murmured, giving Abe's back a few more broad strokes. He swept his fingers down and out, over the ribs, wrapping almost to the front. His right hand felt a tiny ridge under the last rib on Abe's side.

"Oh yeah, my lipoma," Abe muttered under the facerest. "Had it forever, just ignore it."

Jackson bent over for a closer look at what Abe was calling a lump of fatty tissue. Smooth skin over Abe's side, nothing to indicate any problem. He ran his hand over the bump once more to be sure, then finished up without a word.

They set up a more aggressive schedule than Griff —two massages a week for the first month. "Gotta max out the benefits, you know, that's my philosophy," Abe informed him. Jackson had no argument. He said his goodbyes and headed for the next patient.

That evening he fired up the old Dell. Jackson had a fistful of research to do on supplements he'd never heard of before and wanted a larger screen than his phone.

He also had something to think about. Abe had lied to him. Jackson knew what lipomas felt like, every massage therapist did. The coder's lump didn't feel anything like one.

It did, however, feel a lot like the bump under the ribs of the man on the Seabus.

Chapter 18

Certainly not some semi-intelligent rube

Georgia contemplated the steel-framed artwork at the end of the upstairs hall. The exquisite plaster cast deep-set behind thick glass, simply titled Raven and signed by Bill Reid, had been her mother's last gift to the house before she passed on. A single halogen spot recessed into the ceiling made it glow.

The house was an ongoing, living sculpture, passed down by each of the Buckley women to the daughter with the single instruction to add her touch. Her great-great-grandmother had chosen the plot and drawn the plans for her husband to build. Each succeeding generation of family women had embellished and improved it in their own way.

Georgia had grown up watching and admiring as her mother chose fine art for her own addition to the house. Georgia had come into ownership of the home when her mother was taken by a quick, sudden infection six years ago. Now it was her turn to make the house her own.

The Raven was a beautiful example of Bill Reid's work, clean lines and sweeping curves, not a stroke out of place. Georgia shifted a little and caught her reflection in the frame's protective glass. The line of her cheek matched up with the raven's outswept wing.

Her curves were beautiful, too. For now.

Abe Tremblay's card, loudly proclaiming him CEO of yet another groundbreaking tech concern, glittered in her hand. She flipped it over to look again at the phone number scrawled on the back in light pencil. Above it were the words Ponce de Leon. "Erase this sucker after you call," Abe had told her. "This outfit is totally confidential. We're getting in on the ground floor."

She'd already used it once, wasting little time talking her way past the gatekeeper and setting up a second call with the one who mattered. Precisely on time, the phone in her hand trilled.

The man on the other end of the call sounded professional and polite. No trace of an accent. She had the sense, almost at once, that she was talking to the source. He was one of the medical professionals behind the discovery.

"I have your application in front of me, Mrs. Ashton, and everything looks fine. Once we have your deposit we can prepare the implant. Then we'll perform the final procedure once we have the rest of the payment."

Not too bad as far as pre-emptive closes went, but Georgia knew more than this fellow ever would about making the sale. "Sounds nice, Dr. Phillips, but we're not quite there yet. I'd like to know a bit more about the treatment."

The brief silence on the line betrayed Dr. Phillips' surprise. "I'm so sorry for the confusion, I thought your decision was made. Of course. Ask any questions you might have."

"How does it work?" Might as well start with the basics. "I mean, I've read your papers and seen the website, it all sounds pretty marvellous, but they're a little thin on the medical details."

"Oh." More silence. "Well, of course, I'm limited in what I can say by our intellectual property department, but let's see if I can summarize it. You know what fascia is?"

"Yes, of course. Connective tissue. It's what holds us together."

Phillips' voice warmed to his topic. "It is much more than that, I assure you. Fascia provides the underpinning and the support system for every part of us, down to the cellular level. If it's healthy, so are we. If it's not, we suffer. When we age, we get stiff and creaky because our fascia does. We get high blood pressure because our blood vessels are no longer elastic. Our immune system slows, in part, because our fascia gets hard to navigate. Our skin gets thin and wrinkled because the underlying fascia degrades. In short, Mrs. Ashton, we are exactly as old as our connective tissue.

"The Ponce de Leon treatment, delivered slowly over a year through our custom implant, renews the health and youth of your fascia. It revitalizes the cells and structures that create your fascia and keep it young. And that makes everything work better. I do mean everything, Mrs. Ashton. You are as old as your fascia. And we stop your fascia from getting old. Permanently."

Despite herself, she felt her pulse quicken. A giddy thrum started up at the back of her mind. The Spanish explorer, Juan Ponce de Leon, had spent his life searching for the fountain of youth. This could be it. In fact, if the videos were to be believed—and she was certainly not some semi-intelligent rube to be convinced by cinematic sleight of hand—this really was it.

She marshalled her poker face and got her feelings under control. "Sounds pretty impressive. Also far-fetched. So you're telling me that the hype is real? Your treatment actually does what they're saying?"

He didn't bother asking who 'they' were. He knew. When he spoke again, it was with the simple depth of conviction. "Yes, Mrs. Ashton. The treatment works. Once you get the implant, you stop aging. Your body works perfectly again. It's as simple as that."

Time. She needed time to digest this. The first rule of negotiations, never make the decision in your first round at the table. Always step back and take a breather. "All right. It is a lot of money you're asking, though. I'll have to think it over. Can I call you back at this number?"

"Of course," he said, "I completely understand. I just want to make sure that you're aware of two things. Firstly, you know that you have this opportunity to be one of the very first because of your connections? You are an influencer, Mrs. Ashton, with a wide audience of people who might be receptive to this therapy. Part of the condition for your early entrance to this program, at a discounted rate, is that you help us spread the word. Only to the right ears. To those you believe could benefit most from our service."

She nodded to the phone, but put a little incredulity in her voice. "Discounted rate? Is that what you call it?"

Now Dr. Phillips was smiling, she could tell. "I see you haven't been given the whole picture," he replied. "I usually don't talk figures on this call, but let me be plain. You are providing a $10,000 deposit, then placing $40,000 in escrow for when you receive the implant. That may sound precious, but consider what you're buying. Will it seem like a good investment in 20 years? In 50? And yes, this is the discounted rate. Once our production goes mainstream, the fee will quadruple. To help us cover our extensive development and testing costs."

He was right. If his claims were true, then any amount of money would seem paltry once enough time had passed. "You said two things?"

"Yes," he said. "You must also understand that our implant keeps you from aging, but it does not roll back the years. If you receive it when you're forty, then you remain forty. If you receive it when you're sixty, then you will remain sixty. Now, I empathize with your wish to think it all over," he continued, "but please remember. Every day you wait is a day that you will never, ever get back."

"I can have the entire payment to you in two hours." She knew an art collector in West Vancouver who had been wanting her Bill Reid for years. "What account shall I wire the funds to?"

Chapter 19

NO TRUCK WITH REMORSE

"Here now, this will help." He emptied the syringe into the port of the IV line that snaked from a saline bag through the bars and into the test subject's thin arm. Three rows of tape held the needle in place; the vein it was inserted into had long since lost any ability to grip.

The subject, a young man he'd scooped off the street with promises of drugs three months before, was beyond speech, but the eyes betrayed a fatigued distrust. With good reason, he could admit that much. When the human trials had begun showing signs of failure, and the subjects had started demanding to leave, he'd had them all confined to the animal lab. Not his favourite decision, and not a popular one.

He'd worked the puzzle with everything he had, and he was the best. Removal of the implant was useless; by the time anomalies became obvious the damage was done. Half a hundred variations of the original formula, a full system flush, even transfusions had no effect. The problem had defeated him. He and Sachs came up with more ideas than he could count and they'd tried them all, working long into the nights.

For nothing. This subject was the only one left. Now all he could offer the medical martyr was temporary relief.

This time he'd added a touch of fentanyl. To take the edge off, and to make the next job easier. The subject whispered a wordless surprise as the solution found his bloodstream, then closed his eyes and fell asleep.

He sighed, turned from the row of cages and closed the door as he went back to the front room.

A butterfly of—unease? regret?—stirred somewhere inside his chest. Anyone paying for the new implant was lighting a fuse on the last three months of their life. Sure, he'd known that before shipping them. But the look in the subject's eyes had slipped past his professional objectivity and landed somewhere soft.

He stomped on it. No time for that. No place for weakness. The Uncle wouldn't have any such qualms; the Uncle had built the Croats with a will as hard as granite. Now he had his own reputation to build, and it was starting here. His initiative was going to land the family back on their feet. Then the Uncle would take a bow and hand over the reins.

He was going to bring them millions. He'd use the project's windfall to rebuild the Croats, make the family strong enough to reclaim the city. Strong enough to show the new gangs what dread really looked like.

If that meant a few setbacks along the way, oh well. A true leader had no truck with remorse.

Another week, maybe ten days, and everything would be fine. He walked down the empty corridor of the tiny lab to the kitchenette and made a cup of tea. Five thousand longevists around the world had placed $50,000 in escrow to secure a spot in one of the handful of discreet medical-enhancement clinics scattered across the globe. They were lining up for their chance at eternal youth. Within a week of the product's launch, after expenses and the clinics' cut, over $200 million dollars would funnel into the family's bank accounts.

The Croats would be back. Then he'd burn down the lab and remove all of his careful cutouts before the new immortals discovered that their once-in-a-lifetime deal had placed them all on borrowed time.

The project was on track, on time. Beautifully seamless. Except for the one loose thread. Even the most perfect plan had at least one. This thread might be nothing. Or it could unravel all he'd worked for. The massage therapist knew more than he was letting on.

He took a sip of tea and burned his tongue. Blowing air in and out to cool it, he ran through the problem. The boy had talked with Sachs before the ambulance picked the old man up. No way would the scientist waste those moments in idle chatter. By then, Sachs had known his time was short. The boy had been in possession of Sachs' papers and the implant for almost a whole day before turning them over. Registered massage therapists got some level of medical training; the boy might have figured things out.

Or maybe not. Following him had been useless. Searching the boy's apartment had given them nothing. He really had no way to know what Jackson Teague knew and what he planned to do about it. But he needed to, and badly.

The project depended on secrecy. He'd spent months dropping hints in just the right ears, on the right dark web chats, whispers of a new therapy called Ponce de Leon. The name had been Sachs' brilliant idea. He'd lured in the elite of the life extension crowd, desperate to lay their hands on a cure for death and wealthy enough to pay anything for it. They all knew the price for getting in on the ground floor—the cash, of course, but also his demand for total silence.

Which made news of the new treatment spread like wildfire to more of the right ears, and none of the wrong ones.

But today the project balanced on the thinnest of razor's edges. He'd convinced the Uncle to give him everything. The Croats had paid for this lab. They'd paid for the best clinical researcher in the world with the right set of ethics for the job, and smuggled Dr. Sachs into Vancouver. The implant development, the trials, the production and distribution, all of it. The last of the family's wealth was spent.

Life extension clients were rich, desperate, entitled fools, but they weren't stupid. If any evidence of the Ponce de Leon's failure leaked they would scatter like leaves, and their money with them.

Sachs had diligently and professionally recorded that evidence, against direct orders. Too much a scientist. Then, in his last moments, passed it to a massage therapist. Maybe.

Did the therapist know? Did his girl, the policewoman, who'd come with him to Blast Dynamics and seemed just as nosy? Were they a threat? The risk was monumental. He had to find out.

He put down the tea and picked up his phone.

"It's me," he said. "I have a new job for you. I want you to pick them up." He listened to silence, then a burst of static. "Yes, I meant it. The girl, too. Take them over to the old machine shop off Pandora, that will be the right atmosphere for our little chat. Don't let them see where they're going." More static. "Yes, I said blindfold them. I don't care that it's daylight, take the Nissan, it has tinted windows. I'll see you there in an hour. I have something to take care of first."

He cut the call as one of the Stooges—Donnie, with that ridiculous Irish accent—was gearing up to complain some more. They still hadn't gotten used to taking orders from a scientist. He'd have to make that attitude adjustment soon.

But first, the other business. The butterfly started up in his guts again. He stared at his phone. Franko had been the one to make all these calls before. The ambulance team was a vital tool, like a scalpel in an operating room, but both times he'd met the freelancers he'd been deeply shaken.

Shaken and envious. It had felt like coming nose to nose with two sharks. He'd only walked away because they had decided to let him. Something to be profoundly respectful of. And to aspire to.

Bracing himself, he made the call.

"I'm at the lab," he said. "I have a pickup for you. It'll be the last one from this location." He thought about it, then added, "But I might have another call for you later on today."

Chapter 20

No decorum at all

"Uncle," said Markovic, and in that one word conveyed a level of tension the man hadn't shown in almost a year, "it's Franko." He held out the phone and the Uncle took it.

Three children were running around the house today, Daniella playing with two of her cousins from across town. His wife and their mothers chatted and laughed together in the kitchen, one or another of them constantly peeking around the corner to keep an eye on the kids. The spiced-meat smell of sizzling cevapi filtered through the house. It was a warm and happy home, and the Uncle had felt himself slipping into a comfortable lassitude in his favourite chair.

An old man's lethargy. He should have known better. Such things were not for him. He glared at the phone and said, "What?"

"Sorry, Uncle, I know you said he was the boss and we should do what he says, but this thing, I dunno, I thought you need to hear this, soon better than late, so—"

"Just say it, then," he prompted, keeping as much irritation out of his voice as possible.

"He, uh, well. He wants us to take them. Both of them, right now, and bring them to the old machine shop."

"What!?" He made no effort to hide the anger as he rose out of the chair, all lethargy gone from his bones. The house's laughter and yelling fell off a cliff into nothing, three kids and three moms staring at him with wide eyes. He waved a palm at them, everything's fine, as he headed for the office and closed the door. "Tell me everything."

"Not much more to tell," Franko said, the relief palpable in his voice. "No idea why he wants to see them, but he does, and now. Said to pull them off the street, bag them and take them to Pandora Street. Use the Nissan with the tinted windows. But, you know, people will notice such a thing. And the machine shop? No idea what he has planned, but it's still got everything in it. You know, hammers. Punches. Saws." He swallowed through the phone. "I thought you should know."

Franko's explanation had given him the moment to calm down, or at least let his rage settle deeper. "You did well. Now I need to think. Be quiet."

Franko waited in silence. He was a good man. All the Stooges were, for what they were. Reliable and trustworthy tools. They were right to bring this to him. Franko, like him, knew an error in judgement when he heard one.

The arrogance was off the scale. The blindness, the sheer ugliness of it. No decorum at all. No attention to elegance, to protocol. Did he think this was what the new way of doing business looked like? Then he was wrong, dead wrong, and the Uncle knew it. The Croats would not sink to the level of barbarism.

Leave that to the barbarians.

He paced the length of his office from the bookcase to the statue of Venus and back. The man was a scientist, lived in his head. What was he thinking? Obviously, the answer came back, he considered these two a threat. Now, at the project's most vulnerable point. He would need to find out what they knew, of course, but there were ways you went about these things. You didn't make waves. You didn't terrify ordinary citizens on busy streets in the best parts of town.

You most certainly did not antagonize the police, not unless you needed to. And unless you were prepared for the war to follow. Which the Croats most definitely were not.

He decided. The day was warm and pleasant, the grapevines outside his office window deepening their autumn yellow. "Bring them here," he told Franko. "To the back gate. Be polite. Deferential. Make it an invitation, not an order. Do you understand?"

The man sounded almost happy, the old order restored, the universe back to making sense again. "Yes, sir. What if they refuse?"

"They won't. Or rather, the young man might. He has no context. But make sure his woman is with him. She will not refuse, and she'll make certain he does not, either."

"Yes, sir. We're a block away from them now, they are out for a walk. We'll see you soon."

He left the office, handed the phone back to Markovic and strode into the kitchen. His wife, daughter, and her friends stopped talking and turned to him. "I need enough coffee for three," he said, "and a brunch. Make sure there's a tray of figs, grapes, nuts. Also," he pointed at the cevapi in the pan, "some of those. I apologize for interrupting your plans, my dears. In the garden in twenty minutes."

Chapter 21

Take a swing at the crime lord

Jackson stuck out a hand and gave a wink as he and Marilyn strolled past a shoe store on Fourth Avenue. She laughed and took it. The morning was warm for October. Plenty of people were on the sidewalk taking advantage of the sunshine. They got a few grins as they held hands and windowshopped.

"Didn't take us long to get your place back in order," she said, admiring a pair of Gucci pumps behind the glass. "Ahmed told me they're putting extra patrols through the area. Yours was one of six forced entries in Kits over the past week, and that's too many. It's got our attention."

He smiled at the implication behind her words. Marilyn loved being a cop. Her department was all over it, her team was going to make the world safe again. Four years on the VPD was enough to sour some people. He knew she was only getting started. He gave her hand a squeeze.

She caught something in the shop window and tensed, squeezing his hand back hard. His peripheral vision caught the movement, too. A thick, aggressive red streak of irregular motion flashed across the reflected traffic as a car accelerated hard out of a parking space and headed their way. Before they could turn, dodge into the store, run, a black SUV with tinted windows pulled up fast and jammed to a stop beside them.

The passenger window rolled down and a bowling ball of a head popped out, round and fleshy, topped with a blond frizz.

"Mr. Teague? Ms. Mathers? Sorry, my friend can't drive for shit. Can I have a word?" Jackson caught the broad, tinny vowels of an American accent.

He knew their names? Jackson would bet good money this goon also knew the exact layout of his apartment. His boot probably fit the dent in Jackson's door. A rush of outrage rose up and burned his face. Words rose with it, he didn't even know which ones, and he was taking a breath to fuel them when Marilyn stepped in front and cut him off.

"Johnnie! You old dog. When did they let you out? Harassing little girls at the mall, wasn't it?"

The man—Johnnie—looked offended. "Little girls? Please. I was collecting for paid protection and your prosecutors couldn't convince the judge it was anything different."

She walked over to the car. Traffic was piling up behind it. A horn bleated from a Kia a few windshields back. Behind her butt she waved a calming hand at Jackson. Keep your cool. "So, what's up?"

Johnnie's face slid from offended to a little upset. Embarrassed, even. "Can we talk? Not here, too many cars. We're causing trouble. Get in, please, and we'll talk." The rear window rolled down to show an empty seat.

Marilyn's voice was casual, but Jackson could see the tension in her back and shoulders. Again, she waved at him to stay calm. "I'm out for a walk with my guy, here. How about we meet at a cafe later?"

Another horn honked behind them. Fourth Avenue had two lanes for each direction, but the shuffle to get around the stopped SUV had backed up eastbound commuters for a block already. Johnnie's face twisted with even more embarrassment. "I need to talk with both of you, actually. Right now. Please. It's important." He reached back and opened the rear door to enhance the invitation.

"You want me—us—to get in there with you? Come on, Johnnie, what's this about?" The horns were growing into a chorus. Marilyn and the big man, eyes locked on each other in some kind of casual intensity Jackson didn't understand, ignored them all.

Johnnie sighed. He leaned out farther, as if he was whispering a confidence. "The uncle needs to see you. Both of you. Now. Please, and thank you very much."

Jackson saw Marilyn jerk. The tension in her shoulders migrated to her spine. She straightened, gained another inch that he hadn't known she had, and practically rose up onto the balls of her feet. Still she kept her voice lazy and relaxed. "The Uncle wants to see us. Really." The way she said it gave the honorific a capital letter.

"Yes," replied Johnnie. "With respect. And I guarantee the coffee will be better than anything here." He waved a meaty arm at the busy avenue.

"Well, that settles it, then." She turned around. A hard glint of excitement sparked in her eyes. "Come on, Jackson, let's go have the best coffee in the city."

"What?" He tried to take a step back but she had a firm grip on his hand again. "You actually want to go for a ride with this guy, right now? He probably broke into my apartment! You've arrested him before, for hell's sake!"

She stepped close, right up against him, and whispered into his ear. "The Uncle wants to see us, and he's being polite about it. That's really weird. It's also not optional. Say no now, and we'll be seeing these men again very soon, in much less friendly circumstances. Come on. I want to hear what the old man has to say. Just let me do the talking." Stepping backwards and dragging him along, she shepherded them both into the back seat of the SUV.

"Thank you both," said Johnnie from the front. He sounded

genuinely relieved. The driver took off into traffic the moment the door was closed.

A hand floated up from the SUV's third row of seats behind them, giving Jackson a heart-thudding surprise. It held a wad of crumpled bills, including some hundreds. "For the damage to your place," said a third man in a gruff, Eastern European accent. "The Uncle sends his apologies." Jackson wordlessly pocketed the cash.

They left Kitsilano and drove in silence towards East Vancouver. Marilyn vibrated with energy on the seat beside him. At last he asked the question. "Okay. You all seem to know. Who is the Uncle, and why are we going to see him?"

Johnnie glanced back. "You tell him," he said to Marilyn.

She turned to face him. "Branislav Zupan. He's the head of the Croats, an organized crime family that's been operating in Vancouver for many years."

"We prefer 'independent entrepreneurs,'" said the voice from the back seat.

"Sure. Keep telling yourselves that. The Croats really are from Croatia, and they really are a family, mostly. Zupan picked up the nickname the Uncle somewhere along the line and it stuck. Makes him sound all soft and cuddly, doesn't it? Don't be fooled. He's as ruthless as they come, and he has his fingers in all the pies."

"Had," corrected the driver.

"Right," Marilyn said. "The Croats were one of the bigger organizations on the West Coast until the new gangs moved in. Trans-national, well funded, and evil as they come. Remember all those stories of shootouts in the streets? Cars filled with bullets and bodies? Some of those bodies were Croats. These new guys are the reason 'ultraviolent' is a word. If a few of their members went to jail they just ordered up more. They draw from all over the world. From places that make the worst Vancouver has to offer look like a pretty good day."

"We hated those feckers on sight," said the driver.

"Yeah. So Zupan, the Uncle, decided enough was enough. He went to war with the New Canadians. And got his ass handed to him. We're still finding body parts." Marilyn paused. "The Croats fell off the radar. Most of their business interests were taken over by the New Canadians. Some people figured the Uncle had packed up and gone home."

"Not likely," Johnnie said. "Vancouver is his home. In fact, we're here."

They'd drifted into the residential area between Nanaimo and Renfrew Streets and down a back alley. This was post-war suburbia, neat little lots with single-family clapboard and stucco houses that dated back to the forties. Built with some level of care and individuality, and renovated multiple times, the neighbourhoods had kept much of their original character and developed more of their own. Each house, Jackson figured, would fetch close to two million on the open market. More than a massage therapist could afford, that was for sure. From the back alley, each lot sported a chainlink or cedar fence surrounding a scrap of yard with rhododendrons and a few kid's toys, or maybe a garden.

The house they pulled up to was worth four mil at least. Nestled unobtrusively in the middle of the block, it was somehow three lots, all fenced in higher-than-code cedar. Over the fence Jackson could see the gables and filigrees of a solid European chateau, the point of an actual turret sticking up on one end. Several trees grew over the fence. One of them fairly dripped with ripe figs. The driver stopped next to a chauffeur's gate built into the cedar.

"He's waiting for you," Johnnie said from the front seat. Jackson guessed the thug's training in etiquette hadn't included opening the car door for his guests. He cautiously stepped out of the SUV, Marilyn behind him, and lifted the latch on the gate.

Grapevines! The spacious garden behind the high fence was a maze of vines and huge, yellowing leaves, trained to three levels of wire. Gnarled trunks as thick as Jackson's arm anchored each set of vines and spoke to the vineyard's age. A path followed the fenceline to left and right, passing the ends of innumerable rows, but the way forward was clear: a wooden-arch arbour directly in front of them, fully overgrown with thick vines, created a leafy tunnel extending into the garden.

It was lovely. Marilyn led the way into the warm, green-and-gold light. Jackson's pattern sense admired the hidden symmetries of the riotous vines as they passed.

The tunnel of vines curved gently towards the house. As they rounded the corner it opened onto a large patio—terrazzo, perhaps—in the middle of the vineyard. Two trees, an apricot and another fig, graced the far corners. In the middle of the tiled space sat four comfortable-looking teak chairs around a wrought iron table that was laden with a sumptuous brunch.

Standing next to the table was an old man. Hard and brown as a grapevine's trunk save for a waved and pomaded crown of silver hair, he stood easy and elegant in a weekend shirt and trousers that looked torn from the pages of The Rake and would make most Burrard Street money managers look like sartorial amateurs. He walked over to them, extended a hand and said, "Welcome to my home. Thank you for agreeing to come."

His voice, with just enough Croatian accent to sound as exotic as his clothes, was relaxed and pleasant. Jackson took one look into his eyes and remembered Marilyn's caution. They were deep brown and as hard as the teak chairs. The old man's handshake was warm, firm, and unbreakable.

Marilyn spoke first as she swung a long leg over the back of one of the chairs and sat down at the table. "We didn't exactly have a choice. But thank you for making it an invitation. So, first things first. What shall we call you?" She snatched a dark, purple grape off a tight bunch and popped it into her mouth.

A shiver passed through Jackson as he sat down next to her. Easy there, he thought, although their relationship was nowhere near the telepathic level. Of course she'd want to seize the conversational advantage, get on top of things right away. But this man lived and breathed a certain level of class. Jackson was sure they didn't want to piss him off with bad manners.

The old man took the seat closest to the house and spread his hands. A smile touched his lips. "Well, I am sure you are not interested in calling me Uncle. Just Branislav will do. And you are Jackson Teague, a fine massage therapist, so I am told. Of course, you are Marilyn Mathers, up and coming in the Vancouver Police Department."

A woman, maybe mid-sixties, emerged from the house carrying a tray. She set a steaming urn and three small espresso cups down next to a tiny pitcher of cream and a dish with three sugar cubes.

"This is my Milanka," said Branislav, touching the back of her hand with obvious affection. "Thank you for the coffee, Mila. You must try her cevapi, it is one of her specialties." He waved at a dish of what looked like small sausages, accompanied by soaked grape leaves and a dish of tzatsiki.

"You be nice to our guests," Milanka warned him, "no hard words. It is a beautiful morning, and they are good people." She kissed him on the forehead and went back inside.

Branislav poured them all some incredibly black coffee. He picked his up, ignored the cream and sugar, and took a sip. Marilyn did the same, so Jackson followed suit. The brew was hot, rich, and invigorating.

"She always gives me good advice. I shall do my best to follow it. Please, have some food. The grapes and figs are my own."

Jackson took a cevapi, a small pastry, and a couple of grapes.

The cevapi was hot and delicious, made with a mix of spices he couldn't name. The grapes were obviously from the vines all around him, incredibly dark clusters with the occasional failed green raisin among them. He tried one and found it a surprising mix of tangy and sweet.

Marilyn loaded up a plate. Seeming to get Jackson's silent warning about etiquette, she spoke before trying anything. "So, Branislav, what brings us down here on such a fine day?" She tried a cevapi, mmmed in surprise and had another.

"See? I did not lie to you. You're a police officer, that would be unwise, am I right? And quite a policewoman, from what I have heard. Four years on the force, a good clearance rate, and most importantly a good head on your shoulders. A nose for the job, as they say. Even some time with the Emergency Response Team! Exciting, I'm sure. All too brief, though, and you have my condolences for that." He reached for a fig, sniffed it, and ate.

Marilyn took her time answering, although Jackson could see the glitter in her eyes. "Yes, it was fun, and I wanted to stay, but circumstances dictated otherwise. You didn't have anything to do with that, by chance?"

Jackson remembered the story from the news. A dark and foggy night. An ERT training exercise on the Lions Gate Bridge. A large explosive accidentally detonated in the middle of Vancouver Harbour. No one was hurt. No damage at all, except to Marilyn's big career move.

He also knew the real story. They'd been on the bridge to stop a professional bomber. A pedestrian had materialized out of the fog and blown the takedown. The bomber—a nasty piece of work named Borden—got away, and crossed paths with Marilyn and Jackson a week later.

Branislav smiled and tilted his coffee cup before taking another sip. "No, that was not me. I understand the saboteur was a professional? That his target was a natural gas transport ship, and no one knows who hired him, or why?" He waited. Marilyn slowly gave a nod. He smiled again. "Unfortunate. But a moment's reflection tells you it could not have been me. This man would have destroyed much of the city. My life, my work, are here. Vancouver is my chosen home. I would never do such a thing."

Marilyn considered that as she refilled her demitasse. "All right. So it wasn't you. Thanks for your condolences."

"Excellent. We are making progress, you and I. So, no more emergency response. But that cannot be all, is it? You still have ambition, I can see it in your eyes. Ambition brought you here today, no? So tell me. What's next for the ambitious Marilyn Mathers of the VPD?" He examined a grape for blemishes and then ate it with obvious enjoyment.

Don't tell him, Jackson thought, bad idea. But he could see the pride behind Marilyn's carefully casual posture and knew she hadn't heard. "I'm thinking about Organized Crime," she said, then levelled a steady gaze at the old man.

He wasn't surprised. But acted like he was, and delighted, too. "Organized Crime! Ah, you want to go after the big fish! That is bold. Very noble. And what about you?" He turned abruptly to Jackson as Marilyn was taking a breath for her next turn in the jousting match. "A traveling massage therapist, such a unique take on your profession. Working on any interesting cases lately? Anything challenging that sends you back to the books?"

He almost jolted at the conversation's sudden shift. "Uh, well, yeah. I mean, yes, sir. Branislav. I'm working with a woman who lost all her toes to frostbite and is still relearning how to walk. Some of my patients take all manner of supplements for life extension. And I'm studying new advances in geriatric massage, which is kind of a specialty for a traveling therapist." Why was this man even asking? But his interest seemed genuine, and Jackson felt himself warming to the topic.

"Such varied work! The day may come when I require my own

elder care, who knows? I am happy that you keep up on the latest research. But I do not know this life extension. You say they take pills to stay young? Tell me more."

Marilyn shoved some more food into her mouth, irritated. Jackson leaned in and put an elbow on the table. "All right. Longevists try to stay healthy for as long as possible. They see the diseases of old age, even ageing itself, as unnecessary and curable. Keep the body supplied with everything it needs, give it a few chemical nudges along the way, and who knows? Some of these people, my clients included, think they can reach 120 and still be healthy and strong."

"Fascinating! I will have to look into this. Tell me, what is the latest and greatest? What should I investigate first?" Branislav leaned in, too, an elbow on the table, the food forgotten in his eagerness.

Jackson laughed. "Well. I'm no expert, in fact I'm just beginning my research into all this. But from what I can tell, there is no clear winner. Not yet. The best advice is to eat like this," he waved a hand at the table, "get plenty of fresh air and exercise, and avoid accidents. Beyond that, the range of supplements and treatments is dizzying. Do your own research and make your own choices."

Branislav had spent the last minute peering into Jackson's eyes, riveted on his words. He kept up the stare for a bit longer. It was intense. When Jackson started to get uncomfortable he blinked, leaned back in his chair and laughed again. "An old man's dream! Just whisper the words 'fountain of youth' into our ears and watch us salivate. Please excuse my inquisitiveness." He pivoted his gaze back to Marilyn. "Organized Crime, you said! Tell me, why would you choose such a path for your career?"

Jackson felt his toes curl. He held his breath and waited for Marilyn to explode. Shout, storm out of the garden, take a swing at the crime lord across from her, he didn't know what. Instead, she slapped the table and laughed.

"Branislav, that question! The confidence you must have to even ask it. I can see why your family looks up to you."

She lowered her gaze at him. Jackson didn't see fury in her face. Not disgust, or righteousness. To his surprise, he saw humour. And a grudging respect.

"I want to stop men like you, of course. I'm tired of catching pushers and pimps. Sick of seeing the human destruction left behind by the things you do and trying to patch it all up. I want to make a real difference and stop it all at the source." She pointed a finger. Thankfully, Jackson thought, not a finger gun. "That's you, Branislav." She popped a grape between her teeth. "These are excellent."

The old man shrugged and looked around at the greenery. "An old Croatian varietal. A grapevine can produce magic. If it is properly trained, you understand. Only so many spurs, guided along the trellis. Too many leaves and it picks up mildew. Too many branches and it does not fruit. Too much water and it drowns. And regularly, the vine needs a hard prune." He sighed. "That time came for us, I suppose. All the things you say may be true, my dear policewoman, but they are not the whole truth. And not true of the Croats any longer.

"Your Organized Crime department is very good, did you know that? And your Combined Forces Special Enforcement Unit even better. But they have not stopped all of what you said, have they? Perhaps slowed it a little, here and there, but does it stay slowed? Does the crime, as you call it, go away? You and I both know the answer, so it does not need to be said. But do you know why?"

He plucked a grape and held it between his thumb and finger. "It is because we do not create the need. We are in a business that needs no marketing, Constable Mathers, because the market already exists. We simply supply it. And when your departments and units stop us, when others hurt us so badly that we cannot go on?" Jackson heard the gangster's voice shake a bit. "Then others step in to take our place."

"We get them, too," Marilyn said, her anger a touch closer to the surface. "And in the meantime, a lot of ordinary people get to breathe a little easier."

"Do you, though? Have you?" The old man had helped himself to a pastry and talked around a mouthful. "These others who stepped in to replace us, the ones who destroyed my family. Have you punished them? Stopped them? The briefest glance at the headlines tells everyone you have not. They are worse than we ever were. Killing in the streets. Bystanders hurt. Tainted drugs that kill the customers. These newcomers have no decorum, no respect. There are laws on my side of the table, too, Marilyn Mathers, and these people break them. They are breaking everything."

Silence settled into the terrazzo, the echo of the old man's words ringing through the vines. All three of them ate in silence for a minute. Jackson cast a wistful glance at his empty espresso cup, but he sensed the meeting was drawing to a close.

Marilyn chewed another cevapi, wrapped in a grape leaf, and waded into the quiet. "You haven't answered my question yet. Why are we here, Branislav?"

The Uncle rumbled a laugh. "You are everything I thought you might be. I invited you here, Marilyn, to ... let's say, establish a relationship. It is an old way of doing things, a nod of mutual respect. I guarantee you the newcomers will not offer anything of the sort."

"What kind of relationship? What did you have in mind?"

The Uncle shrugged again. "Oh, nothing too involved. Nothing to get either of us in trouble or violate your principles. Not that I could, am I right?" He chuckled again at the expression on her face. "Simply an understanding between us. Occasionally, perhaps, a sharing of information. Something might come along that is of no use to me but you might find interesting. And vice versa." He waved a hand before she could object. "Again, nothing against your principles or your judgement. Just something to keep in mind, and in your back pocket."

She considered it. "I'm going to tell my superiors, you know. This won't be our little secret."

"I knew that before you stepped through my gate. By all means, tell them. You may be surprised at their response."

Silence dropped into the grapevines again. After a long moment Marilyn nodded at Jackson. "You invited both of us. Johnnie made a point of it. You've been following Jackson around, broke into his place. Why?"

The Uncle's gnarled, dark face pinched into a grimace that made Jackson's knees water before he recognized it as a look of chagrin. "That was clumsy of me. The truth is, I was looking for information. You see, I have heard news that the newcomers are up to something. I do not know what, which irritates me. They brought in a contractor from overseas to help them somehow, but that man has vanished. He was last seen on the Seabus several nights ago." He turned to Jackson. "In your company. I had to make certain you were not involved with the newcomers' plans. You are not. But you spent some minutes with him. I was curious if he had told you anything, or passed you anything, that I could use."

Jackson remembered the envelope, now in Jonathan Harrowman's desk drawer. The photos on his phone. He remembered the shambles of his apartment after the break-in and made his decision.

"Nothing you don't already know about," he replied. "Your men were pretty thorough. That's all."

The old man took that in, then gave another shrug. "Well, it was worth asking. I have detained you both long enough. This has been most pleasant. You will find my men waiting for you at the gate." He stood, and they followed suit. Two firm, deliberate handshakes and they were back in the SUV. Johnnie and Marilyn kept up an aimless banter all the way back to Fourth Avenue.

When they were back on the sidewalk, right where they'd been picked up, Jackson turned to her as they continued their interrupted walk. "What the fuck, Legs? Did I just wander onto the set of the Godfather?"

"I know, right?" Marilyn walked so fast he struggled to keep up. "That was freakin' awesome! I can't wait to tell Ahmed and the rest. But all that, the whole 'mutual regard' thing? That was secondary." She stopped and spun to face him as he piled into her. "He wanted to grill you. Whatever that guy on the Seabus was into, he's worried about it, and he didn't find what he was looking for when they searched your place. Are you sure you've told me everything?"

He nodded. "You know what I know. I have Charles looking into the medical side of it."

She started walking again. "Okay. Pay attention at Blast Dynamics, and let me know what Charles comes up with. Keep your eyes open, Jackson. You find out anything more, tell me right away."

She was gone, barrelling down the Fourth Avenue sidewalk with him almost running to catch up.

So this is what it's like to be with a cop, he thought. He wasn't sure he liked it.

Chapter 22

IT CURES DEATH

That didn't take long, Georgia thought, as she stepped out of the bedroom to find Charles staring at the artwork at the end of the hall. She'd hung a John Horton original, a dark scene of tall-masted ships riding out a storm, in the spot vacated by the Raven. The change from spare, white lines to vivid nautical colours might not have been her best choice.

She took a deep breath to settle herself and walked up to stand beside him. Even that small motion felt easier, like her lungs were fresh and new. The implant didn't even hurt, less than a day after Dr. Phillips had slid it under the skin on her right side below the last rib. She was so thrilled she felt like dancing, but kept herself reined in.

"What do you think?" she asked. "I thought the hall could use a dash of colour."

"I liked the Raven. What did you do with it?" Charles sounded disappointed, as she knew he would. He'd always appreciated Bill Reid's clear, strong lines.

"Oh, I sold it to a collector. He's been pestering me about it for a couple of years."

"Really?" Charles pivoted and looked at her. "That must have netted you a boatload. But wasn't that your mother's? I thought the Buckley women weren't supposed to get rid of their forebears' additions to the house."

She laughed. "No, silly! We're supposed to improve the house and put our own personal flair on it. Like I have." She waved at the Horton. "Besides, I can always buy the Raven back later if I want to."

They headed downstairs to get breakfast going. "I don't know, Georgia, those things go up in price, not down. How much did you get for it?"

"Sixty thousand. You're right, that's a lot more than my mother paid for it." She knew what the next question would be, and the one after that. Although she pitied him for his lack of understanding, she still braced herself for the storm.

Charles had his head in the fridge, so his whistle was muted. "Pretty good! Got any plans for it?"

She felt it get closer. "Oh, it's already spent."

He came out with a grapefruit and some yogurt. "Holy snap, Georgia! What did you buy, a new car?"

"No, of course not. Ten thousand went to the new art. The rest," she paused and hated herself for the tell, "I spent on my health."

Charles plucked a small paring knife from the block and headed for the grapefruit. "Fifty thousand? On your—" He jammed the knife into the cutting board and spun, his eyes wide. "Georgia, what have you done?"

The tempest had arrived. But she would survive this storm. And every storm after it. She turned to face the wind. "It's called the Ponce de Leon treatment. In a year everybody will know about it, but only the richest will be able to benefit. I'm getting in on the ground floor because I can help spread the word. It's revolutionary, Charles. I've seen the proof, the clinical trials. Test subjects improved within weeks. Days. Old injuries went away. They didn't need glasses anymore. Diseases disappeared."

He grabbed her by the shoulders, hard, and stared into her eyes from inches away. She let him look for whatever he was scared to find, knowing it wasn't there. After a moment he released her, growled an inarticulate roar and threw himself into a chair by the table.

"We had an agreement, Georgia! You find something new, you run it past me first. That was ironclad. That way I'd know you were at least safe. Now this? The 'Ponce de Leon'? Fountain of youth bullshit? That's a tailormade sales pitch right there. If I heard about anything with a name like that, I'd laugh and walk away. So tell me, then. What the hell is it? What have you done to yourself?"

She kept standing. Kept a little distance between herself and the waves of anger coming off her husband. Her first husband, she reminded herself. There would be more as the decades went by. "It's a supplement, timed release. A once a year treatment. It returns every system in your body to perfect health. Keep getting the treatment and you stay that way."

"For how long?" Thunder rumbled under the surface of his voice, and just below that she heard his anguish. It almost broke her heart. Charles was so intelligent, so capable, exactly the person you wanted to see if you were wheeled into an emergency room. And so inflexible in his opinions and rules. She knew he would break long before he'd ever bend.

"Indefinitely."

He exploded. "Bullshit! I don't believe this. Georgia, you're an incredible woman. A top-tier fundraiser, hell, you're a salesperson! You know a pitch when you hear one. How could you get so taken in by something so obvious? And for fifty grand? Really?"

"In a year it's going to be two hundred. And my body would be another year older. It can't make you younger."

"Oh, a time-limited offer! Get it now while you still can! Jump in with both feet and your life's savings right now, before it's too late and the train has passed you by! Fucking hell, Georgia, that's 3 a.m. infomercial tripe. It's so industry-standard it's laughable. You know why you didn't tell me?" He was standing now, his words rattling the dishes on the shelf. "You know why you didn't tell me! Because it's such obvious snake oil that a ten-year-old could see through it!"

He got quiet and soft. "The only reason you got taken in was because that particular sales pitch was targeted right at your weak spot. I love you, Georgia, and I understand. We all have them. Me, too. I'm glad you told me about this. But get them on the phone today. Get your money back. You're not getting whatever this supplement is, not until I've had a chance to really look into it. That's our agreement, remember? You said you'd do that. And no black market pill is worth fifty thousand dollars unless it's going to cure cancer."

He was through the anger now, and into his doctor-knows-best routine. Which was the real reason she hadn't told him. She sat down next to him, placed a hand on his arm. "This does cure cancer. Charles, it cures death. And it's not a pill, it's a device, just under the skin. I got it yesterday."

The colour drained from Charles' face, actually fell away until he was white as the wall behind him. "You got it? Somebody stuck something into your body? For Christ's sake, I can't believe this. Where?"

Of course he'd want to inspect it. She lifted up her shirt. "Here, below my rib. Look at it, Charles. Really look."

He did, bending close to her side. He felt around the incision, tenderly at first and then with increasing vigor. He glanced up. "When did you say you got this?"

She smiled down at him, just a Mona Lisa touch to her lips, no need to exaggerate it. "Yesterday afternoon. Four o'clock. The entire procedure took about five minutes. Yes, he sterilized the area and yes, he wore gloves and yes, he used sterile instruments."

"That's not possible." He poked at it some more.

"I took the dressing off before you got home last night. I took the steri-strips off at bedtime. The Ponce de Leon is real, Charles.

It's already working. The incision is half-healed. In a week I won't even have a scar."

She bent over to see it again. A single red line on the side of her abdomen, an inch long, already knit back together into a neat, raised scar. Visible, incontrovertible proof.

Charles straightened up. His face had gone from white to grey. "Who knows what else that thing is doing inside you? You should have let me check it out. That's my job, to keep you safe. It was, anyway." He waved at her scar. "That's—impressive. But it's not the point."

She let the full, beaming smile that took over her face speak volumes for her. Because, of course, it was.

Chapter 23

COULDN'T HURT TO LOOK

Jackson waved goodbye as Marilyn jumped onto the Burrard Station bus at Cornwall Avenue, then headed home and changed into cycling gear. He was ahead of schedule; Charles wasn't due to swing by for another hour.

Which was good, because his nerves still vibrated from their morning visit to the Uncle's vineyard.

Marilyn's excitement rang in his ears. 'Watch out at Blast, keep your eyes open.' Right. Like he'd see anything interesting from the upstairs boardroom. Did she want him to quietly pry the company's IP out of the scientists during their fifteen minute sessions? Fat chance.

He stuffed some dried mango, cashews and a banana into his cycling bag and filled a water bottle. He'd rather talk hockey stats at Blast Dynamics tomorrow. The weather. Politics, religion. Anything that would keep trouble from darkening his doorstep again. Because this whole weird mess was getting way too serious for comfort.

He sank onto the couch, waited for Charles to call and stewed. This was ridiculous. All of it. A clandestine handoff in the middle of a rainy night? A mysterious biotech company making outlandish claims about a world-changing breakthrough? Plucked off the street for brunch with a mob boss and grilled for what he knew? He laughed into the empty air of his living room. All of this, and the real joke was that he knew nothing.

Which was also maddening. Outside his window, past the shoreline midrises, the waves of Burrard Inlet sparkled in the autumn sunshine. He knew nothing, and he didn't like it. There was something to know, that was for sure, because all sorts of very important people either wanted to find it out, or wanted to keep it to themselves.

"Couldn't hurt to look," he muttered into the silence of the apartment.

Years of massage therapy training had made him a decent researcher. According to his dad he'd inherited the gene for extreme curiosity; he figured he just liked to know things. Right now, something he knew practically nothing about was steamrolling through his life. Looking into it would at least give him some feeling of control.

He took out his phone. Then reconsidered and moved over to the laptop for its bigger screen. It was old, but it could handle Google.

What to research? He could look up the history of the Croat crime family, headed by Branislav Zupan, but that wouldn't get him anything pertinent. The Uncle had sweated him for information, which meant the elegant old European didn't know, either. Jackson needed to look at the people who knew more than he did.

The Seabus guy? That was a dead end. He chided himself for the bad pun but conceded the point. Without at least a name, there'd be nothing to research.

That left Blast Dynamics and its two founders, Jonathan Harrowman and Harold Dunn. He cracked the lid on the computer and got to work.

Blast Dynamics was easy to find and not at all useful. They had a beautiful website, full of lab photos and background information, a few promotional videos featuring Jonathan Harrowman against the white walls and floor of a much smaller lab saying vague and fancy things with his magnetic enthusiasm. The entire site was nothing more than a fancy pitch for venture-level investors.

The two founders each had a bio page. Dunn's publicity shot showed the big man in a lab, bent over a microscope, a glass panel to one side covered with chemical notations in black Sharpie. Harrowman's photo had him in front of the building below the Blast Dynamics logo in pressed, beige khakis and royal blue polo shirt, complete with an actual white sweater sleeve-tied over his shoulders. Jackson had to admit the two made an effective combination: the brains and the money.

Harrowman's bio page even featured one of his fascia drawings, this one a study of the superficial fascia of the abdomen. Jackson studied it. The black and white pencil sketch was lovely and meticulously detailed. Harrowman could easily have pursued a career in the arts. He grabbed his phone and pulled up his picture of the fascial hand from the Seabus documents.

Definitely two different styles. Harrowman hadn't drawn the hand.

Jackson tried a few tricks. He did advanced searches for various document types, to see if the Blast website had any accidentally-unprotected files. He checked the sitemap, scrolled through the source code for several of the site's pages. No back doors presented themselves. The website had been professionally built by someone with an eye for cybersecurity.

Next he tried Harrowman himself. The man's bio gave a brief timeline of his life and career, about what you'd expect from an Ivy League scientist. Degrees in biochemistry and business management from Princeton, advanced degrees and some postdoc work in molecular biology at the University of British Columbia. A few years at a major pharmaceutical firm in Illinois, a stint as Chief Research Officer for a smaller drug company

Jackson had actually heard of. Then he'd started Blast Dynamics.

Dunn's bio was a bit longer. The full suite of science degrees, with his interest focused on structural biochemistry. That specialty was a new one for Jackson, but a side trip to ChatGPT gave him a pretty good explanation. Structural biochem examined the physical structure of molecules, right down to the atomic level, to see how they interacted with other molecules. Like how an antibiotic would match up with the bacterium it was supposed to attack. Or, presumably, how a new chemical would influence the behaviour of fibroblasts.

He flipped back to Dunn's bio. It listed several papers he'd cowritten or authored on his own, with titles Jackson had to struggle through word by word. Very impressive. The man could probably build a molecule from the ground up, given the right kind of lab and a bit of time.

Dunn had worked at the same small drug company as Harrowman. They'd formed a friendship, said the bio; they'd realized the remarkable synergies of their two skill sets and gone into business together.

Jackson sat back. Nothing obvious here, but then, there wouldn't be. Still, it told him where to search next.

He dug into the company they'd both worked for. It was based in Toronto, and today had several popular and effective medications in production with more in various stages of development and approvals, according to its website. Neither Harrowman or Dunn were mentioned at all as past executives. "Hmm," Jackson said, his interest picking up. The absence of information was sometimes as good as a signpost.

He searched for their names in association with the company. Several research citations came back, but he ignored those. They'd gotten mentions in the news for advances in the company's success, but that wasn't what Jackson was looking for. He swept them aside and tried something a little more targeted.

He found them buried in the archives of the local newspaper of the small city where the drug company was based. Just one small article, deep enough in the document tree that the web's larger search engines had never picked it up, that mentioned both of them in a three-line sidebar. "Arrow Pharmaceuticals announces that J Harrowman and H Dunnai, senior scientists with the firm, are leaving the company for personal reasons. Arrow Pharmaceuticals wishes them well in their future endeavours."

And that was it. Had they left to start work on Blast Dynamics? The date on the article was a full two years before the new company had been formed. The stub of an article was completely devoid of detail. Nothing about their accomplishments, no mention of where they were going next. The absence of information practically pointed a finger at itself, yelling, 'look here.'

He dug deeper. Following a hunch, he paid for access and did a search through Ontario's justice records.

And found it. A single record, a civil court case. Arrow Pharma vs Dunnai and Harrowman. The page was riddled with black bars, the information heavily redacted. He was surprised the entire thing hadn't been restricted, but sometimes things slipped through the bureaucratic cracks. He gleaned what he could from the visible leftovers.

A picture emerged. The two scientists had been working on a research project. What medication they were researching, and why, was covered with black bars. The action that landed them in court was not.

"They tried a shortcut," Jackson said into the quiet of his apartment, shaking his head.

One of them—the lawsuit blamed them both equally—had decided their project needed a sample of Nipah virus. Jackson went back to the search bar and looked it up. Nipah virus was a highly infectious and particularly lethal pathogen, native to the Malaysia–Singapore–India triangle, carried by bats and occasionally passed to humans. Very unfortunate humans, he thought, judging from the photos that he quickly scrolled past.

They must have been working on a treatment or cure. They should have been working in a Level 4 biohazard lab for something like that, but the small firm didn't have anything that fancy. They couldn't import samples of the virus itself. That would have triggered alarm bells from halfway across the globe.

Instead, they'd imported bats. Live ones, a half-dozen of them. Smuggled them in, from what Jackson could interpret from the online documentation. Very much without the knowledge of the pharmaceutical company's CEO. She'd found out, of course, and had them clapped in legal irons.

He dug some more, trying to find out the verdict in the civil case. No dice, it was hidden behind an impenetrable layer of nondisclosure. Settling the suit must have cost them a pretty penny, he thought. Plus all the academic credibility they'd spent years building. By the time they left the courtroom, opening their own firm would've been their only remaining career path.

How had they avoided a criminal case? Jail time, for endangering themselves and everyone around them? The Internet had no answers. Harrowman must have leaned on some very high connections, Jackson figured.

There was one last thing to investigate. Harold Dunn had changed his name. Dunn, the internet told him, was a relatively common surname of Scottish and Irish origin. Dunnai, on the other hand, came from Eastern Europe, primarily Hungary.

Had Dunn shortened his last name for convenience? For some perceived greater acceptance in the academic world? Or some other reason altogether?

His phone pinged, a message from Charles. Outside. Let's go. The guy's in a hurry today, Jackson thought, he's not usually this terse. He closed the laptop, grabbed his bag and headed for the bike storage room.

Maybe he would keep his eyes open at Blast Dynamics tomorrow. Not stir up any more trouble, of course, that was the last thing he wanted. But, as every scientist knew, digging up information often produced more questions than answers.

Chapter 24

THE PONCE DE LEON

"Uh, hey man, want me to drive?" Jackson held onto the Jesus bar above the passenger door as Charles took the turn onto Cornwall at speed, the tires of his older Lexus chirping their complaint. The bikes rattled on their rack.

Charles was angry. That had been Jackson's first assessment on seeing his friend's dark face outside the apartment building. Charles' body was tense enough to warrant a dangerous red shimmer from Jackson's pattern sense. As they got into the car, Charles behind the wheel, he was muttering to himself. Actual words. His lips moved, but too low for Jackson to make out. He'd left their parking spot without checking traffic.

"Yeah." Charles yanked the car to the curb and jumped out. They changed places, and Jackson threaded eastward through town towards the Ironworkers Memorial Bridge at a more sane pace. Charles kept up the thundercloud impression for the entire drive.

Not angry, Jackson reinterpreted. Well, not just angry. He knew his friend. Charles was devastated.

Definitely relationship trouble.

Today's ride was North Vancouver to Deep Cove, part lung-refreshing roll through lush temperate rainforest and part death-defying traffic rodeo. Jackson coasted into a small parking lot tucked into the trees beside Lynn Creek. As they unstrapped their bikes he broke the conversational ice. "Want to talk about it?"

"Later," Charles growled. He slapped his water bottle into its cage and swung the bike around, ready to mount and take off. Jackson sighed and laid a hand on his shoulder.

"You're in no shape to ride. Let's sit for a minute." He nudged Charles' shoulder around and towards the big rocks along the creek bed. In silent agreement, Charles lifted his bike over to the water.

"It's Georgia," he said. No great surprise. Jackson sat down on a boulder and waited.

Charles spilled it. Georgia had always been one for taking good care of herself, Jackson knew that from their massage sessions. She had the loose, easy flow of a longtime yoga practitioner and the quiet poise of her instinctive, old-money aristocracy. He'd always noted her uniformly excellent skin, from callus-free feet to unlined face, and knew that it spoke to both good hydration and plenty of spa time. But he marvelled as Charles laid out the multitude of health improvements she'd tried over the years.

He'd had no idea. Georgia was a longevist, like the two clients she'd introduced him to.

Charles told him about their agreement—she never took a new supplement or tried a new therapy without running it past him first. Sensible, Jackson thought, and a decent compromise with her doctor husband. But he knew what was coming next.

"She broke it," Charles said, his hands bunching into fists in his lap. "She knew what I'd say, and she did it anyway. She didn't tell me until it was all done, on purpose."

It was something called the Ponce de Leon, he said, some kind of device stuck under the skin. The treatment was long-term but highly lucrative. You replaced it every year at a massive, bank-breaking cost. The whole deal was a masterful, high-end scam that had nailed Georgia right in her weak spot. She'd fallen for the sales pitch like a shot duck.

"Wow, hey, that's harsh. I can see why you're so perturbed." A niggle of professional interest sparked in his brain. "What does it do? Supposedly?"

Charles glared out at the creek. "Get this: it cures everything. Including death. It's the fucking fountain of youth." He picked up a rock and smashed it down onto another, then again. "Her biggest wish. You see what I'm up against? And she's convinced she has it now." He did it a third time and the rock in his hand cracked open. "We're married. Known each other since forever. We had an agreement, Jack. She broke it. Ah, man, I don't know what to do."

Charles' eyes welled up and spilled over as the cry of his heartbreak rose into the creekside trees. Jackson threw an arm around his back and held on while Charles leaned in and soaked the shoulder of his jersey.

When the tears began to ebb he tried to lighten things up. "So a funny thing happened this morning. Marilyn and I got kidnapped and taken to a mobster's house for brunch."

Charles's sobs gave way to an explosive laugh. He pulled away to stare at Jackson. "Mind repeating that?"

He handed Charles a tissue for his nose and told the story. It sounded crazy, even though he'd lived it. "That cevapi was to die for. But let me tell you, this whole thing is too weird," he concluded. "Marilyn's sure excited. The old guy—apparently he's known as the Uncle—mainly invited us over to talk to her. I think they made some kind of deal. You know, back channel information sharing, like in the movies. She's practically levitating."

Charles had listened, open-mouthed, through the entire adventure. When Jackson finished he shook his head. "You don't do things small, do you? First that nurse, now this. At least it explains those cars following you around. So, what are you going to do?" He blew his nose, then walked over to Lynn Creek for a handful of water to wash his face.

"About what?"

Charles snorted. "Don't give me that. You get a mysterious package, deliver it, and suddenly you're breaking bread with an inquisitive mob boss. He didn't just talk to Marilyn, right? I know you, Jackson, you're not going to leave it alone. What's next?"

He wasn't sure he should answer. Charles was his oldest friend. He was also Jackson's mental health monitor, and as by-the-rules as they come. "Uh. You sure you want to hear?"

Charles' anger resurfaced, or at least an edge of it. "Today's already shot to hell. You could tell me you're going to slash someone's tires and I wouldn't care. Lay it on me."

"Well. Okay, then. I looked into the two scientists who founded Blast Dynamics. They both got fired from their previous jobs for doing unauthorised research into a very nasty disease."

That caught his friend's professional attention. "Damn straight. Sounds worth getting fired over."

"Yeah. And they imported live bats to do it."

Charles whistled. "Amazing they didn't get jailed. That kind of cowboy science could endanger the whole country."

"I think Harrowman must have pulled some pretty big strings to get them out of it. I bet the civil case cost them a bundle. But hey, maybe they learned their lesson. From what I've seen at their company they're doing everything right, going through all the steps."

Charles snorted again. "Right. People change, Jackson, but not that much. If you think shortcuts are fine, that's more than just a bad decision. It's a mindset. The temptation to cut corners in medical research can save you a boatload of time and money. That urge won't go away, and a court case isn't going to dissuade you." He stood up. "Thanks for the story. I needed a distraction. Let's ride."

They spun out to Deep Cove, a town perched above the water

on the slopes of the mountain, breathing rich, moist air and dodging the occasional passenger mirror. They took a moment to admire the quiet finger of ocean that extended into the mountains, then rode back.

As they dismounted at the car Charles said, "I have something for you, almost forgot."

He reached into the back seat and pulled out a manila folder. "My colleague came back with the details on those notes you gave me. Interesting stuff."

They sat down on the rocks again. Lynn Creek had swelled with the runoff from the last night's rain and now rushed past their feet, cold and clear. Jackson examined the copy of the papers given to him by the injured man on the Seabus. Still a dense forest of chemical notations, incomprehensible to his eyes, ending in a long, complex formula. Another paper lay beneath them in the folder with a few printed notes.

'Notations, calculations and final formula for a bioactive compound. Appears to target and modulate cytokine receptors, with strong preference for fibroblasts. May have potential use in wound healing. Patent applied for, still pending.'

Jackson butted the papers together and slid them back into the folder. "Wild, but not really anything I didn't already know. Thanks for looking into it."

"That company has a long way to go," Charles cautioned. "Don't go getting any investment ideas, Jackson, not yet. Even with AI simulations to narrow things down, a drug's journey from bench to bedside can take a decade or more. Maybe ten percent of all pharmaceuticals make it through the process. I wish them well, but don't count on Blast Dynamics being the next big thing."

"Oh, they're not getting added to my portfolio, even when they go public. Still. What's with all the skulduggery, the organized crime interest? They must have something special, don't you think? Or it wouldn't be worth all this fuss."

Charles shook his head. "Remember, a successful medication can be worth billions. Even at this stage, when something's just been discovered, there's big money at stake. They're right to have locks on the doors. A lot of people are going to come sniffing around."

After the bikes were strapped down Charles headed for the driver's door, but paused. Jackson saw that look of devastation blanket his face again. "We've been together since we were teens," he said. "For the first time ever, I don't want to go home."

Chapter 25

KEEP YOUR RESUME HANDY

Jackson arrived at Blast Dynamics a few minutes before nine, headlights on and his wipers thumping hard to beat back the rain. He looked for a parking spot close to the building but the staff had already snagged them. The canopy of trees kept him somewhat dry on his way to the front door.

Tucked in against the trunk of a large chestnut close to the funky bench, hunched into a long, grey trench coat, Jackson saw Harold Dunn's blocky form. He hugged a phone to his ear. Having a conversation that was too personal for his office and worth getting soaked for? Jackson filed it away and kept moving.

Kelly the receptionist checked his ID and clipped his badge on. "My turn today," she said as they headed in. "I hear you've got good hands."

"I'll look forward to it," he said, and headed for the elevator.

More sandwiches and treats, the same dim lighting. Kelly's doing, he guessed. As he clicked the massage chair together he thought about the day's challenge. Dunn's behaviour aside, how was he going to keep his eyes open and find things out from the confines of this boardroom? And, most importantly, without bringing even a shred of suspicion his way? He flipped over the Visitor badge, now beside him on the table. Reggie had said they were tagged to monitor everyone's movements. Was he right? Was that even possible?

Kelly opened the door. "I'm first," she announced.

"Says the keeper of the schedule." That got him a laugh. He adjusted the chair for her stature and invited her to sit.

Kelly was farm girl strong, a bit rounded in face and body but not soft, and had the usual collection of tensions through her back and shoulders. She'd worked the desk at Blast for almost a year. Ex-military, to Jackson's surprise, hired by Dunn fresh off a decade in the Canadian Forces. Loved her current job, which mainly consisted of being the professional face of Blast Dynamics and keeping an eye on the place.

"A quiet building on a dead end street, you probably don't get many visitors," he said.

"They come in rushes," she answered. "Big entourages of investors the CEO brings in to tour the labs. Sometimes clumps of worried investors Dr. Dunn takes around to show them what their money is doing. Not very many drop-ins."

"Not much to do on the security side of it, then."

She tilted her head in the facerest. "Not yet. I'm told that may soon change."

That was all he could get from her, and was afraid to push for more.

He'd brought several water bottles for the day. Bathroom breaks, he'd decided, was how he would at least get beyond the boardroom door. After his second session he ducked out to go find one.

The upper floor was quiet. Dunn was back in his office, the door closed. He heard Jonathan Harrowman's voice discussing something with a few others in another boardroom. The maintenance guy was killing time with a hammer checking the baseboards in the hallway for loose nails. He bypassed the upstairs washroom and went to the first floor to find another.

Okay, he was keeping his eyes open. Now what? The doors to the two active labs were closed, and only opened onto the anterooms. He'd be spotted on the office wing in about three seconds and redirected back upstairs. He could hear Kelly doing her thing at the front desk around the corner.

The door to the first lab opened. The lab tech with the snappy comebacks, Dorey, emerged carrying a tray of tiny plastic boxes. She headed for the second lab and spotted him.

"Massage guy! I'm up to see you this afternoon, can't wait. The pressure around this place is giving me migraines." She winked. "Anything I can do you for?"

He gave her his best apologetic grin. "Uh, looking for the facilities. Guess I got lost."

She laughed. "I'll say! There's a set upstairs, end of the boardroom aisle. And by the way, don't let Dr. Dunn catch you without your Visitor badge. He'd send you on your way, head-first."

"Really?" He made a show of slapping the empty spot on his chest. His badge, with its RFID tag, was still on the table by his massage chair. "Thanks. What's that?" He jogged his chin at the tiny boxes.

"More leads," she said with a shrug. "We find maybe a dozen a day, work out the promising ones, and cart them over to the torture chamber." She waved the tray at Door Number Two. "Reggie tests these puppies to within an inch of their molecular lives to see which one wins." She got quiet. "No luck with any of them so far."

"Oh. All right, then," he said, and made to head for the stairs, when something about Dorey's expression stopped him.

Still quiet and stepping close, she asked, "You see the bosses, right? Have they ... um ... told you anything?"

He lowered his voice, too. "Like what?"

"Anything. We're kind of siloed from the pencil pushers and decision makers, you know? But things have seemed kind of, I don't know, tense. The bosses making calls in the corners, people coming and going at all hours, the new security. It's got us lab rats kinda wondering. And the results," she waggled the tray gently.

"Well, they're not. Not yet, anyway."

She shrugged again. "Outfits like this are great while they last, but you kinda want to keep your resume handy, know what I mean?"

Thankfully, she didn't wait around for an answer but stepped past him and into the second lab. He was late for his next session and took the stairs two at a time.

Just before noon Jonathan Harrowman showed up for another massage. "Jackson, good to see you, how have you been keeping?" He led with the glittering smile and the outstretched hand, but some of his natural ebullience was missing.

He looks tired, Jackson thought. Stressed. He also looked like he was waiting for an answer.

"Pretty well, thanks," he said, pulling out a standard response.

Harrowman swung a long leg over the massage chair and took a seat. "So, what's new and exciting in the life of our favourite masseur?"

Behind Harrowman's back, Jackson raised an eyebrow as his hands got busy. The CEO's tension was still evident in his back and neck. "Oh, not much," he lied. "I picked up some life extension patients with the longest list of supplements I've ever seen. They've sent me back to the books. By which I mean the Internet."

Harrowman's ribcage rippled with a chuckle. "I've no doubt. Find anything Blast Dynamics might be interested in?"

"Everything I'm researching has already been invented. But I guess whatever you're working on will eventually make most of them obsolete."

"Hah!" Harrowman seemed to regain some of his humour. "This is me crossing my arms and saying 'intellectual property.' But I think it's safe to say," he lifted his head to glance over his shoulder, "yes."

Despite himself, Jackson again felt a thrill of possibility. "You're quite the salesman. I bet investors fall all over themselves when you speak."

"Hah!" This time Jackson felt the man's neck ratchet tight again. "In my dreams. They're not nearly as patient, or generous, as I need them to be."

The session got quiet. Jackson did what he could in the short time they had. As Harrowman left he said, "Come find me when you're done."

After the last session Jackson packed up his chair and left the boardroom. The balcony walkway looked out over the lobby. He spent a moment leaning on it to watch the Blast Dynamics crew leave for the day.

A few of them spotted him and waved goodbye. Harold Dunn carved a slow path through the exiting staff and spent a minute with Kelly at the reception desk, their heads close. He saw Jackson at the railing, looked up with an expression that might have been a scowl, and tapped the ID card on a lanyard around his neck. Jackson pulled his out of the pocket he'd put it in and clipped it back on the front of his shirt.

Reggie, who he hadn't seen all day, came in as the rest were going out. That got another, more visible scowl from Dunn, but nothing worse. Reggie mimed a 'forgot something' as he passed and ducked out of Jackson's sight towards the labs. A moment later he was back, rain jacket slung over one arm, then gone.

Jonathan Harrowman was in his office, examining papers and sorting them into piles on his desk. A cup of tea steamed on a side table by his elbow next to a small bunch of dark purple grapes and a plate of cookies.

"Jackson, come on in," he called, and came out from around the desk. "Wonderful reports from all quarters, myself most definitely included," he exclaimed. Some of his energy had returned, or been dredged up for the occasion. "This is my personal treat to the staff, so let's settle up for the week." Jackson gave him the figure and Harrowman pulled out his phone to transfer the funds.

"Let's do one session next week. Mustn't get too much of a good thing, right?"

It was his dime. "Of course. Same time next week, then."

Outside the rain had stopped. More yellow leaves now littered the ground than still clung to the trees. On his way to the parking lot Jackson considered what he'd seen. Dunn's rainy phone call, his scowl. The flicker of tension across Harrowman's face when he'd limited next week's appointments.

The pile of papers on the CEO's desk; Jackson knew overdue bills when he saw them. The grapes, with a few pale, dry raisins tucked into the bunch.

He'd kept his eyes open. That evening he filled Marilyn in over dinner. After some discussion, they agreed—he'd seen a whole lot of interesting things that didn't really tell them very much at all.

Chapter 26

MY WEEK FOR MOB BOSSES

Jackson had coffee and blueberry buttermilk muffins ready by the time Marilyn woke up. "Think I might keep you around for awhile," she mumbled through her breakfast. "These are fantastic. Say, I don't work until later. A crazy new art gallery just opened on Main Street, want to check it out?"

He shook his head. "Can't, I have a new client this morning. My schedule's really filling up." He downed the rest of the coffee, grabbed his toothbrush and pointed the Subaru for Southlands.

A block away from Marilyn's he caught movement in the rear view mirror. A silver Honda compact pulled out of a side street and into traffic behind him. "For hell's sake," he muttered, "what now?"

An urge to step on the gas washed through him in a rush of adrenalin. He could see a faint, curving line of electric blue point the way to an opening between apartment buildings coming up on the left. He could lose them again.

His better self told the urge to get lost. The VPD was never far away in the middle of downtown Vancouver, and having a cop for a girlfriend didn't give you immunity from traffic fines. The suggestion from his pattern sense vanished.

Instead he decided to ignore the tail. Nothing he could do about it anyway. If the Croats wanted to chase him through the city on his rounds, they were welcome. It wasn't like he was up to anything.

He checked his scheduling tablet to confirm the address, crossed over from downtown to Westside on the Burrard Bridge and turned down Arbutus Street. Southlands, he thought. Should be fun. Trips to the tony neighbourhood where the north fork of the Fraser River brushed past Vancouver before dumping into the ocean were like stepping into an adjacent world. Southlands was horse stable country and golf heaven, the only place in the city where you could still measure your back yard in acres. Whenever he got a call to a residence in Southlands, he knew he'd have plenty of room to set up his table.

The estate off West 55th didn't disappoint. He pulled in at a white iron gate set into a ten-foot hedge, then around a sweeping drive to the front of the house. The silver Honda sailed on past, and good riddance.

He paused a moment before getting out of the car. "Well, would you look at that," he said, staring out the windshield. As a traveling therapist he made it a practice not to form opinions about his patients' living circumstances. He'd given massages in mansions and hovels. But this home merited a minute's appreciation.

The place was modern, and not. The body of the house was serious grey concrete walls with an abundance of straight lines and hard angles. Pale rock pillars, sculpted in an ancient, flowing style that didn't look Greek, flanked an expansive front door of banded oak and held up gleaming steel-and-glass balconies on either side. The doorway was surrounded by cut crystal stained glass in striking geometric patterns.

The stark lines of the house were relieved by traditional accents with a decidedly Persian flair. The steps up to the door were overlaid with a tiled mosaic in an intricate, intertwined vine and flowers pattern that led upwards and inwards to the doorstep. Each window ended in a peaked arch, and more filigreed arches and adornments graced the balconies. He'd driven around a small pond set into the grass in front of the house, and an eight-pointed island of blue and yellow mosaic tile sat in its exact center. In the middle of the island was a fountain that resembled a tiny dome, spraying a perfect mushroom of water into the morning air.

Jackson's pattern sense leaped out of hiding to devour the scene with a warm thrill that threatened to unseat him. "No," he muttered, and forced it back under control.

He checked his scheduling tablet. Shaheen Kiani. Sure enough, a Persian name. Shaheen had probably built the place, and he obviously had good taste. It also looked like he'd have no problem covering Jackson's fee.

A man in a black suit and tie materialized on the top step and came down to greet him. Apparently Shaheen was rich enough to have security. Jackson had seen it before, but not often. He got out of the Subaru before the man opened his door for him.

"Welcome, Mr. Teague," he said, with the slightest of Eastern accents. "Mr. Kiani is waiting for you in the east wing. May I help you with that?" He reached for the strap of the massage table.

Jackson was about to say no, I've got it, when something about the man's bearing told him that might not be the right answer. "Sure." The guy shouldered the strap of the bulky table without seeming to notice it and led the way up the mosaic steps.

As they got to the top step before the big front door, the man deked left and passed between two pillars set close together. Ah, Jackson thought. His table had just been scanned.

So. Either kidnap rich or assassination rich. He filed that away as an additional data point in his professional assessment.

He removed his shoes inside the entrance, as did the man with his table. He was led down a marble hallway to an archway on the left, which opened into a sumptuous living room the size of a basketball court. Dark wainscoting counterpointed desert sand walls and a gleaming hardwood floor. A fire crackled in a black-marble fireplace on the far wall, with a grouping of comfortable chairs in a semicircle around it. To the left was another set of chairs around an oval table, these of fine woodwork and braided brocade. To the right, under a smallish chandelier, a stack of cushions lay at the edge of a soft rug, ready for a more intimate gathering. The center of the room, directly in front of Jackson, was warmed by the largest and most ornate Persian carpet he'd ever seen.

Over the fireplace mantel was a huge painting, seven feet wide at least. It was an abstract, an unsettling mess of black and red that, to Jackson's eye, held no pattern or rhythm whatsoever.

A tall, slim man, mid-thirties and fit as a dancer, stood waiting for him under the painting. He said, "Jackson, welcome! Call me Shaheen. Come on in." He walked over from the fire, hand extended. Lithe, thought Jackson. Moves like a big cat, a panther. With his Mediterranean complexion and loose mop of jet-black hair he looked the part, too.

Jackson let his pattern sense out. Not enough to sweep him into obsession, which was a real danger in such a pleasing room, but enough to serve the purpose. It told him something in the four strides Shaheen took from the fireplace to Jackson's hand. Sure enough, most of Shaheen shimmered in a vibrant green, full of energy and strength. But he caught tiny shots of red that wrapped around the man's midsection and flickered down his left leg.

He's got a lower back limitation, Jackson thought. It's old, he's compensated for it, but it still bothers him. He shook Shaheen's hand, which was warm and sensitive.

"It's a pleasure, Shaheen, thanks for booking a session." He launched into his patter and prep, a reflexive routine by now. "I'll just set up here? And I think you have some paperwork for me."

He began snapping the massage table into place in the middle of the carpet as Shaheen produced the case history form. "As requested," Shaheen said. He stood back and watched Jackson set up. A smile flickered at the edge of his lips. Was that a glint of amusement in his eyes? Jackson filed that away in his mental assessment folder, too.

He looked over the man's history. Nothing out of the ordinary, until he got to the section titled, 'Previous Illnesses or Injuries.' Shaheen had listed two words: Burn and Gunshots.

Well. "Tell me about the burn," he said as he clicked the headrest into place. "Lower back, I'm guessing."

Shaheen laughed. "Very good! Yes, in fact. It happened when I was ten. I keep myself fit, but the scar tissue never grew as fast as I did and it has always bothered me."

"I've seen that before," Jackson said. "How did it happen, if I can ask?"

The humour on Shaheen's face glinted harder. "White phosphorus. My father was stationed in Fallujah in 2003 and brought his family with him. Very unwisely, and I remember my mother shouting at him for it, but I was only ten at the time and was not allowed an opinion. The Americans attacked the next year, rooting out insurgents. I remember the entire city shaking with the bombardment. They fired white phosphorus bombs into the air to light up the battlefield at night. A tiny shard of burning phosphorus flew through my bedroom window and onto my back."

"That's terrible. What an awful experience to have as a child."

"At any age," Shaheen agreed. "White phosphorus does not stop burning until it stops. No matter what my mother did. But I survived."

Jackson flipped the sheets onto the table. "And you mentioned gunshots?"

The tall man gave a light, pleasant laugh. "Oh, yes! Here, and here." He tapped his right shoulder and left thigh. "Nothing too serious, they were poor marksmen. I included it only because you'll see the evidence."

Not even worthy of being called scars, Jackson noted. "So,

Shaheen, what can I do for you today?"

He wanted stress management, with a bit of extra work on his left leg if Jackson thought he could help. Easy peasy. Jackson spent a bit of time doing his visual assessment and ran a few tests to check Shaheen's back and hip mobility, then left the room to let him get situated.

He started on the left leg. As promised, a star-shaped wound on Shaheen's outer thigh showed where a bullet had gone in the front and out the back. He probed, but found minimal restrictions from the insult. Shaheen's fitness regimen, and maybe a good massage therapist, had kept the fascia from knitting everything together into a tight mess. He did find plenty of fascial stiffening and tension from the leg's valiant efforts to compensate for the burn scar, and he went to work on that.

Shaheen seemed okay with talking about his past. Jackson decided to take the lighthearted approach. Working around the bullet wound he asked, "Dangerous line of work, or jealous husband?"

That got him another laugh. "The holes? Those came from my work, although," he lifted his face out of the cradle, turned and winked, "it could have been either."

Jackson smiled. "So, what do you do for work? I noticed the security, so don't answer if you're not comfortable talking about it."

Shaheen's chest rumbled with another chuckle. "Can you keep a secret, Jackson?"

He worked into the fascia of the hamstrings where they were adhered to the wide tendon that stretched from hip to knee and said, "Everything here is confidential."

The man's chest vibrated under the sheet again with another laugh. "I am the Chief Executive Officer of the New Canadians. Perhaps you've heard of us."

Jackson's hands faltered. He recovered and continued the

session, but it was a plain and obvious tell and they both knew it. His mind reeled with an echoing What The Fuck as he tried, oh lord he tried, to integrate this new data point into his ongoing assessment. No luck. It took all he had just to keep his hands moving.

"This seems to be my week for mob bosses," his mouth said. That does it, I'm dead, he thought.

Shaheen took the label in stride. "Indeed. And yet I did not conceal my identity, and here you are. Since I booked under my own name and you kept the appointment, either you are an uncommonly curious man or you don't pay much attention to the news."

"I didn't make the connection," Jackson said. His mouth added, "Although it could have been either."

Shaheen, still face-down, roared a laugh and slapped the table. "And balls as well! I guarantee your woman friend knows my name. But your recent acquaintance with mob bosses, as you say, is exactly why you are here, my friend. I would love to know what you have been up to. Why have the Croats taken an interest in you? The Uncle even invited you to his home. What did you discuss? You are doing wonderful work, by the way."

Jackson switched legs, his massage now entirely on automatic. He might not be a news junkie, but he'd heard of the New Canadians. Everybody in the Lower Mainland had. The multi-ethnic gang had developed a reputation as ruthless and vicious. After two years of bloody, public takeover wars that had frequently made the headlines, they had carved out a solid niche in Vancouver's illicit trades and were making inroads into the rest of Western Canada.

They were rumoured to be led by a charismatic, sadistic psychopath.

Jackson had never paid much attention. He'd seen Shaheen's name once or twice. But the idea of a transnational crime lord calling him up for a massage had never even entered Jackson's paradigm. Now here he was.

His hands ironed out a tight spot in the right calf. Shaheen was curious about the Uncle, not specifically Jackson. He wanted to know what was up. Fair enough, given the context, and booking a session was a remarkably efficient way to find out.

"There was this guy on the Seabus," he began, and spun out the entire tale. He insinuated that the brunch was all about him and left out the Uncle's deal with Marilyn, but nothing else. By the time he was done he'd finished the second leg. "So they dropped us off where we started and that was that. Oh, not quite. I noticed this morning that they're following me again."

He pulled the sheet down from Shaheen's shoulders to his hips, exposing his back. "Holy mackerel," he said, "one piece of phosphorus did this?"

The left side of the man's lower back, from ribs to pelvis and spine to side, was a mass of keloid scarring, wavy and blotched with odd patches of skin pigmentation, the characteristic appearance of a bad icing job on a cake. It was old, completely healed or as much as it would ever be. But it was a permanent part of Shaheen's life.

Shaheen shifted on the table. His left arm rose halfway towards his back and then dropped. "As I said, phosphorus just keeps burning. It was a very bad night."

Jackson could imagine it, barely. A modest home, the city outside the windows dark except for the flash of bombs and fires. The noise would have been the worst, a sickening mix of booms and sirens and guns and screams. Then one blindingly white firefly floating in through the window as a boy was trying to sleep.

"How were the rest of your family?"

Shaheen stayed quiet for a moment. "My father's command bunker was erased by a tank round that night. We did not bother looking for the pieces. My mother and sisters stayed with me in

Fallujah until I was healed enough to travel. Then we went back to Isfahan."

They both let silence settle over the room for a minute, the only sound the gentle hiss of Jackson's hands on Shaheen's skin. Then Shaheen lifted his head out of the facerest and twisted around to look at him.

"You know, don't you? I can feel it coming through your hands. You are missing the same piece. What happened to your father? Tell me."

His hands faltered for the second time. "Nothing," he answered, and it came out as a petulant mumble.

Shaheen didn't laugh at him. "Come now, my friend," he said with some actual softness, "we are sharing confidences. Tell me."

Why not. "Some street kids pulled a knife when he tried to talk sense into them. Five years ago. He died on the sidewalk."

"Ah." Shaheen settled back into the facerest again. "You still miss him. But, if I may say so, it sounds like a good death."

"Yeah."

Jackson kept his mind on the work. He massaged the minor spots of tension out of Shaheen's right side as he examined the burn scar. It refused to move with the massage, a thick and stubborn mass of tissue. As he watched, Shaheen's left arm twitched halfway up towards the burn again, then fell back down. "Does it ever get in your way?" he asked.

"The injury took three years to heal and almost killed me twice. It does not bother me so much now. It pulls, but the worst is the itch. I have a badger-hair brush by my bed to help.

"Thank you for your answer to my questions, and for telling the story so completely. That is quite an adventure for you. One that, I think, is not over yet. But I cannot believe the Croats' backwardness. Manned surveillance? Searching your apartment? Kidnapping, no matter how polite? Those are Neanderthal tactics, Jackson, and that, in a nutshell, will tell you why the New

Canadians enjoy the position we do, and why groups like the Croats are part of the past. Or soon will be."

Jackson lifted the folded-down sheet back up, bunched some of it in his left hand, and rubbed the wadded fabric briskly over the scar. Shaheen gasped, then relaxed into the table. "Better?" he asked, folding the sheet back down.

The man muttered a few words into the facerest Jackson didn't understand. Persian swearing, perhaps. "Yes, thank you." They both lapsed into silence as Jackson continued with his work.

He didn't seem to be in any immediate danger. Shaheen had asked for information, gotten it, and that was that. Jackson always kept his pattern sense a bit open during his sessions. Now he widened the crack. 'Curiosity is going to get you killed someday,' he heard his father's voice say in the back of his mind, but he wanted to know. As he worked gently but firmly with the burn scar, easing the tightness of its adhesions, he gave Shaheen a good look.

Could he see evil? The man on his table was known as a sadistic bastard. A psychopath. Thankfully Jackson had never heard any details, but Shaheen's reputation was solid enough that there had to be some truth to it. Did it show?

The room sprang into a beautiful symphony of coordinated lines and curves. It had been designed by someone with an impeccable eye for detail. Shaheen? It was possible, he supposed. He focused on the body on his table. Shaheen was nearly symmetrical except for the burn, head squarely on his neck, shoulders even, spine straight. His ribs flared in and out with his breath.

Nothing. All he saw was a body.

He finished Shaheen's back and lifted the sheet for him to turn over. He remembered his first impression as Shaheen had walked over to him from the fireplace. He'd reminded Jackson of a big cat. A panther. Maybe a tiger.

That was it, he decided. He couldn't see evil in a person's form. But he knew how to spot a predator.

"Why hurt the Croats?" he said, starting on the front of Shaheen's right leg. He immediately felt a massive rush of heat suffuse his face, and knew his freckles had just turned beet-red. But the question couldn't be pulled back. It hung in the air between them.

Shaheen kept his eyes closed, but smiled. "How refreshing," he spoke at last. "An innocent, honest question. I am so deeply involved with my work, my friend, that sometimes I forget that such questions exist. That people like you inhabit my world."

He opened his eyes, staring at the ceiling. His smile didn't so much as twitch, but turned into something that made Jackson uncomfortable. "Why hurt the Croats? Or the Scorpions or the Keepers? I could list off a dozen plausible reasons. Supply and demand, control of the market, territory management. But you've given me truth today, and that demands truth in return."

He lowered his gaze to Jackson. "I hurt them because they are. Because I am. Because if I did not, you can be certain they would hurt me. Oh, occasionally we may work together for the common good, when our goals intersect. But even then, we never turn our backs to the other."

He closed his eyes again. Jackson finished up with Shaheen's neck, keeping his face as far from the gangster's as possible, and was glad it was done. Overall, not his best massage. Maybe one of his worst. He left the room again to let Shaheen get dressed.

Shaheen had paid in advance for the session on the appointment app, but he grabbed Jackson's hand in a double handshake and pressed a sheaf of cash into his palm.

"I like you," he said. "I am certain we will see each other again."

The Subaru waited on the circular drive where he'd left it, the quiet security man holding his door open. As Jackson drove out of the gate, finally letting himself break into a cold sweat, he tried to rid himself of the feeling that he'd just been adopted as some kind of mascot. Halfway to his next client he saw the silver Honda slide into his rear view mirror, three cars back.

Chapter 27

AM I SAFE?

He called Marilyn from his apartment. She answered on the second ring. "Hey, Freckles, what's up?" She sounded calm, relaxed. He thought he heard chewing.

"Hey, Legs," he said. "Um. I had another one this morning. It's got me—a little freaked."

The chewing stopped. "Another what?"

"Gangster. A guy called Shaheen had me over for a massage."

A chair fell over on the other end of the line. "Tell me you're joking. Are you okay?"

"Well, no, I'm not. Joking. And not really okay about any of this."

Her voice got all business. "Ahmed and I are at Bean Around The World by Tenth and Sasamat. How fast can you get here?"

The cafe was packed, the big front windows steamed over from all the espresso and conversations. She met him at the front door, paid for his coffee and practically dragged him out the back to the patio. Her partner Ahmed sat at one of the small wooden tables under the only opened umbrella. Nobody else braved the late-October chill.

After his first sip Marilyn said, "Start from the beginning. Don't leave anything out."

He told them about his morning. Shaheen's interest in the Croats, his curiosity about their visit with the Uncle. He kept the Persian's medical history to himself. This report was bending enough ethics as it was.

"What did you tell him?" Marilyn's question carried an edge.

"Nothing about you, or your deal with the old guy," he reassured her. "I told him about the handoff at the Seabus, our visit to Blast Dynamics, all of that. Basically what I told the Uncle. Nothing more." He sat back against the wooden lattice surrounding the patio and drank his cooling coffee.

Ahmed spoke up. "You two, I really don't know how you do it. But you certainly do. Marilyn, you know we're going to have to report this up. I mean, on the surface of it there's nothing wrong. A massage therapist had a session with a person of interest. Still, we'll send it up the chain."

Marilyn laid a hand on Jackson's knee. "I bet you almost jumped out of your skin when you discovered who you were working on. Brave of you to finish the session, and you did the right thing by calling us." Her words, and their tone, carried the perfect amount of caring and concern. She's learned her training well, he thought. But he saw the unabashed excitement in her eyes.

"Sergeant Rockford needs to be there when we brief Dilly. He'll want to know."

Jackson asked the question he'd walked in the door with. "Am I safe? Do I have anything to worry about?"

Neither Marilyn nor Ahmed jumped in with calming reassurances, professional or otherwise. Instead they looked at each other for a long moment. Finally Ahmed said, "I think you're fine, Jackson. You're an outsider, not a player in their world. You had a bit of information, and gave it to both of them. I don't think they'll have any more use for you at all."

"What he means," Marilyn corrected, slapping Ahmed on the

shoulder, "is that they won't be interested in you anymore. I think they'll leave you alone now."

Jackson drained his mug, the last swallow bitter and grainy. "That's good," he said. "Because I'm certain that black Nissan SUV tailed me here. And the silver Honda followed me to Shaheen's this morning." Ahmed and Marilyn glanced at each other again, but had no answer for that.

Sergeant Dilly stood up from the boardroom chair and waved them in. Rockford, looking like he'd rather be anywhere else, was beside her. "Constable Mathers, Constable Uphram, take a seat. You said you had something to report, and that Sergeant Rockford would want to hear it. We both have a full schedule today, so give us the short version."

Ahmed laced his fingers together on the table and turned towards Marilyn. So did the other two. Show's on, she thought, and took a breath.

"The day before yesterday, my boyfriend and I were invited to brunch at the Uncle's. This morning, my boyfriend gave Shaheen Kiani a massage. He's a traveling massage therapist."

Rockford ran cool, she'd give him that. He sat up a little straighter in his chair, and Marilyn could see his schedule rearranging behind his eyes, but his face showed only an interested curiosity as he glanced over at Dilly.

Sergeant Dilly, on the other hand, did a full-on double take as surprise widened her eyes. She caught Rockford's glance and they both nodded at each other. "Okay, now the long version," she said.

Marilyn let out the breath she knew full well she'd been holding and allowed herself to take another. "It started with an incident on the Seabus on the evening of the 5th."

"What incident? I don't recall anything on the briefs." Dilly started jabbing at her phone.

"By itself, it wasn't enough to report. My boyfriend helped a stranger in medical distress and got handed a package. We delivered it the next day, to a research place called Blast Dynamics. Mission accomplished, until Jackson noticed someone following him."

Dilly held up a hand. "That's Jackson Teague, your boyfriend? We have a bit of a file on him." She scrolled. "Quite a bit. Not the most reliable witness, is he?"

Marilyn felt a flush of anger and tamped it down. "He's unconventional, not unreliable. Then his apartment got ransacked." She continued the story—getting picked up by the Three Stooges, the offer from the Uncle to open a quiet line of communication with her, and Shaheen's grilling of Jackson about the meeting. "The Uncle is still having him followed. He noticed them this morning on his way to Shaheen's." She leaned back in her chair and waited for the questions.

Dilly had stopped pecking at her phone. Sergeant Rockford was gazing at the table, listening intently and deep in thought. He spoke first. "Did you agree to anything?"

"Not in so many words. But I didn't tell the Uncle no, either."

He nodded, absorbed it. "Go over the brunch again. As verbatim as you can."

She did. When she was done, Sergeant Dilly leaned over to Rockford and the two had a whispered conference. When they were done she straightened up.

"Thanks for bringing this to our attention. As you both know, we allow our constables a certain amount of latitude. Although you were taken by surprise, Marilyn, you've pushed that latitude pretty far. Nevertheless, no harm seems to have been done."

Rockford leaned in. "As interesting as this is, there's nothing actionable in your report, Constable. You got invited to brunch and had a polite conversation. I imagine the food was decent, too.

And your Mr. Teague got a new massage client and had another conversation. On the surface of it, that's all that happened.

"I can see the Uncle's motive here. You're an eager and upwardly mobile officer. He leads a criminal organization that's critically injured, probably dying. He wants whatever leverage he can get. He spotted your ambition and appealed to it."

He frowned at Marilyn to stop her objection. "That's not a bad thing, Constable. The old family-oriented gangs used to do that fairly often. There was some back-and-forth information exchange, which meant we occasionally told them things, but we always made sure the balance was in our favour. Now he wants to do it again. We might be able to use that. I'll let you know."

"Yes, sir." She could practically feel a spot in Organized Crime opening up for her. Exactly as she'd hoped.

Dilly scowled her best. "Don't get ahead of yourself. Ahmed, make sure you tie a string around her ankle and keep her from floating off. Marilyn, you are to report to us any further developments. But for now, there's nothing to be done. We'll open a file and see what comes along to fill it." She put her phone back in a pocket. "Dismissed."

Chapter 28

WAY ABOVE YOUR PAY GRADE

Jackson had to trust Marilyn and Ahmed's professional judgement, but he could feel the tension buzzing along his nerves. His second session with Abe Tremblay was set for the afternoon. As he headed for Quebec and Third the tension was displaced by anticipation. After Charles' revelation about Georgia's new adventure he had questions, and he suspected Abe Tremblay might have the answers.

The coding genius greeted him at the door to the elevator, starting in on his rapidfire torrent of words and ideas almost before the doors opened. Jackson stole glances around the open-concept living area as he set up. A few rooms, bedrooms and bathroom probably, were walled off in one corner, and some ricepaper shoji screens blocked another corner from view. He scanned the living area, a bit untidy but definitely not a pigstye, and didn't see any empty cans of Red Bull or Monster. No coffee-mug stains on the table, no jumbo bags of Twizzlers, not even a discarded Twinkie wrapper. None of the usual stimulants. Unless the village of pill bottles in the corner of his kitchen contained some major amphetamines or a vial of cocaine, Abe came by his energy honestly.

Unless his vitality came from something else altogether.

"Jackson, my man, great rub last time, did me a world of good. Let's do it again." Abe was undressed and face down on his table almost before Jackson was finished setting it up. He floated the top sheet down over the nude form and got to work.

Another relaxation and maintenance massage on that marvellously soft and pliable body. The minor knots he'd treated on his first visit were still gone, and no new ones had taken their place. Jackson settled into a basic but thorough Swedish therapy session, throwing in a few passive limb stretches to make it worthwhile.

"Still taking that forest of supplements?" he asked as he lifted Abe's foot off the table and eased it towards his butt in a quadriceps stretch. "Add any new ones?"

"Nah, got a routine that works for me, I'm open to new ideas but haven't seen anything worth it lately. I do the research, you know, anything I add has to be better than everything I've already got. Pretty high bar, right?"

Jackson chuckled and edged into the oh-so-subtle interrogation he'd planned. "See what you mean. From what I can tell, you've latched on to the fountain of youth."

He was feeling for it, and there it was, a tiny ripple that went through Abe's body and was gone in the blink of an eye. Surprise, for sure. Maybe even excitement. He pushed the quadriceps stretch a little more, until Abe's heel touched his butt. It took hardly any effort at all.

"Right, you know it, I bet you can tell. Fountain of youth, yeah, that's the Holy Grail."

Jackson lowered Abe's leg and took his inquiry the next step. "Yeah, right. You're a regular Ponce de Leon."

That shock went through Abe's body again, stronger this time, practically a jump. "Don't you know it, massage man," Abe said, and that was definitely a tinge of excitement in his voice.

"Well, I don't know it," Jackson corrected. "Know of it, more like. I'm open to new ideas, though."

Abe gave him a thumb's up. "I got you. Once we're done here, I have some things to show you." For the rest of the massage, by some minor miracle, he was silent.

Jackson made himself give the full hour's treatment, although he could barely control his impatience. Not all that hard, because he was working on a truly exceptional body. If anything, Abe's skin was even softer and more elastic than he remembered, gliding smoothly under his hands. The coder's musculature felt perfect, loose and supple. When he bent Abe's legs and arms into various stretches the man was flexible as a gymnast. Jackson could find no restrictions anywhere. Abe's body was perfect enough to be almost spooky.

Abe was impatient, too, he could tell. The moment the massage was over he jumped up, threw on his clothes, and said, "You pack up, I'll get some things ready over on the command deck." He hustled to the far corner of the spacious apartment and ducked behind the trio of shoji screens.

When Jackson stepped around the screens a minute later, a strong rush of tech envy widened his eyes. A sweeping, curved desk supported three monitors, two of them as big as Jackson's TV. Two keyboards were suspended on swivel arms, leaving the desk available for mountains of paperwork ranging from dense code to spreadsheets to financial reports. A bank of humming black boxes, their fronts bedecked with flickering red and green LEDs, warmed the space underneath.

Abe had stationed himself in a chair that looked like it belonged twenty years in the future. He saw Jackson gawk. "Like it? My own design. Check this out."

He caressed a keyboard and waved his right hand over a black pad. The center screen came to life with a pattern of stars on a black field. He moved his hand around some more and the screen dopplered in to one point of light until it filled the screen. The white circle resolved into an image of rows of tiny drawers, made out of oak, complete with brass pull handles. An old-fashioned library card catalog. "My file system," he grinned, "had to keep my ideas straight, you know? Each of those stars is a different topic, and each has a catalog like this. These folders here are my longevity research."

He reached with his fingers. A barely-visible hand opened a drawer and pulled out a library card. On it were the words, Ponce de Leon. Jackson's pulse quickened. Below the words lay a single black line. Abe staccatoed the keyboard and the line filled with asterisks. "Major encryption around this puppy. Only the passcode gets you in."

He jabbed the Return key and the card catalog disappeared. In its place bloomed a four-square block, each square showing the same picture of an ornate fountain. Inside each square was a simple line of text. One said, Research. Another said, Video. The third said, Bloodwork. The last said, Testimonials.

The title over the top of the page read, in large ornate letters, Ponce de Leon.

"We're down the rabbit hole here, Jackson, deepest of the dark web. The only way you get here is by invitation." Abe's quick, easy hipster patois had dropped away, his demeanour suddenly serious. He glanced over, and his tiny, Mona Lisa smile had an edge. "You haven't been here before, have you?"

So much for Jackson's careful interrogations. "First time," he admitted. But his answer carried the ring of curiosity. Because he was curious, intensely. He leaned in to the screen.

Abe chuckled. "Well. Consider yourself invited. Where to first?"

He pointed. "Research."

Abe clicked. All three screens lit up with reams of documents laid out in fans of white rectangles. Jackson pointed. "That one."

The center screen filled with a list. The document's title read, 'Indicators of Aging in the Human Body.' The list read like a directory of decrepitude: loss of muscle mass; decreased bone density; loss of joint cartilage; hardened blood vessels; thin and flaccid skin; stiffened corneas in the eye; decreased cognitive functions. It went on for the entire page, and each entry contained a link to a scholarly article or medical paper.

Another column, on the right side of the page, was titled, 'Cured.' Every line on the page carried a check mark.

"This," he said, jabbing at another file.

The list was replaced with a series of graphs. They sported titles like, 'Average Onset of Heart Disease,' 'Typical Mobility Loss,' or 'Average Lifespan Relative to Species Norm.' Each of these showed different lines in a rainbow of colours, tagged with the names of various animals ranging from fruit flies to rabbits. All the graphs showed some level of data normalization or logarithmic scaling. Only to be expected, Jackson figured, when you were trying to compare the lifecycle of a nematode to that of an orangutan.

Each graph showed the expected senescence and decay associated with age. Each graph also had one extra line, titled 'Enhanced.'

This line, shown in gold on every graph, went straight across the page. No heart disease. No mobility loss. A lifespan that went beyond the edge of the graph. The end of every 'Enhanced' line ended in a tiny, but unmistakeable, infinity symbol.

"Jesus Henry Christ," Jackson muttered.

"Right? Blew me away, too. Where do you want to go next?" Abe backed out until they saw the four squares again. Jackson pointed to Bloodwork.

These were lab reports, of course, mostly beyond the limit of his knowledge base. They looked to be tracking all sorts of indicators, from basics like white blood cell and platelet count, through various hormone and disease markers such as testosterone and uric acid, to acronyms he didn't recognize—GDF-15, TNF-Alpha, and others.

More important to Jackson was the patient information. They

were testing humans.

The lab reports followed a series of people, called only Patient G, Patient N, and so forth, through about eight weeks of testing. Each string of reports followed the same trajectory. One week to establish a baseline, which showed varying levels of disease and decline. After that, each report began with 'One day after procedure,' 'Five days after procedure,' up to six weeks.

All of them showed impossible results. Within a month, every single marker went back to optimal levels. Every one. And for the last weeks of the test they stayed there.

"Videos," he said, once he'd had his fill. Abe clicked over to the new folder.

These files were organized by patient, with three videos in each section—Pre-Procedure, Three Weeks, and Six Weeks. He chose Patient J.

The first video was a one-minute clip of a middle-aged Asian woman sitting on a plain chair in a small, nondescript hallway. Bright ceiling lights banished all shadows. Jackson saw white walls, tiled white floor, and two wooden doors at the far end of the hall, and that was it.

The woman appeared nervous, but not in any distress. She wore a tight-fitting spandex shirt and yoga pants over her generous curves that obviously made her uncomfortable and self-conscious, and she squirmed under the camera's gaze. The video had no sound. Someone off-camera directed the woman to stand, turn, bend over towards her toes, go through a couple of other stretches, and walk down the hall and back again.

She was more worn than her years. Her Asian heritage had kept most of the wrinkles from her face, but strokes of grey touched her black hair and lines were beginning to etch in beside her mouth and eyes. Her hands bore the telltale, blue-veined look of thinning skin. She had trouble with the stretches. Her walk was a stiff-legged, side to side clomp. Jackson's pattern sense kept overlaying flashes of orange and streaks of red on her as she moved, revealing the bad knees, stiff back, and sore hands of a lifetime labourer.

Three weeks later, the second video showed a changed woman. In the same hall, wearing the same clothes but no longer self-conscious, she was grinning and laughing and talking an entire monologue, although the video still had no sound. She'd lost weight. She'd lost the crow's feet by her eyes. She sat tall and easy in the chair. When directed to go through the same stretches, she jumped up and bent into each pose with the flexibility of a practiced yogini. Her walk down the hallway and back was light, buoyant, and quick.

Jackson's pattern sense didn't flash once. When the video ended the woman was still laughing.

By six weeks the woman had dropped more weight. She looked twenty years younger. Her skin glowed. There was noticeably less grey in her hair. She was no longer laughing, but the smile on her face had settled into a look of deep joy. She stood, ran through the same stretches with no trouble whatever, added a couple of her own, and walked down the hall and back with an easy stride. As the video ended she looked directly into the lens and mouthed, Thank You.

"Run it again," Jackson ordered, and Abe clicked the replay arrow. He let his pattern sense out until the clutter on Abe's desk chafed at his nerves, locked his eyes on the video and watched. The woman in the video glowed with vitality, a shimmering blue. She was straight, poised, perfect. Only when she fell into her stretches, and once during her walk down the hall, did he see anything, and even then it was only the ghost of something, a brief flicker of violet around her knees and hips. He couldn't tell what it was that his pattern sense was seeing.

He closed his eyes, willed his obsession to get back where it belonged, and took a deep breath.

"Want to see the testimonials?" Abe asked.

"No. I've seen enough." He waved a hand at the screen. "Any way these videos are doctored?"

Abe gave him a snort. His coder vibe returned. "Who am I, man? Look at this setup. I took the panties off these files. Made them bend over and cough, know what I mean? Nah, they're virgin. Exactly as originally recorded." He sat back in his incredible chair and let it all sink in.

Jackson thought about where to go next. "So this is that thing in your side, right? How long have you had it?"

Abe patted the spot under his ribs. "Four weeks. I'm the earliest of early adopters. It's working as advertised, Jackson." He grabbed Jackson's hand, and the gleam in his eye was unmistakeable. "I'm a hundred percent. My old scar from falling out of the tree as a kid? Gone. My eyesight's better. I don't get sore, no matter how hard I work out. I barely get tired. I'm good as new."

Keep it in, Jackson told himself. Get the information. He looked at the screen, back to those four squares. "I don't see any place to sign up."

Abe laughed. "More security. They have a one-pixel doorway, you have to be told where to find it." He waved his hand over the computer's pad and the mouse traveled up to the right hand corner. There, at a precise spot in the undifferentiated black close to the edge of the frame, the mouse briefly changed to a clickable hand. He clicked.

A new page opened up. Words at the bottom of the screen said, Singapore—New York—Perth—Mumbai—Bruges. The top of the screen was filled with a plain, white countdown timer.

It read 3 Days—14 Hours—27 Minutes—36 Seconds. The seconds rolled.

"You get on the waiting list for one of these clinics," Abe said. "Top flight places, elite and discreet. No other way to get the Ponce de Leon."

Only one more question to ask. "How much?"

Abe shook his head. "Sorry, my man. Way above your pay grade. In order to get on the list, you put $200,000 in escrow. That's US greenbacks. It's not for the average joe."

Jackson ignored the implied slight and whistled. "Yeah. What, maybe a hundred people around the world might spring for one of these?"

Abe looked surprised. "You're kidding. Longevity's a game for the well-heeled, my man. Of all the longevists in the world, I figure probably seven or eight thousand will line up for one of these in the first few weeks. Once the results become obvious," he popped a bicep, "you bet your ass ten thousand more will be scraping their bank accounts clean."

A minute passed in silence, then Abe closed out the Ponce de Leon site. He swivelled his chair around to face Jackson. "I showed you this because I know you're a professional," he said. "I knew you'd grasp the science. I also know you can keep a secret. This stays under wraps for another four days. Nobody else, my man. Nobody."

"Right. Got it." He must have sounded sincere, because Abe held his gaze for another moment and then relaxed.

"See you in a few days! Love these massages, should have done them long ago." Jackson packed everything up and headed back to his car.

He barely registered the traffic on the drive home. Numbers swam through his vision. Huge numbers, with long strings of zeroes. And a dollar sign in front of them. So many people, willing to pay so much.

All because of a load of crap pseudoscience Jackson could have whipped up on his laptop at home. The research, and those bloodwork reports, weren't worth the pixels they'd been printed on. The proof behind the Ponce de Leon was hokum.

Except for the videos. He trusted Abe's skill set and believed his claim to their veracity. If the videos didn't lie, then what did they show? Jackson had no answer for that. Because what they appeared to show was impossible.

Donnie parked the silver Honda and pulled out his phone, shaking his head. He called the number from memory and said, "We might have a problem over here. Teague, yeah him. He went to see the tech guy for a session, carried his massage table in and the whole shebang. No, nothing wrong with that, but get this. It's a one-hour appointment, right? He spent two hours in there. When he came out he was real distracted. He drove like a feckin' eejit, blew through a red light on the way home."

He listened, shook his head again at what he heard. "Like I said. We might have a problem, then again we might not. Yeah. We'll stay close, see what he does. If he so much as whispers the wrong word we'll let you know."

He put the phone down and made himself comfortable in the Honda's driver seat to watch the apartment building. He liked watching, it told him things. He wasn't much of one for going on instinct, trusting his gut like the other two. But right now his gut told him that the skinny redhead was definitely going to be a problem.

He laid a hand on the slim Walther tucked under his jacket. Shame, he thought. He almost liked the boy. After watching him for a few days he'd come to know Jackson Teague as an upbeat, friendly, pretty smart kid. A little hotheaded, a little clueless sometimes, but what what could you expect from a flaming redhead with that many freckles. Donnie had plenty of those in his own family tree. But the family he was with now, his found family, was everything, and even a soldier like him knew that this project meant life or death to the Croats.

This was their last shot. No busybody therapist was going to get in the way. He settled his eyes on the kid's apartment windows and kept them there.

Chapter 29

You've got hyenas on you

Sunday dawned bright and beautiful. Jackson had been enjoying a full work schedule, and now he was going to enjoy a day off just as much. Besides, it had been a hell of a week.

Marilyn was at work, so he and Charles met their friend Leaf for a stroll-and-wheel along Cornwall Street and the wide expanse of Kits Beach. The grassy park next to the long, log-strewn beach was pretty much across the road from Jackson's apartment block. He considered it his back yard. During the summer Jackson, Charles, Georgia and Leaf got together every week for picnics on the sand. Leaf had practically lived on Vancouver's beaches, a child of the wind and waves.

Until a falling rock last Spring had missed Jackson and put Leaf in a wheelchair.

He was recovering from the brain injury better than most, gaining new mobility every week. They got to the bus stop just as he whirred his motorized chair off the bus ramp.

"Hey," he called to them, lifting one arm off its rest in a stiff-handed wave. "Good to see you both." He canted his head to one side, sending a cascade of blonde curls over his cheek. "Jackson, Charles. Both of you look kind of frayed around the edges. Wild. What did I miss?"

Jackson gave his friend a professional top-to-bottom scan as Charles leaned in to give Leaf a hug. Leaf had been lean, strong, and fast, a natural athlete. He'd introduced Jackson to several sports. He'd signed up for the Vancouver Police training program days before saving Jackson's life and landing in the hospital. Months in bed, and the profound shock of the injury, had stolen his physique. Used up his reserves, Leaf would say. He was still too thin. His legs and left arm still didn't work well. But his hair, which had fallen out after the incident, was full and golden again, and that was a sign of the body's energy returning.

"What did you miss?" Jackson glanced at Charles, saw the same expression of incredulity that must be on his own face. They both burst into a laughing fit so hard that it hurt his sides and drew looks from the people on the Kits Beach grass.

Where to begin? Jackson said, "Pop quiz. It's a busy day at the beach, right? Lots of people on the sidewalk, more on the sand? Three people don't belong. Tell me what they look like."

Leaf broke into a lopsided grin at the challenge. He twirled his chair around in a slow pirouette on the sidewalk and ended up facing them again. He shook his head, a look of amazement twinkling in his blue eyes. "Jackson, brother, you've got hyenas on you again. I really don't know how you do it." He wheeled in closer. "Tall, thin dude trying to look like he's part of that big chestnut tree, tan windbreaker and golf cap, head like a melon." That would be Johnnie, Jackson thought. "Smaller one, strawberry blonde with the black Stormtech coat that's too large for him, half a block up the sidewalk. He's carrying, I'd bet money on it, right-hand pocket." Donnie, for sure. Jackson paled a bit at the mention of a weapon. "Bullet-headed bruiser in a dark Nissan with tinted windows, parked across the street. He hasn't had a good day in a long time." The one Marilyn had called Franko.

"Bingo," Jackson said, "you get the prize."

"And bonus points, my man," Leaf added, the amusement falling off his face. "Asian in the cafe window on the corner, where he can see everything. Face like a hatchet, eyes like a coyote. Cafe's full, but nobody wants to sit next to him. All of these baddies are on you like burrs on a sock. So. What did I miss?"

"Let's walk." The three of them strolled down Cornwall then along the Kits Beach pathway, Charles and Jackson on each side of Leaf's chair. They filled Leaf in on the week's events, starting with the Seabus handoff. Leaf took it all in with a serious face and no comment, but even as he told the tale Jackson could hardly believe what he was saying. It was all too outlandish. Things like this didn't happen to real people.

Charles got to the point where Georgia had broken their agreement. "One sec," Leaf murmured, and did another slow twirl in his chair, then continued on. "All four are following. Asian hatchet-face is watching the other three, not you two. He's got a phone to his ear. Bullet-head is in the lead. Brother," he glanced at Jackson, "Bullet-head's got a shotgun mic sticking out of his jacket. He just heard me tell you that."

A flash of outrage electrified Jackson's limbs, but before he could even form the idea to turn around and confront the three gangsters Leaf's good hand rose off the chair and rested on his arm.

"So, Charles, what did you do?" Leaf asked, moving his chair forward again. Jackson had no choice but to keep pace.

"I moved into the guest room," Charles said. "I'm looking for an apartment."

The conversation fell into a black silence. "Oh, man, I'm sorry," Jackson managed at last. Charles and Georgia? His heart broke for his friend, but it felt like a sinkhole had just opened up under his own feet, too. They were a mainstay of his life. Those two separating would be like the sunshine parting ways with the warmth.

"I knew she thought well of herself," Leaf said after a moment. "Didn't know it went that far. You said it was some kind of new thing?"

Before Charles could answer Jackson jumped in. "Yeah, it's

called the Ponce de Leon. Charles, I've got more to tell you about it. A client showed me around their website yesterday."

He laid out everything Abe had shown him. The dark-web site with the heavy encryption, the research and bloodwork reports, all of it. He was launching into a description of the videos with the woman's impossible improvement when Charles waved a hand.

"Stop, stop," he said. "A meta-search of existing studies? They went from there to bloodwork? Either they left out a crap-ton of important details or something's very wrong. I've told you what it takes to get a drug to clinical trials."

"News to me," Leaf commented. "Sketch it out."

"It takes years. It takes millions, sometimes billions of dollars. Exhaustive lab work. In vitro studies. Careful experiments on tissues, on isolated systems, on progressively more complex animal subjects. Multiple redundant checks to validate the results. Peer-reviewed papers and oversight approvals every step of the way. And for something as supposedly revolutionary as this? No possibility they could keep it under wraps right up to human trials. Unless they skipped every safeguard in the system."

"I'd agree with you all the way," Jackson said. "Until I saw the videos. Charles, that woman got better. I'd swear she actually got younger."

"Bah!" Charles spat. "Videos are useless! They're faked every single day, you know that. I could make a video of you sitting in the Oval Office pressing the big red button and it would look real."

Jackson remembered what he'd seen. "Yeah, I know. But I was the one watching them, Charles. When that lady walked in the first video she was hurting in ways you can't fake, not to me, not to any decent massage therapist. By the second video her body had gone from worn out to fully functional. I have a client with one of these implants, too. I tell you, it's like working on a teenager."

"So they're better," Charles said, the disdain thick in his voice. "At what cost? I don't know. They don't know. Maybe even the people giving it to them have no idea. I've heard stories of clinical trials going wrong, even after all the testing that came before, and trust me, you don't want any part of that."

"I might," said Leaf from his chair. "If it could help with this?" He knuckle-rapped the side of his head. "Yeah. I just might step up for something like that."

"Exactly why these things are so tightly controlled," Charles glowered at them. "To keep freethinking zealots from throwing themselves off a cliff."

Leaf started another slow circle with his chair.

"Whoa, heads up, guys," he said when he was halfway through his spin. The tension in his voice stopped Charles' monologue cold. "Bullet-head's stopped, he's on the phone, waiting for the other two to catch up. Hatchet-face is closing in. We've got a new player—Adonis dude, in the parking lot, standing by a sweet ride."

They all pivoted, any pretense of casual ignorance gone. Most of the leaves were off the huge chestnuts and elms, forming a thick blanket on the ground. Jackson heard them swish from a hundred feet away as Donnie and Johnnie hustled along the path to catch up to Franko.

A bolt of fear poured like fire through his veins. With a sensation almost like a tearing in his mind his pattern sense rocketed out of confinement, cranked to a maximum he never willingly allowed.

He staggered back a step. His focus on the immediate threat was destroyed as everything came alive, all at once.

The trees, oh, the trees. A moment before they'd been rough trunks sprouting tangles of branches. Now he could see their strength. Broad pillars of iridescent power curved up from the ground, splitting off with an inevitable geometry into limbs, branches, twigs. Each tree had become a continual, flowing cascade of lovely and intricate symmetry that took his breath away.

Beyond the trees the broad, grey-green thumb of Burrard Inlet shushed quiet waves onto the sand with the rising tide. Enmeshed within each wave he saw the shimmer of the ocean's restless, unstoppable pulse, advancing and receding with the planet's own heartbeat.

It was all thrillingly beautiful, and utterly mesmerizing.

He wanted to lose himself to the patterns of the trees. He felt a tingling, terrible urge as the waves beckoned. He hadn't been this overwhelmed in a long time. But he remembered. This same fascination had landed him in the psych ward.

He clamped his teeth together, forced himself to take a breath, and ordered his condition to Knock. It. Off. Or at least make itself useful.

Donnie and Johnnie were a few steps behind Franko now, moving in fast. Jackson's pattern sense, in a minor miracle of obedience, refocused on the trio. Bright swaths of electric yellow swept forward from two younger men showing their beeline to Franko, who was vibrating in glints of angry red.

All three of them reached inside their jackets. As one, they turned to stare at Jackson. And he saw, clear as a painted line, three curving swaths of laser-red intent arc from each of their jackets to a line that was going to point directly at him.

"Oh my fuck," he breathed.

He, Charles and Leaf were in the open. There were trees within twenty feet of either side of the path, but Jackson knew that neither he nor Charles would run any faster than Leaf's chair. Not that any of them could outrun a bullet.

The Three Stooges pulled their hands clear of their jackets. Each of them held a boxy, black pistol. Beside him Jackson could feel his two friends reaching the end of their moment of paralysis. They would have to run. Somewhere. Anywhere.

A frisson of silver movement pulled Jackson's eyes left. The Asian man, the one Leaf called Hatchet-Face, was threading between the trees off to the side of the three others, at just enough of a backward angle that they didn't see him. He was whippet-thin, dressed in black jeans and a dark fall jacket. He moved with the spare grace and purpose of a master, so beautiful it was terrifying.

One arm hung down by his leg. The black gun with the extra-long barrel was nothing more than a dark smudge against the man's black jeans.

Sweet fucking Jesus.

The three men on the path spotted Hatchet-Face as the Asian levelled his gun and fired. A chunk of thick bark exploded off a tree behind Donnie's head and all of them scattered, taking cover.

"There!" Jackson pointed at a massive chestnut a short distance off the path towards the beach. With the Croats busy they could make it. Without a word Leaf spun his wheelchair and kicked it into turbo. Charles and Jackson raced to keep up.

The Asian's pistol had been quiet, little more than a handclap. The Croats' guns were not. Multiple cracks startled the beach into action as they shot back. The Asian, seemingly oblivious, kept on coming and fired again. All around them people screamed, shouted and ran away.

Jackson kept his body behind the big tree but peeked around it at the battle, entranced. Bright flickers and lines shifted and glimmered among the trees as the Croats and the Asian dodged and fired at each other. The three gangsters had chosen three tactics, he saw. Donnie was behind another trunk, flashing around the side of it to shoot and then pulling back. Johnnie was a moving target, running a broken-field pattern across the grass and among the trees. Jackson saw an uncertain, disorganized mess of flickering lines around Johnnie as the man fought competing urges to stay out of the Asian's range but get close enough to fire back. Franko had stayed put and thrown himself to the ground. He held his gun in a two-handed grip, elbows against the grass.

Hatchet-Face took in the dynamic scene and, in a mercury-smooth maneuver, slid to the right as he fired another shot towards Johnnie. He didn't even look at the young man, just kept him busy and off-balance. Johnnie cursed and backed up some more.

Franko's gun cracked and missed as the Asian flowed behind one side of a tree. Jackson, who could see both men clearly, saw Franko settle in, take aim, and shoot past the trunk's far side.

The Asian knew it was coming. In a breathtaking display of precision timing he continued his course behind the tree, paused for a fraction of a second, then kept on moving into the wake of Franko's bullet.

He emerged from the tree's other side as Franko's pistol was still recoiling and shot the Croat between the eyes.

Jackson saw it. His condition flashed a scarlet line from the Asian's gun to the prone form. He saw Franko give a full-body shudder as the back of the man's head took flight. Then he slammed his eyes shut and pulled back against Charles. No good, he thought. I'm never going to unsee that.

More suppressed thumps, more cracks. They got fewer, with spaces of silence between them. Jackson had to look. He peeked around the edge of the rough bark and saw a crumpled form. Donnie was gone, no doubt hit as he ducked out from behind cover. Johnnie and the Asian were both on the move, circling each other through the trees. The Asian's left arm hung limp. Johnnie was favouring one leg. Johnnie fired again as Jackson watched, a wild shot that continued past his target towards the now-vacant beach.

A shrill, loud whistle pierced the air from the parking lot. Leaf had mentioned another man. An Adonis, he'd said. Jackson jerked his head towards the sound.

Shaheen Kiani stood tall and easy beside a charcoal-grey McLaren. His gaze was locked on the gunfight. As the Asian turned towards the whistle he twirled one hand in the air. Hurry the hell up.

Jackson watched as the Asian nodded. Hatchet-Face stopped circling. In one swift motion he bladed his thin body, held his weapon out straight from the shoulder and marched directly towards the last remaining Croat.

Johnnie got off two more shots, both misses, before the Asian drilled a hole through his chest with enough force to knock him off his feet. Hatchet-Face kept moving forward and shot Johnnie again as he passed by on his way to a Tesla double-parked on the side street.

Jackson turned to the parking lot. Shaheen stood by his sports car, gazing back. He gave Jackson a smile and a nod of the head. Added a freakin' sultan's wave. As sirens blared in the distance he sank into his car, peeled out of the lot and was gone.

Jackson's knees gave out. He thumped to the grass and waited for the police, Leaf right beside him, as Charles ran towards the three bodies on the grass.

Chapter 30

JUST A BYSTANDER

The sirens and lights arrived from everywhere all at once. Jackson watched, from the detachment of shock, as the performance played out. The first cops bumped their Chargers onto the grass and leaped out, scanning everywhere with guns drawn. The second wave, hard on their heels, went to check out the still forms. More cars sealed off all the streets. Once the scene was peppered with officers they let the ambulances through.

Charles had rejoined Jackson and Leaf after he'd confirmed the three men as dead. They were the only people left on the scene; everyone else had run for the hills when the first shot was fired. It didn't take long at all for the police to spot them. Two officers, weapons still in their hands, peeled off from the main action and hustled over.

That woke Jackson up. "We were bystanders," he muttered to the other two, hard and urgent. "Out for a walk when the shooting started and we took cover. That's all." He shushed Charles' objection with a stern look and the cops were on them, asking if they were all right.

His two friends stuck to the script. They were all dumbfounded, horrified, that their innocent walk could be so violently interrupted in such an upscale and peaceful part of the city. After a few minutes Jackson thought they might be sent home, but they didn't get off that easy. An older officer with sergeant chevrons walked over from his car and murmured something to the two cops watching over them. Suddenly they were all being politely but firmly escorted to the growing forest of police vehicles on Cornwall Avenue. They found themselves headed for VPD Headquarters at 2120 Cambie, Jackson and Charles in the back of a car and Leaf in a ramp-equipped van.

Jackson knew what had changed. They'd run his name. Which, thanks to Marilyn's sense of duty, was now firmly linked to two of the worst criminal gangs in the city.

"Easy," Charles said under his breath in the back of the cop car. Jackson hadn't realized he'd begun breathing hard. A sheen of sweat was making his face cold. He forced his breathing down and got it under control.

He knew that the VPD were good people, doing thankless and essential work to keep the city safe, of course he did. But in a very deep part of his mind, a place where threats carried a weight he couldn't ignore, he remembered a police car just like this one driving him from the Lions Gate Bridge to the hospital. He remembered a uniformed man, just like the one in the driver's seat, grasping his arm and guiding him through the heavy doors of the psych ward. That entire, terrible time would be part of his file. And it blasted a permanent hole through any credibility he might have.

Stick to the story, he said to Leaf and Charles in his mind, and maybe to himself, too. Just bystanders. No connection to the shooting. No reason to keep us. He said it over and over again, all the way to the fourth floor boardrooms with the windows overlooking False Creek and the Cambie Street Bridge. Leaf was already in the first boardroom, behind a closed door with two cops asking questions. They steered Charles into the second. Then the big cop ushered Jackson into the third.

Marilyn stood against the windows in the far wall, flanked by a woman with sergeant chevrons, desk-slouch posture, ash blonde hair and no smile lines, and an older man in plain clothes with deep, dark eyes and the slow flow to his movements of water cutting through rock. Her face was dark with worry. She broke away from the others and wrapped him up in a solid, warm hug. "I'm so glad you're okay," she murmured. It felt wonderful.

"Terrible way to start the day," said the man in a voice like black velvet. "I'm Jim Rockford, from Organized Crime. This is Sergeant Delores Dilly. And I believe you know Constable Mathers." He and Marilyn both smiled at that. "She's technically in a conflict of interest here, but I figured you could use the support."

"Jackson Teague," he said, shaking their hands. Rockford's grip was careful and warm. Sergeant Dilly's was more powerful than he expected. "But you already know that."

Rockford waved them all to chairs. He and Dilly sat on the far side of the conference table. Marilyn sat in the chair next to Jackson, which was a surprise and a comfort. Rockford gave a one-huff laugh as he took his chair. "I guess we do, Mr. Teague. However, there's a lot about this morning that we don't know. We were hoping you could fill us in."

"Not much to tell, really." He'd refined his story on the ride over, and reeled it out now. "Charles and I met Leaf for a walk. We're old friends, and Kits Beach is our usual hangout. We were partway down the path behind the beach when shooting broke out. We ducked behind the nearest tree and stayed there till it was over."

"That's awful," Rockford said, and sounded like he meant it. "You must be fairly rattled, anybody would be. We have an excellent Victim Services team. I recommend you connect with them later today."

"Uh, thanks for the offer. I'll think about it." Or not. Stifling the urge to fidget, he kept his hands planted on the boardroom table.

"That's good advice, Mr. Teague." Sergeant Dilly had a voice like one of his elementary school teachers, the one who'd whacked the side of his desk with a ruler whenever she caught him daydreaming. "For now, why don't you step us through it. Tell us everything you remember."

The interrogation went on for almost an hour. He gave them every detail of the morning that supported his story, and Rockford and Dilly stopped him a hundred times to ask questions. Who was Leaf? How did they all know each other? What were they talking about? Did he see anything out of the ordinary? What did he do when the first shot rang out? The second, and the third? He told them about seeing the Asian's deliberate assault, and Shaheen's guidance from the parking lot. He called Shaheen Kiani by name, Rockford interrupted, did he know the man? Of course Jackson did, and he knew they knew. He told them of his appointment at the gangster's house.

He did not tell them that Shaheen had looked at him, smiled and waved. He'd simply got into his McLaren when the last Croat fell and taken off.

Marilyn, who'd been a silent support until now, jumped in. "I don't know about you, but I'm sure Jackson could use a coffee." They all pushed back from the table and walked with Jackson to a break room down the corridor.

Marilyn walked with him, two steps behind Dilly and Rockford. She glanced over at him and raised her eyebrows, lips pursed. What the hell? she was saying. You're holding back? With the police? With my superiors?

He shook his head infinitesimally, once, and frowned back at her. Not going there, he tried to communicate. Just a bystander. That's all.

Rockford kept up an easy banter about city politics and cop jokes, even telling one story that made Jackson laugh a little. The coffee wasn't bad, strong and hot. Before long, however, they were back in the boardroom.

Dilly dropped the hammer the moment they were all settled. "Thank you for giving us the event from your perspective,

Jackson," she said, in that voice that carried no thanks whatsoever. "Now tell us everything you didn't say before."

"Uh … what?" He tried to make it sound convincing.

She scowled across the table at him. "Puh-lease. You've already told us you know Shaheen. You knew the three victims, too. They took you to the Uncle's house, and they're most likely the ones who have been following you around. You've spotted them at it before, according to Marilyn. You saw them again today, even before Shaheen's hitter showed up, didn't you? Hell, you probably know him, too. What's he, your cycling pal?"

He didn't have to fake his confusion, or his growing outrage. "What are you talking about? Those were the Uncle's men? I saw the back of their heads for a few minutes when they drove us to his house. And yeah, I saw their cars when they followed me. Their cars, not them. That was—oh, wow." He pulled up the memory of Franko's death, a sight he'd hoped to forget, and felt his face turn green.

Then he rallied. "The Uncle pulled them off me after we had our little visit. He said so. Why chase a massage therapist all over town? They must have better things to do. Well, not now, I guess." He took a drink. The coffee had turned cold. "If that was them, I have no idea why they were in that park. I do know that Shaheen has it in for them."

Rockford leaned forward. "How do you know that, Jackson?"

Jackson put his own elbows on the table and glared back. "Twitter, Reddit, the freakin' CBC evening news, that's how. The New Canadians pounded the hell out of the Croats last year. They don't seem to mind being public about it. I guess they're finishing the job." He crossed his arms over his chest and sank back into the chair. "And I had to see it."

That seemed to end things. The boardroom filled with silence for a minute or so. Rockford and Dilly shared a look. Marilyn slipped her hand onto Jackson's knee under the table and gave a squeeze. Finally Rockford stood and extended a hand.

"That's all, then. You have some kind of connection to both these groups, Jackson, but I think you might have nailed it. I believe Mr. Kiani is tidying up. A word of advice? If you get any more invitations to the Uncle's house, decline. Can I give you a call if I get any more questions? Thanks for coming in today, you've really helped. And consider Victim Services, please. Marilyn can show you out."

"You did really well up there," she said as they went down in the elevator. Both Charles and Leaf were long gone. "I'll be over the moment I'm off shift."

They gave each other a rib-crushing hug at the exit, then Jackson made his way home. For the first time, he wasn't eager about Marilyn's visit.

Chapter 31

POISED ON THE KNIFE EDGE

"We need to do something! This is intolerable. In broad daylight, in front of everybody! Those three morons barely got off a shot, and it was three to one. We have to ..."

"Respect!" The Uncle slapped a hand onto his desk and the man shut up at last. He'd been frothing at the mouth since the moment he got through the door, even in front of the children, and the Uncle was tired of it. "They did their best. I know of the one Shaheen sent, he was born in a war, killing is all he knows. They stood their ground. They wounded him, which is impressive in itself. We will miss them. We will mourn them."

The other man stormed around the side of the desk and glowered down at him. Were he any other man, anyone else than the one he'd chosen to lead the family forward, Branislav would beat him into the carpet for such an affront. But he saw the anger in the man's eyes, felt its equal deep within his own chest.

He also saw the other thing. The fear, lurking just behind in the dark, pushing the anger forward as a shield. He felt that, too. Fear, and suspicion. The devil Shaheen should not be interested in the Croats anymore. He should be on to other things, confident and comfortable in his supremacy. The fact that he was not, and that he was suddenly involved in their affairs, was bad. They were poised on the knife edge of the project. Vulnerable. Everything depended on their complete invisibility.

"It's that massage therapist," the man said. "The Stooges

tracked him to Shaheen's home. He went inside with his massage table. Either Shaheen called him or he called the Persian, but either way it's the same. They talked, and now the devil is on us again."

Branislav nodded. "So it would seem. And? What would you have me do?" He sat back in his desk chair and folded his hands over his belly. "What would you do?"

The man got larger with the gift of authority. He grimaced, the fear pushing his anger to a fever pitch. "Answer them! Go to war, of course. Call the entire family, everyone that's left. Call in favours from the others. Empty the arsenal. Let's go down to Shaheen's lair and wipe it off the face of the world. Hunt every New Canadian we can find. It's time, Uncle. They've pushed us far enough. I say we answer."

Branislav nodded and considered, giving the plan all the thought it deserved. "And the massage man?" he asked. "The one who comes to your place of business? Who has worked on your colleagues, had his hands on you? Tell me what you would do about him."

"The same." The quaver in the man's voice was well concealed by hardness and grit, but Branislav heard it. "He has to go, too. He started all this. He knows far too much."

Branislav nodded again. "That would seem to be the right thing. All of it, a public and bloody war, flashes and bangs and bodies everywhere. As you say, it would seem to be time."

He lifted his eyes and let some of his own anger show. "It would also be the last action the Croats ever took. Our family would be done. We could never win such a fight, not against the New Canadians. We have few weapons. Level Shaheen's club? What firepower do you think that would take? Do I have a warehouse of bombs, a plane to drop them? We have few people left, and now three less. We have no more favours to call in."

He lifted himself out of the desk chair and salted his anger with disappointment. "Even if we did have the men, the guns, everything you say, it would still be the wrong thing. It is inelegant. Messy, brutal, public. The police would be forced to act. They can be slow, but they are thorough, and once they move they do not stop. We'd be gone, one way or another. If you are to lead you must see this. Think your plans through, and then think again. You have brought the family a daring and original plan, and if we keep quiet for another week then we will have everything we need. But not now! We must be silent now."

The man took the chastisement well. He kept his mouth shut for a moment, thinking. "So we do nothing?" he said at last. "Take the loss, collect our bodies, and slink away? Wait for Shaheen to kill more of us? Because he is not done. Surely you know that."

"No," Branislav said. He was happy to see a bit of sense come to the man. "I said we must be silent, not still. We will not slink away, as you say. But we will be smart, and use what tools we have. Tell me. Blast Dynamics has not fired any of its maintenance staff?"

The man's eyebrows went up. "No. Shaheen's spy is still there, even though he's a terrible fixer. I make sure he knows nothing."

"Not precisely true. The man knows nothing about us."

He saw the light of possibility and vengeance return to his successor's eyes and was pleased.

Chapter 32

TO ABSENT KIDNAPPERS

Marilyn buzzed the intercom at six as Jackson was putting the finishing touches on the meal. He watched as she came through the door. She made it two steps into the apartment before she stopped, her nose twitching.

"What is that smell? It's heavenly."

He took her jacket. "Something new. It'll be ready in a minute."

He poured them two glasses of dark red wine. She surveyed the table and took another deep sniff. "All right, what do we have here?"

He pointed around the plates. "Pasticada, a beef and vegetable sauce over gnocchi. Cevapi, although probably not as good as we had at the Uncle's. And this is just salad." He raised his glass and she did the same. "This is Plavac Mali."

Marilyn was quiet for a moment. "This is a tribute, isn't it?"

He nodded. "Yeah, I guess. It just seemed right to have a Croatian meal tonight." He glanced down. "I might have overdone it on the meat, though."

She looked over the meal again and pulled out her chair. "Well, it smells wonderful. I'm sure Franko would have approved. To absent kidnappers." They clinked glasses, drank, and tucked in.

Their plates were almost empty before the conversation began. He started it off. "I hope I never go through anything like that again."

Her fork paused, then resumed its journey. "The shooting? It must have been awful. And scary. After you left the station Rockford told me some stories about that Asian guy, he's straight out of a nightmare." She chewed some more. "So. I think I know why you lied today, but tell me anyway."

He'd known the question would come, and was ready for it. "Because I want to keep as low a profile in that building as I can. My file there is thick enough already. You know, you've seen it. According to the official records, I'm unreliable. One bad day away from another trip behind a locked door. They have every reason not to believe me, and the crazier I sound the worse it gets." He put his fork down with the last oval of gnocchi still on it. "And the truth is starting to sound pretty damn crazy, don't you think?"

She sighed. "I figured as much. Yeah, I see what you mean. Still. You lied to my superiors. You left important details out, details that I know. Do you have any idea the conflict that puts me in?" She poured them both more wine. "This is amazing, by the way. So. The Three Stooges were following you this morning, weren't they?"

He nodded. "Definitely. Not being subtle about it, either. Leaf spotted them right away. Franko had a microphone pointed at us, can you believe it?"

"Really?" She pushed her empty plate away and took a sip. "Why the hell would he do that? And what's for dessert?"

He brought out a basket of tiny, deep fried balls dusted with icing sugar and they headed for the couch. "Fritules," he said. "I have no idea what they were listening for. But at one point, they stopped listening and got serious." He crunched a fritule. "Those three seemed kind of embarrassed when they picked us up the other day. Almost friendly. Could they ever, you know, hurt someone?"

She snorted. "They're gangsters, Jackson. Part of the Croats family. Donnie, Johnnie and Franko might act harmless, but the

Croats have been involved in drug import and distribution, prostitution, human trafficking, organized theft, you name it. They held their own for years against half a dozen gangs as vicious as they were. Each of them has a list of felonies going back to the Stone Age, and not for littering." She frowned. "Or had. Why?"

He hesitated, anticipating her reaction. "Because the moment before the Asian opened up on them, all three were headed right for us. Reaching for their guns."

"What!?" Marilyn jumped up, glaring at him. "You kept that little detail to yourself? Jackson, how could you? That puts a whole different spin on things. It changes the entire investigation."

He glared right back. "It puts me right in the center of it all, Marilyn. Not a witness. A person of interest. A target. If I'd said that, I'd still be in that boardroom. Or somewhere worse. Right?"

She stomped over to the window, looked out at the night, ran a hand through her hair and strode back. "So let me get this straight. Franko was listening to you. The Asian was following Franko and the others. Suddenly the three of them are headed for you, guns drawn. Then the Asian attacks them?"

He nodded, feeling his freckles heat up with a blush. "That's pretty much it. Uh, one thing more." She crossed her arms and waited, refusing to sit again. "Both Franko and the Asian were on their phones."

"Bah!" She threw her hands wide and headed for the kitchen. He winced as she started clearing the table with a clatter. "So they were both getting directions. That's just great!"

He got up to help. "You see how it looks? Like I was somehow involved in all of it. You know I'm not, right? I sure as hell do. I haven't done anything wrong, Marilyn. There's no reason for any of this. Besides," he added, placing dishes in the washer, "they have plenty of reason to go after each other."

"That's not the point and you know it. You lied, Jackson, I mean really lied. You thought you were keeping yourself out of trouble? A little fib to avoid being the center of attention? Wake up, boyo." Marilyn stopped putting food in the fridge and whirled to face him, her voice rising. "It sure sounds to me like two of the very worst groups of people in the city have you at the center of their attention. If that was the Uncle on the other end of Franko's phone, then he wants you gone, and he has more people he can send. And the Asian? Shaheen's trigger man? Was he told to rub out some Croats, or to protect you? I don't know which is worse. My God, Jackson." She slapped him on the chest hard enough to send him back a step. "I don't know whether to haul you to the shop right now, or call in some protection."

"I'll be okay. At least from the gangs."

She shoved the last of the cevapi into the fridge. "Oh yeah? And how did you deduce that?"

He shrugged. "Like you said. The Asian was either there to kill Croats or protect me, although who knows why. And if the Uncle wanted me ... gone, he's had plenty of hours since I left the police station this afternoon."

"As many murders happen between ten at night and three in the morning as the rest of the day combined," she growled. "But yeah. That's fair. Still." She went into the bedroom and came out a moment later with a small, black pistol in her hand. As he recoiled into the back corner of the kitchen she slipped the magazine, checked it and cracked it back into the handle. He caught a glimpse of a gleaming copper round and his mouth dried up.

"Jesus! What the hell is that?"

She hefted the small weapon, which almost disappeared in her hand. "My purse gun. Springfield Hellcat, if you're interested. Don't tell anybody. You're getting a good night's sleep in the bed tonight. I'm taking the chair."

He got hold of himself and eased out of the kitchen. "Sorry, I guess I'm a bit nervy. It's just, I've had enough of those things for one day, you know?"

She got a look on her face, something halfway between compassion and challenge. "I guess you have. You really jumped when you saw this. Come here."

She wrapped one long arm over his shoulders in a warm side hug. With the other, she placed the Hellcat firmly into his hand.

"What the—I don't want ..."

"Feel it," she said, her voice soft in his ear. "You're good at that. See that button right there?" She pressed his thumb against it and caught the magazine as it fell out. "Now we pull this back," she helped his other hand slide the top of the gun back. A brass cartridge flew out and she snagged it out of the air. "There! We're unloaded and safe."

"Marilyn, I don't like these things. I know what they can do."

"You've seen what bad people do with them," she said, her arms still around him. "These things are machines. They shoot bullets. That's all. And now you're going to learn a bit about them."

For the next half hour she took him around the small weapon. She demonstrated what the various buttons and slides did, how to load and unload it, how to check that it was empty. She got him to aim it. Pull the trigger a few times. Gradually, towards the end, it began to feel less like an evil menace and more like a tool.

An extremely dangerous tool. But one that could be managed.

He yawned and handed the Hellcat back. "Okay, lesson over. Thanks, I guess. I might even get some sleep tonight. What about tomorrow, when you go to work?"

Some of Marilyn's glower returned. "You're coming with me, that's what. You're telling Dilly and Rockford everything you told me so they can do their jobs with the right information. One word," she held up a finger against his protest, "and I'll drag you down in cuffs. I'm not even kidding."

He stifled the complaint, gave the table a final wipe and straightened out the placemats. "I suppose. Cuffs, eh? Um, want to practice?"

"Jackson."

So that was a no.

"Oh, by the way." She headed down the hall to check the door locks. "We're invited to Ahmed's for dinner tomorrow. You're going."

He paused by the bedroom door. "It's my dad's birthday tomorrow. But I should be back in time."

A flicker of compassion passed over her face. "Your visit, I forgot. Looks like you'll have a busy day."

Chapter 33

AN IRON-HARD OPINION OF RIGHT AND WRONG

The next morning he followed Marilyn into the Cambie police station and back up to the fourth floor boardroom, where he elaborated on his story again and endured a half hour of tongue-lashing from both Sergeant Dilly and Sergeant Rockford. They spent the hour after that rifling so many questions at him that by the time they were done he felt as wrung out as an old dishcloth. They didn't offer him any coffee. During the entire grilling, Marilyn stood in the corner with a smug 'I told you so' expression on her face. Eventually, after some more stern warnings about not withholding information from the police, they let him go.

The trip over to North Vancouver on the Seabus was a welcome respite, with only the drone of the boat's motors to break the quiet. Still, he found himself subtly unnerved to be back where this whole crazy trip had started. Several times during the trip he jerked his head around, looking for watchers. On the way out of the terminal building he kept an eye out for slim, fast-moving strangers and the glint of a knife.

Knock it off, he told himself.

Russell Sortland waited for him in the terminal parking lot, his moon-faced grin and cheery wave chasing away the drama. Jackson picked up the pace and shook hands with his father's office-mate.

"It's great to see you, Russ," he said, standing back and looking the man over. "Gained another few, I see."

Russ laughed, and every part of him got into the act. "Never get a desk job, my boy. Six months equals six pounds. Looks like you're still punishing yourself with that road bike, you're thin as a rail. Come on, let's head back to the shop before somebody misses me."

Russ was standing next to his car, a comfortable Mercedes sedan that listed a little to the driver's side, parked in the first blue-squared accessible spot. They got in and drove the four blocks to the plain, stucco building down a narrow side street off Victory Ship Way. Few people outside the marine shipping industry ever came down here, and few of the ones who did knew anything about this building. Russell maneuvered his bulk out from under the steering wheel, made his way to the building's sole door like a topheavy container ship coming into berth, and slipped a blank white card past the card reader to get them in.

Jackson knew without even looking that Russell's back was stiff as a steel plate and his feet were killing him. The man's gut was big enough to make his belt buckle disappear. The laws of leverage meant that his back had to hold on for dear life, and impact dynamics had long since flattened his arches.

"Place hasn't changed much since your last visit," Russ said, squeezing through the opening. He led Jackson through the shabby reception room with its criminally ugly lime green polyester carpet and dark, faux-wood wall panels, behind the abandoned and crumbling secretary's desk, and through another card-locked door. "Hasn't really changed all that much since Aidan was here five years ago, come to that." They went down a similarly dingy hall past two more doors. Russell opened the end door with a regular key.

The room beyond looked like the command deck of a starship. It took up the entire seaward half of the building and held enough bleeding-edge technology to bankrupt a small country. The humming, blinking collection of computer hardware dwarfed Abe

Tremblay's setup. A solid line of monitors ringed the far side of the room, some of them stacked two high, linked by thick cables to neat stacks of winking black boxes underneath the curved desk. The sound of half a hundred fans created a ceaseless white noise. Even now, in October, an air conditioning unit worked nonstop to dispel the heat.

"Anomaly headed our way out of Shanghai," said the brushcut triangle of a man seated at the left terminal, black boots firmly on the floor. "Hey, Jackson, welcome back."

"Hey, Carl. Still keeping the free world safe, I see."

"For all the good it does. Here, Russ, see what you think." Carl flicked a mouse and three screens near the right side of the room changed their displays to a spreadsheet, a map of the Pacific crisscrossed with lines, and a live feed of what looked like a huge and busy container dock.

Russ sank into an oversized office chair and wheeled over to examine the information. "See what you mean," he muttered. "No way that should have stopped there. Look at this, Jackson." He pointed to the map of the Pacific. A red line crossed back and forth between North America and Asia, hitting a number of ports on each side. Smaller yellow lines extended inland from Seattle, Vancouver, Los Angeles, and several spots in Asia Jackson didn't know. "These lines show one shipping container's voyages. Yellow lines are for drop-offs and reloads, red ones for ocean crossings. Right now, this container is on the dock at Shanghai Guangdou, getting loaded onto Maersk for Vancouver. But catch this." He pointed to a yellow line that snaked inland from the stop before Shanghai. "Obscure port on the Russian coast, some container traffic but nothing big. And this pickup doesn't go to any industry I recognize."

He played his fingers over a keyboard and another screen lit up with Google Earth's satellite view of the world. He zoomed down until he'd located the Russian port, then followed a road inland to where the container had spent three days last week. A small group of buildings ballooned into view.

"Gotcha." Russ checked the spreadsheet. "Says it got loaded with stuffed bears, part of the Easter rush. Destined for Vancouver. And, sure enough," he pulled up a search on another screen, "that's a tiny little toy factory right there. Last check." Back to the spreadsheet, then over to another one with the Maersk logo on top. "The weights match. It's legit, Carl. But worth looking into."

Russ pivoted his chair around. "That took me, what, four minutes? Your dad would have called it legit or not in ten seconds. I really don't know how Aidan did it, but he could just stand back and take in all this realtime data," he waved his hand at the screens, "and spot the anomalies."

"That sounds like Dad." Jackson had never told Russell about how the patterns of the world had once swept him off his feet and could again if he wasn't careful. He could never be certain, since his father wasn't here to ask, but he suspected he'd come by his obsession honestly.

He'd loved his visits to this room with his dad. The Overwatch, as his father had called it, was a very quiet partnership between the major shipping companies, the Canadian Border Service, and US Customs. A handful of small rooms like this monitored all the container traffic headed in and out of North America. Any suspicious cargos were flagged to the port authorities for inspection. His father had stopped everything from a container full of stolen Ferraris to an incoming shipment of contraband chickens.

"Still miss him, eh?" Russ pulled two Mars bars out of a drawer and handed one to Jackson. "So do I. If he hadn't gone and got himself knifed, I wouldn't be saddled with this hunk of beef."

"Heard that," said Carl without apparent rancor, his eyes still on half a dozen screens.

Jackson felt the too-familiar ache bruise his heart again.

"Yeah, I do. I went up there last week. To the intersection. Had a look around. I don't know, reminiscing I guess." Jackson gazed at the screens without seeing them, revisiting the gloomy, rainsoaked sidewalk in his mind.

"Looking for answers, you mean. Like you do every year." Russ shook the Mars bar at him. "It's just a street corner, Jackson. There is no answer. Your dad couldn't leave a problem alone, you know that, his tongue had poor impulse control. He saw those young punks wasting their lives. He told them so, one of them pulled a blade, and that was that. Your dad went to his greater reward and the punk ran away. That's all."

He wheeled his office chair over and laid a hand on Jackson's shoulder. His breath smelled like chocolate. "Let it go, son. Five years is long enough. We love having you visit, but maybe pick another day of the year, okay? Are you going to eat that?"

Jackson shook his head, forced a smile and handed back the unopened Mars bar. Russ clapped him on the shoulder again, spun around and got to work.

The big guy was right, of course. His assessment was spot on. Aidan Teague had an iron-hard opinion of right and wrong. He rarely let a mistake go unchallenged, a trait that had caused Jackson plenty of headaches as a kid. Jackson needed to let this morbid habit go. Let his dad rest. Maybe put the unanswered questions to rest, too.

But they were big questions. Jackson knew how his father's mind had worked, maybe better than anybody. Aidan Teague saw every mistake and never tolerated wasted potential, but he'd also had an excellent radar for trouble. More than once, when the family was out for a walk, he'd steered his wife and son across the street to the opposite sidewalk when he saw a problem ahead. Once, an actual fight had broken out as they passed. They would have been caught in it without his father's nose for danger.

The question bothered him. Kept him returning to that quiet

corner. Aidan Teague would want to correct those boys, yes. But he'd have seen the potential for violence from a mile off and not gone anywhere near them.

Unless. Maybe he'd been preoccupied, or tired, or his guard was down. Maybe he'd simply made the wrong choice. Jackson didn't know, and he never would.

"Drug shipment," Carl muttered across the room. "Shanghai again, ready to load. Came from the usual factory but made an unscheduled stop." He flipped the details over to Russ.

The map came up again, this time focused on mainland China. Russ highlighted a single line that snaked from a spot on the outskirts of Zhengzhou south and east to the Shanghai container docks. The snake had a tiny bump in its back. The container had made a detour, and been tagged at a roadside station.

Russ zoomed in on the bump, switched over to the satellite view. Nothing but fields and the occasional single house or barn for the entire detour.

"Either the driver went home for lunch, or he picked up something extra," Russ said. "Good catch. Call it in. Soft approach, it's only a maybe."

Carl rattled off a message on his keyboard and hit Enter. Russ pointed the second Mars bar to the biggest monitor in the center of the array and said, "This never gets old."

The live feed from the Shanghai container pier filled the screen. They saw the center third of an incredibly long ship being loaded by three massive orange cranes. Tiny loaders ferried containers back and forth from a field of them that went on forever.

A car swerved into view, blue light flashing on its roof. It pulled up close to a loader that had a container off the ground, halfway to one of the cranes. The loader stopped and lowered the metal box. Two uniformed figures emerged from the car, one of them reading from a tablet in his hand. They checked the seal on the container's door, then broke it and opened up the box. A moment later, both of them backed away. One figure spoke into a radio while the second tapped on the tablet.

Carl's monitor pinged. "Hah! Vacuum-sealed pouches, about a hundred of 'em. White powder. Gotcha, bastards." He wheeled over to Russ and they high-fived.

Jackson whistled. An idea lit up his mind. "Impressive. You guys track outgoing stuff as well, right? Can you check out some packages that left Vancouver maybe a week or two ago?"

Russ and Carl both spun their chairs to face him. Carl had a bodybuilder's chiselled physique, but a face that had been carved by an apprentice, all odd angles and sharp edges. "Maybe," Russ said. "When did they leave?"

"Uh, not sure," Jackson said, starting to feel foolish.

"All right. What was the destination?"

"Multiple destinations. Elite medical clinics, all over the world."

Carl and Russ glanced at each other. "What size was the shipment?"

Jackson thought about the small lump he'd felt under Abe's skin and in the Seabus man's side. Pictured a hundred of them. A thousand. "Not big," he admitted. "Shoebox to microwave."

Carl shook his head. "Too small, not our department. Those probably went FedEx."

"Interesting request," Russ said, his eyes two gleaming points in his round face. "I know there's a story behind that. Do tell."

Jackson wheeled over another chair, sat down and told the story. Everything, from the Seabus man to the Ponce de Leon to the shootout, even his interviews with the police. The sharing felt like a relief, an offloading of some of the tension he'd been carrying around his neck and shoulders. Halfway through the tale Russ opened the drawer and handed him another Mars bar, which he devoured.

"So that's it," he finished. "A bunch of these implants are floating around out there somewhere, about to get released to anyone rich enough to pay for them. Someone's about to get very, very wealthy. The hell of it is, they might actually work. But that's just the thing. Nobody really knows."

The room fell into the soft, rushing silence of overworked computer fans. At last Russ slapped his knees and let out a sigh. "Whew! I have to hand it to you, my boy, when you see trouble coming you run towards it as hard as you can. Just like Aidan, and I'm seriously not joking. Did you know how tough it was to keep that man in his chair? Our job was to report what we found. But if it was local, and the port cops didn't react as fast as he thought they should? You dad would head right down to the docks and crack the container himself. Nearly got arrested I don't know how many times."

"I didn't know that," Jackson said. "He never mentioned any field trips."

"Of course not. He blew the protocols all to hell, put himself in danger and flat out broke the law, because he had to fix what was wrong. Not exactly dinner conversation to be proud of. Now listen to me, Jackson."

Russ wheeled his chair as close as his bulk would allow. "That outrage and moral high ground is what got your father killed. I've always seen the same thing in you, and that story you told proves it. Your dad got himself knifed for sticking his nose where it didn't belong." Russ' voice, a high tenor to begin with, gained a plaintive, earnest edge. "Don't make the same mistake. The Croats? The New Canadians? These aren't street punks, Jackson, they're serious badasses. Don't get on their bad side, and for sure don't get in between them. Let them kill each other. You forget all about this stuff, turn yourself around and walk away. Hell, run." His eyes welled up and he gave a sniff. "I'd hate to lose you, too."

The three of them fell silent again while the machines winked and blipped around them. Jackson felt the truth of Russell's words. Coming hard on the heels of a scolding by Marilyn and the VPD, it convinced him. He needed to be done with all of this.

His eye caught a clock on the wall as its big, red numbers changed. "Whoa!" He jumped up. "I have to go, busy day, dinner date. Thanks for the visit, Russ. Carl, good to see you again. Sorry, I've got to go."

"Want a ride?" Russ made to lever himself out of the chair.

That made Jackson smile. "No thanks. I can run there faster."

"Smartass. Don't be a stranger."

Once outside he ran for the terminal. Trying, with every step, to convince himself he was running away from danger and not towards it.

Chapter 34

We need to have this little talk

Jackson scooped Marilyn off the sidewalk in front of her Yaletown highrise with a driveby double-park that had traffic behind him squawking. She was coiffed, lightly dusted with makeup, and wearing a jet-black tuxedo shirt and jeans ensemble over spit-polished Doc Martens. He'd thrown on a button-up plaid shirt and his good khakis and run a comb through his curls.

She levered herself into the passenger seat of the Subaru, looked him up and down, and said, "At least you made an effort."

Still angry, then.

Ahmed and Gordon lived in one of the few actual houses left between Broadway and the water of False Creek, close to Cambie, tucked in amongst the townhomes and office blocks. They had an understated home with Art Deco accents set back from the street and finished with a modest, tan stucco. It was easy to miss, but unmistakeably elegant once you saw it. Gordon, Jackson knew, was an architect with the city. He'd designed the house from the ground up, and probably pulled a string or two for the permits. They were both waiting at the door when Jackson and Marilyn stepped past the rhododendrons flanking the walkway.

Ahmed looked the same as when Jackson had first met him. A doorframe-filling six foot two with the shoulders to match, he'd struck Jackson as both contained and formidable on that visit. Now he knew that Ahmed had a dry sense of humor, an infectious laugh, and a mad love of soccer.

Gordon stood next to him, one arm around Ahmed's waist and the other giving them a cheery hello. He was everyone's picture of the architect at home—sandy hair, John Lennon glasses, cardigan over button-down shirt and slacks. He and Jackson had actually met several years before at Jackson's aikido class, where Gordon was a Third Dan instructor.

"Come on in, I'm just about to plate the salmon," Gordon called. "Drinks are at the bar."

The house was truly a home, warm and solid, with just enough chairs on the floor and art on the walls to wrap you in a warm embrace without smothering. Mouthwatering smells drifted from the kitchen. A basket of fresh rolls perfumed the dining room. Ahmed got them all glasses of wine as Gordon bustled back and forth with the food.

The conversation took about a minute and a half to get around to work. Ahmed wanted to hear all about the Kits Beach Carnage, as the news was calling it. Jackson tucked away his irritation and reeled off the details around forkfuls of poached salmon and roasted veggies. He glanced at Marilyn in the middle of his retelling, wondering what he'd see on her face. Boredom, from hearing the same tale? Still a boatload of indignant condemnation?

To his surprise, he saw worry.

"So they hauled Charles, Leaf and I off to the boardrooms and grilled us till we were crispy, then that was that." He took a sip of wine and sat back.

"Almost," Ahmed replied with a ghost of a smile. "Marilyn brought you back in this morning to, uh, fill in a few more details."

"Leave the poor man alone," Gordon said, slapping Ahmed's arm, "he's barely had time to eat." He reached for a roll and added, "That sounded very scary. I'm glad you're all right."

Talk drifted to Gordon's work with the city, then the latest soccer scores from the runup to the World Cup. Jackson regaled them with a couple of stories from his growing roster of massage clients, but stayed away from the gangsters and longevists.

They spent a few minutes clearing the supper dishes. Gordon loaded them up with fresh drinks and a communal chocolate and cheese plate and they retired to the living room.

"So, any more news on the career move? Rockford must be getting impressed by now," Ahmed said, turning to Marilyn. She'd taken the seat next to Jackson on the curved, supremely comfortable couch. She sipped her wine before answering.

"I can't say. No, really, I actually can't tell. Rockford plays the closest game I've ever seen. I told him I was interested in OCS and he said, 'Uh huh.' I got an invite to the Uncle's house and given a frickin' inside track, and he said, 'Uh huh.' Now this whole shootout thing, and he barely even blinks. Honestly, Ahmed, I don't know where I stand with that guy."

"But you do stand somewhere," Gordon pointed out, snapping off a square of dark chocolate. "He knows you exist. He knows you're interested. You just have to be patient."

"Patience is an essential skill for Organized Crime," Ahmed mused. "Gordon's right. Wait a bit, see what happens."

"I hate waiting," she grumbled, and they all laughed. Then Ahmed turned to Jackson.

"What do you make of it all?"

Lulled into a relaxed and peaceful doze by the food, the wine, the couch, and Marilyn's warmth, he started at the sudden attention. "Me? I don't know. It's Marilyn's career choice, not mine."

Gordon nodded at his partner. "Told you so," he said. "He hasn't faced it yet."

Jackson sat up straighter, Marilyn shifting to accommodate him. "Faced what?" Had he just walked into another trap?

Ahmed laid a hand on his partner's knee. "Come on, Gord, be gentle. It's never come up before, that's all." He tipped his wine glass at Jackson and Marilyn. "You two are getting pretty close, aren't you? Marilyn tells me you're doing the toothbrush thing."

Jackson felt a tinge of irritation rise up his spine. He glanced over at his girlfriend. "Anything he doesn't know?"

She shrugged. Almost an apology. But not quite. "Probably not. He's my partner."

He swept his eyes over them all, saw the evening in a new light. The warm room in this lovely home. The great meal, delicious wine. Gordon, composed and quiet on his chair, was folded in upon himself except for the polite and interested ray of attention he directed towards Jackson.

Ahmed and Marilyn were intensely focused on him. Ahmed in his wingback chair next to Gordon, and Marilyn next to Jackson on the couch, were pretending to be relaxed and conversational, but every scrap of their attention was riveted on Jackson. He felt pinned under a dual spotlight.

He answered Ahmed, curious to see where this was leading despite his irritation. "We're pretty close, yes. Apparently not to the point of keeping confidences. But close." Marilyn, her side still nestled into his, didn't react at the criticism.

Ahmed nodded. "It's plain. Both in the way she speaks about you, and in how you sit together." He waved a hand at the couch. "She loves you, Jackson. And that's beautiful, it's magic. But she's a cop. That means ..."

"It means we need to have this little talk," Gordon picked up when Ahmed faltered. "Don't worry. I had to go through it, too."

Jackson didn't relax. "What talk?"

"About some special considerations. Being in a relationship with a police officer." Ahmed spread his hands. "Nothing you don't already know, on some level. But some things you need to be more aware of."

Jackson nibbled some chocolate, then waved the melting square at Ahmed and Marilyn. "Let me guess. It's a rough life. My girl will occasionally come home with bruised ribs. It's shift work. Some days I'll have to be quiet around the house. Like that?"

Ahmed nodded. "Like that, but more. Deeper. Sure, police work is shift work. But it's more than a job, it's a duty. We're sworn officers. If something happens during our shift, we stay and see it through. If you two are out to dinner, maybe visiting your mom, and her phone rings, she's off to work. Middle of the night, middle of a movie, it doesn't matter. That's police work. The job comes first. Always."

"Yeah, sure, I get that. It's already happened once or twice." Jackson did get it. But he started to see where all this was going.

"Tell him the other thing," Marilyn said. Her tone was serious, subdued.

Ahmed shook his head. "You tell him."

She lifted herself away from his side and pivoted on the couch until she faced him. "You know I don't mind mixing it up, right? Those bruises the other day? They were, well, kind of fun. But it's a dangerous job, Jackson. I know that, and if I end up in hospital I'm ready for that. I sure as hell don't want to, and we all protect each other out there. But shit happens. Sometimes we get hurt. Sometimes, worse."

He saw Marilyn's sinuous geometry as she sat curled up beside him. She was calm, dark, perfectly still. She really was okay with it. He'd always known that about her, sort of. Peripherally. Now it sunk in a little more.

"I see," he said at last. "So the job takes a toll on relationships. She might be late for dinner. She might get broken. Anything else I should know?"

Ahmed leaned forward until his elbows were on his knees. "Yes. One more thing. Not often, but every once in a blue moon, the danger lands close to home. We keep our personal lives off the Internet and out of the public record, but if a punk with a grudge wants to find out where we live, he can do it."

Marilyn chimed in. "Rockford told me that if I get in with Organized Crime, that danger ramps up. Gangs are more organized, better resourced. It's baked into the definition. Mostly they know better than to go after a police officer or their family. But it's been known to happen."

Jackson frowned, pursed his lips in concentration. "Right, now I get the picture. So if Marilyn and I make a go of it, there's always the chance—slight though it is—that a gangster might find out who I am. Might, I don't know, call me up. Invite me over to his house to find out what I know about my cop girlfriend's work. Even grab me off the street. I know it's a one in a freakin' million chance, but I could even find myself in the middle of a running gun battle." He nodded sagely. "Something to consider."

The room was silent as a held breath for three long seconds. Then they all, Jackson included, exploded into laughter. The tension of the conversation, and some of the stress of the recent days, left him as he laughed hard enough for his ribs to hurt.

Gordon got himself under control first. "Oh wow, we needed that. These talks can get so heavy. Well, the easy part's over. We've told you what the life's about. Now you just have to decide if it's for you."

Jackson pointed at the two men. "How do you handle it?" he asked Gordon. "Knowing what you know?"

Gordon finished off his wine. "I accept what I can and hide the rest," he said, straightfaced. "I'll admit, some of what he does scares me. Some days, when the headlines are full of bad shit, I don't want him to step out the door. But I put it away where he never gets to see it, give him a kiss and send him off to save the world. That's who he is. And when he's at work, the last thing I want is for him to be distracted by my feelings."

"As if," Ahmed snorted, and endured another slap from Gordon. They all laughed some more.

"We're doing great," Marilyn said, still face-on to him on the couch. "Before we take the next step, you just needed to know what you were getting into. Thanks for listening."

Later, as they all pitched in to tidy up, Ahmed stepped close to him in the kitchen. "I don't know if this move into Organized Crime will work out," he murmured, "but Marilyn is going places. She's going to find a ladder and start climbing. You just need to decide if you're going along for the ride."

He deposited a stack of plates on their shelf and said nothing. Much later in the night, as Marilyn was in the bathroom brushing her teeth, he thought it all over again.

A decision, Ahmed had called it. But it was so much deeper than that.

Chapter 35

A fine serendipity

Marilyn grabbed her toothbrush and overnight bag before Jackson woke up, slipped out the door and headed back towards Yaletown. She had a few hours to freshen up and relax before her shift.

She was thrilled at how the evening had gone. Well, maybe not thrilled, but cautiously optimistic. Jackson had taken 'the talk' like a champ. Which meant he hadn't melted down or run screaming into the night. On the contrary, they'd gone back to his place and romped into the wee hours. She smiled at the memory.

Of course, Jackson hadn't gone into the evening totally cold. As he'd so aptly pointed out, their warnings of possible danger were, if anything, too little and too late.

Now she just had to wait.

She glanced over at the passenger seat as she pulled into her highrise's underground parking. The overnight bag slumped there. It was saggy from overuse. Her silly backup toothbrush was inside under the rumpled tuxedo shirt, still damp and no doubt picking up lint. She sighed, frosting the windshield with a moment's fog. Their relationship would evolve past this point sooner or later. Sooner, actually. Because, as she well knew, she was shit at waiting.

After a hot shower she headed out for a quick walk down Hamilton Street. She had time for a coffee and biscotti before work, and her favourite café was owned by an Italian couple who knew how to do both right. Three minutes at a fast march took her to the small tables outside the Cafe Burrata.

Branislav Zupan sat at one of the sidewalk tables, fork in hand, a plate of tiramisu and an espresso cup on the table in front of him. He saw her, lifted his other hand in a wave, then lowered it to gesture at the chair opposite.

She stopped dead in the middle of the sidewalk five steps from the cafe. The Uncle's lips spread into a grin, which broke into a laugh as she felt someone bump into her from behind. A teenager, huge headphones on his ears and eyes glued to the screen in his hand, mumbled an apology and skirted past her. The Uncle gave a good-natured shake of the head, repeated his welcome gesture, and added a pointed finger at the tiramisu.

It was barely past eight o'clock. Zupan was shaved, combed, dressed in a pressed shirt and trousers with a whip-thin tie and a tailored blazer under his autumn jacket. He was having coffee a block from her house. An accidental meeting? Or something else? Her curiosity warred with her survival instincts and her feet stayed still for another second.

He waved at the tiramisu again. She walked over, pulled out the second chair and sat down. No one else had braved the October morning chill to sit outside. They were alone.

Zupan waved his hand in the air and an older gentleman sporting an apron around his midsection opened the door to the cafe. "What will you have?" Zupan asked her. "Allow me to treat you."

"They know what I drink," she said.

"Ah, a regular! You have good taste in cafes." He turned to the waiting server. "Her usual, Dominic. Plus another tiramisu." The server—who Marilyn knew was the father of one of the owners— nodded once and went back inside.

"You're up early," she started things off.

He sighed, and some of the welcoming smile fell away. "Up

very late, in fact. I am having trouble sleeping. You may have heard, we've recently suffered some deaths in the family. It weighs on me."

Dominic eased open the cafe door, placed a dish of cake, a steaming cappuccino and a chocolate-dipped biscotti in front of her, actually bowed to the Uncle, and headed back inside. "I heard something about it. My condolences for your loss." She paused, and added, "I'm only glad there weren't more deaths that day."

"Yes." No other mention of his men drawing their weapons on her boyfriend. He took a bite of tiramisu, chased it with espresso, and changed the subject. "I am happy we met, Officer Mathers. A fine serendipity. I was going to call you this morning."

A smirk came to her face and she let it show. "Oh, yeah. A wonderful coincidence, to be sure. What did you want to talk about?" The tiramisu was excellent, rich and creamy with soft mascarpone, and she got busy with her fork. A decadent way to start the day.

"To fulfill our agreement. To begin the mutual sharing of occasional tidbits." His smile was gone now. This close, across the tiny table and the two blocks of cake, she could count the grey hairs in his eyebrows. See the faint tracks left by his morning razor. He had a face of old leather; not scuffed and cracked like a too-old shoe, but more like a steamer trunk that had seen too many long voyages. It had cracks, certainly, but much of it was worn smooth. Still thick, however, and tough as elephant hide.

Now that the veneer of friendliness had fallen away she could see the truer emotions underneath. The ones that had given his face its hard miles. Branislav Zupan was devastatingly sad, all the way to his bones. Of course he was, she reflected, he'd lost much of his power and family the year before and three more in the past week. But also, right there in equal measure, he was furious. She saw it in the set of his eyes, heard it behind his voice. That also made sense. The Uncle was a gang leader, used to being an apex predator, and now he was bloodied and backed into a corner. Nothing was more dangerous.

She sipped her latte, leaned over the table and peered, faintly amazed at her own bravado. She pushed in until her nose was inches away from his. He sat still and let her. She held his gaze for two long seconds, staring into the very back of those black eyes, and in the last instant she saw the hidden emotion, the deepest one. A tiny flicker in the muscles of his lower eyelid, at the same moment as his eyes danced away and came back.

Branislav Zupan was sad, sure. He was angry. He was also desperate. Thoroughly, existentially afraid. She sat back and took another drink.

The Uncle sipped his espresso. "I think, at last, we see each other, Officer Mathers. This is good. We should have honesty between us."

She took another bite. "Marilyn. You called our—agreement—a mutual sharing. You wanted to see me today. I don't have anything I can tell you that you don't already know. Do you have something for me?"

He pulled a folded piece of paper out of his blazer's breast pocket. It had been torn from a larger sheet, one of cream-colored paper made from linen. "You have a good memory, I assume," he said, and unfolded the paper on the table. Two of his fingers anchored the top corners.

An address, printed out in Times New Roman, large enough to easily read. She ran through the maps in her head and had it in a moment. A location on the north shore of Mitchell Island, a large chunk of flat sand in the north arm of the Fraser River on the boundary between Vancouver and Richmond. Mitchell Island had dead car scrapyards, a jumble of small, dirty industries that weren't welcome in the city proper, and not much else.

The paper also showed a time: 2:30 a.m.

"What day?"

"This one. Tonight."

"Let me see." She reached for the paper, casual as could be, but he slipped it back and made it disappear. She grinned, shrugged. "Had to try."

"Of course." The Uncle put an elbow on the table, which angled his face away from the sidewalk, and lowered his voice. Ever the careful one, she thought. "At this time, this location, a small barge full of derelict delivery trucks will be pushed upriver to a dock and moored for the night. The trucks will be cube vans, mangled and rusted. Useless for anything but scrap. Empty. Except for one."

"What will be inside?"

He told her. He told her how much, and her eyebrows flew up. His own brows flicked into the ghost of a frown and she got her face under control. Still, her pulse had quickened. That much product could supply the streets for a month.

This was what she'd wanted. To really help, not one person at a time but in heaping handfuls.

"How did you get—wait, I don't want to know, do I?" The Uncle remained impassive. She thought it over. "I've no idea if we can action this, it's not my call. I'll send it up the chain. But," she leaned back and polished off the last of her cake, "like I said, I don't have anything for you."

He took his elbow off the table and sat back as well. Put his smile back on, and the predator was again concealed behind its camouflage of faded elegance. He shrugged and lifted a palm. "A show of goodwill," he said. "To, as you say, get the ball rolling."

She laughed. "Branislav, I thought you said there'd be honesty between us. You're giving me this. It'll help the department, help the city. Maybe even my career, who knows. But if this comes off, then it will help you, too. Right? One action, and we both benefit."

This time his smile was genuine, and wide. "Yes, we understand each other very well. I think we shall do good work together, Marilyn." He rose to leave.

She held out a palm to stop him. Gestured, as he had, to take his seat again. He did, and she leaned forward until her nose was once more inches from his.

"Thanks. I hope this works out. But, Branislav, the next time you want to chat, invite me to a cafe that isn't right on my fucking doorstep. I can think of a few down by your place that should work just fine."

She saw the expressions flow across his features. The feigned surprise, the mild outrage at being told what to do, the hurt feelings at the very thought that he would intrude on her privacy. But he settled for honesty, and the predator under the surface crinkled the corners of his eyes.

"Of course," he said. "If you will forgive me, I have funerals to arrange. Enjoy the rest of your coffee, Dominic has put it on my bill. Happy hunting tonight."

He rose and walked up the sidewalk, presumably to where a car was waiting down a side street. Two dozen people passed by him in the full of the morning rush, and not one of them registered the old man strolling against the current as anything worthy of their attention. Not one of them had a cop's eyes.

She finished her coffee, sent Ahmed and Sergeant Dilly a text with the new intel, and headed back to her place to get ready for work.

Several passersby did notice her. Probably because of the wall to wall grin.

Chapter 36

Half a hundred men

"Position those two next to the dark grey warehouse. Remind them to face out." Shaheen pointed down off the rooftop at a smudge of darkness beside a structure to the left of the dock and listened as his lieutenant mumbled the command into a tiny radio. Two shapes flowed out of one shadow and into the deeper dark beside the warehouse, filling a hole in the protective net that guarded the night's delivery. Trained by Shaheen himself, they moved as if part of the night.

He took one more slow look around, crabwalking below the flat rooftop's parapet from one side of the roof to the other, then said, "Good. Bring them in."

Two dark vans, both electric, backed up close to the dock, soundless except for their tires on the gravel. Even that crunching was muffled by the hum of Vancouver to the north and Richmond to the south, and the louder buzz of traffic on the Knight Street Bridge that arched high above them between the two cities. The vans stopped. From the darkness of the river Shaheen heard one more sound: the slow, rhythmic coughing of a harbour tug pushing a barge.

The rocks of the rooftop pricked his knees. His scar was giving him hell, pulling and itching like it remembered the fire that had birthed it. He took the irritations and folded them into the sharp edge of his awareness.

He did not, strictly speaking, need to be here tonight. The

shipment was large but not exceptional. His teams could handle the transfer. The New Canadians used Mitchell Island to land the shipment every couple of months, they knew the territory. But he had started to notice something disturbing since he'd come to this cold, wet city and finished the initial fun of conquering the locals. His life had fallen into a routine—running the club, overseeing distribution, placing the right people in the right positions, reporting to his superiors.

He'd become a bureaucrat. And he was getting bored. He needed to get out more.

The chugging got louder. A large, boxy shape emerged from the river's darkness. From his elevated vantage he could see the jumble of wrecks on the barge, and the one slightly less-damaged truck between them. The tug's high bow was wedged into a tug-shaped notch at the stern of the barge. Its engine slowed, the chugging less insistent. The barge drifted in close to the dock, not in any kind of a hurry at all. Three of his men grabbed the lines thrown by three more on the deck of the barge.

Shaheen crawled closer to the edge of the parapet to the corner of the roof where he could see the widest view of the dark streets.

The tug fell quiet. For a long minute, nothing happened. He nodded in satisfaction. His men remembered the training he'd given them. Before exposing your position, wait. Smell the night. Listen. Let your enemy make the first mistake.

After the minute had passed, six more men flowed out of the darkness and formed a line from the barge to the waiting vans. The men on the barge opened the back of the truck and began unloading the cargo.

Lights! A blazing white beam shot down at them from the Knight Street Bridge, illuminating the dock, the men, and all the nearby buildings. More light caught them from the other side of the river, so intense that Shaheen imagined he could feel its heat.

The roof he was on lit up with the edges of both beams, dazzling his eyes.

Voices! Loudspeakers boomed from the island, the bridge, the water itself, shouting orders to stand down and surrender. Under the crackling words Shaheen heard the sound of running boots. Half a hundred men burst from buildings all around the dock, black armor replacing the banished blackness of night, adding their own shouts to the overwhelming din.

A galvanic lance of jubilant excitement electrified his cells. At last! A real battle, enemies everywhere, the darkness alive with energy. He leaned over the edge of the parapet to see what his men would do.

Most of them remembered their training. The rearguard, surprised by the sudden appearance of the shock troops, were taken and disarmed in the first moment. He saw one man next to the dock dive into the murky waters of the Fraser River, saving himself at the expense of his team. The rest of them, after the shock of the first moment, scattered into cover and fired. His nerves practically sang as the night glittered with crackling gunfire.

The police retreated around the corners of their buildings and shot back. One of his men, thinking tactically, unleashed a long, controlled burst of automatic fire into the night and the light across the river flicked out with a shattering of glass. He saw one of his men fall, then two black-helmeted police.

The shipment was lost. His men would find their own way home, or not. "Time to go," he told his lieutenant.

They had broken all three door locks between the road and the wedge of the rooftop stairwell in case they needed to leave quickly. Shaheen heard boots on the stairs coming up. His fast exit meant their fast entry.

He felt the lion's grin take over his face as he swept his lieutenant behind him, crouched down behind the door and pulled his dagger. A holstered pistol weighed down the back of his belt, but he wanted this first one to be personal. The leather-wrapped grip nestled into his hand as the metal door swung away with a crash.

A black-suited figure jumped onto the roof and sideways to the left, rifle panning across the open expanse as the man behind him pushed forward to go right. The barrel of the gun swept right over Shaheen's head. He rose, grasped the man's weapon with his right hand and used it to pull the cop further onto the roof, off balance. He twisted the barrel. The gun went off past his ear with a tremendous crack as he broke the man's finger with the trigger guard. The cop yelled, and the rifle sailed away across the rooftop.

On the other side of the doorway he heard a pistol bark, saw the second policeman sink.

His opponent recovered from the loss of his weapon with commendable speed, ramming his back against the wall of the tiny shack and pulling a pistol. Shaheen batted it to the side with his free hand and lifted the dagger for a high plunge.

A hard boot caught his shin. Bright sparkles of pain pulled a shout from his throat as the cop pressed the advantage and swung with his other hand, grazing Shaheen's cheek with an armored glove. Shaheen danced back and parried with the knife. The cop let out his own curse as the tip of the blade scraped along his forearm.

They paused for a microscopic fragment of time, half an armlength apart, and Shaheen saw his opponent's eyes. They were hazel, and hard, overshot with thick brows and couched in rough folds of skin. A seasoned soldier, confident and determined. The cop saw him, too, and whatever he saw in Shaheen's face produced no bolt of fear or doubt in him.

Marvellous. The pause expired. The cop jerked his gun around for a point-blank shot from the hip. Shaheen admired the boldness of the move as the gun fired, close enough for the heat to scorch his belly. He twisted sideways, thrust his dagger up under the man's chin and deep into the helmeted head. A fast pull jerked the blade free. The man was dead before he fell to the rooftop stones.

His lieutenant stood in the doorway. "Our path is clear, but not for long. We need to go now." He reached forward and shoved his finger through a hole in Shaheen's jacket, blackened and still smoking. "You take too many chances, Shaheen."

Shaheen laughed as they raced down the stairs. "Perhaps. But it was worth it." His dagger was back in its sheath, gun now in his hand. The fun was over. Now he had to survive the night.

The dark green Jeep he'd chosen as his ride, parked two blocks away in an auto graveyard, would not get them past the Knight Street Bridge blockade. They turned into the shadows between buildings and flowed along the ragged shoreline, headed for the alternate departure plan. Ten minutes later they were leaving Mitchell Island behind them underneath the deck of a second harbour tug.

Shaheen made himself comfortable on a roll of wrist-thick rope, kept his feet out of the oily water beneath it, and considered the night's events. His lieutenant perched on a wooden crate, face glum.

"The shipment is lost," he said in Farsi.

"Obviously," replied Shaheen.

"So are the men. Killed or taken."

"Either way, they won't talk. Their families will be compensated and the principals will send us more."

"Bit of a setback for our operations. The principals won't like your report."

"Naturally. I expect I shall receive a lecture."

That brought a laugh out of both of them, a welcome vent for the tension. Afterwards, the lieutenant's face settled into a scowl. "So tell me, then. Why have you been grinning like a fiend since the first shot?"

Shaheen slapped his lieutenant on the knee. "Because, my friend, it means I have work to do. Real work, not managing people and filling out spreadsheets. Think about it. Why were the police there tonight? They knew the exact place, the right time. They were prepared, which means they knew in advance."

The big man shrugged, his gloom deepening. "It means we have a leaky ship. Somebody talked."

"Yes!" Shaheen would almost be embarrassed at his own excitement, if he had any familiarity with embarrassment. "None of our crew would be stupid enough to talk willingly. So tell me. Who might have talked unwillingly?"

The lieutenant shifted on his wooden crate and considered. "The maintenance man," he said after a minute. "We have not heard from him in two days." Another moment, and he added, "He was at that research place watching the Uncle's man. The Croats must have discovered him."

"And instead of returning him to us piecemeal, the Uncle leveraged his advantage. That, my friend, is the mark of a general."

"And he gave the shipment to the law?" He waved a hand back at the receding island. "That's over a million dollars of product in the police lockup. Pah! It makes no sense."

Shaheen laughed. "A million is not what it used to be. And think of what he bought with it. His own army is in splinters, so he used someone else's! A brilliant move."

His lieutenant picked up a length of rope and started unraveling it. "So what now?"

"We remember the training," Shaheen said. "We wait. Watch the shadows, smell the night. Our eyes on the lab are gone, but we are watching the massage therapist and the Uncle. We stay close to our enemy and let him make the first mistake."

Chapter 37

THE VERY WORST OF CRUELTIES

The machine shop on Pandora Street had not been well maintained by the company that went bankrupt and abandoned it. Grime covered the windows with a brownish, opaque smear. Half the lights over the long, low workbenches were broken. Tools lay where they'd been dropped. An engine block hung from a chain hoist, its crankshaft clamped in a vise nearby. The stale air inside the long, low building reeked of oil and burned metal.

Branislav had instructed his people to leave it that way. Less incentive for any trespassers to walk across the greasy concrete and open the basement door. He maneuvered past a pile of steel shavings next to a derelict lathe and down the murky stairwell.

The basement was as large as the upstairs but held nothing. Clean, white-painted drywall and a swept concrete floor expanded the room, making the regular lines of boxed-in support columns seem to march on forever. All the ceiling lights worked.

The hunched figure strapped to the room's single chair had a splendid view of the vast, empty space his life choices had led him to.

A table next to the chair held various implements borrowed from upstairs. Pretty much the list Franko had given him, Branislav observed with a pang of grief. Pincers. Saws. Pliers. A few tools he didn't recognize, but which looked more than adequate for their new purpose.

The chair itself was bolted to the floor over top of a drain. The concrete had been rinsed in advance of his arrival. A thin stain of pink still ringed the grate.

Markovic leaned against the wall next to the bottom of the stairs, waiting. Branislav nodded to him. "Uncle," he said by way of greeting.

Marko appeared relaxed. Unhurried and unbothered by the work he had done. They'd used this room numerous times over the years and Branislav had always secretly marvelled at his friend's comfort with this aspect of the job. Like it was just another task.

"It was beautiful," he told Markovic in Croatian. "The shipment was where he said it was, at the right time. The police gave them a fine welcome. The police suffered a few losses, which will only make them more determined." He paused, gave Markovic a clap on the shoulder. "Two of their arrest team died on a rooftop overlooking the dock. One of them by a long, thin blade." He mimed a thrust up under the jaw.

"Shaheen was there," Marko said. "Overseeing the delivery. He got away." He pushed himself off the wall. "Still. The spy told us the truth. That deserves some consideration."

The figure on the chair stirred, the first sign of life Branislav had seen from him. A meatless, older Filipino man, still in his loose-hanging Blast Dynamics work coveralls, he lifted his damp mop of black hair that was shot with streaks of grey and turned his face to them. Or, to where he thought they must be. His swollen eyes weren't nearly as useful as they'd been the day before.

Hope, thought Branislav. Even in the blackest of days, it so easily sprang to life. Hope could be a man's salvation. Or sometimes the very worst of cruelties, a betrayal from one's own heart.

The custodian mumbled something. Markovic leaned down, close to the Blast Dynamics logo on the shoulder of the ruined uniform, and asked him to repeat it. Another mumble, louder. "Truth," he managed.

"Yes, that's right," Branislav said. "Marko here promised you something if you spoke the truth, didn't he? What was it?"

Another mumble. The man tried again, making an effort to lift his shoulders, regain a shred of power. "Free."

"Of course." He thought it over for a moment. Then waved at Marko, who still hovered over the old man. Marko hesitated only a moment, his surprise getting the better of him, but his lieutenant was loyal beyond all else. Marko produced a knife. Ignoring the seated man's terrified flinch, he bent down and cut the straps that held feet and hands to the chair.

Branislav waited. Markovic stepped back and closed his knife. The seated man did nothing for a moment. Then he turned his reddened, pulped face to each of them. Then across the room, towards the staircase.

"Go on. We are done with you."

The custodian rose on unsteady legs, found his strength. He stepped clear of the chair and hobbled his way to the bottom of the stairs. Each step was stronger than the one before. Powered by his growing hope.

Branislav came up behind him. The man smelled terrible, a mix of sweat and blood and fear. He went to grasp the railing, discovered the sorry shape of his broken fingers, and took the first steps up. "Come on, I have other places to be." Branislav reached out and placed a helping palm on the back of the old Filipino's uniform.

His Blast Dynamics uniform. The man, with help from the hand, made it to the top of the staircase and into the darkness of the old machine shop. Light streaked through the dirty glass of the doorway to the outside. He stood a little taller at the sight, found the ability to walk a little faster.

"Of course," Branislav mused, still close behind him, "you did betray the New Canadians. You were stupid. Shaheen will not soon forget that. I have heard rumours of what he does to those he dislikes. Perhaps you will soon tell me if they are true." The maintenance man's steps faltered, but he continued towards the door. "Or perhaps not. Then again, you also spied on us. Told Shaheen as much of our plans as you could discover. Did you record phone calls? Listen at doors? Steal documents?" He tsked. "As if we would be so careless. But still."

He charged. The spy, hearing his footsteps, uttered a wordless cry and tried to run for the door. Branislav snatched a miniature sledgehammer off a cluttered workbench and threw it, catching the honourless sneak in the middle of the back and sending him sprawling. He charged forward, sweeping another tool off a rack as he caught up to the prone form.

"You worked for us, got paid by us, all so you could find our secrets." Branislav landed a knee in the center of the betrayer's back and felt the old energy flood through him, the determination and singlepointed fury that had won him this town. "You have no respect. None of you do. No manners." He lifted the tool high—a chain wrench, a heavy handle anchoring three feet of dark, brutal links—and brought it down across the man's head.

"No dignity." It rose and fell again.

"No ethic." Smack. "No culture. No. Decorum."

He dropped the wrench. His arm was tired, and the tool's work was done. The man had not made it to the door, but he'd very much left the building.

Markovic stood to one side. "Uncle," he said, and held out a towel he'd dredged up from somewhere. As Branislav wiped the custodian off his hands Marko asked, "Shall I deliver the body?"

He huffed. "To serve as what? A warning? A shock? They get no warning, and they would not be shocked. Make it disappear. Leave them guessing. Animals that they are, they'll probably think we cooked and ate him."

Markovic pulled a dusty tarp off an old bandsaw and got to work. He glanced up as he laid it next to the cleaner's body. "What do we do now?"

"The hardest thing," Branislav answered, checking his fingernails for blood. "We wait. Tomorrow the product will launch. The idiots will get their immortality and we shall have their cash. Enough to crush the New Canadians and drive them back into the sea. Until then, we wait. We know where the masseur goes. We shall make sure he stays quiet, and we will stay quiet ourselves. Do nothing to disturb what is already in motion."

Marko rolled the body onto the tarp. "Yes, Uncle," he said, and folded the heavy canvas over to conceal the mess.

Chapter 38

THE SOONER HE KILLED IT THE LESS IT WOULD HURT

Jackson readjusted the anatomy texts on his bookshelf and wondered if he should take an extra pill today. Sighed, decided against it. He had clients to see and didn't want to be messing with his meds. He moved on to the plants by the window.

His condition had been giving him hell for two days now, ever since the dinner at Ahmed and Gordon's. No great mystery why; even a waffling, indecisive, uncommitted lunkhead like him could figure it out. The evening's message had been crystal clear. Marilyn was going places. He could either get on board the train, or get the hell off. The really fun part: Marilyn's train would be moving fast, through dangerous territory.

So what was he waiting for? He loved Marilyn, that much was clear. Her energy and physicality were a perfect match for his. They had great fun in bed, and loved talking with each other, sometimes long into the night. Best of all, Marilyn knew about his condition. More than anybody else, Charles included. She took it in stride as part of the overall Jackson Teague package. Even more, she'd shown him how to use the patterns in new ways, even have fun with them. She'd changed his relationship with himself.

He flicked some dust off the ficus, tearing a leaf. His reluctance was no great puzzle, really. He was waiting for the emotional soap opera in his head to calm down and make room for common sense.

Jackson knew how these things went. He'd seen it plenty. Read about it in countless books. He and Marilyn were in the honeymoon phase of their relationship. They could see no wrong in each other. They glossed over any irritations and insufficiencies with the raw heat of new love. It wouldn't last. It never did, not with anyone, ever, in all of history. And once the glow faded Marilyn would see him for what he was.

Damaged goods. A weird, wiry kid who'd spent time in a psych ward for an illness he still had. Probably always would. A crazy young man she'd come really close to locking up for his own good. If they stayed together long enough, no doubt they'd face that moment again.

Best not. Ahmed and Gordon were right. His dalliance with Marilyn was living on borrowed time, and the sooner he killed it the less it would hurt.

The hallway flared into his vision. An angry, red glimmer spiked his eyes where the line of the pencil next to its pad of paper on the little shelf wasn't right. Not at all. He left the plants to go fix it.

A sweet, trilling notification from his cell phone pulled him back into the living room. Marilyn's message tone, which he'd set up in a moment of optimism and hope. Hearing it now, with the dismal thoughts running through his head, welled up a twinned emotion of delight and dread. As they fought for dominance, he tapped the screen awake.

It wasn't a text. She'd sent him a photo, an image from her computer screen zoomed in on a headshot from some kind of identity document. Maybe a passport photo, or a security badge.

It was a grainy message of a scan of a photo, but still clear enough. Staring back at him, looking considerably healthier than the last time they'd met, was the man from the Seabus.

"His name is Dr. Luca Sachs," Marilyn said, both to Jackson on the phone and Ahmed, who stood over her shoulder. "I was flipping through the BOLO files and ran across his sheet. He looked like the man you'd described, so ... are you sure? How sure?"

She tried to keep the excitement out of her voice and quell the sound of her pulse thumping through her ears. "It's him," Jackson was saying, "clear as day. Who is he, does it say?"

Marilyn glanced up at Ahmed, who nodded assent. "He's seriously bad news. Like, Nazi prison doctor bad. He's got all sorts of degrees and doctorates, some kind of expert in biosciences and chemistry. He's worked all over the world, with major pharmaceutical firms and companies I've never heard of. Interpol wants him, Jackson. He's infamous for skipping steps in his clinical trials. He tests things on people long before they're ready. They say he's responsible for hundreds of really nasty deaths. Interpol has him on all the no-fly lists. He was last seen," she scrolled down the long bulletin, "in Munich, a couple of years ago. There's no way he should be on this side of the pond."

Jackson had that eager edge in his voice that she loved, which was good. He'd sounded depressed when he first answered. "That's him! And it fits perfectly with Blast Dynamics, the implants, the supposed evidence I saw, all of it. Marilyn, the countdown I saw on the Ponce de Leon's website? It ends tomorrow. So is this enough to get the department's attention? What can you guys do about this?"

She was already rising from her seat. "Stand by. I mean that, Jackson, stay in your place. Sit on your hands if you have to. Ahmed and I are running this up to the brass right now."

"It's a workday. I was about to head out the door."

"Cancel your morning. I'm saying this as a cop, all right? We'll see about the afternoon."

She closed the call. Ahmed was right beside her. "Let's go," she said, and led the way to Sergeant Dilly's office.

Delores called up the Inspector as soon as Marilyn said 'Interpol's Most Wanted.' The moment she mentioned Jackson's name, Delores also messaged Jim Rockford to join. She spent the five minutes while they waited reaming out both Marilyn and Ahmed for not following procedure and presenting Jackson with a photo six-pack.

Once everyone was present Marilyn sketched out a condensed version of the case—the man on the Seabus, the handoff which they'd delivered to Blast Dynamics, Jackson's discovery of the Ponce de Leon, the impending deadline.

"How does all this square with the gang interest?" Delores asked.

Rockford picked it up. "Not sure of the specifics, but the motivation is easy. An immortality pill? Even if it's snake oil and dreams, it could be worth millions. If there's actually something to it ... well, it could be the most lucrative drug launch in history. Hell, I'd be interested."

That got a moment's silence from the room. Then Delores said, "Get your man in here. We'll put a team together while we wait. Time for Blast Dynamics to get a high colonic."

Jackson met Marilyn at the entrance to 2120 Cambie. She looked even more excited than him, so full of energy she practically sparked. "They want to see you," was all she said. No boardroom this time; she took him directly to Sergeant Dilly's office, a glassed-in square around the corner from Marilyn and Ahmed's desks.

Rockford was there. Dilly's wall-mounted monitor showed five screens. Patrol Section Inspector Fromme was on the call, as well as the Deputy Chief Constable. Another man, decked out in the

VPD's tactical uniform and built like a compact steel wall, was introduced as ERT Inspector Takeda. The Interpol bulletin on Dr. Sachs graced one corner. A judge occupied the square next to the bulletin, a serious-faced woman seated in a plush, book-lined office.

The interview took all of five minutes. Jackson got the impression it was mainly for the record. He confirmed that Sachs was the man on the Seabus, told the story of the handoff, gave a precis of their visit to Blast Dynamics, and detail on the Ponce de Leon research he'd seen. He was about to go into the Uncle's interest when Takeda raised his hand and stopped him.

"Enough?" he asked the judge.

"Yes. Warrant granted." The woman signed something on her desk, then left the screen. Takeda looked around the room. Sergeant Dilly said yes, and after a moment's consideration the DCC agreed as well.

"Good," Takeda replied, reaching for his keyboard to leave the call. "Five minutes."

"Threat level low?" Dilly asked.

Takeda paused. "You mean him? Yeah, sure." Then he was gone.

Dilly turned to Jackson. "You're with Constable Mathers," she said. "Stay back, stay quiet, and answer questions."

"Uh, ma'am? Constable Mathers already told me to rebook my morning clients, but I have afternoon ones, too. I, um, really need the work."

Dilly glanced at a wall clock. "You're deeply involved in this, but you're not under suspicion at the moment. Please come with us, at least until noon, in case you see something we don't. I'll see if we can release you after that."

He agreed. Marilyn and Ahmed hustled him out of the office, swung by their desks for jackets, and took him down to a line of waiting cruisers in the basement parkade. "Watch your head,

Freckles," Marilyn quipped as she opened the rear door for him and placed a hand on his curls. He swallowed a visceral shot of residual anxiety as he slid into the back seat.

Five police cars and a black van paraded through East Vancouver to the border with Burnaby and down the Kootenay Street dead end, no lights or sirens but not wasting any time about it. Three blocks from Blast Dynamics they picked up another few cars—a forensics team from the VPD's investigations building close by.

What have I got myself into, Jackson thought. He'd never wanted any of this, right from the start. He should have dropped the package in the mail and been done with it.

The first two cruisers bracketed the block as the van pulled up outside the front of the long, unassuming building. Ahmed stopped by the funky park bench. The van's doors flew open and Jackson saw an actual freakin' SWAT team storm the building, several to the front door and more to either side.

Rockford, Dilly and Takeda did the knock. The conversation through the intercom took about ten seconds, with a few more for the warrant to be waved in front of the camera. Jackson imagined Kelly handling it with cool efficiency. Then they were in. The doors were propped open and a swarm of uniforms took over Blast Dynamics.

"Stay close," Marilyn murmured to Jackson as they went inside. "I'm not kidding. Say nothing, touch nothing, and don't wander."

"Wouldn't dream of it." She gave him something between a scowl and a smirk. Then their attention was pulled elsewhere as loud shouting filled the air.

Harrowman was yelling at the two sergeants, with Dunn glowering at them over his shoulder. "We haven't done anything! This is delicate work, proprietary intellectual property! If you come barging in here now, disturbing my employees, taking files, contaminating the lab, you'll set us back weeks. Months! My investors ..." And on, in an endless stream of red-faced outrage. Dunn stood in front of the door to the Compound and Archive Lab, looking like he'd stop them by sheer bulk.

Sergeant Dilly tried to get a word in edgewise while Takeda and a squad of cops behind him stood and listened. After a minute, with Harrowman not even showing signs of a pause for breath, Takeda slapped the warrant on his chest and pushed Dunn out of the way. Police entered all three labs simultaneously. Jackson heard more of them rummaging around on the second floor.

Ahmed joined the search. Marilyn held Jackson back by the front door reception area until Dilly stuck her head out of Harrowman's office and waved them up the stairs.

Jonathan Harrowman was back behind his desk, seated now, with Harold Dunn in another chair beside him. A patrolman had pulled in more seats for Dilly and Rockford. Marilyn and Jackson remained standing.

"You two have quite the colourful history," Rockford was saying in his slow, cool voice. Not accusing, just voicing an observation. Dunn's thunderstorm scowl deepened and Harrowman beeted up.

"Ancient history and you know it. A lesson learned. I've already told you, there is nothing wrong with our work here. Every single aspect of our research is documented, approved, by the fucking book."

"Then why'd you hire Sachs?" Rockford looked puzzled.

"I don't know that name."

Rockford gestured, and Sergeant Dilly threw a printout of Dr. Luca Sachs' wanted poster onto the desk. Harrowman and Dunn both leaned in.

Jonathan Harrowman glanced at the paper, slapped it with the back of a hand and sat back up. "Never saw him before in my life."

Every part of him, from the expression on his face to the set of his shoulders to the casual disdain in his movements, rang true.

Harold Dunn's thick, rugged face, red with anger, dropped ten shades to ashen shock. He jerked back upright hard enough for his chair to wheel back from the desk.

"All right, you never saw him before." Rockford tilted his head over towards Dunn. "Anything to add?"

Dunn shook his head. "I've never met him, either. I have heard of Dr. Sachs. Believe me, he's the last person we would ever allow into our facility."

"Harold Radoslav Dunnai," Rockford read from a notebook. "Great name. Where's it from, Croatia?"

"Hungary," Dunn growled.

"Hmm. Why change it?"

"I hate Hungary."

Dilly pitched in. "You changed it right after you and Mr. Harrowman, here, were fired for—what was it?—taking shortcuts."

Jackson stared hard. Dunn had closed in on himself. His face was a slammed door, shoulders thrumming an electric green with tension. His hands were below the desk, but he saw the man's forearms ripple with the tension of clenched fists. Barely-visible rays of potential movement lifted off him in every direction. Dunn was poised to run the moment an opportunity presented itself.

Chapter 39

It'll be a double

The cops were finally gone, their raping and pillaging satisfied for the day. He yanked another sample out from the collection tray, disposed of the candidate and placed the empty glassware into the autoclave for sterilization. The Optimization Lab, along with all the work in it, was hopelessly contaminated. The clean room was so far from clean it might as well be a back alley behind Hastings Street. The entire facility stank of law enforcement.

He flushed another, then another, pausing between each for the assistant to record them in a notebook. Even the computer files had been compromised by the raid. They were reduced to writing things down by hand.

It was all moot, of course. His own work at the other lab was about to make everything here obsolete. But even in the midst of his barely-containable excitement at the pending launch, he was still furious at the invasion. The police raid on Blast Dynamics had been a personal affront to all of them.

"That's the last from this rack," he told the lab assistant doing the recording. "I'm taking a break. Go get yourself a coffee or something." He stomped out of the clean room, fuming at the door hanging open. None of them had bothered with the white Tyvek suits. The rest of the group in the main lab took one look at his face and cleared a path.

He went out front, across the grass to the springy fascia bench under the chestnut tree. Nobody else was around; the police had left at noon, satisfied with their destruction and temporarily out of questions. After another scan of the area to make sure, he pulled out his phone.

The massage boy. He'd been there, in the middle of it all, right from the first day of the trouble. The police had held him like a trump card this morning, in the background but in plain sight while they asked their probing questions, as if to say, look what we have. He'd had to restrain himself from plunging a scalpel into the boy's neck the moment the redhead slid through the front door.

Now they were gone, except for two uniforms stationed in the lobby and a cop car down the street. Teague was gone, too. He'd heard the rat talking about clients, and work, and heard one of the cops tell him to go. With her thanks, of all the insulting things to add.

Well. He knew where Jackson Teague was headed. He owned the boy's online calendar, since Johnnie had installed the snooper on his laptop. He was off to see the tech bro. Who also knew more than was strictly good for him.

He punched in the number. It was answered on the first ring with silence. "I have another ambulance job for you. It has to be this afternoon. And it'll be a double."

After he closed the call he realized that making it was getting easier. He pulled up the next number. This call was getting easier, too. He'd tell the Uncle what was going on. It was a courtesy. Also, for the moment, still the smart thing to do.

Chapter 40

CHAIWALLA

Jackson shook his head as he hustled his massage table down to the car. The cops, with Marilyn front and center, had torn Blast Dynamics apart. All their resources were bent on finding the Seabus man, Dr. Sachs, and revealing what he'd been doing in this country. They believed Jackson, at last. Sort of.

They'd taken their sweet time about it. And now that they were moving, they'd focused on the wrong target. Sachs was most likely gone; Jackson had seen the men who'd taken him and was pretty certain about what had happened next. The real issue—the real emergency—was the countdown. The implants, already at clinics around the world. Waiting for tomorrow.

He sighed as he pointed the car toward Abe Tremblay's tech heaven of a condo. He'd done his best. Much more than he was comfortable with. The police were welcome to take it from here. Now he needed to focus on his own work.

Abe greeted him as the elevator doors opened onto the cavernous living room, bouncing on the balls of his feet. "Jackson, my man! Great to see you, come on in. It's a beautiful day, freakin' fantastic." He clapped Jackson on the shoulder and speedwalked over to the kitchen for a drink of some violently green concoction directly from the blender.

It was like being welcomed home by a puppy, Jackson thought. The man had energy bursting out of him. The only thing missing was the sloppy licks, for which he was mightily grateful.

Abe's walk to the kitchen set off a red flag in Jackson's vision. His stride was loose and freeflowing. Jackson could attribute it to the good massage work of a few days before, but his professional sense overruled his ego. Two sessions couldn't produce what he was seeing. Abe's walk kind of resembled the rolling, supple gait he'd seen in lifelong yoga practitioners. But not quite. It was that, and somehow more.

The session began as usual. "Nothing to report, massage wizard. I'm fit as a fiddle, better than ever. I mean, wow! It's like I'm a kid again. I'm a hundred percent plus." Abe hopped up on the table and said into the face cradle, "I'm really gonna like the next hundred years." Jackson threw the top sheet over him and began with the right leg.

Abe's skin was as remarkable as before. Smooth and soft, pliable, some of the finest he'd ever encountered. His hands felt clearly down into the structures beneath. The muscles inside their fascial sheaths moved smoothly and easily against each other, no restrictions at all as they narrowed down into tendons and attached onto the bones. Jackson could feel every striation of every muscle. The tissues of Abe's calf and thigh were so unbothered, so perfectly relaxed, his fingers could trace the bone structure underneath.

He finished Abe's right leg and moved on to the left, which felt the same. It should have been delightful. He should be rejoicing with his client over such sparkling good health. But he couldn't quite shake off the feeling that it wasn't right. It was somehow too much of a good thing.

He noticed a tiny dark spot on Abe's butt cheek, right where the ischial tuberosity—the sit bone to lay people—rested beneath the surface. He leaned in and looked it over. "You have a bit of a bruise here," he remarked, feeling over the spot.

"Really? Well, long hours in the captain's chair, you know. Sometimes I fold up my right leg, puts pressure on it." A reasonable explanation. Jackson moved down to Abe's thigh.

He made a long, firm swipe up Abe's iliotibial band, the broad tendon on the outside of the thigh that connected the gluteal muscles to the knee. Almost everyone had a tight ITB. On Abe it was just a thicker version of marvelous. As he made the powerful stroke with his left forearm, he placed his right hand below Abe's knee for support.

Abe's knee bent. Sideways. Only a little, but more than it ever should.

Frowning, Jackson placed a finger on the inside of the knee joint and stressed it again. The thin indent between tibia and femur turned into a gap. The ligament that should be holding the bones together felt more like a rubber band than a rope.

Abe hadn't squawked, hadn't even noticed. Struck by an idea, Jackson left the knee alone and carefully pinched up some of the skin over the back of Abe's hamstrings. The fold of skin lifted smoothly, and kept on lifting. One inch. Then two. When it became two and a half, he let it fall back.

"Have you ever heard of Ehlers-Danlos Syndrome?" he asked, moving on to Abe's back.

"Nope," came the answer through the facepiece. "Sounds like something that's either really good or really bad."

"No syndromes are good," Jackson replied. "This one can be inconvenient, or not very good at all. It's a disorder of fascia, your connective tissue. Ehlers-Danlos makes the fascia really loose. Tendons, ligaments, everything. If you've ever seen a circus contortionist, most likely you've seen Ehlers-Danlos at work."

"Cool."

Jackson worked along Abe's back from pelvis to neck, encountering more of that too-supple skin. Now that he knew what to feel for, the ribs and vertebrae felt springy, not quite fully connected. "Not cool, actually. Fascia is your body's scaffolding. If you have Ehlers-Danlos, you can dislocate your joints. Your skin gets fragile. Your internal organs don't have the support they need. Sure, you can bend. But it's a net loss, in a big way."

Abe was silent for a minute. "So what's the word, Jackson? You're the hands-on expert back there. You saying I have this thing?"

Jackson knew the professional thing to say. "I'm a therapist, not a doctor. All I can say is, you might want to get it checked out." Then he said what was really on his mind. "But no, Abe, I don't think you have Ehlers-Danlos Syndrome. I think you have an implant that's messing with your body."

Abe tensed up under Jackson's hands. "That's not reflected in the evidence, my man. Nowhere in the data, and not in the live environment experience. I'm A-1, Jackson, like I told you. Better than I've ever felt." His voice carried the clear emotional charge behind the message: don't go any farther. Jackson shut up and kept on working.

Abe turned over and kept his eyes closed as Jackson began on the front of his legs. More soft skin, more buttery flesh. He smoothed out the nonexistent knots, pushed Abe's circulation through the deepest reaches of his muscles, and worked in silence.

Abe's left quadriceps had an actual tight spot. He placed his forearm above the knee and gave Abe's thigh a deeper stroke. At last, a chance to do some real therapy.

The knot flattened out under his pressure. In its wake, as Jackson moved further up the leg, a fresh bruise formed. Damn, Jackson thought. What the hell? I wasn't working that hard.

"You doing some heat thing down there? My leg's warming up." Abe frowned and opened his eyes.

The bruise, fresh and bright red, spread. It went from dime-size, to a quarter, to the size of Jackson's palm. It shaded from crimson to burgundy. A low hump began to form as the welling blood pressed upwards against the skin.

"Holy fuck," Jackson muttered, and dashed across the room for his phone.

"What?" asked Abe, and sat up to look at his leg. "Holy fuck."

"Sometimes Ehlers-Danlos weakens the blood vessels," Jackson said, his fingers moving to dial 911. "That's the most not-good of all. Hello? We need an ambulance, now."

He sped through the 911 operator's questions as he raced for the bathroom. A first aid kit under Abe's sink delivered what he needed. Back at the massage table he wrapped a tensor bandage around Abe's thigh as tightly as he dared.

"Not feeling a hundred percent anymore," Abe said, the words slow. "Kinda woozy over here." He sank back onto the massage table, his face losing its colour. "Hey, you wanna throw some clothes at me? Sweats in the top drawer."

Jackson did as instructed. He ran to the big windows overlooking the street and saw the boxy, white ambulance, lights flashing, pull up in front of the building. "They're here," he called over his shoulder, "I'll go down and ... " His condition flashed a warning as the two ambulance attendants opened their doors and hustled to the back of their truck.

Shoulders wider than hips. Military precision to their movements as they yanked the gurney out from the back of the ambulance. Shimmering, steel-grey intent radiating off them. The same colour he'd seen at the Seabus terminal. The same colour as circling sharks.

"Oh shit. Wrong ambulance." His heart dropped through the floor as a bolt of primal fear watered his knees. The surge of adrenaline right behind it electrified his spine and got him moving.

"What you mean, wrong ambulance? Talk to me, Jackson."

"We're leaving. Now." He ran to the elevator door and pushed the call button, then grabbed Abe by the arm and pulled him bodily off the table. "You have access to the second floor?" He limped the game developer to the elevator and threw him in as the door opened.

"Uh, of course. Why?" Abe had caught Jackson's urgency, and punched in the code for the second floor as he talked.

"Those aren't paramedics. They're bad, and they're connected to this whole mess somehow." He prodded the implant in Abe's side. "We really don't want them to find us."

Abe caught Jackson's vibe. He came back from his slow fade to level his intense, piercing CEO gaze into Jackson's eyes. He stared, and whatever he saw made him believe. "Jackson, I need you to get solid with me. How much trouble are we in?"

"They're killers. Anyone who goes into that ambulance doesn't come out. Their job is to keep the truth about this," he jabbed the implant again, "from coming out. Clear enough?"

A look of incredulity, then determination, flashed over Abe's face before the sickly pallor returned. "Strange days, for sure. All right. And this?" Abe touched his thigh, which was now bulging around the bandage. "I really don't feel great."

"We'll take care of it. Let's dodge these guys first." The door opened onto another huge, columned expanse. This one was carpeted in industrial-strength burbur and decorated with a profusion of cubicles, open areas dotted with comfy chairs and gaming consoles, a full kitchen setup, and rows of glassed-off rooms down each side. The lights were off, the floor deserted. He pulled Abe onto the carpet. The elevator door closed, then went down. "Where can we hide?"

"One sec. Chaiwalla, here boy." A chest-high robot, resembling an oversize trash barrel with a flat top and too many flashing lights, whirred off its charging station and came over. Abe glanced back at Jackson as he kneeled down to the robot's height. "Don't you tell a soul about this. Chaiwalla, ID check."

The robot's screen face lit up. Abe held his eye close. A cheerful, young-male voice Jackson vaguely remembered from an old 1980's movie said, "ID confirmed, Abe Tremblay. I hear and I obey."

"Scan my friend here." The robot turned its face to Jackson. A moment later it spun back to Abe. "Okay. Whew. Chaiwalla, Westworld protocol. 'You can't play God without being acquainted with the Devil.' Confirm Westworld protocol."

"Westworld protocol confirmed." The robot's voice had deepened, roughened. Jackson realized, with a shock, it sounded a lot like Ed Harris.

"Protect," said Abe. He pointed at the elevator, which had begun to hum up from the ground floor. "The next people through that door are fuckin' hostile." He stood, balancing on his good leg. "Now we hide."

They ducked into an office that could only be Abe's, with a large, clear desk surrounded by an utter chaos of books, boxes and consoles. Jackson tucked behind a stack of boxes. Abe hunched down under the desk. They both peeked out as the elevator doors opened.

The two men, balanced and ready as they pushed the gurney into the room, flared steel grey to Jackson's eyes. A tiny hitch in their stance produced red flashes at their sides, the telltale accommodation of three pounds of metal under their jackets. Guns.

"Ambulance," called the man who'd spoken to Jackson at the Seabus terminal. "We're here to help."

Chaiwalla rolled up to them. A hatch opened in its head and a long stalk emerged, with two cylinders attached at the top like eyes. "Coffee? Tea? Chai?" it said, still using Ed Harris' voice.

The two men stared at it. "No. Go away." The one on the left waved a hand to shoo it off.

Chaiwalla said, "You first." The eyes on the stalk turned to look directly at the man on the left. Two red beams strobed the room into a scarlet brilliance that dazzled Jackson's sight. He heard a terrible scream, and when the dots cleared he saw one of the men kneeling, hands clamped to his face.

Smoke curled out between his fingers.

The man on the right was fast. Before the robot could refocus he had a pistol out from under his jacket, barrel elongated by a suppressor. It spit fire three times. Chaiwalla, its brains blown out the back of its hemispherical head, fell over and died.

Abe and Jackson pulled fully back under cover as the second man said over the first man's continued screams, "We know the elevator stopped here. Come on out, we just want to talk."

Jackson glanced over at Abe, making sure the verbose CEO wouldn't fall for it. He gasped at what he saw. Abe's leg strained at the sweatpants, swollen all out of proportion. Whatever vein had ruptured under his quadriceps, it wasn't sealing off.

So much blood in Abe's leg was so much less for everything else. As if to prove the point, the tech CEO gave him a long look from the footwell underneath the desk and passed out, crumpling the rest of the way to the floor.

His shoulder thumped into the wall of the footwell and nudged the desk sideways. Out in the main room the gurney creaked as the second man stepped out from behind it.

Jackson's hiding place wouldn't survive ten seconds if the ambulance guy searched the office, and the tower of cardboard boxes definitely wouldn't stop a hail of bullets. Frantic, he looked around. No other exit from the room. No windows that opened. No grenades. Just boxes, computer junk, and cables everywhere.

Cables. Red, blue, iridescent, and black. An insane, terrifying idea jumped into his mind. He peered at the closed door of the office, let his condition show him what was there. In a burst of desperation, he asked it to show him the geometry beneath his plan. He was amazed, and relieved, when a phosphorescent web of curves and angles overlaid the office door and showed him what to do.

He commando-crawled out from hiding and over to the door, dragging two of the black cables with him. He looped one around the steel I-beam column next to the office's far wall just above floor height and tied the other end to one leg of the desk, pulling it as tight as he dared.

The steps drew closer, checking out the cubicles and rooms on this side of the building. "Nasty trick on my coworker," the man said. "We're only supposed to pick you up and take you to the man in charge. That's all. Come on out, you two, and we'll go for a short drive. You'll be back here before you know it." An office door opened, sounding close.

Jackson checked in with his pattern sense again, making sure of the angles. He found a shelf with a cabling hole through the vertical panel and shoved the second cable through it. He pulled both ends over to the wall nearest him. There was no anchor point for the thick double strand of wire, nothing to tie it to. Feeling a fresh jolt of dread, he wrapped the loose ends around his forearm until they formed a crisscrossing gauntlet, tucked back in behind the boxes, braced his feet against the carpet and pulled the cable taut.

Was this actually going to work? He looked again, letting the full force of his condition wash through him and show him everything. He adjusted his hold on the cable and moved it up slightly. Yes, it would work.

Was he actually going to do this? That was the bigger question, no doubt about it. His stomach roiled at the thought.

He risked a glance out the office glass. The second killer appeared in silhouette as he moved to the next room over and opened the door. A long barrel jutted out of his upraised hand. Yes. He needed to do this.

The man was being careful. His partner had descended into a quiet moaning over by the elevator. Not wanting the same fate, the man opened the door to the office next to Jackson and peeked in.

Not good. Jackson's plan depended on momentum. Steeling himself and offering up a silent prayer, he let out a low but loud moan. Letting the predator know that his prey was just around the corner, and it was injured.

The hunter pulled back from the door he was in, focused on Abe's closed door, and ran. He crashed the door handle and flew through the opening into the office, his eyes everywhere, pistol following.

Everywhere but directly down. His leading foot caught the tripwire with a hard twang. With a grunt of surprise, and a thwip as his pistol went off, the man rotated forward around his ankle's pivot point.

Jackson's pattern sense was flaming, shimmering, illuminating every millisecond of the inevitable fall. He saw the man's sweep towards the floor in an arcing wash of vibrant green. He made a last adjustment to his hold on the second cable and hung on for dear life as the predator caught it just underneath the chin.

The impact seared marks into Jackson's arm from the wrapped cable. It jerked him almost to standing. It slapped the man's head back until his occiput connected with the spine between his shoulder blades.

Jackson heard and felt the crack. He let go of the cable as the man fell chest-first into the floor, the gun sailing into the far corner. He spun around to one side and lost his breakfast onto the carpet in a single, burning rush.

He had to check. Needed to look. The form lay still in the semidarkness of the crowded office, chest to the floor and face, horribly, to the sky. Jackson got up, unwrapped the cable from his arm, and made himself take the two steps.

The killer's eyes blinked. Jackson almost lost whatever meal he still had, choked it back down. The man's chest wasn't moving, but he was conscious. A break above the C4 vertebra, then. He was a respirator-dependent quadriplegic.

He rolled his eyes towards Jackson. With an obvious effort, he beetled his brows into the ghost of a scowl. He was working around to a glare of supreme hatred, Jackson could tell, but he never got there. Halfway into the frown those shark's eyes went wide. Then blank.

He went over to the desk and examined Abe. Still breathing. Still unconscious. Thigh still massive, but no larger than before.

A siren wailed up from outside, a sound he'd never been happier to hear. The real ambulance. Jackson had to get down there, warn them, redirect them to the second floor and Abe.

He had to get past the other guy. He briefly considered searching for the dead killer's gun, but tossed that idea away with a shudder.

The first attendant slumped against the wall next to the elevator. Beside him the perforated remains of the brave little robot and the overturned gurney filled the space in front of the elevator doors. On the man's other side was a door with a crash bar and a green Exit sign. The stairs. Jackson approached slowly, making no noise on the office carpet.

"Did we get 'em?" the man asked. He lifted his face towards Jackson. Both eyes were bleeding and charred, the sockets beginning to fill with grey pus. Instead of answering, Jackson continued his course around the blind man.

"Oh. You got him." The man patted around for his pistol, but it was nowhere nearby. He gave it up and sat back against the wall. "Is he dead? Nah, don't tell me. That's an ambulance downstairs, right? A real one? Do me a favour. Send them up here."

Jackson was at the door, hand on the crash bar. "On one condition," he said.

"What?"

"Choose a different line of work." He popped open the door and ran down the stairs.

Chapter 41

NO IDEA HOW LATE IS TOO LATE

Another crime scene. Another rush of police, with a constable paying close attention to Jackson outside Abe's building until Sergeant Dilly, looking a bit frayed around the edges, emerged and took him aside. "In here," she said, opening the sliding door in the side of a police van. He climbed in, took a seat on the bench against the far wall, and she joined him and rammed the door shut.

She pinched the bridge of her nose between two long fingers, then glared at him. "What is it with you? You're seeing more action than most of my officers."

He shook his head. This was the last place he wanted to be, and his nerves were practically on fire at being stuck in the back of a police van, but the only way out was through. So he answered her. "I really don't know, Sergeant. If I did, believe me, I'd have whatever it is surgically removed. Uh, how's Abe?"

"The resident? The paramedics—the real ones—tell me he's alive, but in bad shape. They looked puzzled, tell you the truth. They should be bringing him out now."

"Get one of them over here. Right away." Dilly looked irritated at being given an instruction, but keyed her radio. A moment later the van door opened and a paramedic stuck his head inside.

"He has an implant in his right side, below the last rib," Jackson told him. "The doctor needs to get that out of him, first thing. It's turning his fascia to jelly."

The paramedic's eyes widened. "That explains a thing or two. I've never seen anything like this. Thanks."

The sergeant sighed. "All right. You killed a professional assassin in an obvious case of self defence. Your tech bro sicced a robot on the other one and burned out his eyes, and let me tell you, our forensics team is going to have a field day with that piece of hardware. You gave a full statement to the constables outside?" She waited for him to nod. "We've already interrogated you twice. Is there anything more you can add?" He shook his head, for once keeping his mouth shut.

Dilly considered her hands for a moment, then looked up with something like compassion. Maybe even concern. "You've been through a hell of a lot in the past few days, Jackson. I've read your file. I know about your ... thing. How are you? Are you holding it together?"

He pushed his back a little further against the hard wall of the van, taken by surprise. "I'm freaked the hell out, but I'm doing all right," he said. "Thanks for asking."

Her concern shifted gears. "Okay, a more usual question. Again. Would you like to talk with Victim Services? I mean, you've been kidnapped, witnessed a shooting, and now this." She waved her hand out the window. "That would knock anyone off kilter. I can make a call."

"Thanks again. When you lay it all out like that, yeah, it's been a pretty weird week. But really, I'm okay. Give me a few days and I might be asking for that call." He added a rueful but solid smile and made sure it dimpled his freckles.

She peered at him for another second, then relaxed and sighed again. "You're free to go, Jackson. You want me to set you up with a counsellor, just ask. Better yet, tell Mathers. But also this. I have your phone number, and if I get more questions about anything at all you'd better answer, and you'd damn well better be within the city limits. Got it?" He nodded once more. "Then get out of here. Go home. Have a cup of tea and stay the hell out of trouble."

He scrambled out of the police van and waited till he was three steps away before pulling in a breath. He was out and free, which was a very good thing. The cops had helpfully moved his car outside the police cordon, and he went straight for it. He'd get his massage gear later.

The second he was in the driver's seat he pulled out his cell phone. Sergeant Dilly had told him to go home. He really, really wanted to. But not yet.

"Charles? It's Jackson. Meet me at your place, I'm on my way there now." Some squawking on the other end of the call. "I don't care if you're at work, this is urgent. Get someone to cover for you. No. No, Charles, listen to me." He rose his voice over his friend's complaints and let a sliver of his shredded nerves come through. "I'm coming from a crime scene, people are dead, a patient of mine is dying, and it's all those implants." He took a deep breath and dialled back the shrillness as his emotions threatened to turn him into a quivering mess. "The implant's poison, Charles, I've seen it with my own eyes. We have to tell her. Meet you there, I'm going now."

They got there at the same moment, Charles screeching to a stop with the grill of his car facing Jackson's and that professional-intense ER doctor look on his face. He still wore his scrubs. Together they rushed up the steps.

Charles led the way through the front door. Georgia was in the kitchen, a glass of orange juice and a plateful of avocado toast on the marble counter. She jerked her head up from the ebook reader next to the plate and said, "Hello, Charles. Jackson. Where's the fire?"

She looked gorgeous. Even just sitting there, Jackson marvelled at her flawless skin, clear eyes, and the pale yellow shimmer of perfect ease and vitality he saw all around her. Her body was well and truly a hundred percent. But not for long.

Charles looked over, ceding the floor to him. "I just came from Abe's place. His body's falling apart, he's in the back of an ambulance headed for the hospital." At that Charles started, no doubt irritated at not being on duty for a critical patient. Too bad. "Two professional killers came for us, Georgia. The same two I saw take away Dr. Sachs. The cops raided Blast Dynamics this morning and they haven't found anything yet, but they will."

She held up a hand, folded her Kobo closed, and said, "You're babbling. Start from the beginning."

He took a moment to organize his thoughts, then started again. "It's the implants. They're bad, and a lot of very bad people are involved with them."

He caught her up. She'd heard the basics of the shooting in the park from Charles and Leaf. He told her about Shaheen Kiani's involvement. He filled her in on Luca Sachs, wanted the world over for shoddy medical trials, and the VPD's intense interest in finding him. The raid at Blast Dynamics, his certainty that they were behind the implants somehow. About Abe, and his Ehlers-Danlos symptoms, and the attack at his home.

"Those implants are huge money, Georgia, and they don't care who they hurt. They're garbage. Worse, poisonous. The research on the dark web is paper thin, I could have doctored it up on my own laptop. Dr. Sachs is wrapped up in it somehow, and I'm pretty sure he was trying to do the right thing by handing me that package. They'll never find his body, I saw the men who took him away. I killed one of them today." His voice began to shake. "You have to get rid of it, Georgia. I have no idea how late is too late."

Charles kept his silence, waiting. Georgia stood in one fluid movement and paced around the long counter to stand in front of them. Her right hand brushed the spot where the implant nestled underneath the skin and subcutaneous fascia, slowly releasing its payload into her bloodstream. He didn't think she was even aware she'd done it.

The second he saw the gesture, he knew they'd lost.

"So, to recap. To make things perfectly clear. The three of you got caught in the middle of a gang warfare shootout, and you think one of them looked at you. I'm sure that was quite flattering. Someone who resembled a person of interest to the police handed you a package before getting taken away in an ambulance, an innocuous set of things you delivered the next day. A company in the initial stages of chemical research, years away from any kind of actual therapy, got raided. You saw the body of evidence to back the Ponce de Leon and disagree with it. Armed men dressed as ambulance attendants came to the home of a leading tech entrepreneur who, I can tell you, has made more than a few enemies in the industry. And you injured your patient with an over-enthusiastic move. I'm sorry about Abe's ruptured vein, but I'm sure he'll pull through." She reached for an avocado toast, took a nibble, and waved it at them both. "A busy week, I'll grant you that. Now tell me this. Where's the proof?"

Charles threw up his hands. "The hell, Georgia! What more do you want?"

She pivoted to him, and all of a sudden there was fire in her eyes. "What do I want? You, of all people, ask me that? I only want what any medical professional would demand, Dr. Fixall. Real proof. Real evidence. Because I've seen the real evidence that the Ponce de Leon does what they say it does. You think I'd fall for the sales pitch? You think that little of me? I studied it, Charles! I went over that research with a fine tooth comb and a sceptic's eye, and it held up. So I got the implant, and you know what? It works as advertised! I feel better than I have since I was twelve, Charles, and you can't fake that!"

She paused, out of breath, her cheeks flushed rose-red. Charles, equally furious, slammed a fist down onto the marble. "I knew it would be no use. Come on, Jackson, let's go. She's found her ticket to eternal life and no way in hell is she going to listen to reason. I'm going back to work. Where I stand a chance of actually helping someone."

Jackson grasped his arm before he could leave. Everything was falling apart, desperation thrummed like high voltage through his veins, jangling every cell. "Wait, just wait! Georgia, come on. I know this feels fantastic right now, but trust me, soon it won't. There has to be some way I can convince you. What will it take?"

Without turning away from her teenage sweetheart she glanced over at him, her anger cooling a little. "The only sensible thing you've said since you came through the door. Longevists follow evidence, Jackson. Bring me solid clinical evidence of what you're talking about. Prove it to me with science, not circumstance. Because I've seen the science that proves the Ponce de Leon is effective. It followed all the protocols: chemical analysis, animal testing, blood work, refinements, clinical trials. Only after all that, they're releasing it to the public. Tomorrow. Some of my like-minded friends have chartered a jet to Singapore to go get it.

"You say you've seen negative effects? Then show me the clinical trials evidence, Jackson. That, I might believe."

Charles jerked his arm free from Jackson's grip and stormed out of the kitchen with a growl. Jackson turned to go, but gave it one last shot. "Georgia," he said, as soft as he could make it, "don't you get it? You are the clinical trial."

The stubborn expression remained on that perfectly unlined face. He sighed and followed Charles. She needed evidence. With his heart sinking into his shoes, he jumped back into his car.

The proof existed, he knew that. And he had to go get it.

Chapter 42

SWALLOWED BY A STORMCLOUD DUSK

He'd finally gotten free of the police mess and shocked aftermath at the Blast lab and driven the hell out of there. By the time he pulled up behind the Uncle's house and made his way through the grapevines to the back door it was getting dim.

Mrs. Zupan let him in. "He's in the study," she said, totally unperturbed by the tension that must be showing on his face. "My daughters and I will take the children for a walk."

The Uncle stood behind his desk, hands linked behind his back, gazing out the window. "Uncle, I—" he began, but the old man raised a hand for silence. Didn't even bother turning around first.

A minute later the sounds of young complaints, rustling coats and shoes, and the closing of the big front door signalled the departure of the household. "Now begin," said the Uncle, turning around at last.

The old man already knew. The Uncle's knuckles were white where they gripped each other. Well, this was no fault of his. "The police came to the lab. Blast, not ours, but they're getting close. The massage therapist was with them. He's been visiting the tech influencer, and I'm sure that hyperactive ass told him too much. I heard Teague say he was going there again this afternoon. I sent the cleanup team to remove them both. Even if they weren't responsible for bringing the cops to our door, it's time for the tech bro to start showing symptoms, and the therapist won't miss that."

He swallowed and hated himself for the tell. "They failed. One of the crew dead, the other wounded and in custody."

The words settled to the floor between them like dry autumn leaves. The silence in the study grew, thickened, coalesced. Outside the window the hazy sunset was being swallowed by a stormcloud dusk. The Uncle did not reach for the pull cord on the Tiffany lamp beside him as the daylight faded.

"What now?" he broke the stillness. "The launch is tomorrow. We'll have all the capital we need within a week. Are we good?"

"You are asking me?" The muscles at the Uncle's temples rippled under the skin, but the old man's voice was soft in the semidark, almost kind. The implications sent a shiver down his back. "This is your mission. You had the vision to conceive it. You had the expertise to bring it into reality. You have used knowledge, skills, tools that I cannot. You," and his soft voice hardened, "are the future of this family. My family. So I ask you. Are we good? Is the project safe? Is there any danger at all?"

He knew better than to lie to the Uncle, and he knew the answer. Had known it all afternoon. "There's still some risk. Life extenders are proud of their intelligence. They love reports and research and evidence, so we gave it to them. Even though it was desperation that made them sign up for the implant, if they see any of the real evidence they'd reconsider. If one or two sound the alarm and pull out of the launch the rest will follow. Their money is all in escrow, so if they refuse the implants we get nothing."

"Where would this evidence come from?"

He grimaced. "Sachs, damn his soul. He must have saved records when the trials began to go sour. He was a stickler for documenting everything. I thought he'd passed the records to the therapist, but I examined the envelope myself. Nothing. Still, there's a risk. He must have put the proof somewhere."

"The massage therapist," the Uncle said. "I have looked into his eyes. He sees what others do not. He has an inflexible moral compass. He carries the inborn stubbornness of both the Irish and the redhead. His curiosity has been fired. If Sachs did conceal something then young Mr. Teague will keep looking until he finds it."

"I think so, too. Which brings me around to my first question, Uncle. What do we do about it?"

The Uncle reached over and pulled the cord on the lamp. A hundred muted colours from the stained glass shade bathed the old desk and bookshelves in a quiet glow. The wash of dappled light over the Uncle's face made him look like the oldest thing in the room, ancient and hard as the mountains outside the window.

"We? No. This is your venture. What is to be done is plain. So." He lifted one hand, just a little, and turned the palm up in invitation. "You tell me."

He felt a sweat begin to slick his palms. "The Stooges are gone. The contractors are gone. Who else do we have?"

The Uncle pulled open a drawer in the desk. He placed a thick, black pistol onto the green blotter. "We have you," he said, that dangerous softness back in his voice. "This is your project, your problem. You will fix it."

He wanted to take a step back from the thing. Three steps. He kept his feet rooted where they were. The Uncle hated weakness above all else, and the Croat was within reach of a gun. Besides, he was right. It was time to wade fully into the family game.

He bent forward and picked up the pistol, an HS2000, the chosen compact killing machine of the Croatian Army. He'd shot one at an indoor range once, years ago. It was heavier than he remembered. "All right. I know where he lives. He's probably having supper. His cop girlfriend might be with him, that will complicate matters."

"No," the Uncle said. "Young Mr. Teague is not at home. I am still watching. He is in his car, headed towards Blast Dynamics."

"What?!" The news electrified him. "He's looking for it! I have to stop him."

"Yes, you do." The Uncle was holding out something else. A black box, the size of an old-style satellite phone. A thick, black circle of some kind of composite jutted from the top on a thick stalk. "Take this as well. Call it a failsafe."

He grasped the thing. A single light embedded in the case glowed red above a recessed switch, the box's only features besides a simple belt clip. "A radio?"

"A jammer. Better than most. Turn it on, and nothing within three hundred feet will send or receive a signal." A tiny smile lifted one corner of his mouth. "Don't carry it too close to your jaja."

He'd been about to clip it to the front of his belt, but eased it around to the back. "Anything else, Uncle?"

The Uncle placed both hands on his desk and leaned into the words. "Don't fuck it up. You know what is at stake."

He swallowed again. "Everything."

No one saw him out the back door as he hustled through the grapevines to his waiting car, and from there to Blast.

Branislav breathed out as he heard the man slam the back door and hurry into the dusk, carrying the hope of his family with him. The man had been equally angry and scared, but he'd said all the right words. Taken the gun and the jammer, the only help Branislav had left to give. Would he carry it through? Do what it took to safeguard the Croats' last chance?

The heaviness in Branislav's heart was the answer. His protégé had ambition. Pretentions. At the day's end, however, he was a scientist.

Branislav opened the drawer again, pulled out his own HS2000, checked the load, and grabbed the car keys out of the bowl by the door.

Chapter 43

AN ICE-COLD BITCH OF A DAY

Jackson got a message from Marilyn as he left Georgia and Charles' house: Helluva day. I'm at ur place. Where R U? He texted back: Not over yet. Meet you, front door, 3 minutes.

He cracked open the door to his condition. The flow of traffic around him transformed into a swishing series of waves and lines, dopplering red and blue as the rush hour mosh pit of cars jostled for advantage. Fourth Avenue was two constant lines of vehicles in each direction, but green flickers showed him where to insert the corner of his front bumper and slide between the lanes. He made it to Balsam Street in four minutes, not three, but it was still some kind of record.

Marilyn stood outside, holding an umbrella against the Scotch mist of rain that was light enough to be almost pleasant, but dense enough to soak you before you knew it. Her black jeans were darker where the rain had reached them above her Doc Martens. Her face bore an expression halfway between puzzlement and irritation. "Where are we going?" she asked as she levered into the passenger seat. "Why are we going there?"

"We're going to get some answers," he said as he slipped back into the line of cars, ignoring the horns. "Georgia is in trouble and she refuses to see it. The only thing she'll believe is hard evidence. We're going to get it."

Her irritation morphed into something close to alarm. She placed a hand on the dash and turned to face him. "Jackson! Tell me we're not going back to Blast Dynamics."

"Yep," he said.

She snorted. "The department has been all over that place! We have the files, the servers, we're going to get the answers. If there are even answers to be found. What the hell makes you think they'll talk to you when they've spent the day not talking to anyone else?"

"Because we know what questions to ask," he answered, giving her a half-grin as he sideslipped at speed between two lanes, getting a chirp from his tires on the wet pavement. The day's light was gone now. The black pavement glistened as the streetlights came on. He faced front again, the grin fading. "And because Georgia needs those answers."

"Hah!" She settled into her seat, and of all things, she looked pleased. "Welcome back, Freckles. It's about time. Step on it."

The parking lot of Blast Dynamics was nearly deserted but the building's windows shone bright. Every light in the place must be on, Jackson thought. Good. He pulled to a stop on the street out front and they threaded past the trees and benches to the front door.

No one answered the intercom. It was after 6:30, so not unexpected. Marilyn tried the handle of the reinforced glass door.

Unlocked. It opened without a sound. With a glance at each other they entered the reception area.

"Hello? Anyone home?" Marilyn called into the empty space. Jackson jumped at her volume. He had no clear idea of exactly how to proceed here, but he'd had a vague idea it would involve sneaking. Her way was better, he realized. Less chance of being arrested for trespassing. Or shot.

He'd had more than enough of that for one life.

The reception area was a mess. The cops had rifled through every drawer and dumped the contents onto the floor behind the desk. They'd opened every cupboard and closet. And left them open. Jackson's pattern sense marked the line of each item, the jumble of angles they made with their neighbours, the wall, the design on the floor, and the absence of any pattern at all set his teeth on edge. A more normal part of him bristled at the show of disrespect. He half-shut his eyes to diminish the view.

He realized, with a sinking feeling, that the entire lab might be like this. He might have a very hard time being in here.

"Sucks to be me," he muttered under his breath, and steeled himself for the next move.

Footsteps sounded from the floor above. Harold Dunn—Dunnai, according to the Internet and the cops' paperwork—poked his head around the corner of the upstairs doorway, his expression even more dour than Jackson remembered.

"You two," he said, not a trace of warmth in his voice. "What the fuck do you want?"

"We need to talk with you and Mr. Harrowman," Marilyn said before Jackson could open his mouth. Her tone was apologetic, almost plaintive. "We know it's been a challenging day, but it's really important." She hesitated and glanced at Jackson, then back upstairs. "Lives could be at stake."

True, Jackson thought, impressed. With just the right amount of drama to ring an alarm bell in Dunn's brain.

The big man scowled at them for another moment, then hmphed. "Come on," he said. "While you're here you can help clean up the mess your colleagues left behind."

His shirt sleeves were rolled up. His lab coat was missing. Clunks and shuffling sounds drifted from the first office. As they rounded the corner, Dunn first, Jonathan Harrowman wrestled a banker's document box back onto the top shelf of an otherwise empty storage closet. More boxes spilled onto the floor.

"They want to talk," Dunn told him as Harrowman slammed the box into place. "Say it's important."

Harrowman's sky-blue shirt, impeccably tailored to follow the lines of his slim, squash-toned waist, had dark stains under both arms. When he turned away from the cupboard to face them Jackson's condition flared more electric blue around the guy, brighter at the shoulders and condensing to solid swaths of energy over his legs. The CEO was tense as a frat boy on exam day, practically quivering. His expression was far from the confident, serene man they'd first met. Now his face was pinched, hollowed, all lines and shadows. He was distraught.

Jackson began to doubt his plan.

"What now?" Harrowman kicked another box on his way to the office's desk, perching on its edge. "I've answered enough nonsense questions today to last a year. Haven't you two done enough?"

Marilyn gave Jackson an invisible nudge in the ribs. This was his show, and the curtain had risen. "We know about the Ponce de Leon," he started.

Harrowman waited. Jackson waited, too. Dunn's glower deepened. The executive finally shook his head. "Bully for you. What the hell does a Spanish explorer have to do with anything at all?"

Strike one. A bead of sweat trickled between his shoulder blades as he forged ahead. "Not the explorer. The Fountain of Youth. Except it isn't, is it? And tomorrow, a whole bunch of people are going to find that out."

Dunn looked like a thundercloud ready to burst. Harrowman cast his eyes to the ceiling and gusted a humourless laugh. "Hah! I thought the rest of today had been nonsense. This tops it all." He jumped off the corner of the desk and levelled a glare at them both. He fished a cell phone out of his pocket and wielded it. "Mr. Teague, either you explain what the hell you're going on about or I'm calling the men in white jackets. Because it sure as shit sounds like your reason has fallen off a cliff."

He was serious. Dunn, off to the side, was saying nothing.

Strike two. Marilyn had gone all loose and relaxed beside him, which was her way of getting ready for a fight. She nudged him again, this time so all could see. "Lay it out," she told him.

So he did. "The Ponce de Leon. The magic implant that will make anybody live forever in perfect health. You remember that, right?" He turned to Dunn, his anger taking over. "The research you're doing, on something that will cure everything? Except you're not in the early stages like you tell everyone, are you? The journey from lab to market takes forever, costs millions. Surely there'd be some way to shorten it. You found Dr. Sachs, who was willing to test your formula on actual people, implant them with it and watch what happened. And it worked, didn't it? Made them better. Made them better than better, practically young again. Melted the years off their joints, their circulation, their skin. But it didn't stop, did it? The implant kept going. Until it started melting them."

He heard himself getting louder but couldn't stop. "You didn't care, did you? All you saw was buckets of cash. But you didn't count on Dr. Sachs sampling the wares. He gave himself an implant. I know, I felt it in his side. And when he saw his test subjects fail, when he felt the breakdown in his own body, he had a crisis of conscience. Who knew? A doctor the Nazis would have loved turning good? So you had him knifed. Taken away and killed. But not before he slipped me a package."

Outrage threatened to leap his heart right out of his chest. He moved to take a step towards Harrowman but Marilyn's hand on his chest held him back. "Still, you needed financial backing. Another lab. A network of clinics around the world that wouldn't ask questions. Big money. That meant organized crime.

"Funny, thing, though. Gangs can smell profits. Especially when it's millions. Billions. We brought you the package Sachs gave me, knowing nothing at all, and they came after me. In my house! On the street! Killing each other to get a leg up on—

whatever this is."

He wanted to bull his way through Marilyn's hand on his chest, but resisted. "Now a friend of mine has fallen for it." He pointed a finger at Harrowman. "She refuses to listen. She'll only believe hard proof that your medicine, your Ponce de Leon, is poisonous garbage. Well, Mr. CEO, we're here to get it. Now."

He stopped for breath, feeling the heat in his face. His pattern sense shuddered at the disordered mess in the small office, highlighted the off-kilter angle of the desk pushed out of its divots in the carpet. It washed over Jonathan Harrowman and illuminated the straightened spine, the thrown-back shoulders, the slackening of all the lines etched so deeply into his face.

Harrowman's mountain of tension had washed away under a deluge of pure, unadulterated astonishment.

He knew nothing.

Dunn, at the periphery of Jackson's vision, glowed as a single block of red. Rigid with anger from his brush-cut hair to his size twelve shoes. "How dare you," he said, the words strangled and hoarse. "You, a—a masseuse, accuse us of research misconduct? Blast Dynamics does not cut corners. Jon and I tried that once. It didn't end well and we'll never do it again. When I told you we're doing lead optimization lab work, I did not lie."

He got redder, fists clenched but still at his sides. Jackson worried the old guy might stroke out right in front of them. "It's slow going. Frustrating. Because it has to be. As for Dr. Luca Sachs, and I use that honorific with utmost sarcasm, we'd never hire him in a million years. Everybody in the industry knows about Sachs. If we told each other bedtime stories Sachs would be the bogeyman."

He was pulling another breath to continue his tirade when Harrowman interrupted.

"Our formula? In clinical trials? It works?" He leaped to his feet. Marilyn dropped her arms to her sides and stepped forward.

Harrowman saw her stance, lifted his empty hands, changed trajectory to skirt around her, and headed out the door into the hall.

"Come on," he called back to them.

They followed, Dunn last, into Harrowman's office at the end of the long hall. By the time Jackson caught up Harrowman was at his desk holding a sheet of paper with dense notations on both sides.

The sheet from the package.

Harrowman scanned the paper front and back, moving a finger along the hieroglyphics. "Here, look at this," he told Dunn, and the molecular scientist stomped over to the desk. "Here, and here. It's almost identical, but ..."

Dunn looked, then scrunched his brows together and leaned in. "They changed it," he muttered. "That might actually work." He straightened up and glared at Jackson. "This came from Sachs?" He got a nod. "You say it's been used? You've seen it? Tell me."

Dunn was furious, still deeply red to Jackson's gaze. Not the fury of being discovered. There was no hint of nerves, no tension in his legs from a concealed urge to run. Or to spring forward and tear them apart. He was ... Jackson tried to put a label on it.

Harold Dunn was glowing with righteous fury.

Strikeout. Neither of them were behind the Ponce de Leon.

"It looks pretty good to start. Miraculous, even." He told Dunn what he'd seen on the dark web videos and in Abe Tremblay. "Eventually it all goes too far, starts looking like Ehlers-Danlos. I can only imagine it gets worse from there."

Dunn and Harrowman were both focused on his words, taking it all in. They bent to the formula again. "Sounds right," he heard Dunn murmur. "See here? And this alkyl shift? That would kick it into high gear. But," he flipped the page over and back, "there's no brake. No competitive inhibitors, no terminal group, nothing. The effects would just keep going."

Jackson saw both the men lose some of their colour.

Dunn's fists relaxed. "This drug is a disaster waiting to happen."

"Not waiting for much longer," Marilyn said. "The implants are set to go to market tomorrow morning. Hundreds, maybe thousands of people are lined up to get them. You wouldn't believe what they've paid for their chance at immortality."

Harrowman straightened up and regained some of his patrician composure. "Mr. Teague, Ms. Mathers. I swear to you, on our professional honour, we had nothing to do with this. These implants," he pulled the ziplock bag from his pocket that contained the dull, silver cylinder, "horrify us as much as they do you. Worse, perhaps. You've seen some of their effects. We have some idea of how bad they could get."

"So help us stop it," Jackson said.

"Of course. How?"

Jackson thought of Georgia's words, the obstinate look in her eye. "Proof," he said. "We need hard evidence to counter what the longevists have already seen. I'm sure Sachs knew that, and I'm sure that's what he gave me. The formula, that sheet. We could post it to the dark web."

A whole new kind of horror overtook both the men. "No, we can't, that's our life's work," Harrowman began, but Dunn thumped a meaty hand onto his shoulder.

"Jon's right, that would be the end of Blast, but I'd do it if giving away our formula would help. It won't."

"Why not?" asked Marilyn.

Dunn handed her the paper. "Tell me what you see."

She didn't even have to look. "Oh. Right." Nobody without an advanced degree in molecular chemistry would know what they were looking at.

"What else was there? The implant," Jackson said.

"So what?" said Marilyn at his side. "They're going to see a hundred of them tomorrow. It just proves the things exist."

"And this." Harrowman pulled the sketch from his desk drawer. A beautiful rendering of a hand, thumb and forefinger curled under and the other three fingers outstretched, skin removed to show the webs of fascia underneath. They all crowded the desk to examine it.

It was a hand. It was a lovely work of art. The pencil sketch cut off at the wrist bones, with a few curly flourishes around the fingers and a few small circles below the wrist to give depth and style. Nothing more.

One by one, they stood up again. Jackson was last, peering at the thing for a full three minutes. "It's gorgeous. Anatomically correct. Nothing else that I can see."

Harrowman sighed and wiped a hand over his face. "I am sorry, Jackson. Thank you for telling me what the police wouldn't. Now, at least, I have some idea what they were looking for. I don't know how we can help you stop all this. But it's been an ice-cold bitch of a day, and I still need to restore some order here before I head home. You know where the exit is. Oh," he managed the ghost of a smile, "you're fired."

Dunn's voice stopped them on their way out the office door. "One thing. It's been altered, but that is our formula. It came from this building. Ms. Mathers, if you don't mind my saying, you move like a barroom brawler. If you run into that weasel Reggie," his voice dropped into a deep, black well, "fuck him up for me."

Chapter 44

Islands of trees in the night

Dunn saw them to the front door and closed it behind them. They huddled under the small roof over the steps while Marilyn fished out her umbrella.

The Scotch mist had upgraded to a fairly decent rain that lent the October night a chill. Jackson gazed out at the landscaping and the deserted street beyond, his thoughts as dark as the night. He'd failed. He had no way to convince Georgia to get rid of that damn implant. Maybe—and he hated even the thought—he should talk to Charles about ambushing her with a chloroformed rag and a scalpel.

His condition, given such frequent free rein today, was refusing to go back into its cage. The patterns of the night intruded on his mind. Tiny meteor trails of phosphorescent light streaked down from the sky, marking the raindrops' paths and showing where they'd land. The concrete slabs from the door to the parking lot formed a neat, pleasing ladder of lines that called to his feet, urged him to follow. The scattering of trees on the grass had mostly lost their leaves. The branches, outlined by the streetlights, jutted stark fingers into the black night, following an intricate and inevitable pattern that he could stare at for hours.

He forced his gaze to the ground, dispirited and desperate. The proof of the implants' danger existed. It had to. It just wasn't anywhere Jackson could find.

Faint, shimmering lines glowed from the base of each dimly-lit tree trunk to all the others. The landscape designer had known what they were doing. The trees were placed in a pleasing, careful symmetry, a pattern anchored and made whole by the addition of the benches.

It was lovely. Beside him, Marilyn had managed to pop open the umbrella with a muted curse. He indulged in another glance at the masterful interplay between the trees, felt the glow as a warm, familiar comfort.

Islands of trees in the night, their crooked black fingers reaching to the sky. The faint lines between them, connecting them. He'd seen this pattern before.

"Let's go," said Marilyn, taking the first step.

"Wait," he said. He pulled his cell phone out and jabbed at the screen.

"We're done here, Jackson. You gave it your very best, really. Maybe the department will find what we missed. Tomorrow's not too late."

He stood where he was and kept jabbing, swiping through screens. "The package. Think of what Sachs went through to get it here. He knew his body was in trouble. Knew he was in peril. When they got him, he shoved it into the hands of a complete stranger. It was that important."

She tugged on his arm, gently. "We've been through all this. Come on, let's go to bed."

He had them now. The photos he'd taken of the envelope's contents. "Here, look." The first photo was the sheet of chemical notations. "The formula. Harrowman and Dunn's formula, but altered in a way only they could see." Flip. "The implant. See? He was telling them, your drug is out in the world. It's launching."

Marilyn sighed. "Jackson, we know all that."

"Right! But then this." The last photo, the sketch of the hand. "Artwork? Really? Sachs was vain, I'm sure, but if it was in this envelope it had to be important. Had to be part of the story. Look."

He held the image out to her.

She watched his face instead, her expression soft. Sad. "Let's go."

"Look." He lifted the phone's screen in front of her face. She sighed and glanced at it. "Is it familiar?"

"Of course. We just finished staring at it upstairs."

"No, not that. See?" He held the phone horizontally, the image facing the sky. The fascial hand glowed up at them, its fingers pointing towards the empty street. Tiny raindrops landed on it. "Oh, wrong way. Now?" He reversed the image.

"Still a hand," she said.

"No, it's not. Here." He circled the main part of the hand, wrist to exposed knuckles, then waved at Blast Dynamics. "And here." He swooshed his index finger along the three outstretched fingers, then waved at the building again.

The skin between her eyebrows was now creased by a hint of curiosity, that was at least a start. "You see something?" she asked.

"This!" He did all the motions again, image to building. "The main block, offices and such. The three labs sticking out behind it. Marilyn, this is Blast Dynamics."

She peered at the image with new interest, but gave up after a moment. "Could be. But so what? We've been all over this place. And I doubt that Dr. Sachs was ever inside. Dunn would have murdered him on sight."

"Yeah, but no one's had a map." He pointed again. Wavy lines flowed away from the fingers, the artist's flourish. Little circles and diamonds highlighted the space below the wrist. He zoomed in on them. Pointed at a circle, then at a tree. Another circle, another tree. "It's the landscaping. Circles are trees. Diamonds are benches. Right?"

He saw the light dawn on her face. Then saw the second realization strike home. "Yeah! They're a match. And this one," she said, pointing to one square. The only one that had been filled in, a tiny dot of black where the rest were just boxes.

They both turned towards the street. Jackson already knew, and it took Marilyn less than a second. "The fascia bench." They squeezed together under her umbrella and headed for it.

The pale pink, semi-rigid bench, formed of tough but flexible composite plastic in the form of a web, glistened in the rain. "Sachs must have walked by here. Of course he'd choose this bench to sit on."

"Okay, hotshot, you've impressed me. Do it again." Marilyn stood back and folded her arms, the picture of impudent challenge. A smile touched her lips. "What the hell are we looking for, and where do we look?"

He grinned back, then got serious. They were good questions. He needed the answers.

He checked over the entire bench, then the ground around it, quickly getting soaked through from the pattering rain. The bench had been well used. A lot of butts and shoes had created shiny spots on the plastic and a grassless trench in front where feet had scuffed and rested. Nothing was hidden underneath, behind, or close to it. The bench was a weird, arty, but eminently useable seat.

He got up off muddy knees and shook his head. "I don't know," he muttered.

"Change your focus," Marilyn suggested. "Walk me through it."

Worth a try. He thought about it, went a few steps down the sidewalk. Sachs had been old when Jackson had seen him walk up the Seabus ramp, but still spry. The doctor's gait, once you factored out the knife wound, had been the pace of a professor, an easy amble. Jackson took a few more steps away from the bench then turned and walked towards it. Easy, relaxed. Like he had a head full of thoughts and not much attention on anything else.

He could feel it. This was a quiet neighbourhood, ideal for a stroll. The fascia bench beckoned. Not only was it right out front of the very lab whose work he was stealing, and a design his inner medical geek would appreciate, it was also a bit removed from the line of the sidewalk. Not enough to be inconvenient, but enough to feel like you were closeted inside the big trees.

Jackson drifted over to it. He pictured Sachs again, in the long ramp of the Seabus terminal, walking ahead of him. Remembered helping the old man up the ramp after he'd slumped to the floor. Jackson had stood almost straight as he placed his arm under Sachs' shoulder. The scientist was a large man.

The dirt in front of the right side of the bench had sunken more than the left, exposing a few roots from the tree nearby. More leg room. Jackson sat down in Sachs' preferred spot.

Evidence. Reports, scans, clinical notes? No way could the doctor have hidden papers here. Once he thought about it, that part of the answer became obvious.

His right hand hung down outside the bench where the thick strands of the collagen web terminated in blunt stubs. A longer arm from the fibroblast he was sitting on reached the edge as well. He swung his hand back and forth, feeling each stub as he went.

The rubberized plastic was smooth, almost slippery. The strands had been poured over a solid steel framework which gave the bench its strength.

The fibroblast had caved a little as he sat down. Like it was a very stiff pillow. He ran his fingers over the end of its long arm and tugged.

It flexed a bit. It was hollow.

He bent the tip of plastic this way and that. As he lifted it up, his index finger felt a thin slit opened in its underside.

"Here, help me out."

He lifted hard, turning the slit into a gap. Marilyn knelt down and reached in with her slender thumb and finger. Came out with a black metal wafer, squared off at one end.

"If you ever get tired of massage, we could use you on the

force," she said. "Let's get this thumb drive back inside and see what we've got."

Neither Harrowman nor Dunn were particularly surprised to see them again. They both seemed to be dulled by the events of the day. The sight of the tiny thumb drive, blocky USB connector slimming down to an inch of metal casing that was wide as a pencil and thin as a credit card, perked them up.

"We found where Sachs hid it," Marilyn said without elaborating. "Let's plug it in."

"Your colleagues took everything electronic that wasn't nailed down," Dunn grumbled. "Not a laptop or tablet in the place."

"I'll be right back," Jackson said.

He ran downstairs and out into the rain to his car. His scheduling and clinical notes tablet took USB drives. He plucked it from its hiding place and hustled back to the building, shielding it from the rain with his jacket. The entire night glistened under the streetlamp glow, Vancouver now blurred by another Pacific Northwest drenching. As a solitary car drove past its tires hissed through growing puddles.

They gathered around Harrowman's desk as he set the tablet to full screen display and plugged in the drive. The screen hummed to life and a folder structure appeared.

"Bingo," Jackson whispered.

Three folders read, 'Bloodwork,' 'Interviews,' and 'Tests.' Below them was a single file, a video with the title, 'Watch Me First.'

Without a word, Jackson clicked it open. Dr. Luca Sachs appeared large on the screen, backdropped by a long room lined with sturdy silver cages. Marilyn gasped. Most of the cages were empty. The last three on the left held people. Details were scarce at this distance, but none of them were standing. None moved. All of them flickered a nauseating green to Jackson's eye, something about them subtly wrong.

Sachs, wearing a lab coat over a shirt and tie and looking

considerably better than the last time Jackson had seen him, glanced around and then back at the camera. He opened his mouth, hesitated, closed it again. He was ... Jackson tried to identify the expression. Embarrassed. Maybe even a little concerned.

"Dr. Harrowman, I hope this finds you well, and I hope it finds you in time," Sachs said in that light, sandy voice with the touch of German accent. "I appear to have miscalculated. Your formula works, with some adjustments, as my notations and early records will show. However, there are side effects that present over time. Excessive flexibility gains. Internal organ laxity, then prolapse. Vascular fragility." A briefest of smiles flickered across his face and was gone. "Death from cascading organ failure. These results are, obviously, unfortunate. My experimentation with this iteration of the formula has ended."

"No remorse," Dunn muttered, fists clenched again. "Unfortunate, he calls it. Try murder."

Sachs continued. "My investors, though, have decided to capitalize on the short-term gains and take the product to market. Over my objections, let me assure you. They are adamant, and have used the early test results to generate significant interest. So I am providing you with the records of the side effects. Please publish them. I hope you are in time."

Sachs coughed, a wheeze that kept on coming and turned into a breathless gasp. He glanced around again and continued. "I must be brief, but need to tell you one more thing. A mea culpa, if you will. I have made a critical error. The initial findings were so favourable that I gave myself an implant. I know," he waved a hand at the camera, "unprofessional in the extreme. But I will pay for it. For four to six weeks after implantation, the patient has nothing but improvements. Then, for roughly two weeks, symptoms begin to show—lax skin, spontaneous dislocations. They get progressively more serious, then debilitating. Then severe. No subjects have survived past twelve weeks."

He shifted on his chair and leaned in. "This is important. Once negative symptoms show, you have days to remove the implant. After that, the decline is irreversible. And if you remove the implant after six weeks, the sudden removal of stimulus pushes all the body's fibroblasts into a massive autoimmune response. A cytokine storm. The subject expires within hours."

The office was silent as midnight. On the screen, voices could be heard approaching from a distance. Dr. Sachs dropped his voice to a whisper. "Publish these records. Stop the project. Best of luck in your future endeavours." The screen cut off.

"Bloodwork," Dunn ordered. Jackson complied, opening the first of a dozen files. Page after page of charts and graphs meant nothing to him, although most of the graph lines went down. The two scientists got grim.

"Video," Dunn said again. Jackson switched folders and started the first one.

"Turn it off!" Harrowman yelled. Jackson was already fumbling for the button. The screen blanked out.

The afterimage of what he'd seen burned his eyes until it faded away. The video had shown a single person, a young man. He'd been walking down a hall. Or trying. On the first step his ankle folded in. Halfway through the second stride his knees had bowed. Jackson's pattern sense had strobed red and orange flashes of alarm as the poor man's hips, even his pelvis, defied every arc and angle of their normal range. In the last frame before he'd killed the video, the young man's upper body had canted sideways as his spine turned to wet spaghetti.

"Is that thing connected?" Dunn pointed at the tablet. "Post it where people will see. All of it. Hurry!"

Jackson opened up a browser and pecked in the address of the dark web chat room Abe had shown him. The browser came back with an error message. He frowned. "Your wifi was here a second ago. Now it's gone."

"Damn police messed with everything," Harrowman growled.

Marilyn had her phone in her hand. "The department needs to hear about this. Right now." Then she peered at the screen, shook the phone and peered again. "No signal."

"Well, look at that. This gizmo actually works."

Reggie stood in the doorway to the office. His left hand held a black box with a circular antenna mounted on top. His right hand held a gun, pointed into the center of their group.

Jackson's condition showed him a scarlet line of intent from the tip of the pistol's barrel across the room to the tablet on Harrowman's desk. And through it, to the other side of the desk and Jackson's navel.

He dove out of the way as Reggie screwed up his face and fired.

Chapter 45

THE NEPHEW

The room erupted into chaos. A chunk of oak flew past Jackson's head as the gun's blast punched his eardrums. He hit the floor and rolled away from the desk. Dunn roared like an enraged bull and went for Reggie, arms outstretched, hands reaching for the boy's throat. Marilyn had her back up against the far wall, yelling at Reggie and Dunn both to stop. Harrowman opted for the visitor chair and thudded down onto the seat.

"Hey, hey!" He heard Reggie's voice through the buzz in his ears. Reggie put both hands up to fend off Dunn's crushing attack. The gun cracked again.

Dunn's momentum carried him almost to the doorway despite the cloud of red that burst through the back of his shirt. The big scientist got his hands around Reggie's neck, but had no strength left to finish the job. He thudded to the floor at the boy's feet.

Jackson's ears rang from the dual thunderclaps. The smell of gunpowder and blood filled the office with a choking reek. Reggie stood, openmouthed with shock at what he'd done, both gun and black box loose in his hands. Marilyn kept her back against the wall, yelling for him to drop the weapon. Harrowman, out of Jackson's sight on the far side of the desk, made no sound.

Fuck. Shite oh my god feckin' hell, his father's old Irish cursing rushed through his head in a nonstop stream. Dunn was dead, no question of it, and Jackson had maybe one second before Reggie recovered enough to do something even more stupid. He crabbed over behind the desk again, reached up and scooped the tablet.

It was unharmed. Reggie's first shot had gone wide. The thumb drive still protruded from the tablet's side, the browser still hunting for a connection. He hugged it to his chest and risked a peek around the desk's far side, past Harrowman in the chair to where Marilyn stood in plain view of a murderer with a gun.

Harrowman's voice from the chair in front of him sounded calm, relaxed. "Reggie, stop this now. You've got what you want. That's enough."

"What I want?" The lab rat's words were shrill, almost squeaky with panic and adrenaline. "Not yet. When five thousand implants are bought and paid for, then I'll be happy. And that's only the first week." He waved the pistol, black and boxy with smoke still curling from the barrel, at everything in the room. "So Jackson," he narrowed his focus to the desk, "I'll be needing that drive."

"Genius work," Harrowman said, still calm.

Jackson took his focus off the gun long enough to glance at the back of Harrowman's chair. A thin stream of dark red trickled down the armrest.

"Think so? Better than you two could manage, not that that's saying much." Reggie's voice came out stronger. He was back on familiar ground and proud of his accomplishment. Jackson snaked an arm up by Harrowman's side and began feeling around.

"Right side, underneath my ribs," Harrowman said, as if making conversation. "I don't think it's too bad."

"What? I got you?" The boy was edging back into panic again. Jackson ignored him and felt around the CEO's waist. He found sticky warmth. Harrowman hissed but didn't complain as he probed the gunshot as best he could while staying behind the back of the chair.

A chunk of flesh was missing. The bullet had plowed a furrow about an inch wide and an inch deep. It was bleeding, but a seep and not a gush.

"Deeper than a graze, but you should be okay," he murmured into Harrowman's ear.

Harrowman nodded and kept his eyes on Reggie. "How'd you do it?" he asked, his words brimming with sincerity and admiration. "We've been trying for years."

Reggie laughed. The pistol lowered a notch. On the side of the room, Marilyn shifted her left foot back against the wall. "You know how much fun I've had, watching you two fail and knowing that I'd already done it? I didn't even have to botch any Blast experiments or contaminate samples, you were so far off track. The answer was obvious to anyone with an actual brain. You and OverDunn here were so busy examining that formula from beginning to end and back again, you never thought to look at it from the side."

Jackson heard Harrowman gasp. Then the CEO chuckled, making the chair vibrate. "Touché. Brilliant work. Really. Too bad you had to fuck it all up, though."

Marilyn tensed, a yellow shimmer in Jackson's eye that passed by Reggie unseen. The boy, still in the room's only doorway waving a pistol, was busy getting outraged.

Reggie's gun hand came up a notch. So did his voice. "I did not! The formula works exactly as advertised, thanks to me! Not my fault it doesn't know when to stop."

Harrowman shook his head, sad at his apprentice's naiveté. "Not your fault? Reggie, you know better. You took the lead on your own little project. That makes everything your fault. The problem would have become apparent with nematodes, and if not, then with the mice. Certainly no farther up the ladder. But you skipped all that. You brought in that monster, Sachs, and cut every corner in the book. Went straight to human trials." He sighed. "Now look where you are."

The gun was back to pointing everywhere at once as Reggie

huffed out a brittle laugh. "No time for all that. I have a family to save. Sure, Sachs came with a reputation. So did you two, as I recall."

Harrowman nodded. "True enough. But we learned from our mistake. Luca Sachs? He couldn't. That piece was missing inside him from the day he was born."

Marilyn joined in, drawing the boy's attention. "Why the Croats? You're not part of that family. You're not even Croatian. Mancini is about as Italian as it gets."

Reggie glared at her. "Cops. You're as stupid as these two. So busy researching their checkered pasts, you never once thought to look around them at who really does all the work here."

He stood up straighter and jabbed himself in the chest. Realized he was doing it with the pistol and swung it around to face Marilyn again. "The Mancini's are fourth-generation Little Italy. We helped build this town. But who the hell wants to grow up and run a laundromat? My great-aunt Teresa wanted a bigger life, so she found herself a Croat. Aimed high, too. Got hitched to Branislav Zupan's older brother. It almost started a goddamned war, but you cops never even heard about it.

"I hung out with the Zupan kids. Had Sunday dinners at their place. The Uncle took a shine to me, and right out of high school he sat me down and told me I was going places. Paid my way through two degrees. So, guess what?" He gave that brittle laugh again. "The Uncle really is my uncle."

Marilyn whistled. "Missed that completely. Well, my bad, I guess. Tell me, did your Aunt Teresa survive the purge? I mean, after what the New Canadians did to you guys, there can't be many of you left. The Organized Crime Section doesn't even have a file on you anymore. There aren't even enough Croats left to qualify as a gang." Marilyn was very careful not to let a sneer into her words, which made her contempt ring through the room like a gong.

Reggie didn't look as rattled as Jackson expected. "That's the

Uncle's greatest trick yet. You can really get stuff done when everyone thinks you've disappeared. When this payday comes through, we'll buy the people we need. We'll shove Shaheen into the ocean, kick his ass all the way back to Iraq."

Marilyn nodded, a picture of someone seeing the big picture. "Right. So the Croats will rule all the poverty and misery in the whole city. And in a few years, when the Uncle gets too old, what then? The Nephew?"

Reggie brightened at that, gave a smile. "Sure, why not? I like the sound of that."

They were leading the murdering, psychotic weasel in circles, but not getting anywhere. Reggie had to step away from that door if they were to have any chance of getting out. And they needed to get out, Jackson knew, far and fast. Out of range of that signal jammer long enough to send the truth into the faces of those who wouldn't believe anything less.

He knew how to get Reggie's attention and get him moving. Once the boy was refocused Marilyn could do her cop thing and take care of him, Jackson had no doubt of that.

Tiny downside. For a few seconds, Reggie and that too-capable gun of his would be headed in Jackson's direction.

Sucks to be me, he thought.

He backed away from Harrowman's chair and rose from behind the desk, tablet in hand. He held it up and worked an expression of elated surprise onto his face.

"A signal! We got a bar, it's sending now."

Reggie did what Jackson hoped he would—forgot all about the gun and rushed forward to stop the transfer. The boy vaulted over the unmoving lump that had been Harold Dunn and charged the desk.

Marilyn sprinted off her back foot to intercept but Harrowman, with his squash-tuned reflexes, beat her to it. He pushed out of the chair and slammed into Reggie, chest to chest.

Both of them yelled and then went to the floor in a blur of swinging arms and legs. Marilyn danced around them, looking for an opening.

The pistol went off again, another explosion in the too-small room and a bright spark between the two bodies. Harrowman stood up like he'd been pulled by the red volcano that arced out of his back. He took a step back and crumpled. An unidentifiable clump of the CEO splatted against the front of the desk.

No time, Jackson told his stomach, gotta go. Reggie had frozen in horror but was recovering fast, swinging around wildly. Marilyn took in Harrowman's departure, glared at Reggie, but didn't continue her rush. She pulled something from her pocket and threw it at him. Reggie, amped beyond maximum, did a full-body flinch.

"Door!" she yelled. Jackson was already there. They rocketed into the hall and ran for the stairs.

Reggie leaned over the balcony railing as they slammed out the lobby door into the night. Another crack. Jackson flinched this time, but Marilyn ignored both the report of the gun and the sharp splintering as the round hit a window off to their right. "Four," she muttered. They both turned towards the parking lot and sprinted for the Subaru.

"We have to get out of range!" he huffed. The tablet, thumb drive still attached, was under his left arm. "Just one minute, then the evidence is out there."

Reggie blasted out the door of Blast Dynamics and shot at them. "Five," Marilyn said, then, "I'll do the tablet. You drive."

He got the Subaru running as Reggie reached his own car, parked on the street by the fascia bench. "Still nothing," Marilyn announced from the passenger seat, eyes fixed on the connection bars. "What kind of range does that jammer have?"

He said nothing, just power-turned the car out of its parking spot and raced for the exit. As much as he wanted to crank the

Subaru around and ram Reggie head-on for what he'd done, the game was to get away.

And the kid had no idea who he was playing against.

The rain drummed a steady beat on the car's roof and made a thousand splashes every second on the black, shining pavement. Ahead of them, past the windshield wipers, the empty night came alive to Jackson's sight as an intricate web of myriad angles and curves, phosphorescing in the black. He had an inside track on the geometry of the world and he knew how to use it.

As he pulled into a controlled hydroplane around the first corner he glimpsed Reggie's headlights, two carlengths behind and coming on fast.

Chapter 46

NO IDEA HOW TO PULL THIS OFF

Marilyn laid the tablet aside and jabbed frantically at her phone. "Shit, shit!" she growled, then, "Lay on the horn. Do it!"

He was kind of busy. Blast Dynamics was on a dead end side street. Three fast turns past a handful of low warehouses and an eight-storey office block took you back to First Avenue, and he was taking them at speed on wet pavement. She reached over for the horn herself but couldn't get past his forearms as he wheeled them onto the main drag and pointed them west.

"Damn!" She threw her phone down and picked up the tablet again. "That was the VPD Services building back there. I can't call them. If we'd caught someone's attention ..."

"On our own," Jackson said. He clicked the windshield wipers over to high as the rain intensified. "We're outgunned. But he's outclassed."

The first of the true winter rains—relentless, cold, like a million dropping icicles—had chased everyone inside for the night. Which was a very good thing, Jackson thought, as he skidded off First and onto the residential streets, taking both lanes to make the turn.

"Nothing yet," said Marilyn in the passenger seat, eyes glued to the tablet in her lap. The Ponce de Leon chat group was still open on the screen. The Upload Files box showed the little spinning circle, patiently waiting until the device made a connection. Her hands worked her phone. "No signal. Can't even call for backup.

How close is he?"

Jackson risked a glance back in the mirror. Reggie careened around the corner. His black VW was angled all wrong for the turn. Jackson saw a wobbly green swoosh of possible trajectories as Reggie strongarmed his car back under control, almost clipping a parked Kia. "Too close."

Boy's got game, he thought. Let's see how much. He punched the gas to the floor and the Subaru rocketed through the quiet neighbourhoods of East Vancouver.

The city had spent years of brainpower and millions of dollars making city drivers miserable. Swaths of residential streets had been turned into alternating one-way roads. Concrete islands, most with decorative shrubbery in the middle, forced cars to slow at random intersections. They'd dropped the speed limit to a tooth-grinding 30 kilometers an hour. Over in Kitsilano they'd gone so far as to place concrete jersey barriers across entire lanes to keep drivers from escaping the congestion on side streets.

He'd spent the same years dodging and weaving through every obstruction on his way to massage clients across the city. Now he chirped the Subaru onto Windermere Street, took it up to seventy, and kicked into the fastest side street shuffle he'd ever tried.

"Jesus, man, lights and sirens," Marilyn grumbled from the passenger seat as a swerve down a back alley knocked her into his side. She righted herself, eyes never leaving the tablet screen. "Still no joy," she said.

Reggie was right behind them. Jackson swung left, right, left again, street to alley to street, and the black VW rocked the turns and stayed on his tail. He tried going straight for a couple of blocks. The Subaru whined almost to redline but couldn't pull away from the VW's German love for speed.

A traffic calming island loomed into view at the next intersection. He hated to lose any momentum. His pattern sense, which had offered up a flickering, ever-shifting array of arcs and trajectories that showed him how to take every corner, flashed a spray of red lines over the street ahead. "Come on," he whispered, and feathered the brake. One curve, just at the edge of his ability, flickered from red to pale orange.

Good enough. He touched the brake once more, nudged the Subaru to the left of the intersection and clenched his nutsack.

He clipped the sloped edge of the traffic island at sixty-five and sent the Subaru up onto two wheels. Fingers light on the wheel, feet off the pedals, he locked his intention on the single orange line that he needed to hold amidst the forest of ruinous red trajectories. With a scream of rubber and a yelp from the passenger seat, the car canted up, flew past the island into the street beyond, and bounced back onto all four tires.

Still doing sixty. Jackson unclenched, jerked right down the next alley, and glanced back as the traffic island disappeared from view.

The VW had slowed. Reggie swung around the circle of concrete like a normal human, then sped up again to rejoin the chase. Hah, Jackson thought. Found your limit.

"Remember when we first met?" Marilyn was looking over at him, a mixture of concern, bright-eyed adrenalin, and maybe some admiration on her face.

"Yeah." His apartment. Her and Ahmed in uniform. Questions about his sanity.

"Still not sure I made the right decision." He checked again. Now she definitely smiled, but it didn't last long. She poked at the tablet again, then her phone, and grunted in displeasure. "We seriously have to get away from this guy."

He'd zigzagged them almost down to Hastings Street. "Nothing I want more." He whipped down yet another side street lined with postwar houses. The VW was still close behind, the lab rat proving difficult to shake. He jinked left into another long, close alley.

Thunder clapped through the air. A thunk sounded from the

Subaru's hatchback.

"Oh, no, you don't," Marilyn growled. She threw the tablet onto the dash, took off her seatbelt and twisted around to reach into the back seat. "Nobody shoots at me and gets away with it."

She came back with her purse. Snapped it open and dug out the small, black Hellcat. "Hold it steady," she said, and buzzed down the passenger window.

His body gave a full-on startle, the twitch rocking the car from one side of the alley to the other. She glared back at him and he tried to get it under control. Deep breath. It was just her gun. He'd held it. Seen lots of them in the past week, no big deal. The other guy was shooting at them. She was a cop. It was all right. Perfectly natural.

Except it wasn't. Nothing about the past week had been normal at all, and Jackson knew his nerves were reaching their breaking point. Some deep part of him hated the sight of the dark machine in his girlfriend's hand.

Marilyn spun backwards in the seat and stuck her left arm out the window.

"Turn coming," he called. She braced herself as he powered the Subaru into yet another suspension-rocking corner, across the broad expanse of Nanaimo Street and south.

Bam! At the sound he jerked again, couldn't help himself. The car swerved, pushing him against the door.

"Damn, my gun!" Marilyn was back inside, waving both empty hands in his face. He caught a glimpse of a black lump on the pavement behind them. "We have to get it!"

A solid part of him was glad it was gone; he wanted to get as far away from the thing as fast as he could. The rest of him knew that another gun was right behind them, and that without their own weapon they were in serious trouble.

Nanaimo was a broad street, with plenty of lanes to handle midday traffic. Right now it was deserted and glistening. Jackson flicked his head around and looked, but saw no phosphorescent streaks, no possible moves. Even his pattern sense had no idea how to pull this off.

Don't think, he told himself. He gave the wheel a gut-wrenching spin to the left, held it for one second, then racked it hard to the right.

The Subaru screamed into a four-wheel drift of a turn. Vancouver cartwheeled in front of him. On dry pavement he would have peeled all four tires off the rims. Without letting up on the gas he stickhandled the fishtail until they were headed back the way they came.

Reggie's VW flashed past, his face a furious scowl. Then he was turning, too.

The Hellcat lay in the other lane. As they passed it Jackson whipped his car into a second 180-degree spin. This time he braked.

Marilyn shoved her door open, reached down and grabbed the gun as Reggie flew past them again. "Got it!"

He was back up to 40 before she levered back up and got the door closed. "Looks okay," she muttered, taking things out of the Hellcat and sliding parts back and forth. She glanced at the tablet again, then her phone. "Nothing. You have to get us some distance."

The rain pelted down now, hammering on the windshield. Nanaimo Street flew by under the wheels, his tire spray creating wings of mist behind them. It seemed like the city was deserted, they'd hardly seen another car. He jammed the wipers on high and pushed it, seventy, eighty.

The VW was on his tail. Reggie dodged to the left and put on speed. He was going to overtake them.

The kid stuck his pistol out the window of the VW and aimed across the windshield. A flash, and another crack, but his shot missed.

"Rear window!" Marilyn leaned into the back, gun arm first, aiming. Wanting the shot.

"Wait!" he called back. The big intersection of Nanaimo and First Avenue was just ahead. He heard Marilyn growl, felt her tense to shoot right through the glass. He tried to see the angles behind what he was about to do, but again, they weren't there. This wasn't geometry. It was human nature, and his pattern sense didn't know anything about that.

But he did. And he knew Reggie's limit. The VW's nose pulled level with his back wheel as they reached the big, open intersection. With a vicious yank on the steering wheel that sent Marilyn sprawling, he jerked the Subaru left.

Directly into the VW's path.

Another yank back to the right, then more, no letup on the gas. Marilyn wrestled herself back into the front seat as the Subaru's nose flew around. They were drifting again, this one less precise, a full-on hydroplaning skid at seventy kilometers an hour on a city street. He fought with the wheel, searching for traction, but they continued to slide in a wide arc.

Right for the lone Tesla sitting in the far lane of First Avenue, waiting on the light.

One tire caught a grip. Then another. Jackson had a single glimpse of the Tesla driver, bald head glistening white and black goatee open in a soundless O, as he flashed past and rocked the car down the oncoming lane.

"Signal?" he called.

Reggie had flinched. Soiled his boxers, actually, judging from the wild slew the VW had made to avoid Jackson's sudden move. The black sedan had spun completely around in the rain, almost stopped. The gap between the two cars was now at least a hundred feet.

"Nada," Marilyn said, tablet once more in hand. "But nice move."

Not nice enough. The boy recovered fast, Jackson gave him that. Two bright headlights swerved into place in the rear view mirror. Already the VW was pointed down First and accelerating hard.

He smacked a hand against the wheel as both cars raced down the long, open stretch of the wide avenue. Victoria Street blew past, then Commercial Drive. He peered through the rain, searching for any car or pedestrian in the intersections, but really there'd be no way he could avoid them. This speed was madness in the middle of the city, getting more insane the closer they got to downtown.

Reggie was still coming. That jammer of his was still keeping the truth of the Ponce de Leon's poison from reaching the world.

Another lone car idled at the intersection ahead. Clark Drive, where First Avenue launched out over the train tracks and downsloped into the edge of downtown. Jackson caught a glimpse of it as he shot past.

A silver McLaren. What the hell? Did everybody know where he was?

Reggie was behind him again. Another thunderclap, this time without punctured steel. "Seven," Marilyn said.

"What?"

"He's got an HS2000, Croatian army handgun. Sixteen in the rack, one in the chamber, most likely. Ten left."

"More than enough," he muttered.

"Yeah. And more than me." She hefted the Hellcat. "But it only takes one to end the fight."

Crack, and this time a metallic zing across the Subaru's roof. "Eight," she said.

"Hell with this." A red haze filled Jackson's vision that had nothing to do with patterns or angles. Thousands of people needed the revelations he was trying to send them. Georgia needed it, before it was too late. Dr. Luca Sachs, doing something good for maybe the first time in his life, had entrusted this secret to Jackson. No way was that loudmouth Reggie going to get in the way.

Besides. He was sick and tired of being shot at.

They flew down the slope of the First Avenue overpass, Reggie three carlengths behind. Jackson seriously wanted to slam on the brakes, crumple the front of Reggie's car and make him eat radiator, but that would pit Japanese steel against German engineering. He'd be just as likely to end up sitting in his own fuel tank.

Instead he threw them into a hard left at the first intersection. Then immediately another, back in the direction they'd come but now on a surface-level side street.

"Not many options down here," Marilyn said. Conversationally, just passing along an observation.

"Only takes one."

At the end of the block he jerked the car across the sidewalk and into a large parking lot dotted with cart corrals and naked trees. The concrete and glass monolith of the hardware store it served was quiet and dark. He swung the Subaru into a sideways halt at the far end of the empty pavement as the VW lurched into the lot.

Reggie slammed it to a stop and stepped out of the car, leading with the gun. Even from here Jackson could see the barrel shake as he swung it around to face them.

Chapter 47

Beautifully, unbearably alive

"Get down behind the front tire, keep the engine between you and him," Marilyn ordered as she swung the passenger door open. "I've got this." Jackson stepped into the rain and crouched down, peeking over the hood of the Subaru, as she kept her door open and steadied the Hellcat in the crook of the opening.

"Drop the weapon! You know I'm a cop. Drop it! Now!"

She used the voice Jackson had only heard few times before, bullhorn-loud and strong as an avalanche. It sent a buzz through his shredded nerves right down to his toes. Reggie, a hundred feet away over the puddled blacktop, jerked at the words but held his ground.

"You're ruining it!" he shouted back. "Just another day, a few hours even, and it won't matter. But you couldn't leave it alone, could you?" He turned to Jackson, the nose of his gun tracking with him. "Jackson, what the hell, man? We got along. Come on, all you have to do is give me that thumb drive and we can all go home."

"Now, Reggie, drop it now! Last warning," Marilyn commanded.

"Home? Is that what you think?" Jackson yelled up over the car's fender. He'd been threatened, shot at, chased over half the city by this insane murderous prick. Now he was huddled in the rain while Reggie was talking about calling it a night. He stood up, a clear target over the hood of the Subaru and not caring in the least. "You've killed two people. Tried to kill us. You've—my God, Reggie, I don't even want to think about what you did to those poor people in the videos, and now you want to unleash it into the world! Hate to break it to you, guy, but you're never going home again."

Marilyn, still aiming her pistol, waved at him frantically with one hand, trying to get him to shut up and sit back down. He was escalating the situation. He knew it. Too bad. This all had to end now.

Suddenly, reaching some kind of decision, she stopped waving and stood tall above the car door as well.

"He's right, you know," she called over the empty expanse of the parking lot. She'd dropped the tone of command. "You've been a very bad boy, Reggie. Played at being an actual, real scientist." She let a note of condescension into the words and stood taller. "Played at being an entrepreneur. A visionary." She escalated as well, curling the words into a smoking-hot burn as she took a step to the side. "And now look at you with that big gun. Playing at being a gangsta." Words dripping with disdain, she sidestepped again, bringing her clear of the car door.

He saw Reggie quake as each jeer slapped him in the face. Saw him grip his gun with both hands as the last one pushed him over the edge. With an inchoate roar he began pulling the trigger.

The first shot sent Jackson down behind the car's hood again. A second split the night, and a third, fourth, fifth.

Marilyn hadn't so much as flinched. He'd heard her mutter, "Nine, ten, eleven, twelve, thirteen." Then saw her sidle back behind the door and lay her gun hand over top of it. "Hey Reggie," she called, and all the force of command was back, "this is how you make a distance shot."

She slid one foot back. Added her left hand to her right. Sighted, and pulled.

Nothing. She squeezed again. Nothing.

"Fuck," she breathed, gave the Hellcat's trigger a close look. "Damn." She tossed the jammed pistol inside the car and gave him a look. "Guess we do this the hard way."

Before he could ask what the hard way was, a throaty rumble sounded from the street. The McLaren pulled in with enough momentum to bumper-scrape over the curb. It nosed to a stop beside the hardware store halfway between the two cars and Shaheen Kiani angled himself out into the night.

He took in the scene in one long, deliberate scan and broke into a huge grin. "Well, isn't this wonderful," he announced, as if speaking to a crowd, "we have a showdown." He frowned. "Something is missing, though."

In a cobra-fast move, he flicked a hand forward and threw something at Jackson's head. Jackson saw the trajectory as a long, blue arc through the rain, easy and clear. He recognized the object in time to be prepared for the weight and caught the pistol out of the air.

"No!"

Reggie was running now, narrowing the distance. The black rectangle of the signal jammer joggled against the boy's belt, its round antenna jutting up almost to his ribs. He levelled his gun again, paused to take up a stance this time, and fired.

A ricochet whined off the pavement. Jackson heard another thunk as some part of his car caught the rebound.

No time. No other option. The gun was larger than the Hellcat, heavy, a capable machine. He remembered what Marilyn had shown him. Held it out, finger taking up the slack in the trigger safety, other hand supporting the base. A wild spray of neon red tangents sprouted from the barrel, washed over Reggie and all the pavement to both sides as he fought to steady the thing.

No good. Reggie, emboldened and desperate, was running towards him again, closing the distance. Jackson wouldn't get a second shot.

He yanked the inner door to his condition wide open. Gasped as the night came beautifully, unbearably alive. The hissing rain was a million half-seen streaks of motion, a veritable 3D curtain of energy and kinetic potential that ended in a cascade of tiny starbursts against the ground. A breath of wind tousled the tall weeds at the parking lot's edge and shifted the rain in a shimmering wave that nearly lost him to awe.

He was insane again. Gloriously, dangerously out of control. With all the will he could muster he pulled his fascination back from everything around him to the one thing that mattered, the spray of red possibilities that wavered from the gun in his hand to the young psychopath barreling towards him. He watched the dancing, scarlet paths steady, narrow down, focus into a single terrible line as he breathed out and nudged the gun into a precise and utterly inevitable aim.

The trigger practically pulled itself.

The gun bucked with a heart-stopping boom and an impressive recoil. His hands fought to control the rise and bring it back to level. Forty feet away the black box of the signal jammer exploded on Reggie's hip. He saw the complex, coordinated grace of a human body in motion wrecked by the sunburst blast of the bullet's impact, felt something inside him wail at the shattered geometry as Reggie fell in a broken heap. The boy crumpled to the ground, screams rising to a soprano shriek as shards of the device embedded themselves into his groin.

The shot had found what he'd aimed at. Reggie was down but still alive. At least Jackson's off-the-scale sensitivity had been spared that. Taking a step towards Marilyn, he closed his eyes and shuddered in a long breath, gun hanging limp at his side.

Open your eyes, his fully insane mind called, in a whirlwind voice that whispered with the force of a roar. See the wonder. Everything dances with everything else. You can, too, if only you'd look, follow. Find the one pattern behind them all.

He kept his eyes closed, slammed the pistol against his leg and focused around the pain. Thank you, he told his condition, feeling like he was yelling into the teeth of a storm. Now get back under control. Give me some space. Now.

Please.

It did. Not entirely, not even close. But whether it was the medications or practice or simply blind luck, he felt the unbearable, irresistible pull recede. He eased in another breath and stood up. Opened his eyes.

"That was great." Marilyn was there, taking the gun from his hands, eyes on the still-wailing Reggie. The hissing curtain of energy was again just a cold October rain. He shook it off and they both headed for the downed figure.

"Excellent shot, my friend," called Shaheen from the sidelines, "but first things first, if you please. You have a job to do."

They paused. "He's right," said Marilyn. "The gangsta can wait a moment, it's his fuckery we're fixing. And you stay there!" she called out to Shaheen, who lifted two empty hands. They backtracked to the Subaru.

The tablet, ignored on the dashboard and now covered in broken glass, had gone to sleep. The thumb drive still protruded from its side. Jackson brushed off the screen and nudged it awake.

The connection icon showed five bars. He guided the tablet's browser back to the immortalists' dark-web chat group as Marilyn watched over his shoulder. Started a new thread and clicked Upload Files, then chose every document on the thumb drive and the first two videos.

Small enough to upload quickly. Persuasive enough to crush their dreams of eternity. He jabbed Send.

Another earsplitting bam! startled Jackson right into the passenger seat, Marilyn landing on top of him. Reggie's continuous wails stopped like they'd been guillotined. Through the spiderwebbed windshield Jackson saw the young scientist's silhouette no longer writhing or holding his side.

The Uncle stood where the parking lot met the weeds, a curl of smoke rising from yet another pistol in his dark-veined hand.

Branislav Zupan, the elegant old man who'd once held Vancouver's sins in a bloody, iron grip, turned and glared at the Subaru with a mask of murderous rage.

Chapter 48

No room for grace

Marilyn was quick off the draw. She untangled herself from Jackson to crouch behind the passenger door, Shaheen's weapon front and center. Her cop voice was back. "Police! Lower your—" and then it became obvious that the Uncle would do anything but.

He swung his pistol around from Reggie's still form in a straight-armed arc Jackson could see, vicious and fast. He took a step towards them.

Marilyn's two quick shots echoed the flashes from Zupan's muzzle. The combined explosions and their echoes off the big box store sounded to Jackson like he'd been dropped into a war zone.

The shot was a long one for them both, fifty feet at least. Branislav Zupan held his gun like he'd grown up with it. He probably had. Marilyn handled hers like she'd first touched the weapon two minutes before.

Jackson saw her right leg snap back, the shin flickering a sickly shade of green to his eyes as it suddenly bent in the middle. The pain and impact threw her face-first to the pavement with a wordless howl. Her pistol, Shaheen's pistol, flew out of her hand. He caught it again.

The Uncle hadn't so much as slowed his advance. He marched towards the car, growling words Jackson didn't understand.

"Do it!" Shaheen's order whipped at him from the other side of the lot. "I'd hate to lose you, my friend!" His dark eyes glittered in the rain. He sounded thrilled, Jackson thought. Like he was watching an excellent soccer game.

The Uncle's gun cracked again. The passenger door's inner panel fabric spalled an inch away from Jackson's leg. Zupan was thirty feet away now, the look on his face something out of a nightmare.

I need you, Jackson said to the closed door inside his head. His pattern sense, life-altering curse and occasionally a blessing, flooded back into his mind with a palpable warmth. Once more the scene leaped into shimmering, beautiful, irresistible life.

The Uncle glowed like a sun with the purest intent Jackson had ever seen. Zupan had been reduced to nothing more than fury. No thoughts, no competing priorities, no goals at all beyond Jackson's immediate death. Everything he had was focused through the muzzle of his gun, a tight beam of blazing yellow that terminated on the center of Jackson's chest. His next shot would not miss.

Jackson's pistol wavered in his grip as he reeled from the sheer hatred in the Uncle's eyes. Ghosts of scarlet arcs danced from the barrel of his gun, a spray of potential bullet trajectories that went everywhere. Scared nearly to eye-rolling panic, struggling to remember Marilyn's lessons, he snugged both hands down on the doorframe and breathed out. No time for thought. The mad spray of useless potentials narrowed down, coalesced into a broad wash of red that painted the night in front of him, then to a thick scarlet band that centered over the Uncle's near-run of an advance.

No time for better. No aiming to wound. No room for grace. Jackson squeezed the trigger three times as the Uncle's barrel erupted in tongues of fire.

Chapter 49

A Lion Being Threatened by a Fox

The window under Jackson's arms powdered into a geyser of diamonds. Flecks of glass scored his cheek and forehead. A searing hot poker drew a line of fire across the right side of his ribcage. He tumbled to the soaking pavement beside Marilyn, shocked and stunned by the impressive amount of pain.

He'd been shot.

"Did you get him?" Marilyn's words were tight, insistent. "Check your target. Are we secure?"

Oh yeah. The other guy. The gun, still smoking in Jackson's hand. He was already on the ground, soaked through. He rolled onto his chest in the middle of a growing puddle and looked under the bottom of the car door.

Two black lumps wrinkled the straight and even lines of the parking lot. No movement. Everything perfectly still except for the incessant rain.

A pair of long legs strolled into view from the side of the lot, unhurried but wasting no time, headed towards the larger form. He saw Shaheen nudge the lump with a toe, then bend to retrieve the Uncle's pistol.

"The Croat's, uh, down," he managed. Didn't want to think about what that meant. About what he'd done. Not yet. "Shaheen has his gun."

"Give me that." Marilyn snatched the black thing out of his hand and rolled out from her semi-concealment, prone on the ground and arms outstretched.

"Shaheen Kiani," she shouted, "drop the weapon! You're under arrest."

Jackson pushed himself up to see. Shaheen stood up and turned towards the Subaru. Slowly, like he was supremely unconcerned. A lion being threatened by a fox. He examined the gun in his hand, did something, and let the magazine drop out. He lowered the gun's frame back to the pavement and stood up again. "I was only ensuring your safety. The Uncle is gone, but you would not know that. Wonderful work under pressure, my friend," he said to Jackson. "It makes one feel truly alive, does it not." He tilted his head back to Marilyn. "Tell me, police woman. What am I being arrested for? I am only a witness."

"I'll think of something." She growled under her breath in frustration. Shaheen, Jackson realized, might actually be right.

Sirens bleeped into life from the direction of downtown. Another started up somewhere past Commercial Drive. Finally. Emboldened by the sound, Marilyn grabbed the door and levered herself into a one-legged stand. She recentered her pistol on Shaheen.

"Take two steps away from the gun and on the ground! Now!"

Shaheen was made of stern stuff. Marilyn's command bounced off. "What, onto this filthy, sopping pavement? I do not think so. In fact," he cocked an ear to the sirens, "I believe I will go now."

Marilyn growled again, shook the pistol for emphasis and amped up the volume. "Stay right there! Hands where I can see them and don't move ..."

Her voice trailed off. At the edge of the parking lot, where the light hit the weeds, twenty faces materialized from the dark. Black, white, brown, mostly men, a couple of women. The New Canadians. Shaheen hadn't come alone. Several handguns glinted, visible but not raised.

"We shall meet again, police woman," Shaheen called as he

strode for his car. "Jackson, keep well! Until next time."

The McLaren squealed a doughnut of an about-face and was gone, leaving a puff of burned rubber around the turn onto the street. The faces in the dark vanished. Jackson scanned once more, saw only Marilyn, himself, and two former human beings. He sank back down, planted his soaking ass in the puddle. His ribs hurt a whole lot.

Marilyn was back on the ground, too. She was barking into her phone, about New Canadians and bodies and medical attention. He leaned over and grasped her free hand as the sirens got louder.

Chapter 50

IT'S ALL ABOUT THE ACTION

November rolled in with its usual Vancouver promise of fog, clouds, and biting drizzle. Jackson paced one step at a time along the cobblestoned harbour section of the Seawall and amused himself by people-watching. Carefully oblivious as Marilyn struggled to get used to her new crutches.

The faces he saw were predictably closed and grumpy. The grey months tended to do that, with occasional breaks for smiles when the sun came out. The joggers plodded through their routines with grim intent, feet hard on the bricks. Tourists and snapshotters stayed in tight-knit groups, watching the seaplanes come in for a landing or taking video of the Seabus approaching Waterfront Station. An older couple rested on a bench up ahead.

"Damn sticks," Marilyn muttered as a crutch got in the way of her toe-to-thigh plastic cast. She overcorrected and wobbled. He shouldered her back upright and worked not to laugh.

"At least you're out and about now," he said. "Only six more weeks to go." He hesitated. "Any word from Ahmed lately? Or the department?"

She knew he was asking two questions. "Ahmed says the Croats are done. Like, seriously done. They're scattering. All the Croats still in town are being caught and questioned. Any who knew about the Ponce de Leon are in for jail time. Shaheen's being his usual slippery self, squeaky clean on the outside and black as midnight underneath. They can't hang anything around his neck yet.

"As for the department." She sighed. "Dilly says I'll come back to desk duty in six weeks, then on the street when I pass the fitness tests. Not a word from Organized Crime. I think Rockford was interested in my connection with the Uncle, but that's dead and buried." She glanced over at him. "Sorry. Bad choice of words."

Even that oblique mention of what he'd done sent an electric zing along his nerves. He kept it off his face. "Not a problem. It happened, it's done. I'm glad it's getting wrapped up."

She held the glance for another second, then smirked. "I'm a cop, and you can't lie worth beans. Victim Services is there for you, you know. One call and I can hook you up. Anytime you want."

They'd paused against the railing by the yacht moorage. He leaned on it, careful to avoid the bandage where the Uncle's bullet had grazed his ribs, and looked across the harbour to the terraced slopes of North Vancouver. The tops of the mountains were shrouded in cloud. The tall evergreen forest that seemed, from here, to be a smooth carpet, flowed down to meet the uppermost houses of the city. Farther down the slopes the city turned into rank on rank of roofs and streets, until the houses became apartment buildings and then full-on city highrises.

He let his gaze wander, trees to city and back, losing himself in the view. Until he found himself staring at a single spot. The midtown residential block, invisible at this distance, where his father had met a young punk's knife.

Had Aiden Teague been scared? Surprised? Righteously outraged, which would have been more his style? Jackson would never know his dad's final feelings. But after the events of the past week, maybe, he could now guess.

"I'm good," was all he said.

Marilyn snaked one arm around his waist and pulled him close. "Looks like more rain," she commented. A bank of darker grey clouds to the west were pushing the lighter grey clouds out of the way. "I guess you and Charles won't be riding your bikes for awhile."

"Hah! Fairweather cyclist. All it means is different tires."

"How's he doing?"

Jackson sighed. "Okay, I suppose. Georgia still isn't speaking to him. He's got a place in the West End close to the hospital. They have a long history together, a really deep connection, you know? But still ... we'll see."

"At least she got that thing removed."

"Oh yeah," he said. "They all did. The weight of evidence convinced them." He rolled that out with all the derision it deserved. "The moment those videos hit the chat rooms everyone dropped the Ponce de Leon like it was radioactive. Georgia got the implant out before it was too late. She won't have any lasting harm from it. She even got a few benefits. "

Marilyn squeezed him tighter. "That's good. And your friend?"

"Client," he corrected. "Abe wasn't so lucky. He won't die, but he's ... fragile. The drug messed with his fascia. He'll have to watch every move he makes for the rest of his life."

They stood together at the rail, her arm around him, watching the faraway curtain of rain sweep in from the ocean. After a couple of minutes, though, he could feel her get restless.

He leaned in, his cheek close to hers. "Can't wait to get back to work, can you?"

"Nope." No hesitation at all.

"I bet that desk duty will feel like slow torture."

"You got that right."

"It's all about the action for you, isn't it?"

She turned until their foreheads touched. Her eyes, those startlingly clear brown eyes, held not a single trace of uncertainty. "Yes. That, and the knowledge that I'm doing some good out there."

"Huh."

They spent another minute watching the Seabus pull out of Waterfront Station and chug towards North Vancouver. His arm found its way around her waist. "Pad thai for dinner tonight," he said at last. "Want some?"

"Sounds great." A tiny pause. She leaned her other crutch against the rail and dug into a pocket. Held up her find. "I brought my toothbrush."

He laughed. Couldn't help it, and then couldn't help laughing some more, louder. It turned into a full-on belly roll, the kind that rocked his still-sore ribs and felt like a Spring wind cleaning out the house. Marilyn joined him and they stood like that, arms around waists, shaking with humour, relief, and what felt suspiciously like joy. The old couple on the bench smiled at them.

When he caught enough breath to speak again he said, "Go home and pack a bag. A big one. I'll have a couple of drawers waiting for you."

A small box waited at his apartment door when he got back to Balsam Street. So much for building security. An envelope was taped to the top with a note inside.

'I trust you are well, my friend. I was intrigued by the story you told when we first met. I made some inquiries and found the young man responsible for your father's passing. We had a conversation. He shared an interesting perspective on the evening your father died.

'It was not a chance encounter. The group your father met that evening were looking for him. This young man, in particular, had been paid to end your father's life. He did not know why, or care. He did not know who paid him. He took the money and did the job. For him that was the end of it. Until I became curious.

'I am sorry if this news disturbs you, but it is always better to know. Enclosed are two small gifts from the young man by way of apology. He will not be needing them anymore. S.'

Jackson ripped open the box. Inside, wrapped in newspapers, was a single Reebok runner, white with red streaks around the ankle. The red streaks, already turning brown, were not part of the original design.

Inside the shoe lay a long knife, blade sharp on both sides, with a steel haft and a corded grip.

Marilyn was due soon. She'd see this and have a much more official opinion than him. He repackaged the shoe and took it out back to the dumpster. The knife he tucked at the back of the closet. After a moment's thought—and a silent nod to his dad—he burned the note and scattered the ashes.

Chapter 51

This whole city can burn

Markovic used the light on his phone to navigate the dark corridors between the towering containers on the docks. Left, two rights, another left. The directions he'd been given read like the map for a maze, and that's exactly what this was, he realized. A temporary fortress that had been built, probably in an hour, to protect a ten-minute meeting from prying eyes.

He turned the final corner and stepped into an open pocket of dock with a single seacan in the center. It was the largest standard size, 53 feet long and slightly more than nine feet high. It looked scratched, a little weatherworn and rusted, but solid and serviceable.

Completely anonymous. Perfect.

A second container was being lowered to the ground beside the first from the massive orange crane high overhead. Marko stood back and watched, placing his large suitcase on the ground and shifting the two metal urns from the crook of one arm to the other. Two dock workers murmured into radios and made hand signals to get the container safely down. The clamps on top clanked off and the crane's cables lifted away.

A man emerged from another dark passage a few containers away. Marko was surprised the man fit between the metal boxes. At a pace somewhere between a waddle and a roll, the newcomer went over to the two stevedores and gave them each a small package and a chuck on the shoulder. Then they were gone.

Marko walked over and greeted the fat man with a handshake. "You're on time! Wonderful wonderful," the man said, "your boat will be loading in an hour. Two stops before Rijeka. You understand, right, you'll be on board for almost a week."

Marko refused to let the fear show. If there were no shipwreck, cargo accident, shifting load, or wrong destination, then he'd be back in Croatia soon. Milanka, Daniella and her daughters were already there. Zupan and his stupid nephew would be back home, too, and Marko would have fulfilled the Uncle's final wish.

If anything did go wrong, then Marko was stepping into his own coffin. But there you had it.

"First time, isn't it?" The fat man was saying. "Don't worry. I keep an eye on your container tracking from here. And it's a premium service. You won't even notice the time. But hey! Why trust me when we can ask a satisfied customer, eh?"

With a strength Marko didn't expect, the fat man walked over to the new container, clipped off the plastic seal and levered open the door latch. The door swung open with a hermetically-sealed hiss.

A man waited on the other side. Above medium height, sandy hair, blue eyes and a self-satisfied twist on his thin lips. Marko hated him on sight. Behind the man was a well-lit, comfortable looking living space, complete with wall TV and kitchenette. The top part of the tall container held a loft bedroom. "God I hate this fuckin' place," the man said, and stepped down onto the dock. "I'll be glad to see it go."

"Welcome to Vancouver! You had an easy trip?" the fat man asked. "This gentleman here is about to leave and he's a bit nervy about it."

The newcomer took two lanky steps over. "You leaving? Ever plan on coming back?" he glanced at the two urns. "Sure doesn't look like it."

"No. I will never return here. This whole city can burn for all I care."

The other man laughed hard. "Consider it done! They call me Borden, at least in this sorry town." He stuck out a hand.

Marko glared at it. "They call me anxious to depart."

Another laugh, with all the humour of a sandpaper facial. "Well, you can relax. These things are like travelling in a motorhome. Totally self-contained. Even have a shower back there. Well," he abruptly forgot Marko's existence, "thanks for the trip, big guy. Time for me to de-part." Without another word, the man who called himself Borden headed for the maze, and the city beyond.

"Right this way," said the fat man. He'd opened the door on the second container. "This one's clean and restocked. Bon voyage."

Marko gave Vancouver one last look as the door closed. The Croats had helped run this city for decades. He had personally kept the peace between four of the families, made sure their business stayed out of common sight and off the main streets. Then, overnight, everything had changed. With their last hail-mary attempt at redemption gone to dust, the Croats were no more.

Now Vancouver had the New Canadians and no one to hold them in check. The city would burn, no doubt. Marko was glad for it.

Holding the Uncle's ashes under one arm and the nephew's ashes under the other, he turned his back on the old times as the door clanged shut.

Acknowledgements

My thanks goes out to Sgt. Darren Kikuno of the Royal Canadian Mounted Police for invaluable insight into police procedure and the cop's life. Thanks also to the Facebook groups Cops and Writers, and Trauma Fiction - truly incredible resources for authors.

And, always, thanks goes to Juanita Rose Violini of Mystery Factory, ace mystery plot consultant and First Reader. Check out her work at mysteryfactory.com.

Spread The Word

Rate and review **On Borrowed Time** on:
Amazon
Goodreads
Kobo
Your Socials
and everywhere else!

Thanks so much. It really makes a huge difference.

Get The Newsletter

My list gets early notice of new releases, thriller research gems, and occasional updates on my writing life:

https://tonyberryman.com/newsletter/

BONUS!
You'll receive a free copy of a Jackson Teague short story, *The Covid Shuffle*. What good is a massage therapist in a pandemic lockdown? Turns out he can still touch some lives along the path.